# CACTUS DIVISION

*To Sheila Beck,
Cousin, I hope you
enjoy my 2nd novel !*

## J. MICHAEL BECK

*J. Michael Beck*

*12/01/21*

PublishAmerica
Baltimore

Softcover 9781462678389
PUBLISHED BY PUBLISHAMERICA, LLLP
www.publishamerica.com
Baltimore

Printed in the United States of America

# DEDICATION

This novel is dedicated to Randy Vasquez Cruz, my oldest and dearest friend, and Charlene Beck, my mother. Both are ever in my thoughts. Their strength, wisdom, and family values show me the way.

Thanks to my brother Gary for help with research. Thanks to Gary and my sister Sherry for letting me bounce ideas off you. This novel, in the present form would not have been possible if not for Steve and Kathryn's invaluable editing and story content advice.

# CHAPTER 1

## *Oscar and Buddy*

My name is James Henry, but this story is not about me. In August of 1963 I was nine years old and my grandfather, James Oscar was sixty-nine at the time, having been born in 1894. He was a $2^{nd}$ generation James and I was the $4^{th}$, although no family member I knew of in the line of James actually used their first name. I was called Buddy, which was a nickname for Henry, and grandpa was called by his middle name of Oscar by the adults. During summers, my parents, needing a break from their rowdy and willful oldest son would let me stay with relatives in the Texarkana, Texas, and the Arkansas area for a couple of weeks. The city was split right down the center with Texas claiming one half and Arkansas the other. I had been born on the Texas side but raised in Grand Prairie, Texas. I had family on both sides of Texarkana enjoyed many exciting boyhood adventures in both of the states.

During my visits with relatives, if I were honest I would have to say spending time with my Grandmother Myrtle and Grandpa Oscar was not the most exciting of times usually. However, there were times when grandma was away shopping or walking Lady, their pet Chihuahua, and Grandpa would entertain my cousin Jon Marc and I by telling what Grandma said disapprovingly were, "bawdy stories, not fit for young ears." My favorites were about grandpa's time in the U.S. Army fighting Pancho Villa and other lesser known bandits along the borders of Texas and New Mexico. Grandpa had been in the area between 1915 and 1919 when the bandits were crossing the American border and attacking in large numbers.

During these story times, Grandpa would sit in his favorite overstuffed chair and shuffle a deck of playing cards he kept in an old wooden box. I did not understand the game bur I watched him play as he began a new game of solitaire every half hour or so. Jon Marc and I could always tell when Grandpa was feeling nostalgic because he would get real quiet and turn the television volume down. He grew thoughtful, appearing to look inward instead of out. His face would relax and he would tend to stare at a single fixed point on the far wall.

Before long his eyes would seem to glow with the reflection of a long ago camp fire. While grandpa got in the mood for one of his stories, sometimes, Jon Marc, who was seven, would lose patience and start to fidget. I would usually remind him to lie still with a sharp elbow delivered to his side. Grandpa could tell a good story and I would lose myself in his soft raspy voice seemingly transported back in time to share the excitement and danger of bandits lurking behind every rock.

We would lie on the floor or sit near his chair, prisoners to his every word. On this early afternoon, grandma had gone shopping with her oldest daughter, Marie, Jon Marc's mother. As we lay on the floor in anticipation, I began looking up at Grandma's wood quilting frame drawn up and tied near the ceiling. I had watched her for hours as she tirelessly sewed tiny squares of cloth to quilts that she had cut from decorated flour sacks. My Grandma Myrtle's chair sat empty now beside the bay window, which she used for the light where she would sit endlessly crocheting.

I saw the black and white photographs of grandma and grandpa's almost forty years together. I also had heard from the adults that their lives had not always been so peaceful due to Grandpa's wild youth. Of course the only grandpa I had ever known was the quiet, soft spoken man before me. He was a man who I never saw smoke, drink liquor, or say a curse word, except in the telling of one of his stories.

The old picture that interested me most was of grandpa dressed in a U.S. Army uniform, young, with straight posture, and rugged looking. I do not think anyone would have claimed he was handsome, but his striking bearing and self-assured, cocky grin made him seem bigger than life. He wore three strips and was sitting on a powerful looking horse. My dad had told me Grandpa had at one time held the rank of Sergeant in a U.S Army Cavalry Regiment.

Finally, he began to speak, slowly at first, but gaining momentum and excitement as he got further into his story…At 15 I had run away from home fleeing my pa's strict religious upbringing and, lying about my age, joined the Army. I had no particular bone to pick with religion. The rub was that my pa, old James Henry breathed out *hell fire and brimstone* sermons on his way as a circuit riding preacher, made it his personal mission to save his eldest son. He preached and married folks from Atlanta, Texas all through the Arkansas Ozarks.

With six years of army service behind me, I had been reassigned from Fort Bliss in El Paso, Texas and traveled by train to Marathon, Texas seven months back. Now I found myself in the middle of the Mexican Revolution which had been brewing since 1911. I worried that if a bandit didn't get me, a black bear or mountain lion would. Both were frequent visitors to the edge of our camp judging from the large tracks I had seen.

To make matters worse, while both Texans and Mexicans alike had been victims of bandits, there were collaborators, both Mexican and Anglo selling guns and supplies to the revolutionaries. Some of the rifles sold to the revolutionaries were far superior to our outdated carbines. With violence spilling over to the American side, President Wilson sent soldiers to patrol the borders of Texas and New Mexico.

It was Friday, May 5, 1915, Cinco de Mayo, Mexico's Independence Day. I was assigned border duty in Glenn Springs, Texas, with a population of a little more than eighty people. I had made friends here with some of the easygoing town residents. I was assigned duty with Troop A of the 14th Cavalry Regiment. The town had been founded around 1880, when Herbert Glenn walled up the largest of the natural springs, thus assuring a steady water supply in an otherwise arid landscape. I was twenty-one years old and already called *old man* by the seventeen and eighteen year old *boys* in the Regiment. There was tension on both sides of the border. The Troopers of the 14th were inexperienced in war and were not prepared for the bloodshed coming to the border towns. *

On this Friday evening, we had been playing cards in the only occupied tent out of dozens standing in Glenn Springs. I had won a lucky pot before most of my men went to sleep, and found myself in possession of a nice ruby ring. I slipped the ring onto my left little finger as far as it would fit, proud of my winnings. It was the last luck I would have that night. The rest of Troop A had been, in my opinion, sent out foolishly chasing shadows and rumors of a pending attack. The Mexican bandits were said to be attacking 150 miles south and east of *Ojinaga*, Mexico, with the intention of attacking Presidio, Texas.

I was not alone in strongly disagreeing with Captain Casper W. Cole, my Commanding Officer. Charles David Wood, and his partner, Kenneth Ellis, who ran the town's wax rendering factory, had demanded their wives and children go to Alpine, believing the attack would most likely be at Glenn Springs. Wood's wife refused to go unless her husband escorted her there, which he did. Ellis could not convince his wife to leave and gave up the argument. The men had wanted to take no chances with their family's safety and advised others in the town to do likewise.

Wood and Ellis had prospered with their factory, making wax products from boiling the wild *candelilla* plants in water and carbolic acid, which separated the wax from the plant. The plants were readily available in the shrubby desert area. The little town had grown up around the small candle factory. The strategic importance of the town was not the factory, but the town's location so close to the border.

The company store manager, George Compton lived in a house near Wood and Ellis on top of "Robber's Roost" on the south slope of the *Chisos* River. He was a family man too, but his wife was in Marathon, expecting a baby and staying with friends. Compton's other three children, a nine-year old girl, Vivian, and two boys, Jack and Johnny, seven and five were alone in the house with their dad. The youngest boy, Johnny was both deaf and mute. He was a camp favorite who wondered in and out of the soldier's tents during the day, always smiling his contagious grin, receiving return smiles and friendly pats on the head from the rough soldiers.

* The actual battle of Glenn Springs occurred one year later, May 5, 1916. The date was changed for creative purposes.

Our camp tent was nearest to the small adobe cook house. The cook house was roofed with sheet metal, covered with a thick layer of boiled and dried *candelilla* weed. The idea behind the roof cover was to keep the interior cool against the hot Texas summers. Most of the area was desert, scalding in the daytime and cool most evenings. I had been stationed in rougher country, but this area, although beautiful, was lonely, dusty duty. The high desert might be cool at night, but was scorching hot during the summer months, and yet there could be snow during winter months.

I estimated we were less than 20 miles from the Rio Grande, and just south of the *Chisos*, with mountains rising on all sides. On the other side of the Rio Grande was *Boquillas*, Mexico. Boquillas meant *little mouths* in Spanish. The accepted idea was that it indicated the many streams that drained from the *Sierra del Carmen* into the Rio Grande. *Boquillas* was of financial importance to the United States and another reason for our presence on the border. Silver and lead were mined near the Mexican town and transported back across the border into the United States by cable tramways for processing.

Glen Springs was quiet. I had two men on guard duty and six more in the tent with me. Besides me, only Corporal Eleazar Alejandro, who we called "Alex", to make it easy, and Private William "Bill" Kubitz were awake. The two men had been with me at every assignment for the past five years and were as close to me as my own brothers. Bill had once outranked me, but had lost his stripes more than a few times for fighting, drinking, or insubordination. He was the only Jewish person I'd ever met, but I'm not sure he represented his religion well. If Kubitz was not writing letters by the poor light of our camp stove to his folks back in Fort Worth, he was usually polishing his brass US Army issue belt buckle. I think it must have been the nicest thing he'd ever owned and he kept it shining like a gold bar.

Alex, a quiet confidant man, bull strong, but standing no taller than 5 feet five inches was still dressed in his boots, the bottom half of his long johns, and his army issue shirt. He had been born in Mexico and ran away at 15 years old and joined the service as soon as he was old enough. When he spoke slowly, his English was perfect. It was only in times of stress or when he had been drinking that his accent slipped back to the surface. When he had crossed the border into New Mexico he would sit all day learning English from people on the street, then practice speaking the strange words every night. He had lived *hand-to-mouth*, earning barely enough for food, slept under the trees, and made money with odd jobs for locals.

He sat beside me now cleaning his Springfield 30 caliber rifle and his six shot single action Colt 45 pistol. Double action .38 and .45 caliber firearms and semi-automatic weapons were in use but the Army had yet to modernize the soldiers along the border. Alex was smoking a small cigar, the smoke curling around his face. I was attempting to roll a cigarette. It took me nearly five long minutes to roll the darn things. He looked over and laughed. "Oscar, you ought to give up on ever mastering that. I think your fingers are too thick. My cigars are easier."

"Well for one thing, you always seem to have more money than me. These things are cheaper than your cigars and I don't have to worry about breaking them."

I was barefoot but wearing my long johns against the cool desert evening. I cannot say exactly what the feeling was, but I was *out-of-sorts*, more crabby than usual, and feeling an uneasiness in my gut. We had been expecting a well-armed Cavalry contingent of reinforcements to arrive well before dark. What had happened to cause the delay I had no idea. I kept walking outside to listen and it was too quiet. Sound carries a long way in the desert and I heard nothing. After my third trip outside and cutting my foot on a stone, I decided if I was going out again, I'd put my boots back on. Other than the rocks, the Texas scorpions were large and there were deadly venomous snakes roaming the desert sands.

Around 11:30 p.m. we heard six shots ring out into the still night from one of my sentry's Colt pistol. After the first shots, we were on our feet in time to hear wild shouts, quickly followed by gunfire literally erupting from the north, west and south. We heard no horses and realized we must be under attack from bandits that had arrived on foot, leaving their horses some yards away. One of my two soldiers on guard duty was the first to die, cut down in a merciless swarm of bullets. The other man, Corporal Sean Haltom made it to our tent shouting as he ran, "Don't shoot sergeant, here I come!"

I had never lost a man in my charge, or been shot at myself, but training and self preservation took over for me and my men. I shook off the thought and concentrated on keeping the seven surviving soldiers with me alive. We began slamming out a continuous fire, not bothering to aim since we couldn't see the bandits, just flashes from their guns. I didn't know about the motivation for my men, but surviving the attack was secondary in my thinking to a hot searing torch inside me for revenge over the death of my soldier. We might not live to see the sunrise on our shoulders, but I planned on taking as many bandits with me as possible.

The crazed bandits were yelling, *"Viva Villa!"* and *"Viva Carranza!"* Pancho Villa, real name Doroteo Arango, and Carranza were rivals. Venustiano Carranza was the current Mexican President and at one time allied with Villa. Villa had begun his rise to fame by fighting against Revolutionary forces, attacking the new president's government. Eventually Villa had begun to crave power for himself, creating trouble for President Carranza with the Americans by attacking border towns.

The crafty Villa pretended to champion the underprivileged in Mexico and was mostly loved by the Mexican people, but a feared bandit to the Americans. Even with the confused loyalties of the bandits, I knew we were facing an overwhelming force. I started shouting to be heard above the crash of gunfire, "Retreat to the cookhouse!" I believed the sturdy four foot thick adobe walls would protect us, but only if we had enough ammo to kill near a hundred bandits. The only break I could see we had was by firing in three directions, we were assured of hitting a bandit since there were so *damn* many of them.

My decision to move to the cook house turned out to be a *bad* one. As we made our break for the apparent safety of the adobe walls, I saw to my udder horror, five year old Johnny walking in and out of the empty army camp tents, with murderous rifle and pistol firing all around him. It seemed to me either one of my pa's much talked about miracles was taking place before my eyes, or the rumors were true that the Mexican bandits were superstitious concerning the *touched* who walk among us. Either way, no firing seemed to be directed at the boy. Before I could think about going after him, Johnny walked directly toward the intense firing by the bandits as if it were any other day in the desert. I was horrified and helpless. I had to look away believing the boy would be cut down. Not wanting to see his final moment I forced myself to return my attention to my own peril and that of my men.

The remaining seven men and I made the supposed safety of the cook house and continued to fire through the one door and window. The battle was close up now. We could distinguish only shadows and shapes as Villa's men rushed the door or window in an attempt at a clear shot at us or to overrun our position. The intruders began to fall within inches of the door. We existed only in a world filled with the acrid smell of gunpowder, blinding burst of flames, the roar of guns, and the men around us. The rhythm of firing the Springfield's five round internal clips until we were empty, then reloading became all we knew. There was no time for fear or thought, just action and reaction. Taking a quick count I saw all seven of my men still on their feet and firing. Pride…maybe, but I knew there were no better men to fight with or die beside than these.

Around three in the morning, after more than three hours of fighting, the momentum of the attack slowly ebbed as the remaining bandits stopped firing. Exhausted, I looked around and was vastly relieved to see my men alert and preparing against another attack. I had a moment to believe we might actually be winning. However, after less than a minute of quiet, from out of the dark night, the strong smell of kerosene floated on the light breeze. Seconds later, torches soaked in kerosene were lit and flung toward the adobe roof. We all heard, "*Chemen los soldados fuera!*"

We knew what was coming next, but Alex translated into English, "Burn the soldiers out!" Before any of us could react to the threat, the dried *candelilla* weed caught and roared into flames. In seconds we were coughing and suffering from the smoke and heat streaming into the small interior. Next the tin roof began to cave in dropping flaming thatch on myself and the men. We had no choice but to abandon our position or be burned alive where we stood. I gave the unnecessary order to retreat. It was now up to each man to be responsible for finding his own way from the flaming deathtrap. I hoped there would be no panic, but the dire situation only offered the two options, run into the firing guns of the bandits or die in the flames.

# CHAPTER 2

## Bandits on the Border

Before the firing began, Compton, Teresa, the Mexican wash woman, Kenneth Ellis and his wife Martha were sitting in a brush arbor, enjoying the cool, evening. Compton's three children were asleep at his home. As soon as the attack began, his hysterical daughter Vivian came rushing out of the house screaming uncontrollably. She wanted to go to Teresa's house one hundred yards away, no safer, and exposed to gunfire all along the route.

Now Compton and Teresa had taken shelter with Vivian beside the boiler room of the candle factory. He desperately wanted to check on his boys up at the house, but was cut off by a large group of bandits. He and Teresa were trying to quite Vivian before she directed the bandit fire their way, "Calm down Vivian and we'll make a run for Teresa's." Teresa took charge and wrapped her own shawl around the girl to make her look more like a Mexican child. "Do not worry *Senor* Compton. I'll take her. Go check on your boys if you can make it." Without another word, Teresa scooped the trembling girl into her arms and took off at an amazing pace considering the uneven ground and her forty-five years of hard desert life.

Compton made a break for his house, but tripped over the body of one of his sons just outside his doorway. Anguish struck the man so hard it was as if the bullet that killed his son had hit his own heart. Turning the boy over, his eyes filled with tears, "Jack!" He wanted to lie down beside the boy and die on the spot. He forced himself to leave his son to search the house for Johnny. Not finding him, he could only hope he was safely hidden somewhere. He returned to the door and gently lifted the boy and placed him in a sheltered corner of the room. For the next three and a half hours, grief stricken and in shock, he fired at least 150 rounds from an old Sharps .50 caliber rifle at the bandits. Compton had no way of knowing how many bandits he hit or killed through the tears and sweat in his eyes, but he knew none of the killing would bring his son back.

By 3:00 a.m. Compton was out of ammunition. He was now only a spectator of the events unfolding below him. He felt helpless and worried for his remaining son. He knew that if the bandits returned to his home he was a dead man. The thought occurred that if not for Johnny, he would welcome the death. Looking down the hill and toward the cook shack, he watched powerlessly as bandits threw torches onto the tin roof where the soldiers had taken shelter. The flames caught immediately. The men inside had only moments before they would be roasted like pigs on a cooking spit.

The first man Compton saw exit the burning adobe was Bill Kubitz who was badly burned and desperate to flee the flames. He was cut down by a shotgun blast that tore away the top of his head. Next, Private "Tex" Bronson began running toward the corral, intent on catching one of the panicked horses and riding to safety. He dodged between bushes seeking cover, but rifle fire hit him from three different directions, cruelly twisting him with a shot to the head, chest, and shoulder. Private Hudson Rogers, with his hair and clothes on fire, made an easy target in the night. The man ran hard making a hundred yards before being killed instantly by a rifle shot through the head. Compton, without rounds could only watch in helpless anger and frustration at the deaths of the soldiers. He did not see the fate of the other men, but prayed they somehow made it.

A moment later I made my break for safety as the last man out of the burning shack. I somehow spotted Compton in his doorway and saw the big Sharps in his hands. Hoping he could hear me over the other firing I yelled, "Don't shoot Compton, it's me!" Instead of running toward the man, I turned and ran up the side of a hill, seeking my men. If not for the tragic circumstances of the evening, the whole thing might have been funny. I was running in bare feet, dressed only in long johns. I moved fast, running for my life with at least twenty-five bandits chasing and firing after me. I ducked around boulders making my way toward the strategic advantage of higher ground.

My progress up the steep hill was slowed by the two heavy Springfield rifles I carried along with two extra belts of ammunition. I had my Colt holstered and belted onto the long johns which added to my comical appearance. My surviving men were doing their part to help me make it with deadly accurate cover fire from the hillside. Sporadic fire back and forth between bandits and soldiers continued until the bandits rode away just after sunrise. Surprisingly, few bandits lay dead, but the ground was soaked in blood all around the open areas. It was as if someone had been slaughtering sheep, but that was not the reality of it.

The bandit's plunder was great, including money from the post office, most of our horses, plus stores of canned foods and grain. Several cans of sour kraut were scattered on the ground outside the store. Apparently bandits were disgusted by the smelly contents. The raiders had won this round. I figured their cost was high considering more than one hundred bandits had faced off against a mere force of nine soldiers from Company A of the 14th Calvary Regiment. Of course that old Sharps of Compton's thundering away accounted for some of the dead as well.

As a final irony, later that morning, a reinforcement Cavalry Regiment rode into Glenn Springs. The fifty men Regiment reassigned from Marfa, Texas had been delayed due to darkness and had set up camp near Double Mills Spring. The Double Mills Ranch was owned by George Miller, who had dug two wells and put up twin wind mills. It was a green oasis in the desert, and a favored spot for cowboys driving cattle or horses bought in Mexico to sell in Marathon. The Cavalry Regiment slept peacefully, unaware of the desperate struggle taking place in Glen Springs.

The men of the reinforcement cavalry began the task of restoring order to the camp and burying the dead. The dead bandits were unceremoniously dumped into shallow graves, dug into the hard earth. The four known dead soldiers were buried on a bluff overlooking the town, with white crosses marking their resting place, their names scratched into the painted surface. Only three soldiers came down from the hill Sergeant Draper had run up. It would be more than a year before Oscar Draper and Eleazar Alejandro returned to Glenn Springs. By then a few things would have changed for Sergeant James Oscar Draper, including his rank and name.

Compton, Kenneth and Martha Ellis had been watching the soldier's solemn task with grief stricken hearts. As one they turned away to begin looking for little Johnny, fearing they would have to bury both of Compton's sons. Amazingly they saw Teresa with Vivian and little Johnny, seemingly unharmed, walking across the way from Teresa's house.

With tears streaming down Compton's face, he stumbled toward his children, hugging both in a bear hug that forced them to pull away to catch a breath. He looked up at Teresa and silently mouthed, "Thank you." The moment was short lived however, since he still had to bury his eldest son, Jack. As hard as it would be to bury his seven year old son, he still had to break the news to the boy's mother when she returned.

# CHAPTER 3

## *Up To No Good*

"James Oscar Draper! I can tell by your face you've been filling these boys up with wild stories. You should be ashamed of yourself! They're too young to hear such tales. Oscar, you could at least wait until they're older." Grandma Myrtle had surprised us all by suddenly appearing in the doorway with my Aunt Marie. Marie did not seem upset and actually winked at us as we scurried out of the way. I had never seen grandma so mad or ever heard her raise her voice until that day.

Seeing our fear and discomfort, Aunt Marie said, "Boys, go on into the kitchen and serve your selves some ice cream."

We were quick to flee the room. I found the hand cranked ice cream and dipped out two big portions into grandma's green dissert dishes. Those dishes had an "F" inside a triangle with a three forked crown stamped into the bottom of the glass. We used to take those dishes and press the bottom of the glass to our arms, which would leave the design in reverse temporarily marking our arms. Grandma and Grandpa always had the best hand cranked ice cream, although I could not recall ever seeing anyone actually crank it.

Slowing down to avoid a painful headache I said, "That was one of the best stories ever!"

Jon Marc slurped and said between bites, "Yea, but he takes so long before he gets around to the good stuff." He rolled his eyes and continued, "Also, It may be ages before he finishes that story if he ever does. You know our grandpa doesn't always tell his stories in order either."

"I know, but he is the *only* adult that *will* tell us stories like that. They all think we're *babies* or something. My dad will make my sister and I hide on the car floorboard if someone is about to be shot, kissed, or anything else good. I'm still excited over the story. Do you want to go down to the train tracks or climb the china berry tree first?"

He thought for a moment while he finished his last bite, licked the ice cream dish and said, "Train tracks, then the china berry tree. You know if our parents ever catch us we'll be as dead as those bandits grandpa killed! Let's go while Grandma's still mad and won't miss us."

We went out the back screen door and through the alley between houses. The train tracks were about a quarter mile away. We always looked for a freight train to jump on and ride a few minutes. The trains slowed down while going through town, which gave us the opportunity to hop aboard. To us, it was so exciting and of course forbidden. When we were riding a train, it seemed the ground and buildings were flying by. We would ride for only a half mile or so, then jump off and run back to our grandparent's house, laughing all the way.

The first time I had rode a train it was an accident. My two cousins, David and Danny who lived in Florida, were visiting grandma and grandpa's house with their parents. Their dad, John Ray was my dad's younger brother and was in the U.S. Air Force. David was younger than me by a couple of years and Danny a year younger than David. We had climbed inside the open topped box car to explore interior, when the train began to jerk and move. I think the three of us wet out pants the first time from fright. We had to wait until the train had cleared the area. By then the ground was a blur as we all jumped or more likely fell from the train. We checked ourselves and found no broken bones. After realizing we were not hurt, the past few minutes felt more like an adventure. That was easier to believe once the danger was past.

Today, nothing was moving at the train tracks, so we returned to the back lot behind our grandparent's house to pick some wild green grapes and pull some fruit from the blackberry vines growing along the fence lines. The grapes were sour and full of seed, but the blackberry vines were loaded, full and sweet. We stuffed ourselves and our faces and shirts were stained by the blackberry feast.

After our snack, we moved on to play in a large pile of sand left unattended in a vacant lot, probably intended for a service station construction site nearby. Next we climbed down into the basement of an abandoned house on the corner of Lelia Street, a few houses down from our grandparent's house. Nobody had lived in the house for at least five years after the death of the owner. His name was Jack Walker, a friendly old man who had gone blind long before his death. My parents had taken me to visit him a couple of times when I was about five years old. Mr. Walker seemed to enjoy the company. I remembered sitting in his lap as my parents visited, surrounded by the pleasing smell of sweet cherry pipe tobacco strong on his clothes.

We did not break in, but slid into the basement through a high window with a broken latch. The ten foot drop into the dark and creepy basement seemed endless and the landing was hard. I instantly regretted talking Jon Marc into joining me. I worried we might need help getting out again. If we could not find a way back up to the window ledge would anyone hear us hollering for help?

My cousin looked as scared as I felt, but I put on a brave front and started looking around the dim interior. Furniture was stacked around the room in disarray. It reminded me of a picture I had once seen of the tomb of King Tut after grave robbers had looted it. It certainly looked like no one had bothered to clean out the house after Mr. Walker died. While I looked through a box of old letters, Jon Marc found some old wood carved toys and started playing war. Not being able to read anything in the poor light, I stuck about six of the letters in the pocket of my jeans.

Suddenly feeling closed in I said with the beginnings of panic in my voice. "Jon Marc, I think it's time we get out of here. The dust is chocking me and the light is getting dimmer."

"Oh Buddy, we just got here. Besides, these are neat toys. I want to take them with me? What do you think?"

"Maybe just one, you don't want to have to explain to your mom where you got it. I'm going to take some of these old letters so I can see what they say. I'll throw them away before anyone else sees them. Help me stack up some furniture so we can climb out of here."

It took another ten minutes before we escaped the dark foreboding basement. Once outside, the fresh air felt wonderful. I looked at one of the letters and it was postmarked from Pearl Harbor, Hawaii, dated October 10$^{th}$, 1941. That excited me because I remembered my mom talking about a big World War II battle fought there, although I could not remember which one. Maybe there would be lots of war stories written about in the letters. I would have to save them and read the letters later.

Next, wanting to stay in the open air, we climbed into what we thought of as *our* big old china berry tree that had fat limbs that stretched clear out over the street. We sat in the tree for the next hour throwing the china berries at passing cars. Although we had a few drivers look at the tree suspiciously, we felt safe and unseen from our cover in the thick leaves. The drivers must have believed that nature had done the dirty work. The highlight of today was a shiny new red convertible. We hit the unsuspecting driver with all we had stashed from the leaves around us. There was no damage done to the car, but we scampered out of the tree like frightened mice. The driver stopped a block away to clean out the inside of his car. He stood for a full minute and looked around suspiciously. Not seeing anyone, he got back into his car and drove away.

When we got back to the house, nobody seemed to have missed us. My aunt Marie had left, allowing Jon Marc to stay the night. His house was far into the country. We both loved exploring the woods surrounding his house, or camping out on the edge of the forest, but always within sight of his back porch. My aunt wanted to be able to check on us throughout the night and left the porch light burning all night. We always complained to his mom every time about that light, but secretly we felt safer seeing that small illumination, like a tiny lighthouse of safety protecting us from the dark woods.

Grandma Myrtle made a fuss over our stained shirts. "Buddy, you and Jon Marc are a sight! I don't know if those shirts can even be saved. You two go on and change. There is a big storm rolling in and

I want to get supper out of the way before your grandpa heads out to his storm shelter. What do you think about pot roast, cornbread and potatoes? Sound good to you boys? I've also got some peach pie in the oven for you two if you eat a good supper. I'll bet we can find some ice cream to put on that peach pie."

We answered immediately with excited yeses. I did not know about my cousin, but my stomach was growling. I was glad grandma always made plenty of food. We hurried off to the only bathroom in the house to wash up and change. As soon as we were alone I said eagerly, "That storm coming gives me an idea. I think it could be our big chance to get another story out of grandpa."

Jon Marc scoffed, "Buddy, you know grandma will never let us go down there with grandpa. She is probably still mad at him and she'll think just what you are, that he *will* tell us another story. Besides, you know how jumpy grandpa gets around storms. He probably won't *want* us with him tonight."

"Well…if you want to miss out on another story, stay inside, but I'm getting into the storm seller with grandpa if I have to cry *real* tears of fear to get grandma to let me go down there!" Suddenly remembering the letters I had taken from Mr. Walkers house, I told Jon Marc to go on out and I closed the door and sat on the edge of the freestanding bath tub. I had watched grandma scrub clothes on her wash board many times into the tub before my dad and his brother and sisters had bought her an electric washing machine.

Reading the first couple of letters, I was disappointed to read a bunch of mushy words such as *I love and miss you dearly*, written to someone named, Miss Mary Lynn Taylor. My older sister would love these but I was not interested in romance. What interested me most was the second letter with the date,

*November 20^TH 1941*

*Mary Lynn, I miss you terribly. When this war is over, I'll talk to your father so we can be married. I know a place in Texarkana where we can build our home. Don't worry about me. Although we fear a Japanese attack, Pearl Harbor is far from Japanese waters. I supervise the sentries at the fortified bunkers high on Diamond Head, which is an extinct volcano. Unless fog rolls in, we cannot be surprised. I pray you wait for me and I will write again when I can.*

*Truly yours, J. Walker, Petty Officer, 1ˢᵗ Class, Pearl Harbor, Hawaii*

In a rush, memories came to me of my mom talking about the Japanese attack on Pearl Harbor. She had been only six years old in December 1941. She had been very frightened by the adults talking endlessly about the Japanese attacking. My mom had hid all day behind an old tree stump at the back of their farm. Now I wished I had taken more letters to see if Mr. Walker had written about the battle. I know he survived the war and married a woman named Mary. My dad had said they were married over forty years before she became sick and passed away.

Supper was a silent meal, but delicious as always. Grandma never cooked a bad meal, but she did make us taste vegetables we did not recognize or could even pronounce. Grandpa was normally a little self-absorbed after he had been talking about his old days in the army. This evening his mood was further clouded by the oncoming storm and angry looks from Grandma. Grandpa kept looking off to the lightning visible behind the window seat where Jon Marc and I were sitting. My dad had built that window seat and it was a favored eating place for all of us kids. In fact, if there were more than three of us, a fight might break out among the kids for a chance to eat there.

Nobody knew why Grandpa did not like storms, especially ones that came full of lightning in them, but tonight may have just been a good excuse to get out of the house and away from grandma's disapproving eyes. I had always loved big storms and would go from room to room in my house tracking the storm as it rolled through. He cleared his throat. Looking directly at me like he could read my mind said, "After supper me and Buddy are going down into the storm cellar. The way this wind is kicking up I expect the storm will be blowing all night." He thought a second and then added, "Jon Marc can come too if he wants, although I think he feels a little clammy in tight spaces."

My cousin opened his mouth to protest, but thought better of it. We never talked back to adults and maybe he really did not want to be down there anyway. I held my breath as grandma looked doubtfully between the two of us. I spent the four seconds she took to decide wolfing down my vegetables, which was hard to do while holding my breath and flushing red all at once. I am sure I looked guilty and felt my hands turn to ice as the blood rushed to my face.

Finally Grandma smiled. "I guess if Buddy wants to share a cramped, damp and smelly place with his grandpa, it is okay with me. There is only one bed so I'll get him some bedding for a pallet for the floor. I'm sure that cement will be hard and cold." I thought for a moment we had slipped one by Grandma before she added, "Go easy on those war stories Oscar. If that boy has nightmares because of your scary yarns you'll have to explain it to your son and his ma." Grandma looked over at me and said, "Buddy in case this storm blows on through, I'll leave the back porch light on and you know we never lock the doors so you can come back in."

I had started breathing again and was too excited to sit still. I had never been invited into the storm cellar and did not know if anyone had ever spent the night down there other than grandpa. "Thanks Grandma, but I *want* to stay the night if Grandpa does." For me, any excuse to *rough it*, was exciting. When I was home and the power went down, my mom and dad got out the kerosene lanterns and I was in heaven. The idea of sleeping down in the storm cellar all night with no electricity, thunder and lightning, and maybe hearing another story of a big battle would be a grand adventure.

# CHAPTER 4

## *Night in the Storm Cellar*

At around 8:00 p.m. I said goodbye to my cousin and followed Grandpa down into the storm cellar. I was excited, but a little scared as well. I don't think anyone could have paid me to stay in that cellar overnight by myself. Even now with Grandpa leading the way, the cellar stairs seemed to open into a hellish pit. Fearfully, I forced myself to follow grandpa deeper into the cellar. In the daytime we would run around on top of the cement cellar and make up all sorts of games, but at night with the dampness and shadows the place seemed to close in on me as I neared the bottom. I was reminded that my Aunt Marie had said she never went down there because of scorpions. I had once been stung by one and feared them terribly.

Once inside Grandpa lit the kerosene lamp and some of my anxiety eased. Outside the wind howled like a wounded beast as the storm moved closer. The single wind turbine used for ventilation spun faster and faster. I could hear loud thunderclaps in the distance drawing nearer with each explosion. I now worried that grandma and Jon Marc might be harmed in the storm. However Grandpa seemed relaxed now and I was reassured by his much improved mood.

I settled onto my pallet and watched the shadows play off the lamp. Slowly my senses sharpened in the cave-like space and small sounds came to my ears. I was sure I could hear the ticking of grandpa's pocket watch accompanied by his rhythmic breathing. The air in the room seemed cooler now and static electricity made my hair stand up. As I shifted in my bedding, tiny sparks crackled as the lightening closed in on the cellar creating what my dad had said was called static electricity. Apprehension began creeping back into me, mixed with my excitement of the adventure.

Grandpa got settled into a sitting position so he could shuffle his cards on a small table near his cot. The cellar furniture only consisted of the Army cot, a table, chair, lamp, and now my pallet. During the one or two times I had been allowed to venture into the cellar, I had noticed a much read family Bible placed sometimes on the bed and other times on the table. Storm or not, I was tired from my adventurous day. I was afraid I would fall asleep before grandpa decided to tell another story. I knew there was no rushing him and waited restlessly.

"Buddy, are you still awake?"

"Yes Grandpa." I think I had actually fallen asleep for a moment. My mind was now somewhat dull and confused. I shook it off realizing I had been startled when I heard my name.

"Your daddy, James Vinson is my oldest son and a brave man. He served his time in the Army honorably when he was drafted in 1950. I know he would have fought bravely if he'd been sent to Korea. It was only by happenstance that he was stationed in Germany instead. Your momma going into labor when she did for your older sister's birth may have saved your pa from death in Korea. His Army unit shipped over while he was gone on emergency leave.

After his enlistment was up, he volunteered to serve in the Army National Guard. I am mighty proud of your pa. He was an Armored Tank Commander. He left the service with the rank of sergeant first class. Trust me Buddy; they didn't give away that rank in those days. Your pa earned it by being a leader of men. Anyway, the point I'm trying to make is your pa did his duty proudly and had to leave your sister and mom with family until his return. I guess what I'm saying is, I wish I had always served honorably, but on that dreadful night on the hill with my remaining men, something *ugly* twisted and snapped inside me."

I wanted to protest that he *was* brave, but I could not find the words before the moment slipped past. Grandpa continued to speak and before long I began to realize he had slipped back to the aftermath of the Glenn Springs battle with the bandits…I made my run up that hill with bullets ricocheting off of rocks, some so close a couple of times fragments stung my eyes. Some of my boys at the top began giving me cover fire as they opened up a continuous rain of bullets from their protected position. I trusted my men's marksmanship, but worried about them hitting me in the dark all the same. I didn't know who had survived up there, but just knowing I wasn't alone gave me added courage and strength. My bare feet were burned, cut and bleeding. I knew that if I faltered now it meant certain death.

As I reached the shelter of the rocks Alex reached out a beefy arm and hauled me up next to him. "*Amigo*, you look like shit!"

"Thanks for the hand", I panted. "Next time I've got Villa's men chasing me, I'll ask them if I can stop for a shave and haircut." Turning to business, I could make out the shadowy outline of five of my men hunkered down in the rocks. The firing had ceased for now with the lack of targets. I knew where Alex was since he had spoken, but since it was too dark to make out faces I yelled, "Bill, you up here?"

Alex spoke in a croak with his voice breaking, "I'm sorry Oscar but he didn't make it. Sean saw him take a shotgun blast close up. There is no way he could have lived through it."

As the words registered with me I exploded in sudden anguish, "Damn it to hell! I'll kill all of those *sons of bitches* for this!" I stood up in plain sight and senselessly emptied one of the rifles I had brought scattering shots down the hill into the dark. Seconds before the return fire would have cut me down Alex again roughly pulled me behind the rocks.

"Sergeant, are you *loco*? Don't get yourself killed and don't waste our ammunition. We might be up here for a long while yet."

He was right, but I was in a murderous temper. I had grown to respect the Mexican people, but these outlaws prayed on the innocent and helpless. The senseless deaths of my men, Bill among them, and those living in town cut me to my core. When attacked, most men will fight back if it is in their nature. I knew blind hate, fueled by reckless actions would only result in more death, mine included. Even so, I wanted to kill those responsible for the attack, and I was in a reckless and dangerous rage.

# CHAPTER 5

## *Poor Decisions Have Consequences*

Just before daylight, the rest of the bandits pulled out with our horses and carrying as much spoils as they could pack out. I felt like a fool and a failure as a sergeant. We had given them a hard time of it, but at a personal loss to me and the town. I wrote out a description of the battle by the early morning light on a stub of a pencil and some soiled paper given to me by one of my men. I folded the paper and sent the men down to town to wait for reinforcements. Sean began to protest, but I cut him off with a hand gesture. Without another word, I gathered up a rifle, pistol and gun belt, stood up and began walking toward the Rio Grande and *Boquillas*.

Surprised, Alex caught up to me before saying, "Where in *Hades* do you think you are going *Amigo*?"

"I need some whiskey. I'm betting those *bandit bastards* are headed to the nearest town to celebrate. *Boquillas* is the closest. I intend to kill some Mexicans dead, or make it hard for them to hold their liquor."

Alex looked at me questioningly, "I'm a Mexican."

I snapped, "You're a *soldier*! You know I have nothing against your people. I intend to kill the bandits who killed my men and looted Glenn Springs! We have no idea how many more dead there might be back in town."

"Oscar you're missing the point! We have friends who may be hurt or dying in Glenn Springs and fellow soldiers to bury. Sergeant, we have our duty, and I think your actions are unwise. We can kill more bandits *with* the Army. There will be more battles ahead for us. If you insist, we should go back and get you some clothes, provisions, and maybe find some horses. The Army takes going *absent without leave* seriously. If we go *AWOL* we can't go back to the Army."

I knew he was right, but refused to give in. I regretted the words as soon as I said, "I didn't ask you to come along. Go back! The Army is your home. Damn it Alex, I'm not going as a sergeant!"

Giving up the fight, Alex sighed and said, "I go with you *amigo*, sergeant or no sergeant."

We walked along in silence for several miles, each of us were lost in our own thoughts. I knew what I planned was bordering on madness. I wasn't thinking straight and I couldn't seem to plan beyond my next step. I was walking on bare feet, blistered and bleeding, but the pain helped me focus on my one desire to see the men responsible for my soldier's deaths dying by my own hand. I relived the sight of the innocent boy known as *Little Johnny* walking innocently through the swarm of bullets.

I thought it was the sun playing tricks when I finally saw the Rio Grande sparkling ahead. We were exhausted and dehydrated, but with new strength, we began a staggering run toward the river. As I reached the water, I dropped the heavy guns, stumbled and fell face first into the water. It was like waking from a dream. The water was cold and the current was swiftest near the center, but no more than six feet deep. I drank until my stomach was swollen. I lay for several minutes in the shallow edge of the river, still on the American side, enjoying the feeling of the water lapping at my body.

Once I felt up to it, I retrieved my guns and, holding them over my head, waded across until the water was up to my chest, then I began swimming to the other side. Alex followed, swimming with ease and beating me to the Mexican side. We sat down on the sand to dry.

"Oscar, I know a few poor farmers on this side who have been victims of the bandits and have plenty of cause to hate them and might help us. You can hide nearby and I'll barter us some clothes and shoes for you. I have a little cash on me. It should be enough for a couple days worth of meals and a bed. If the bandits are in town, my friends will know and if we're sane, we'll quit this and head back to Glenn Springs."

Agreeing I said, "Alright, let's find your friends. I'm tired of parading around in my long handles and my feet are hurting me something awful. Some food would taste pretty good too. Say, I didn't know you had ever been this far south."

"My father was a *bad* man, who ruled our village by fear. He used to take me with him on his meetings with others like himself. I think he would have been called an outlaw at the time. If he lives, he will be riding with Villa and his men. My father wanted me to be like him, but I hated the way he hurt my mother. One night he hit her so hard she died. I was there and helpless to stop him. I hit him with my small fist but I was like a mosquito to him. I ran away the next day. If I ever see him again, he will know the boy he slapped around has grown into a *lobo* with sharp teeth."

I had never heard Alex speak with such emotion. I would not want to be his pa if he ever met up with the man. Alex was bull strong and never missed with any weapon he held. "Well, you might get your chance old friend. The Army is patrolling up and down the border from Texas to New Mexico."

We had been talking while we shuffled along and now Alex gestured for me to get down behind some cactus and stay put. He walked in plain sight toward a group of adobe buildings a hundred yards ahead. In these times a man could be shot just for getting too near a man's property. I saw him raise his hands in a universally recognized gesture of meaning no harm. Even still a rifle shot dusted his boots. He stopped, remaining perfectly still. If it was possible to ever doubt Alex lacked in courage it was settled now. I did not comprehend how he could stand there so calmly and not dive for the nearest bush. There was scant cover but I would have made a try for it.

From the center of the buildings, I saw a rifle emerge followed shortly by an old man dressed in a weathered poncho and large sombrero. The man walked cautiously toward Alex. From my position squatted down behind the cactus, I took careful aim as the man approached. The shot would have been the best I had ever made, but became unnecessary when the man lowered his rifle and began talking excitedly. The next thing I knew, he was hugging Alex like he was a lost favorite son returned from the dead. Alex returned the affection. He turned and signaled me to come forward.

As I approached the two men, I understood Alex say in Spanish that I was a friend. He turned to me and said, "Oscar, this is Jose Ortega. He remembers me as a boy. My family is in some way related to his. I remember we stopped here many times. He does not speak English. I told him you were an important man and we needed clothes and food."

We started walking toward the largest of the adobe buildings. The man spoke very fast and gestured frequently with his hands. I could only make out a few of the words. He was a stooped shouldered man of an indeterminable age. The desert ages a man quickly, but he still kept up a good pace and seemed happy to have visitors.

Alex turned to me and gestured to the old man, "He despises the bandits. They took his sons away, not by force, but with promises of wealth and women. He lives here alone now. His wife is dead and he still grieves for his sons. He was born here and fears he will die alone and go unburied."

We stopped at his deep well and I filled a large bucket with the cool water before carrying it inside. The adobe had thick walls and the interior was pleasant. The roof was tightly woven thatch. An involuntary shudder coursed through me at the memory of the burning Cook House. I wanted no part of ever coming close to burning alive again. I pushed the thought aside as my stomach became aware of the smell of beans and some kind of broiling meat. A large growl of complaint was heard coming from my belly.

Ortega shared his food and we ate gratefully. The man noticed the sorry condition of my burned feet and after we had eaten, he brought some of his son's clothes and a smelly salve for my blisters. He indicated I should wash my feet in a tub in the next room before applying the salve. The stink nearly took my breath away, but soothed immediately as I rubbed it on. I did not want to know what I was putting on my feet, but feeling immediate relief, wanted to take some with me when we left for town.

We spent the night and in the morning, after the rest and treatment for my feet, I should have been thinking clearer, but I was still determined to go into *Boquillas*. I saw Alex looking at me expectantly. I knew he wanted me to forget this nonsense and go back. "I'm still going Alex. You've done well for yourself in the Army and should go back. Tell Captain Cole you were lost and confused after the attack. My friend, you earned corporal stripes and could easily fill my boots as Sergeant with Company A."

Alex shook his head as I knew he would. "First we finish *your* business in *Boquillas*. Then we will both go turn ourselves in to Captain Cole." His grin which was never far from his face was contagious as he added, "I think I had rather be shot by bandits than stand in front of an Army firing squad for desertion! Maybe we should *not* go back and open a business together in your Atlanta, Texas you are always talking about."

My mood improved as only Alex could do it and I said, "Yep, maybe the Army would think we were both dead and forget about us?" I really wanted to end this foolishness before I got us both killed. Perhaps it was my southern Rebel ancestry that made me want to take the fight to the devil's *own* house.

We started walking toward *Boquillas*, which Alex figured was still a couple of miles away. My feet felt better and I had learned from Alex the salve was a combination of the aloe vera plant, common to the arid desert and some unknown animal fat. Just having clothes and my Army issue Colt 45 belted on made me feel whole again. Alex had reservations about us wearing anything that indicated we were Army until we had a chance to scout the town for bandits. We might pass for American gunrunners except for my US Army buckle attached to my belt and holster, and the uniform top Alex wore. My impulse was to charge in and kill every bandit standing. However, having studied military tactics, I knew it would be wiser to slip into the small town quietly if we could.

The town was closer to a small village, dusty and dry when we circled both ends before walking in. It was too hot for much movement and there appeared to be no danger present. We made our way to the only cantina which looked to have a small boarding house built upstairs. The single street was unpaved and narrow, with a mixture of a dozen wood and adobe buildings on either side.

Once inside the near empty cantina, Alex haggled for one room and bed for the two of us from a lazy-eyed barkeep and apparently the innkeeper as well. I did not understand more than three words of the negotiation, but I took an instant dislike to the man, which was normally not in my nature. He was several days unshaven and it had been many more days since he'd seen any scrub water. He kept making slow circles on the bar with a dirty rag while eyeing me suspiciously. I seriously wondered if I'd have to kill him before we left town.

After making our way upstairs to our room, I was pleasantly surprised at the size. Compared to our usual Army tent quarters, the room was spacious. I opened the small window that faced the street to air out the place and sat down on the bed which creaked out a loud complaint. "Alex, I guess those bastard bandits must have camped somewhere out in the desert. I don't suppose sleepy-eyes downstairs mentioned any large group of rough men coming through lately?"

"He did not mention any bandits, but he said we were the only men that had been through in weeks. I don't trust him. I'm betting he would know and be friendly to any bandits in the area. We best not sleep too soundly and in shifts, because if I'm to die I want it to be in Texas. For now the town is quiet and I don't think they are here."

We washed up from a large tub on the back porch of the saloon. The water was fed from a small spring which was cool and refreshing. After we had cleaned up as much as possible, we began to scout the town. There was a general store with few supplies, a blacksmith, with an attached barn that doubled as a livery stable, and finally an adobe church with a couple of dozen graves in an unkempt graveyard in the back. I shuddered and hoped I would not end up buried in a lonely grave here. Most of the homes were either attached to the businesses or several feet back of the town's main street to avoid some of the dust.

Alex and I returned to the saloon to wait for the evening meal and rest for the anticipated fight. I did not want to die after surviving the battle in Glenn Springs. Also, I was responsible for bringing Alex into the situation and his life and his career were at risk because of me. I had nobody waiting for me at home, but I had hopes of a wife and family. My current course could mean another close friend's death and my own as well.

Supper was surprisingly good. The food was plentiful and delicious. The barkeep, who I learned was named Pedro Sanchez, owned the place. Pedro liked to eat and had hired Carman Montez, a widow to run his kitchen. She was a happy woman of about forty years, with large sparkling eyes, and a distinctive laugh, which she aired out often. I liked her right away as she brightened any room she entered. Carman seemed to enjoy feeding the hungry men who lived or passed through *Boquillas*.

On this evening two local residents and one traveler were around the single table with Alex and me. Pedro preferred to take his meals behind his bar, which was fine with me. One of the two local men was a farmer who had tired of his wife's cooking. The other local was Jacob, the blacksmith, who appeared to be in love with Carman. Jacob was a quiet man, tall and even more powerfully built than Alex. From his accent and Nordic features, he appeared to be Swedish in ancestry. He never said his last name or why he lived south of the border and no one asked.

The traveler was a small, nervous man who kept his hat on at the table. MY mother would have slapped the hat off his head before he sat down. The man constantly shifted his eyes from me to Alex, obviously nervous at our presence. He had only introduced himself as Joe Leigh, and said he sold supplies from his wagon on both sides of the border. I wanted to know why he was here. Also, his manner seemed a little feminine to me, with no whiskers visible at all. I supposed he might be too young or of Indian decent. However, his handshake was firm and I noticed new blisters on the hand from the reins of the wagon.

I suspected him of gunrunning for the bandits, and wanted a look inside his wagon when the opportunity allowed. Although I had no standing on this side of the border, if this man had supplied guns to the bandits that had attacked Glenn Springs, then I would be duty bound to take him to justice on the American side. It occurred to me immediately that I had an exaggerated opinion of my own importance, considering I had abandoned my Army duties and was now *absent without leave*, and most likely a wanted man myself. That thought aside, I knew there were no courts, or law in Mexico at the time that would stand the man up to pay for his actions.

# CHAPTER 6

## *The King's Son*

The next day was spent drinking in the cantina and I am ashamed to say, we did a lot of it. The town remained quiet and no strangers rode into the dusty streets. In the hottest part of the afternoon, I saw Joe walk out the back of the buildings to sit in the shade of a lone tree. A hand carved bench had been set up under the tree. I managed to slip out the front and make my way over to the stables. At first inspection, Joe's wagon seemed normal to me. I did not know where Jacob the Blacksmith was, but I would use the excuse of wanting to buy horses if he returned.

Peeking under the canvas tarp, I saw *various and sundry* items of hardware and tack neatly arranged. I ran my hand around the sides of the wagon and jammed a sliver of wood clean under a fingernail on my left hand. Cussing and trying to suck out the splinter, I was ready to give up and go back across the street. Glancing back at the wagon I noticed the depth seemed deeper than the amount of supplies inside. Dumbfounded, I figured there must be a foot of hidden space under the wagon.

Now what to do? Should I knock Joe over the head, throw him in the wagon and head back to the border? If it was proved the wagon contained firearms for the bandits, I wanted to shoot him like the coyote varmint he was and leave him to rot in the street. I was mad clean through, thinking again of my dead men back in Glenn Springs. How many more would die or had died because of this man's lust for money?

I crossed the street and found Alex sleeping in a tipped-back chair in one corner of the cantina. Instead of waking him I walked through to the back to confront Joe about the hidden compartment. Once I saw him I said without hesitation, "I need to talk to you mister about that wagon of yours. Looks to me like you have some extra space at the bottom that I suspect is loaded with guns." I expected to see alarm in his eyes. Or at least hear a denial, but he was calm. Obviously the man was confident in his abilities and purpose. I outweighed him by fifty pounds and did not see a gun in sight. Suddenly I was wary.

When he spoke, he seemed no more agitated than if a fly were buzzing his hat. "We seem to have a problem then don't we? I gave you no permission to examine my wagon. Whoever you are, you have no authority here. I do not answer to you or any other man. If you continue to persist with your inquiry, you will most certainly regret your present course of action."

If I had been in a foul mood before, I was over the *moon-and-back* now. I just wanted to smash him in the face for his irksome calm. "Mister, if there are guns in that wagon I'm taking them back across the border and handing them over to the Army. Glenn Springs was raided by bandits and several good people died. If you're selling guns to bandits, I'm making it my business and I don't care much about who has authority in the matter. I thought I had detected a flinch at my mention of good people dying. Maybe he was not so emotionless after all. However, he recovered fast enough.

"I know nothing of which you speak", he said with great formality. "You may inspect my wagon again, but at your own risk." With that, he turned, back straight and walked back inside.

Standing in my indecision, I turned to watch him disappear inside. Alex was standing in the doorway with an irritating grin etched on his face smoking a small cigar. "What are you looking at? While you were napping, I checked out the wagon and I'm sure there is a false bottom storage area."

"Maybe for tool storage you think?"

"No I don't *think*, but you can take that grin back inside. I'll take care of the wagon and the mysterious Joe too. If he is gunrunning, we'll be taking that wagon back across the border or burning it to ashes before we leave."

Suddenly, Alex and I both reacted to a loud roar coming from the street. The sound was rare but distinct, and could only be a motorcycle. The only person we knew who owned a bike in the area was Darwin Dawkins Kilpatrick, the son of the *"King of Candelaria"*. James Judson Kilpatrick, known as J.J. to his friends, owned the General Store and Post Office in *Candelaria*, back on the Texas side. The town had grown up around the natural hot springs in the area. The senior Kilpatrick was an astute business man. He had invested well and was the richest man in any town within a hundred miles.

J.J. Kilpatrick's son, Dawkins, was only twenty three and a local celebrity in his own right. He was known for hell raising antics on both sides of the border. Only his father's influence as the Justice of the Peace in *Candelaria* and his uncle H.H. Kilpatrick as the county judge in Marfa had kept the young man out of jail on more than a few occasions. Dawkins was a hard drinker, who rode both sides of the border on his motorcycle or on one of the horses he used for trick riding. Dawkins was friendly and well liked. He lived for adventure and, having grown up on the border, spoke Spanish like a native. We had shared a few drinks and played poker in Glenn Springs and *Candelaria*.

A small crowd of amazed onlookers rushed into the powdery street in time to cough and spit out the dust created when Kilpatrick sped past us and circled back to the delight of the gathered spectators. His speed was an unheard of thirty-five miles per hour before he engaged the brake and slid to a stop. I was impressed with the bright red motorcycle, with most motor vehicles of the day darkly colored, but could not abide the noise it made.

Stopping in front of the cantina, the dust clouds swirled around him as if he was controlling it as part of his grand entrance. As the dust began to clear, he turned and searched those assembled and we made eye contact. "Howdy Oscar, I heard you fellows ran into an angry hornet's nest of bandits the other night."

"There might be a time to talk about it inside Dawkins. Shut off that inferno thing first so I can look her over."

Dawkins Kilpatrick was a striking young man, strongly built in the shoulders and six feet tall. "She's a beauty isn't she? It's a 1913 Indian twin cylinder. She runs 7 horsepower and has a 2 speed transmission. This girl even has a cradle spring frame which makes the ride smoother. That's important in this rough terrain. I love the bike but my back side takes a beating on every trip. I spend a lot of time bouncing around just trying to stay on her."

Some of the townspeople were drifting away out of the heat. I admired the bike and had to admit it was a nice piece of workmanship, but I could not help teasing Kilpatrick. "Dawkins there isn't a rode around this country that's smooth. You run that thing too fast and you'll break your neck flying over the handle bars and this here bike too. As a cavalry man, I say give me a horse, which will naturally sense when there is a washed out road or gulley. This thing could plant you firmly in a shallow grave."

"Maybe so, but it can keep up with most horses and run a long way further. Let's go inside and I expect you could buy me one of those warm beers Oscar."

We went inside seeking some shade and ordered three beers. Alex had never met Kilpatrick, but like the rest of us had heard countless stories of his misadventures in *Candelaria,* and all around the area. Alex looked at Dawkins across the table and said, "I see you wear two guns *amigo.* Are those for bandits, panthers, or the law?"

I worried the man might be offended by such a direct question, but he answered without hesitation. "I used to travel unarmed on both sides of the border, but ever since Villa started stirring things up, it is wise to argue with a man from a position of strength. As for the law, my pa and uncle are both judges. I respect the law just fine as long as it leaves *me* alone. I would never shoot *at* a lawman and so far, I have gotten along with most everyone south and north of the border. However If I spend much time with you two, my free ranging across the border may be over. As for mountain lions, you'll never see the one that eats you." Turning serious he leaned in and said, "I heard about the dust up in Glenn Springs. You lost some men and they buried some townsfolk, including a child."

At the mention of the child I must have taken in a loud, quick breath because both men looked at me. I knew there was a pained look in my eyes. "I saw that deaf and mute boy Johnny walking around aimlessly during the battle, obviously unaware of the firing all around him. We all liked that boy. I imagine it is a hard thing to lose a child. I lost some good men back there too, including Bill Kubitz, one of my best friends."

Kilpatrick looked at me with sympathy in his eyes. "Well now, I only read about the battle in the Alpine and Marathon newspaper, but I heard the battle was not only written about in Texas, but as far away as the New York City papers. The way the story went, Johnny survived without a scratch. It was Jack, his seven year old brother who was shot. Some say it was not intentional, but a ricochet bullet that did it." Dawkins took a long drink of his warm beer while we all thought about the innocent boy's life. He frowned then continues. "Also, you and your eight men put up a fight that the bandits won't soon forget. There were blood pools all around like someone had been butchering cattle. Only a dozen or so bandit dead were left behind, but the guess is that as many as fifty died, give-or take. Some estimates put the number of bandits as high as a hundred. Four of your men were buried and they don't know what to think about you and Alex."

I was surprised and relieved to learn that little Johnny was alive but still saddened by the news of Johnny's brother Jack. All those people were needlessly killed because of some *bad* men. If anything, my resolve for killing as many bandits as possible was stronger than ever. I said, "I'd appreciate it if you let us cross back and come in without an announcement Dawkins. I dragged Alex along and intend to hunt down some bandits on this side before returning to face whatever the Army has in mind for me. I hope to clear Alex so he can stay in the Army. It's the only home he has."

As I expected, Alex took immediate offense to my trying to claim all blame for any wrongdoing. "Oscar, I'm a grown man. I made my own decision. I'll stand up for whatever I've done. You can stop trying to wipe my nose for me."

Kilpatrick studied the two of us as if judging our *real* intentions. "I'm not about to go telling anyone Oscar. I mostly mind my own business and will live longer because of it. However, I'd hate to see two of the Army's best men get themselves shot down in this dust-infested hell hole of a town!"

I looked at Alex and said, "We have some business to attend to tonight or tomorrow at the latest, then we intend to buy horses and head back across the border. Let's order a round of whiskey, toast the friends we lost, and celebrate being *alive*, because tomorrow…well, one *never* knows."

Alex and I exchanged a look and his previous anger dissolved. Instead he seemed relieved to hear me mention a plan that involved us going back. He was a good soldier and would make a good sergeant someday. His only problem would be staying *far* away from self-appointed *know-it-all-fools* like me.

Before Dawkins left, he laid a hand on my shoulder, but spoke to Alex in Spanish. "*Cuidanse y tengan mucho cuidado. Vayan con Dios.*" He made his way to the door on unsteady feet walking to his motorcycle. He managed to get the bike started. Once the engine caught, he road back out of town and was gone. We waved and watched as another swirling dust storm followed in the bike's wake.

After he had disappeared I looked to Alex for a translation. He shrugged and said, "I think your young friend *Senor* Kilpatrick is a good man. I believe he thinks what we are doing is honorable, but *very* foolish. We may well be killed for our honor. The last thing he said was for us to *take care of each other and go with God.*"

# CHAPTER 7

## *Mysterious Gunrunner Named Joe*

Preoccupied with low-spirited thoughts, I went to my room and tried to nap in the heat. I estimated the time as late afternoon. Even with the room window open, scarcely a breeze moved the burlap curtains. I managed to fall into a troubled sleep. Too many unresolved conflicts made my head ache. I questioned again the path I was taking. It felt like I was caught up in flood waters, swept away and helpless to stop myself. I thrashed around on the bed, but finally dropped into a deep exhausted sleep. I dreamed of men dying and heard the loud thundering volley of rifles and smelled burning flesh. I heard the frightened cries of wounded and dying men. The last thing before I awoke, I saw blood on my hands and did not know if it was mine or belonged to others.

I came awake with a start, the dream fresh and troubling on my mind. I was bathed in sweat. My hands shook as I attempted to shave and wash up as best I could in the water pitcher provided in the room. Feeling a little refreshed, I strapped on my gun and went downstairs. I wondered what to do about Joe Leigh. The man had somehow gotten under my skin. I admitted to myself that he had flat out infuriated me. Hidden guns aside, I wanted to strike out at him for his calm demeanor. Suddenly decided, I knew I would seek proof before confronting him again with the evidence in hand.

I went to find Alex to see if he knew the whereabouts of Joe. I found him playing solitary. I walked directly over to his table and stood expectantly like we were moving out that moment. He knew I was there, but did not look up. I put my hands on my hips and cleared my throat. "Time is short my friend and you're wasting time playing a *silly* card game while I was sweating through a nap. It is a good thing for you I'm not a bandit."

He slid his Colt off of his lap and laid it on the table, and then gestured to the cards. "It relaxes me, takes little concentration, and lets my mind focus on more important things." He looked up, reading my impatience. "You need to learn this game too *Senor* Oscar? You have much on your mind and are often anxious to get killed. I think sometimes you need to look to your own business and not others."

"For your information I plan on dying an *old* man. I just need a better look inside that wagon *before* I confront Joe again. If he is guilty as I believe, we can tie him up and drive that wagon back tonight. Recovering a cache of guns and taking back a gunrunner to Captain Cole might let you keep those stripes."

"Well it must be your lucky day because Joe rented a horse from Jacob and rode out an hour ago. Also, before you ask, Jacob is over at that widow woman's house, Carman. If they're having *too* much fun we may go hungry tonight. Come on I'll go with you this time and we'll do it right this time."

Resisting a sharp retort at his poke at me, we walked across the street and began looking over the wagon. It was dark in the interior and Alex found a lantern and lit it. He examined the underneath looking for some sort of trap door while I unloaded some of the supplies inside. The wagon turned out to have been made by the Newton Wagon Company in Batavia, Illinois. It had been made for the purpose of hauling wheat and other grains on a farm. The wagon was 10 feet long, 38 inches wide and was supposed to be 38 inches deep. I worried that if Joe had ridden out to meet with bandits this might be our last chance to capture or destroy the wagon.

Upon closer inspection, it was clear that another foot of space had been added to the entire length of the wagon giving it a 50 inch depth. The lower section of wood was not as faded and a seam appeared to be where there should be none. Alex and I worked around the hitch closest to the wagon and discovered a small trap door that was only large enough to allow a hand to reach inside. Reaching through into the darkness I felt then gripped a handle. With a small tug we heard a creak before the bottom section lowered at the back on a hidden hinge.

Not surprising the secret compartment contained rifles. Loaded inside were at least fifty guns wrapped in oiled canvas. Pulling one out and removing the canvas I could read the stamped engraving on the side of *Model 1915, 32 Caliber* and *Stevens Favorite* on the top. The stock was walnut and the rifle appeared new. It could have been worse with a larger caliber or repeating rifle, but even a small caliber, single shot, lever action rifle in the hands of a marksman would still be deadly.

Alex had this incredulous look on his face and I could not resist a little gloating. "Do you still think I need to relax and look to my own business Corporal Alejandro?"

We decided to hitch up the wagon and pull it around to the back of the boarding house for a quick escape if things got ugly with Joe's capture. When left the wagon in a shaded spot between two small trees. With the sun setting, only a walk toward the wagon would reveal the wagon was out of place. We walked inside just as Carman was loading the table with delicious containers of fresh made tortillas, beef and a peach pie by the smell. "May I serve you *Senor* Oscar, *Senor* Alex?"

She had a glowing smile and Alex and I exchanged grins when she turned to look toward the door. Jacob had a matching smile as he entered. I imagined the afternoon had been most enjoyable. Before I had a chance to decide whether I should remark on the new development, Joe walked in, dusty, appearing tired and worried. I did not know if he had checked on the wagon or something had happened on his ride. A moment later he settled into a seat and again left his hat on. He seemed even more nervous than the previous night. He acknowledged Alex and the others present and ignored me. I was sure if he had checked on the wagon we would be in a fight about now. It was must be something else, but it could wait until after dinner. I realized I had only eaten some beans wrapped in a tortilla that Carman had prepared around sunrise and left out for the late risers.

After everyone had enjoyed the food for a few minutes, Joe cleared his throat and spoke to the room. "I rented a horse from Mr. Jacob today. While I was out riding I saw a small band of men who I thought might be bandits." He looked to the residents of the town before continuing. "I don't know what standing this town has with the revolutionaries, but they may be headed this way."

Dead silence took over the room. My stomach knotted into a tight ball. As much as I wanted to pay the bandits back for my men, I knew the consequences of my actions might be about to be paid for with blood. I was sure he was lying, but I was not going to give him up in front of others. I still intended to slip out of town with the wagon and Joe unconscious or hogtied in the belly of the wagon. Looking directly at Joe I broke the silence and gave him a hard look. "How many men constitute a small band of bandits to you Mr. Leigh?"

"Seven or eight would be my guess." His voice wavered as he continued. He looked away and would not meet my eyes. His answer seemed evasive and trailed off at the end. "Of course there could be more in the area."

Jacob spoke reassuringly, looking at Carman. "Mostly they leave us alone. They are a rough bunch but we don't have much choice in the matter. If they come in Carman will feed them and Pedro will serve them drinks. I think it might be better if Oscar and Alex stay out of sight. They need me but you two will stand out which will be inviting trouble, although Alex would pass unnoticed if he removed that Army shirt."

The rest of supper was a quiet affair, with each person absorbed in thoughts of their own. Alex and I excused ourselves and went to the room. Jacob probably thought we were taking his advice. Once inside we checked our guns and readied ourselves for what lay ahead. Alex said what I believed was a prayer and then crossed himself. I put a hand on the shorter man's shoulder and said, "Alex, I brought you to this. I know you won't stay out of it, but I'm planning on sitting down in the cantina with my back to the door. If you sit outside you can cover me with a rifle if need be. I'll lean my rifle against the wall and kept my 45 loose in the holster."

As I knew he would, Alex refused to be left outside. "Oscar those were my friends back in Glenn Springs and I won't be left out of the fight. I know you worry you will be responsible if I am killed, but It was my choice to follow you here. The Army is as you say *mi familia*." His grin lit the room and lifted my spirit as only he could when I was facing uncertainty or doubt. "If the Army will no longer have me then, I will come live with you."

I asked Alex to go downstairs and keep a lookout. He was still brazenly wearing his Army uniform top with his two strips showing. The uniform would make him an instant target and he knew it. I was wearing an old scratchy shirt and rough-made pants. The pants were held up by my Army issue gun belt, with my single action Colt revolver holstered. The only visible item that identified me as Army was my U.S. issue buckle.

Knowing what I had to do, I took my rifle and went down the short hall to confront Joe with our discovery. I had seen him enter the room a couple of times and hoped he would be there now. We were running out of time and might have to move fast if the bandits rode in. Room doors in the boarding house had no locks. Seasoned travelers would sometimes block the door by propping a chair tightly up under the knob. If need be, I knew I could shatter the chair but not without considerable noise. I was not normally a praying man, but I said one now. Alex and I needed some luck or what my pa liked to preach about as *divine intervention*. Either way, I would accept what I could get tonight.

Standing outside Joe's room door, I took a few deep breaths and remembered the anger I felt at losing my men. Joe's gunrunning had to be stopped before more soldiers and innocent folks died. I grabbed the knob and prepared to rush in or crash through depending on the set up at the door. In the next moment, events happened so fast it was hard later to remember the order of things.

The door was *not* locked and I almost fell into the room in time to see a half naked Joe grab a shirt and cover up. I saw enough to know Joe was not a *man* and had been hiding a beautiful head of auburn hair under that hat. I stood there a second trying to decide if

I should apologize and leave. To her credit she did not scream which would have alerted everyone in the boarding house that Joe had a woman in his room. As we both composed ourselves, I realized this was indeed the same person I had eaten supper with twice while she was masquerading as a man. The gunrunning was still *her* crime and my intention was to stop it.

Finding her voice for both of us she said flatly, "Close the door fool! Also you can close your big gapping mouth while you're at it."

When I was growing up my momma must have tired of my endless questions when she said, "James Oscar, I will faint *dead away* if you ever find yourself *speechless* over anything!" I would have to write ma a letter real soon for I had surely been struck mute now. It took me some time to locate enough words to begin. "First, who are you and why are you running guns to the bandits? Alex and I found your guns and I will burn them before I let them in the hands of those bandits!"

She sighed and I could see she had been crying. "My real name is Josephine Leigh. I'm originally from Savanna, Georgia, but had been living in New York City, before my husband moved us to Alpine, Texas. I was widowed a few months back when my husband was lost in a mining accident near Terlingua, Texas. He was a geologist for the *Chisos* Mining Company. They were mining cinnabar, a type of quicksilver mercury, when the roof caved in. After several days of digging all hope was lost. They had to fill in the hole and I was widowed, left with almost nothing."

She studied me as she continued to speak, biting her nails nervously between words. "Oscar, I often leap blindly following my heart and not listening to my head. I married my husband too quickly after a whirlwind romance, finding myself here in this desert country, then alone. There are few ways a decent woman can make a living. I was approached by local businessmen because they believed I had extensive investments. I took their idea for my own. The thought of selling guns to revolutionaries, disguised as a man seemed like a high adventure, taken straight from a theater play. Oscar you must believe me, I did not know men and women were dying on both sides of the border. Now those horrible men are riding in to collect what is owed to them. I was supposed to meet them with the guns, but tried to back out of the deal. I was told they would be here after dark and take the guns for themselves. If I am seen I'm sure to be killed as well."

I seriously considered the idea that I was being sold a bushel of rotten apples, or if her story could possibly be true. Either way, I knew where the wagon and guns were located. She did not. "I want you to stay here for now. Gather your things and if you hear shooting, meet Alex and me out back of the boarding house. I won't leave the guns to the bandits and must take you back. Under the circumstances the authorities should not punish you too harshly." She seemed uncertain about my words and I doubted she would meet us. My only alternative was to tie her up. Her being a woman made my previous plan of knocking her on the head appeared improper now. My ma raised me to respect all women, even this one. However, I was a long way from trusting her.

# CHAPTER 8

## *Making Our Stand in Boquillas*

I walked out of her room and headed down the stairs, I shook my head in amazement at the mysterious nature of women. Of course here I stood. I was a deserter from the Army and looking to get myself and Alex killed in a foreign country. I knew I was volunteering for a battle I had no right to be fighting. If God *did* exist, he probably had himself a laugh at the way we tangled up whatever plan he had for us. The human race as a whole I reasoned was a complex and often confused people.

When I finally got downstairs Alex was sitting with his back to the wall and to the right of the front door. I could see his rifle close by and knew his pistol was near at hand as well. I decided the details about Joe, or Josephine could wait. I could see the questions in his eyes as I neared his table. "No, I did not knock Joe out, but he admitted the whole deal and said he tried to call it off, but now the bandits are coming after their guns. He's in the room getting together his things and will meet us around back. Now is the time my *amigo* when two sane men would get up on that wagon and ride out of here."

His answer was matter-of-fact. "Oscar, I do not consider myself insane, but we came here for a reason. We have the guns and now you will have your bandits."

Smiling despite the tension I felt. I took up a position on the opposite side of the door and leaned my rifle against the wall. I could feel the barkeep's eyes on me as I sat. What would the man do if shooting started? I suddenly remembered I should have checked behind the bar. Pedro surely had a gun under there and it would have been an advantage knowing what kind. I ordered a beer for myself and Alex, if for no other reason just to have something to do with my hands. Nobody else was in the cantina and I was sure it was due to the expected bandit visit.

Pedro came to my table and sneered down at me when he set the beer down. His accent was heavy and his breath was foul, flowing through the space where at least three teeth should have been. "*Senor*, I think you will maybe be dead soon. Men are coming who hate *soldados!* They will have even more contempt for a cowardly one like you. I know you are a deserter. It is a shameful thing to run away!"

Before I could react to the man's deliberate provocation, Alex chose that moment to stand up and reach for his beer with his left hand. With his right hand he smashed the man in the left cheek. Alex had brought the powerful punch all the way from his hip. Pedro Sanchez fell immediately as if his leg bones had melted. Alex took a long drink of his beer and proceeded to pick the man up by his belt. He slung his weight over his shoulder and deposited him, none to gently in a pile behind the bar.

When Alex was done, he picked up a double barreled shotgun from behind the bar. He held it up and finding both barrels loaded he said, "It's a 12 gage Remington model 1894. I'd guess it was at one time about twenty-eight inches long. Old Pedro here cut the stock and the barrel down to handle it behind the bar. At least the man keeps his guns clean and I don't think he'll be in need of it tonight." He tucked the shotgun under his right arm and stuffed some extra shells into his pocket that he found. He kicked one of Pedro's boots so it would not show from the door, then walked casually back to his seat and lit another one of his cigars. He offered one to me but I turned it down due to a sour stomach.

I looked at him like I had never met him before. "Alex the next time we need somebody knocked out you've got the job."

At that moment we both stiffened at the sound of horses in the street. From the racket, they were hard ridden and it was impossible to be sure of the number of riders. The horses were reined in outside the cantina and we heard boots on the raised boardwalk, then laughter coming from just outside. Something was said in Spanish and some of the voices drifted away. Other voices seemed to be arguing.

Alex leaned toward me and said in a whisper, "He told some men to go search for the wagon at the livery stable. I can't estimate how many more are out there, but they plan on searching the rooms for Joe. If they find him…" Alex made a slashing motion to his throat. Suddenly remembering the unconscious Pedro, he went behind the bar and set a bottle of whiskey on the polished wood along with six small glasses. He then returned quickly to his position by the door. We were as ready as two fools could be.

The first three bandits came through the cantina door and went immediately to the bar. The apparent leader was a big ugly man with an oversized nose under bushy brows. He called out for Pedro, then seeing the whiskey, poured a round for himself and his men. The drinks were swallowed in one gulp and a second glass was poured for each of the men. After the second drinks were tossed back, *Big Nose* turned around and took in the room. I used my left hand to tip my beer at the man. My right hand hung loosely by my side. My eyes widened when I noticed his belt buckle. My blood seemed to run cold and my hands turned to ice.

The man ignored me for now and stared hard at Alex. A hot challenge was issued in Spanish and I assumed Alex told him he was an Army deserter. Not satisfied by the answer, he moved his left hand closer to the center of his belt. Time seemed to slow to a crawl and my senses were heightened with every minute detail acutely in focus. His big pistol was suspended in a holster on his right, tilted for a cross draw from his left. The man had an oversized sombrero hung from a dirty string around his neck. His greasy hair was uncut and he wore a three week growth of beard.

I suddenly spoke up and my voice sounded loud in the room. "*Senor*, do you speak English? I would appreciate a word with you. I am in need of information." His companions were laughing and drinking, facing away from us at the bar, and appeared to be oblivious to the drama taking place behind them.

He suddenly looked at me closely for the first time. Instant contempt appeared in his narrowed eyes. "*You* dare to speak to me *gringo*! You are on the *wrong* side of the boarder. I am *el jefe* here. You live or die by my orders!"

As he finished speaking I stood up revealing my US Army belt buckle, the twin of which the man wore on his belt. The US he sported shone like polished gold. My right forearm rested lightly on the butt of my Colt, placing my hand inches from the butt. I addressed him, relieved to hear my voice sounded steady. I was jumpy inside but madder than I had ever been and wanted a fight. "*You* dared to cross to the *wrong* side of the border and kill Americans in Glenn Springs, including my friend! You *Senor* have his *buckle* on your belt."

Quicker than I could have imagined his hand blurred as he gripped his pistol and began to slide it from the holster. I felt the gun in my hand buck twice as I shot him slightly above the buckle, framing either side of his navel. He grunted as the air expelled from his lungs in a rush. He leaned back heavily against the bar, with a grimace of pain and fear showing on his face. I was half blind from the smoke in my eyes, and my ears rang from my two shots, followed quickly by two more from Alex to my right. As the explosive report of my firing filled the room, the bandit to the right of Big Nose turned, a drink pressed to his lips. Alex showed him no mercy and shot him in the chest before the man realized the danger of the moment. The next bandit was quicker and drew his gun an instant before he was hit in the neck by Alex's second shot, and my third slammed into his teeth. The man's pistol fired into the wall behind Alex as he sank to his knees and stretched out face down.

I stepped forward and roughly pulled the US buckle from Big Nose's belt and stuffed it in my pocket. I could see the man remained alive, his eyes darting around helplessly. He had no chance, gut shot as he was. I felt nothing at witnessing his suffering. As I stood up I heard running feet outside sounding loud on the wooden boardwalk before three men came crashing through the door. I fired too quickly as I turned and the heavy .45 caliber slug dug a three inch crease on the first man's right cheek. A second later, Alex shot the one in the middle with one barrel of the 12 gage shotgun. The blast took him off his feet and the other two must have been peppered by some of the large buckshot. I fired again and saw the one I had hit before stagger back two steps. Alex fired the last barrel into the ceiling lantern and instant darkness enveloped us.

Momentarily blinded, we finally began to see dim moonlight filtering through the only window and we headed for it. Wild shots were fired blindly into the room. My 45 was empty since I routinely loaded only five rounds for safety. I then realized I had left my rifle by my chair. Alex fired at one of the ribbons of flame and I was satisfied to hear a loud grunt indicating he had hit someone. Before I could think about reloading, strong hands grabbed me and threw me bodily through the window. I landed on the raised porch outside covered in glass and panting for breath. An instant later, Alex landed on top of me and forced out whatever air I had left in my lungs.

I rolled over and tumbled into the street, tasting the dust. I was helpless for the moment until Alex again grabbed me bodily and half dragged me to the rear of the building. My legs were wobbly and I could barely walk but we made it to the wagon. Joe or Josephine was forgotten as I took the reins and urged the two horse team on with a crack from a whip that I found stuck down in a crack of the seat. I had lost my rifle but Alex was reloading the shotgun and his pistol. With no way to judge how many bandits were left in the town, our only thought was to put distance between the bandits. I followed no trail but my instincts told me the American border was ahead.

A somewhat familiar voice came from the covered back of the wagon, though softer and more feminine, startling us both. "May I help with the reloading? I took a half dozen of the rifles from the hidden compartment. My father taught me to shoot. I may live in New York, but I was hunting with my father and brother as soon as I could hold a rifle. My pa was fond of saying, *one bullet,* and *one squirrel* for the table. I will prove a valuable asset if they follow."

Alex looked back and saw Josephine in a dress, with her hair pulled back, topped with a colored ribbon. Her excited eyes reflected in the moonlight. He looked from me to her and I started laughing, releasing the pent up tension of the evening. After a moment, Alex joined in, followed by Josephine as well. "Now I know why you didn't knock her over the head Oscar. She's too darned pretty. Perhaps you were planning on telling me Joe is a woman at some point!"

"I only found out before I came downstairs. I wanted you to concentrate on the bandits, not on the lovely Josephine here and her little masquerade."

Just when I thought we had no pursuit I heard Josephine gasp as she looked back. Three bandits had just sky lined themselves in the fading light. Alex quickly began climbing in the back of the wagon when we both heard the rifle shot, loud in the back of the wagon. The middle bandit was slammed off the back of his horse. The other two men fought their horses and decided Mexico needed them elsewhere.

After checking to make sure we were no longer followed, Alex climbed back up to the seat beside me. He ginned, but still looked confused and uncertain. "I would never have believed it Oscar, that shot must have been a hundred yards up hill."

"She did say she could shoot. One shot is what she said Alex."

Josephine moved back toward the front of the wagon as if nothing had just happened. She calmly tucked away a loose strand of her auburn hair and began reloading the rifle she had used. As I drove she told her story to Alex as to how Josephine had become Joe Leigh, and later, how she had become a gunrunner.

After she finished, Alex said, "Now what do we do with Miss Josephine? If we let her go and Captain Cole finds out, he might go on and hang us on general principle."

Josephine said anxiously, I will go back to New York. I have friends there and you will never see me on the border again."

I looked at Alex for a moment before deciding. "I might have suffered a blow to the head back there, but as far as I'm concerned, the gunrunner was Joe Leigh. He was killed by that big nosed ugly bandit and is buried in an unmarked grave behind the church in *Boquillas*. In the matter of our passenger here, we are two gentlemen helping out a *lady in distress*. I think we should drive Miss Leigh into Marathon and put her on a train, then go face Captain Cole in Alpine. I expect he might hang us after all, or send us to the trenches in that European war over there. Oh and one more thing my friend, I appreciate you saving my neck in the cantina. I only have one request, next time you go through the blasted window first!"

# CHAPTER 9

## *Captain Cole's Hard Decision*

It took us another four hours to reach Marathon. We were not the only horse drawn wagon on the road, but sharing the rough and rutted road with those loud automobiles was a problem. I stopped the wagon in front of the only hotel and helped Josephine down. Alex dug deep and produced one of his gold coins to pay for the cost of Miss Leigh's train back to New York, then pressed four more of the gold coins into her small hand. I think he must have been holding out on me during our last poker game and must have gold coins hidden somewhere in his boots.

I don't know what Alex was thinking, but I stood there looking at Josephine Leigh like I was trying to memorize her in that moment. She looked mighty pretty standing there alone and vulnerable, but sad, as she fought back tears. Before she went inside the hotel for the night, she hugged us both and planted a kiss on each of our cheeks before saying, "There are no words to thank you both enough. I will try to get a letter through when I am settled. What you have done for me I will never forget. I guess there are still princes saving damsels in the world after all. I will pray that it will not go hard on the both of you with the Army."

She turned once and waved before disappearing inside. Josephine was quite the woman. She would be missed. I was satisfied with my decision to let her go. Would I ever see her again? Although I was not much older than her, it felt like I was abandoning a little sister to the wolves of the world. We were in no hurry to get into Alpine and face what the Army had in store for us. I drove the wagon to the edge of town and pulled off the road and out of sight under a huge dead tree. Alex found some coffee in the wagon and I made a fire. We had not thought to bring any food and planned on moving on soon after the break.

Back on the road with Marathon behind us we rode along at a creeping pace. I thought of what Alex had said about running away to Atlanta. He was probably right that the Army might never look for us, assuming we had been killed. Shaking off the useless thoughts, I knew we had no choice but to face what we had done. Alex and I were comfortable sharing time without conversations for long periods of time, but tonight I needed our friendly banter to lift my spirits. "Alex it's possible if we ever see a letter from Josephine we might be reading it from an Army stockade or on a frozen battlefield in Europe."

"Oscar sometimes you think too damn much. I have two cigars left my friend. Let's enjoy what might be out last taste of freedom for a while." He handed me one of the slightly bent and misshaped cigars and lit his and mine before saying, "In my mind, which I'm sure will differ from the Army point of view; I choose to believe we are heroes. We captured a wagon full of guns intended for the bandits from the notorious *bad* man Joe Leigh. We killed a few of those bastards that attacked Glenn Springs, killing our friends, and saved a lady in distress." He was silent for a moment before continuing. "At least that's how I saw the circumstances unfold. Captain Cole may have a slightly different interpretation on the events than I do."

The hour was late when I drove the wagon into the Army fort in Alpine. The fort was considerably bigger than out outpost in Glenn Springs, but far smaller than Fort Bliss where I had been previously stationed. We were challenged by a sentry of the 15th Calvary. I knew we were a sorry sight but used my sergeant's commanding voice to disrupt the man's suspicion. "Private, I am Sergeant Oscar Draper of Troop A 14th Cavalry, we have just returned from a mission across the border into Mexico. We need to see Captain Cole immediately."

The man was confused by our appearance, but recognized the tone and bearing of a military man when he heard it. He sent another private running to alert Captain Cole to our arrival. I said to Alex under my breath, "Good, the quicker we meet with the captain, the sooner we can get some grub brought to us in the stockade. I'm hungry."

In a short while, we were met by a youthful-faced lieutenant, who appeared younger than most of the men in my regiment. When I mentioned the rifles, he took immediate interest in us and directed me to park the wagon next to the blacksmith's shop where Alex and I unhitched the team. He introduced himself as Theodore Barnes Jr. We both saluted and it felt strange knowing we were *out-of-uniform* at the time. I was about to show the lieutenant where the guns were stashed when I heard the unmistakable baritone voice of Captain Cole say my name. The captain and I had butted heads on more than one occasion, but I respected the man's rank, if not always his decisions. He was tall and walked at a fast pace, ramrod straight as always, still in his full uniform. I did not know what to expect now but was startled at the initial reception.

Before we could collect ourselves and salute our commanding officer he said, "Well this is a sight I thought I'd not look upon again. Sergeant Draper and Corporal Alejandro, and what a sorry sight you two are at that. You both were assumed to be dead." The man slapped Alex and me hard on the back and pumped our hands in greeting. "I want to hear all about where you've been and what has happened since the Glen Springs battle."

Before I could collect myself and answer, the overeager Lieutenant Barnes jumped in. "Sir, they have recovered a cache of illegal rifles from gunrunners!"

Looking irritated at the interruption, I knew I shared the captain's sentiment that the young and inexperienced lieutenant should be cached somewhere as well. Captain Cole, his eyes wide and excited said, "Show me Sergeant Draper."

I reached into the small trapdoor and released the hidden release. The hinge dropped and the opening was revealed. Alex reached in and took one of the Canvas covered rifles out and handed it to the captain. I recovered one of the loaded ones from the back of the wagon and held it up. "It is a single action .32 caliber Stevens favorite rifle. They are not a big caliber but still deadly in the wrong hands."

Captain Cole gave us both a surprised look. "Very impressive, I want to hear every detail. Leave nothing out, but first we will eat. You men look hungry." Turning his attention to Lieutenant Barnes he said, "See that we are brought food and otherwise left undisturbed. These men I'm sure are half-starved. See that the armory receives and accounts for these rifles." Dismissing Lieutenant Barnes with a *get-on-with-it* gesture, he turned to Alex and me and said, "We will dine in my quarters where I can hear all about your adventures." Officers and enlisted men dining together, even in remote outpost was a rare thing. Alex and I both nodded then exchanged puzzled looks, both wondering what our ultimate fate would be.

I had to thank the captain for feeding us before getting down to our story. The food was plentiful and we showed our appreciation by eating sizable portions. While we ate, the captain added to what we had heard from Dawkins Kilpatrick by telling us about the overnight delay of our reinforcements. I was angered by the fact, but figured it was due to pure bad luck rather than any deliberate dereliction of duty.

Finally, the meal set aside, the captain relaxed and handed us each a fat Girard cigar. Every soldier liked a little piece of home if it could be had in the rough furnishings on post in the southwest. I gathered these cigars were Captain Cole's private luxury and rarely shared. I might have my differences with the man, but he treated us as equals on that night. After a few strong pulls on the rich cigars, Alex and I began telling our story. We traded back and forth as the telling was better from one or the other's perspective. By mutual agreement we left out any involvement by Josephine Leigh, otherwise we laid it all out. I tried my best to take the reckless decisions onto my own shoulders and leave Alex as blameless as possible. However, Alex would have none of it and spoke to his own personal responsibility.

After we had finished our story Captain Cole sat in unreadable silence as he considered what his men had done in honor and duty, and in reckless and dangerous disregard for Army orders and regulations. I imagined him weighing the military charges against us and the treaty violations we must have committed against Mexico. I studied him and could not discern anything about his coming reactions.

He was a mystery of a man, handsome, married, with his wife and children waiting for him in his nearby quarters. I understood he was an educated man who grew up in Portland, Maine. He was certainly a long way from the lobster-filled ocean on the east coast.

Gradually, a slow moving storm of emotions began to cloud his pleasant features. In a moment he was on his feet, thundering back and forth in the room. He shook his head as if in disbelief and seemed to be having an argument in his head that only he was privy to. His face was an unreadable mask as if he was trying to digest something disgusting. I actually gripped my chair, ready for a quick leap to my feet in case he suddenly charged at me. Facing a firing squad seemed preferable to being beaten to death or strangled by my captain.

His mind made, he turned on us verbally. His face was dark and I could read a storm of conflicting emotions raging through him. "*God damn it* sergeant, I can't save you man! We would have given you both medals for your actions at Glenn Springs. Now…I might be able to keep Corporal Alejandro from the flames, if for no other reason than the capture of the gun runner rifles. Sergeant you were responsible for *your* actions and the actions of *your* men. I personally believe what you two have done was understandable under the circumstances. I might have felt the same in your place, but you knew your duty to the Army should have come first. A soldier's personal feelings are to be set aside and good judgment used. I'm sorry Sergeant Draper; you will be given a *dishonorable* discharged from the Army."

I just sat there and took in what he was saying. The Army had been good to me and become my home, but now through my own hand I had ended that part of my life. Alex stood and began a protest. "Captain, I should share in Sergeant Draper's fate as well. He did not force me to accompany him, participate in crossing the border, or in actions once in *Boquillas*. Sir, I do *not* regret my actions. Bandits are dead who raided Glen Springs and killed our friends and those in town. A gunrunner has been stopped due to the direct actions of Sergeant Draper."

"Do not forget your place Corporal Alejandro. You are still a part of my command. I say who goes and who stays. The battle in

Glen Springs was reported on as far away as New York. There are still reporters in the area. You and Sergeant Draper will have to be accounted for. You will serve two weeks in the stockade and lose one strip. MY decision is final. Sergeant Draper will be dishonorably discharged and sent home." Stepping to the door, Captain Cole called out and Lieutenant Barnes appeared. We were escorted to the stockade. Lieutenant Barnes appeared to be in a fine mood and was actually whistling under his breath as he saw us locked up.

Alex and I were given cells next to each other, the place being empty at the moment. I tried to apologize for getting Alex involved in my actions in *Boquillas*, but he shrugged it off. "Oscar, I have made my own way as a man for many years. I must live with the decisions I made. I would do it again and do not regret my actions." He suddenly broke out in laughter. It was worth it to see the look on your face when I threw you out that window."

Taking up the banter I said, "Ah Alex, I will never forget the expression on your face when you saw Joe dressed as Josephine. The shock and confusion in your eyes was worth ten of the gold coins you keep finding." We both laughed so hard a private came to the outside door and peered in anxiously. He must have thought we were *loco* as a rabid coyote. Despite my dread about tomorrow and my future, I slept contented in the knowledge that somehow things would turn out alright in a crazy world where laughter was still possible.

The next morning we were given clean uniforms to wear and fed breakfast as the sun was rising over the horizon. I looked myself over and decided I would miss the rough feel of the uniform. Honor and duty were represented in this uniform and I had disgraced mine. Next we were escorted to Captain Cole's office. He was in his dress uniform flanked on either side by like-dressed and serious officers. The men acted as judges and jury and consisted of a total of five officers, including Captain Cole. There was no testimony given which did not matter since neither of us would have defended our actions.

We were standing at rigid attention in front of the men, heads up, eyes straight ahead. I felt the men's eyes studying us both in turn. Captain Cole stood and spoke formally. Gone was the friendliness of the previous night. I thought he made a fine and dashing figure, erect and wearing a grave expression. However, behind his eyes I imagined I could see deep regret that had followed a sleepless night. Instead of comfort I felt a hot flush of shame at bringing myself and Alex to this reckoning of US Army justice.

"Corporal Alejandro, the decision has been made to retain you in the Army, but with the loss of one stripe. You will be reduced in rank to a private, and serve two weeks in the stockade. At the end of the two weeks you will be reassigned as the Army sees fit." Shifting feet and hesitating, Captain Cole trained haunted eyes on me. "Sergeant Draper, you will be stripped of your rank and discharged from the Army dishonorably." Even though I knew it was coming, his words enveloped me like a rain filled cloud smothering the oxygen from the room. It was a struggle to keep my legs locked to remain standing. I had brought this on myself and now was the time to face my fate. No one spoke for a long minute. The ticking of a clock could be heard clearly in the quite room.

Finally, Captain Cole began sorting through some papers on his desk as if stalling to collect his thoughts. When he continued his tone was softened and his military bearing broke as he added, "You men fought bravely during the battle with bandits at Glenn Springs. You are both to be commended for your actions. However, my personal feeling aside, this military court cannot accept or condone your unauthorized pursuit of bandits across the border into Mexico. I envision a future day will come when such actions may be sanctioned by higher authority. If that time does arrive, your experience in Mexico will prove itself as a valuable blueprint that the Army can take the war to the enemy in their own country. This court is adjourned, and you men are dismissed."

We were taken back to the stockades and I was given civilian clothes to wear home. Justice moves fast in the Army and arrangements were made for me to leave on the afternoon train. I would be home in one or two days, but where was *my* home? Atlanta, Texas was where I was born and my parents lived. Did I still belong there? What would I do now with jobs so hard to come by? Back home farming and the logging industry were the only jobs where a man could eke out a living.

About one o'clock I said a painful goodbye to Alex as Captain Cole came for me personally. I promised to write Alex and let him know where I was whenever that might be. He did the same since there was no way of knowing where the Army might send him. Before I left, Alex fished in a pocket and produced one of his *magic* twenty dollar gold pieces, pushing the coin into my hand. I tried to refuse but he insisted. "When we meet again *Senor* Draper, you can return my money. *Vayan con Dios Amigo.*

The captain and I saddled horses and rode into town. He certainly had access to Army vehicles, but I was glad to leave with a fine horse under me as a cavalry soldier should. I figured the captain would have known that and I was grateful for the sentiment. The train station was a long rectangular building at the edge of town. I sighed and filled my lungs deeply with the dry desert air. The mountain ranges in the distance shown beautifully in all their glory. I would certainly miss this country, hot and varmint filled as it was, with both man and beast.

Captain Cole paid for my one way ticket. I could only assume it was from U.S. Army funds. Next he shook my hand took a moment to ponder his next words carefully before finally deciding what to say. "Mr. Draper you're a good man. Despite what happened I believe you were a *fine* soldier. Let me leave you with this thought. If you do not find civilian life to your liking, a man might use another name and enlist once more. The Army has many outpost and forts throughout the country. Also I fear the European war will soon be ours as well. We will need many good leaders to fill the Army's ranks. I suspect military records are not kept as they should be. Have a safe journey home to your family."

# CHAPTER 10

## *Grandma Myrtle Remembers*

I awoke suddenly, completely lost as to where I was. It was dark, yet shadowy light was filtering through screened slits in concrete. I finally remembered I had spent the night in my grandfather's storm shelter. Looking around I saw his cot was empty, the bedding rolled up. Grandpa had always been an early riser. As I stretched and began rolling my pallet to match grandpas, I was confused as to how much of his story I actually remembered or had dreamed. I felt bad for him, abruptly recalling the way he had left the Army.

If I was home I would have went to my dad and asked him questions about it. Yet I felt grandpa had shared something with me that was not common knowledge and never talked about in the family. I did not even want to share this latest revelation with my cousin. It would take me a while to sort out all I had heard. Later I could talk to my older sister. She was pretty good at keeping secrets and would not tell mom and dad. I did not want anything to stop grandpa from telling me more stories. Outside I heard grandma calling me in for breakfast. I grabbed my bundle of bedding and ran up the stairs and into the house. I could smell the good cooking smell coming through the back screen door.

Washing up for breakfast, I was disappointed that my Aunt Marie had already picked up Jon Marc before I woke up. I knew I would see him next week when I was supposed to stay with him for two days before I went home. Today, my Aunt Ruby was picking me up to spend two days hanging out with my older cousin Brenda. My sister Sherry was there too. They were older than me by almost three years, but still let me tag along. Brenda was one of my most favorite cousins.

She was certainly the most fun of my girl cousins. She owned a red scooter I wanted to talk her into letting me ride by myself. She also had a friendly German shepherd, a mean duck that chased cars and people, and a big tarantula spider as her pets. I liked the dog, but did not want any part of the tarantula or the testy duck.

With Grandpa off running errands and Jon Marc gone, Grandma noticed I was quiet during breakfast, which was unusual for me. Dad sometimes called me a motor mouth. When I was excited I not only spoke fast but the volume would grow as well. Now Grandma kept looking at me with an obvious cloud of worry lining her forehead. I knew she was thinking I might have had a bad nightmare from one of Grandpa's stories. Not wanting her to be mad at him I tried to brighten up. "Thanks for last night Grandma. It was great *roughing* it in the storm cellar. When I grow up I want one just like Grandpa's in my backyard."

"Buddy I don't think there is a great need for storm cellars in the city. It seems those vexing twisters only hit us country folk."

"Grandma", I protested, "you live in the city too. I don't remember your house ever being in the country."

"Buddy when your pa was growing up we lived many miles out into the country. We moved a few times when your pa was growing up, but here the city came to us not the other way around. Anyway, your grandpa didn't build that thing out back until a few years ago. You ought to remember since you, your sister and your cousins had a fine time running around on top. Your grandpa just has an *unnatural suspicion* that every storm that passes through is looking for him. He never has told anyone why that is as far as I know tell of."

About then I felt something licking my bare feet. Grandma's dog Lady was under the table sniffing around for dropped food. The small brown Chihuahua was not particular if the meal was by accident or on purpose. I knew Grandma did not approve so I slipped a scrap of bacon into my hand and onto the floor. "Grandma what did Grandpa do after getting out of the Army?"

She hesitated before saying in a softer, sort of dreamy way, "I was not with Oscar then. We did not meet until 1925, or meet again I should say. We grew up in the same neighborhood in the small town of Atlanta, Texas, which is where your pa was born in too. Your grandpa was just one of the older boys in town then. I had never paid him any mind. I did not think he even was aware of me back then." I suddenly realized that she had a far off, kind of dreamy look in her bright brown eyes. The look reminded me of when Grandpa was remembering way back.

"Times were hard and jobs were few in those years and Oscar had found work around 1920 with small carpentry jobs. He built chicken coops, houses, and anything else he was hired for. I suspect he was poor more than otherwise. I know he jumped trains when he was without work or money. He never stayed in one place very long. He would move after anywhere from a few days to several months. If I had not met your grandpa when I did, I suppose he would have stayed on the road. It becomes a way of life after a spell. You know your pa traveled around like that working with his brother repairing old rotted track for the Union and Pacific Railroad before he married your ma. Anyway, I was working as a maid in a Texarkana, Texas hotel. I worked hard and was glad to hold any job in those days. I needed hard cash to help out my ma and pa on the family's farm outside of town."

Grandma Myrtle took a long breath and half closed her eyes as she remembered. She finally opened her eyes yet still seemed to be looking back instead of the here and now. I was not sure she even knew I was still in the room. "One day Oscar walked right up to me in the hall and addressed me directly. "I know you Myrtle Wheelington." I guess he had recognized me and it all started right then and there. I felt something I had never known before. We just began talking like we were old friends. After that night he was gone for the whole summer. He wrote me but I figured not to see him again. Next thing you know he was back and took me to a picture show in Texarkana at the Saenger Theatre. They were showing *The Big Parade*, a World War I movie which was very thrilling. I had read the book, *What Price Glory* as a girl."

She paused as if she had lost touch with the memory or was savoring it like hot apple pie after a good meal. She then smiled and continued. "We settled into our seats and the picture show began right away. There was a lot of killing and soldiers dying and Oscar grew anxious, not seeming to like it. He walked out to the lobby a couple of times, mumbling some excuse. It was a fine first date but he had to leave the next day. That night when he walked me to my room in the hotel where I stayed during my work days, he stopped at the door to tell me goodnight. Your grandpa, then as now, was a no nonsense man. On this evening, a funny grin took over his face. He looked me in the eyes and said, "Myrtle…there is only one chance to get a first kiss right.""

As she thought of their first kiss, her face shone in what my mom would have called *high color*. Finally she continued. "After that night he went home to visit his folks for the first time in years. I always worried I would not hear from him again. I admit to fretting over Oscar. Then when he returned he took me out again. He would be gone awhile then return. Anyway, the next time he came back through we went to supper and just like that he gave me this *ruby* ring. It was only our third date and I knew we would be together the rest of our lives. We were married June 7th 1926 at the Oak Lawn Baptist Church in Piney Grove, Texas. My family was dead set against the marriage. Oscar was already thirty-two at the time and I expect that had something to do with it. Now mind you I was no young girl and already twenty-six. I was sure I knew what I wanted, having waited so long to get married." Becoming aware of her surroundings once more she held up her left hand for me to see the ring.

As she had been speaking she seemed more youthful and her voice was higher. Her eyes were bright and her cheeks grew rosy red with the recollections. She shook her head as if to settle the past into whatever place she kept it and changed back to her normal grandma tone. "My goodness Buddy, I don't know why a boy your age would be so interested in old stories and such and all. You go on outside and play until your aunt picks you up. Buddy you are far too serious sometimes for your age. My ma would have said you have an *old soul*. We older folks have an excuse. Living in the past sometimes helps us get through the day. You should be outside enjoying being a boy. I'll pack up your clothes for you."

Setting on a homemade wood bench on the back porch I began to figure. First, I wondered if Grandma knew that her young Oscar had won the ruby ring in a Glenn Springs poker game. Did it matter if a ring was won or bought? Next, hating even the simplest math as I did, I began counting the years on my fingers from 1915 on. I was missing about four and a half years of Grandpa's life. I knew he had worked as a security guard at a Cotton Mill and the Red River Arsenal, both in Texarkana after his marriage to grandma from stories my dad had told. What had happened during those missing years? What interested me was this seemed to be the time nobody ever talked about. In fact, nobody had ever mentioned how grandpa had left the Army. Maybe Grandpa had gotten caught up in his story and did not mean to tell me either. I would have to get my sister alone and show her the letters I had found and ask about Grandpa's missing years.

The next couple of days at my aunt Ruby's house were loaded with adventure. My cousin Brenda let me drive her scooter alone after teaching me the simple break and gas operations. My aunt's house was on the unpaved road of Prospect, on the Arkansas side of Texarkana. I took the scooter down the hilly road and it seemed as if I was flying along. To me the houses I past appeared as a blur. The scooter did not have a speedometer, but I thought I was going as fast as my dad drove on the highway. On my second trip I attracted a scraggly pack of barking dogs that ran up to me. I pulled the throttle wide open yet the dogs easily matched my speed. I kicked out, almost losing control and yelled, but the dogs followed me back to the house where they were quickly chased off by Brenda's German shepherd and her duck. I guessed that I had slightly overestimated my speed. Even though my first scooter ride was thrilling I now knew the scooter only went as fast as the *speed of dog*.

That night after supper I pulled Sherry outside onto my aunt's covered porch. She and I had a *wide-eye* signal, followed by a slight tilt of the head that said we needed to talk alone. The gesture was most often used to thwart our four year old sister Deb, who was a big tattletale. She seemed to overhear every spoken word in the house and swiftly report it to our parents.

Wasting no time I showed her the letters I had found. "They are yucky love letters written by Mr. Walker while he was stationed at Perl Harbor during the war. I thought you might want to read them."

Sherry looked at me with obvious distrust. "Okay little brother, confess. Where did you get those letters?"

"Jon Marc and I were exploring Mr. Walker's abandoned house and I found them. I thought they might be about battles, but they are just *yucky* love stuff. Throw them away after you read them. I'm not going back into that creepy basement again."

"One of these days Buddy you're going to go missing and they will never find you. I know you find caves and old abandoned cellars fascinating, but they are dangerous too."

"Yea, I have found an old empty cellar or two with Jon Marc but the only caves I've been in are in Turner Fall, Oklahoma and I was with you and dad. I seem to recall you used to like to explore with me until you became all *girly* at thirteen. I wanted to find out if you know what Grandpa Draper did after he got out of the Army?"

"I remember hearing some talk about things he did that were not very nice. I can't remember what things. When mom and dad talked about it I didn't pay attention. Maybe you should ask dad."

"They think I'm too young to hear stories about *bad* times and battles with bandits. Grandpa will tell me someday, if I can get him alone and in the mood to talk."

Sherry rolled her eyes as only a new teenager could. "Buddy all you think about are gun battles and adventure stories. Try reading a book about *anything* besides the Alamo, Jim Bowie, Kit Carson or Daniel Boone."

"I do. I also read about lawmen and cowboys like Wyatt Earp, Doc Holiday, Bat Masterson, and Wild Bill Hickok. I naturally read about outlaws like Jesse James and Billy the Kid too."

She made an, I give up gesture and said, "You're hopeless you know that. Let's go inside before these half Texas, half Arkansas mosquitoes eat us alive."

The next day my cousin Charles, Brenda's older brother, picked me up and let me hang out with him while we sold watermelons from the back of his 1955 Ford pickup. It was great fun. He even paid me to help him load his truck at a local melon patch outside town. We would load the truck as high as possible then sell out on the side of the road in about two or three hours.

The day was hot and that helped the melons sell quickly. I liked Charles because we always had fun together. He treated me like I was grown up instead of just a kid. I felt bad when the day ended early because I pulled a nail out of one of his rear tires. I did not know the nail was holding in the air. We had to change the tire and then go by his dad's service station to fix the flat tire. My Uncle Paul bought us sodas and Charles, Uncle Paul and I broke open a water melon and ate it *country-style*, which meant without a spoon. With our faces covered in juice, we laughed at each other. It was a good day and best of all Charles never said a word to me about the tire.

Early the next morning my Aunt Marie picked me up. Jon Marc and I spent the day in the woods surrounding my aunt's property. She had made us lunches and we found ourselves sitting on a large stump eating the peanut butter and banana sandwiches. "Jon Marc, the other night, you missed grandpa's best story ever."

"I don't like that smelly old storm cellar. I'll bet there were bugs crawling all over you while you were sleeping."

Oh yea, well look at your foot. There is a big bug crossing your tennis shoe right now."

He shook the invaded foot to dislodge a beetle who had mistaken the foot for a pile of cow dung. "At least I know about these bugs. I don't want anything crawling up my pants leg while I'm sleeping."

"I guess you better sleep in the house tonight instead of outside with me. Your old pup tent doesn't have a door you know."

"Somehow it's different out in the open. Maybe Grandpa was right and it's the closed space that gives me the creeps."

"Yea my dad has that too. He said some mean older boys shut him in a big whiskey barrow when he was my age. He has felt that way ever since when he feels closed in."

An hour later we were chased off a farmer's land. He waved a shotgun at us and cussed something awful. We had been exploring his old ramshackle barn he was using for hay storage when we heard him coming. We starting running and fairly leaped his gate to get out of there, laughing hysterically despite the real danger. Later we cut across another farmer's field. There was a sign painted in large bright red letters which read;

*If you cross my land, do so in under a minute, my prize bull crosses it in 60 seconds!*

By late afternoon we were tired and started walking back toward his house. I was thinking about Aunt Marie's good cooking and not paying attention to where I was walking. Jon Marc being much more at home in the woods than me smartly sidestepped around an old rotting log. Instead of following his lead, I stepped over the log and must have disturbed a wasp's nest. Instantly a big red wasp planted his stinger into my right buttocks. I had been stung by bees, ants, and I thought every kind of wasp, but this one lit my backside like a torch had been stuck in my jeans. I began hollering and running. I took off down the path straight to my aunt's house and into her bathroom.

Once inside I danced out of my pants and underwear. Then I began spinning around like a dog chasing his tail looking back for the stinger. By this time my Aunt Marie, alerted by all the hollering was at the door wanting to come in. She must have thought I had lost my last marble. After I shouted out what was wrong, she reminded me that, as a nurse, she should remove the stinger. I was too embarrassed to let her help and managed to get it out on my own. The rest of the day was spent sitting on my left butt cheek. That night I slept in Jon Marc's small pup tent on my stomach.

# CHAPTER 11

## *Making the Pitch to Dad*

Back in C. E. Dunn Elementary School in September I waited for an opportunity to talk to my dad about what his father had done after the Army. My dad was a powerfully built man, but I had never seen him use his great strength in anger. He liked to lift his children over his head in play as if we were feathers. James Vinson had been a railroad carpenter as a young man, rebuilding the old rotting tracks and completing small remodeling jobs in local neighborhoods close to the tracks. Dad and his brother John Ray had worked together traveling around the country. After marrying mom he had studied accounting at night and took a job in payroll at a local defense contractor. As a side business, he did bookkeeping and payrolls for small businesses in towns surrounding our neighborhood. He called them *mom and pop* businesses. He had clients who owned everything from lawn care companies to gas stations, and even dry cleaners.

I knew I could not approach Dad directly and would have to be careful in how I asked my questions. My parents always tried to protect their children from the rougher side of life. My opportunity came when Mom sent us out to pick up a bucket of chicken on a Sunday after church. Dad often let me go with him when he ran errands or saw clients. The store owners were always nice to me. I usually got a treat from one of the shop owners. I loved it when Dad would tell stories about working for the railroad or the short time he worked in a salt mine. I had once seen a picture of Dad in dusty miner's garb. The nickname on the back of the photo was *Shorty*. Dad seemed plenty tall to me, but today I only wanted to talk about Grandpa.

Attempting to sound as casual as possible I said, "Dad, what did Grandpa do after he left the Army?"

He looked at me suspiciously before saying. Usually when my father looked at me like that, I was in trouble. It was nearly impossible to get anything by him. Finally he said, "What did you hear Buddy?"

"Well, I know he was fighting bandits on the Texas/Mexico border, but not many details as to what he did in the Army before he met grandma."

"I guess my pa has been telling you stories about those battles." He drove on for a couple of minutes before continuing. I watched anxiously as his forehead creased in thought. "I'm not sure if I should be mad or jealous. He never told any of his stories to me when I was your age or since. I suppose as he gets older he thinks about the old days more often. I just don't think you should be hearing about men dying is all. War is a terrible thing son. They may be stories Buddy, but those were rough times. Those were flesh and blood folks who died, both American and Mexican."

"I know dad. I'll be ten next month. I'm not a baby anymore. Grandpa said he had to leave the Army after him and his friend Alex crossed into Mexico chasing bandits. He said he left his men without permission and went after those responsible. He also said he wished he could have always served honorably like you. I don't understand why it was so wrong if the bandits were bad men."

"Well son that's exactly what I mean. You're too young to comprehend the way of adults. There is no way to predict what a man might do when he faces a kill or be killed situation. Combat training can only prepare you just so far. You and I watch all the John Wayne movies together right?" I nodded. "Well that is pretend but what my pa is telling you about is real." He sighed deeply before continuing. "It has been a closely guarded and unspoken of thing in our family all these years. Now my pa is telling his nine year old grandson about getting a dishonorable discharge from the Army." Dad was silent for a minute and I began to think he would not answer my question. Then he scratched his head and began again with wonder in his voice. "Buddy did you say your grandpa *chased* bandits into Mexico?"

I was excited now. Dad loved history as much as I did and he was interested now. I said in one breath, "Yes sir. There was a big fight with a hundred bandits or more in Glenn Springs. After the battle Grandpa and Alex went across the border and killed some of those bandits over there. They captured a wagon load of guns from a gunrunner and raced back across the border into Texas."

Dad was incredulous. "Do you realize your grandpa has never told anyone what he did to get thrown out of the Army? Are you sure he said it was just him and his friend Alex? If I remember my history at some point during the Mexican Revolution conflict President Wilson sent troops over into Mexico. Pancho Villa and various other bandit bands were causing a lot of trouble down on both sides of the border."

"I'm sure of it Dad. They had a shoot out in a cantina with some of the bandits that had attacked them in Glenn Springs. Grandpa recovered a shiny brass Army belt buckle that a bandit took from one of his friends who was killed. Dad I remember you told me once that Grandpa was an Army sergeant. When all this happened he was in charge of the soldiers on the border."

"Yes I recall your grandpa made sergeant the first time he was in the Army. I guess that was the time he was telling you about."

I was momentarily taken back by his words. "Did you say the first time?"

"Yes that's right. Your grandfather reenlisted in the Army sometime after his dishonorable discharge. The second time he served his full tour and was discharged honorably."

By this time we had arrived back at home. The chicken smelled good and I was hungry. I knew Mom would have mashed potatoes ready and green beans too. My question was still unanswered but I had something else to think about. Grandpa's second time in the Army and what adventures he may have had that time around.

That night after I had said my prayers and climbed into bed, my dad sat on one corner. He wore the same expression I recognized from when I had done something wrong. Dad looked a little sad and disappointed. Most of the time my dad was quick witted and ready with a happy smile. Good humor was usually visible behind his eyes.

Tonight he seemed like something was weighing heavy on his mind. I began to search my recent memory for whatever I had done. I could not decide which thing I was in trouble for this time. When I was about to start confessing to any number of real or imagined wrongs Dad finally dissolved my anxiety with his words.

"Buddy, your grandpa is a good Christian man. However there was a time in his life that he drank too much and lost his way. He was restless and clashed often with his pa, the rather stern looking minister whose photograph hangs in our hall. My grandfather was a master at glowering at you until you jumped to do what he demanded. I was afraid of the man and I could see why my dad had his problems with him. There is one family story that says my pa came home drunk when he was around fifteen. Well it's said my grandpa tied him to the bed face down and whipped him bloody with a willow branch. Pa ran away the next day and soon after joined the Army. He did not return for some years. Of course their dust ups happened long before I was born. I just heard that your grandpa was a troubled man when he was younger."

Dad was quite for awhile and I wondered if he was deciding how much to tell me. He finally continued. "I guess he could not adjust as a civilian, or maybe it set hard in him how his first time in the Army ended. Either way he rejoined using his first name in place of Oscar. His discharge papers had him listed as Jim Draper that time. I'm glad we had this talk. Maybe the family does *not* have to walk so lightly over pa's first enlistment, especially if he is now ready to talk about it. When we see him at Thanksgiving we can both talk to him. Now leave the past alone for tonight and go on to sleep. You have school tomorrow Buddy."

I lay awake another few minutes thinking about Grandpa. I set the one hour timer on my radio clock and heard Elvis singing about his Hound Dog. I was glad Grandpa had a second chance with the Army. Everyone deserved a second chance didn't they? I was also excited that my dad would include me when we next spoke to his pa.

Now I squirmed with excitement in anticipation of Thanksgiving. When Grandpa came in on the train, Dad and I would be waiting at the station. Hopefully Grandpa would be in the mood for talking about his next time in the Army. Of course I knew that the best part about being an adult is they could not be pushed into anything they did not want to do, especially by a kid. Adults were mostly funny about what they were in the mood for sometimes. Over the next few days I told Dad everything I remembered from Grandpa's stories. Dad then wrote to his brother John Ray in Florida and retold the stories as closely as possible. Dad had said John Ray was interested too and glad that his pa was finally talking about the old days.

Fall was my favorite time of year. I had my 10th birthday to look forward to, Halloween, Thanksgiving and then Christmas. Our neighborhood in Grand Prairie, Texas was not the best and if you strayed too far from your own house alone, you might end up donating your candy to some bigger boys. Still, to us Halloween was an all out affair. We would cover several blocks then load up with one of our neighbor parents and go to what we called *rich neighborhoods*. Enough candy was collected to take us through the New Year. That year, my friend Randy and I paid my little sister a quarter for the use of one of her life-sized dolls and hung it from the porch by a hangman's noose. It looked pretty real under our porch light shining on it. Dad took it down when he came home from work. Normally he had a good sense of humor, but he was not amused by our stunt.

I can't leave out the tragedy that occurred after Halloween and before Thanksgiving on November 22nd, 1963. Our school day started out dark and drizzly, but the sun came out before noon and by our recess time it had turned into a beautiful fall day. We were all stunned when the announcement came over the intercom that President Kennedy had been shot, followed a short time later by the death announcement. The students of my school had all stood waving in 1960 when candidate John F. Kennedy had rolled by when he was running for President and giving a speech nearby. Our school was dismissed early and the buses took us home. Even the normally loud and boisterous bus ride was quiet that day.

We were all struck hard by the assassination of President Kennedy, no more than twenty miles from our home. As the events played out on local and national television, my family sat home watching. Even my friends and I were affected. I don't remember my friends and me laughing or playing in our neighborhood for what felt like weeks.

The Sunday Oswald was killed we were in church. My Aunt Retha had gone with us and when we took her home my Uncle Kenneth came out and told us about it. I have to admit I was glad, but dad said nobody should take the law into their own hands like that. Like everyone else, we watched the man die a hundred times on television. A week after Oswald was killed my dad drove the family by the Rose hill Cemetery where he was buried. We were not there long because mom asked dad to leave when we saw his mother and wife, still dressed in black at the grave. Mom said people should realize that Oswald had hurt his own family as well as President Kennedy and Dallas Police Officer J.D. Tippit and his family.

A few days later, we watched President Kennedy's funeral on television. As I sat watching with my parents, what saddened me the most was seeing little John-John, the president's son say goodbye to his dad with a salute. That moment stuck with me more than anything else I saw or heard during those terrible days. My best friend Randy who attended a private Catholic school said he and his classmates were terrified to see their normally strict and stern-faced nuns crying openly in the halls and classrooms.

# CHAPTER 12

## *Grandpa and Grandma Visit*

On Wednesday evening before Thanksgiving at around seven o'clock I was standing with my family at the train station in Grand Prairie, Texas when my grandma and grandpa's train whistled into the station from Texarkana. It was an exciting time when family came to visit, be it car, bus or train. The house would be filled with delicious cooking smells and adult conversations went on late into the night. Even though we might be bumped to a pallet on the floor to make room for family, it just added to the holiday mood. Since both sets of my grandparents lived six hours away, it was always a treat to see them. I was often jealous of my cousins getting to live with, or seeing my grandparents any time they wanted. We had moved out of Texarkana so long ago I could remember ever living there.

Mom had a pot roast already cooked at home. Most of the restaurants in the town closed early on the night before Thanksgiving. Hugs and kisses were plentiful from my sisters and me. Dad tied his parent's suitcases onto the luggage rack of our Buick station wagon. My sister Sherry and I climbed into the far rear seat which faced to the back of the car, our favorite seat. My little sister sat up front between my dad and mom. We were fairly loaded down even in the big station wagon. I wanted to ask grandpa questions right away, but I knew it would have to wait for another time and place.

Later in the evening when the dishes were cleared away, my dad looked straight at me, then at grandpa. "Dad, I was thinking you might want to go fishing with Buddy and me on the Friday after Thanksgiving? We have a favorite and *very* secret spot where we go.

I'm sure Charlene, ma and the girls would enjoy shopping downtown. I know ma always likes to pick up some yarn at Woolworth when she comes to town."

"I don't see why not. Buddy and I had a grand time last summer. We even spent a storm night together in my shelter. I didn't know he was a fisherman too. I could sure go for some fried catfish. Charlene always cooks fish of any kind. She makes that great gravy so well. It makes my mouth water just to think on it."

"Well we might catch us some catfish, big mouth bass, or a mess of perch. Those perch are small but fight like you've caught a twenty pound monster. They are good eating though. The only problem is we will have to catch a passel of them to feed this family. If we don't catch enough fish I'll have to stop by the old man Mathis' grocery store to buy more."

I was squirming at the chance to get another story out of Grandpa but knew Sunday would be my best chance. Now it appeared dad was helping me. I could hardly wait to hear about another battle. Of course I hoped when grandpa went back into the Army he wasn't assigned a boring job. By now I was getting sleepy even though I was out of school tomorrow. When we had company I was afraid to go to sleep thinking I might miss something.

I guess Dad saw me nodding because he said, "Go on to bed son. Tomorrow will be a long day. If you go hiking with Randy don't be late for lunch either."

I shuffled over to my pallet next to Sherry's where she was reading. She loved Elvis Presley. We saw all his movies together. I saw her ever-present transistor radio playing softly near her head. Whenever one of her favorite songs came on she would drop everything and turn it up. She also loved reading and you could usually find a book or two stuffed under her pillow. I knew she stayed up late into the night reading with a flashlight under her covers when mom and dad were asleep. I suspected mom knew but she believed a higher vocabulary was healthy. I loved to read too, but every time I tried reading at night, I always fell asleep before I could finish a chapter. I rolled over and looked at her cross eyed, which she hated, until she noticed. "Want to go fishing with us the day after Thanksgiving?"

She wrinkled her nose in distaste. "Not unless you guys are going to shoot dad's rifles while you're out there. Fishing is smelly and the mosquitoes are still bad since we haven't had much of a winter yet."

As soon as we were old enough, dad had often taken us target shooting with his 4-10 shot gun and his .22 caliber bolt action rifle. We would shoot from the banks of Mountain Creek Lake near where we fish. I could not remember dad ever hunting, but he had told us that he used to shoot squirrels and rabbits for the dinner table back in Atlanta with either the shotgun or rifle. "No we're just fishing this time. Dad is helping me. We are going to get grandpa to tell another story about when he went back in the Army."

She grimaced like I had shoved a worm in her face and did her best rolling eyes routine yet. "I can't believe you and dad *want* to hear those stories. I'm sorry but I don't want to think about some old dead bandits."

Now it was my turn to roll my eyes, although I was not as good at it as her. "Those bandits would not be dead if it wasn't for grandpa. Well, they might be by now. All of the history they teach us about in school is from a book. This is from *my* grandpa and he *lived* it. When he tells his stories, I feel like I'm there with him shooting and dodging bullets myself. It's exciting!"

"Go to sleep little brother. You'll get your stories soon enough and quit crossing your eyes at me. Yuk! Besides the pillow monster will be coming by soon to steal yours."

It would be her loss missing out on a fun time. Teenagers were so weird some times. All they wanted to do was dance and listen to rock and roll. I turned away from her and got a good grip on my pillow. My intention was to make any pillow thieves have to wake me to get mine. I awoke early on Thanksgiving with a sore neck. I guessed Sherry was right about the pillows because mine had disappeared during the night, despite my best efforts to hang onto it.

I hurriedly dressed and ate one of mom's fried chocolate pies for breakfast. I was meeting Randy for a hike down to our favorite spring fed creek. The creek did not have a name and was crossed by a high railroad bridge. I don't think our parents would have been happy if they ever saw us playing on the bridge. My mom caught me before I left and warned me about being late for lunch. Missing a family meal in our home was not done without permission. Today mom had no need to worry. I would be home on time. I had no intention of missing Thanksgiving, or her chicken dressing.

Randy was ready and we walked the mile and a half to the bridge. We were the only boys around today and we started throwing rocks into the creek below through the railroad bridge slats. Off in the distance I saw a speck slowly growing larger. It had to be a train so we made our way underneath the tracks. There was never any thought of jumping a train here. These trains were already moving at twenty miles an hour when they came through. As the train roared over us the ground shook like an earthquake, and the noise was louder than thunder. My ears were ringing when we walked out from under the bridge laughing and found a childhood goldmine.

Our find was a large collapsed cardboard box, which may have held a refrigerator. Whatever it had been intended for, it was now our magic carpet. We dragged the box up the side of the hill and climbed inside. The box was open on the end and we intended to ride it down to the bottom like a sled. The plan had a few holes in it because when gravity took hold we began to roll over and over each other all the way down. Bruised and dizzy we crawled out and could barely stand. We would not try that again, but it must have triggered what dad called our funny bones because we laughed for several minutes. Every time we looked at each other and saw our ragged appearance we would start laughing all over again.

I tried to slip into the house without being seen, but grandma walked right into me. "Oh my heavens!" Her hand flew up to her face in horror. "Are you hurt Buddy?"

"No grandma. I'm just a little scrapped up. I slid down a hill during my hike." I had tried not to lie to her, but I had to leave a few scab-making details out. I did not what grandma to think her grandson was stupid."

"You're a mess. You had better go clean up before your mother sees you. We'll be eating real soon."

"Yes grandma." We only had one bathroom and I went in to clean up and change. My mom had reinforced the knees in all my jeans with iron-on patches, yet I had still torn clear through the material. I would be in trouble for this one. There were *school clothes* and *play clothes* and I knew better. I seemed to be always tearing my clothes or getting hurt. I had fallen out of trees, been stung by an asps, and had scars on my hands and knees. Each scar was a badge of honor shown proudly on the school playground or in the neighborhood. My parents had said more than once I would never make it to adulthood without some broken bones. So far I had not busted anything inside me. I looked at myself in the mirror and saw a skinny kid with a scratched face and hands. I was sure fresh bruises would be in my mirror by tomorrow. I looked like a circus performer whose act was juggling feral cats.

# CHAPTER 13

## *Finally Story Time*

The day after Thanksgiving I awoke before daylight, too excited to sleep any longer. The fishing was one of my favorite things to do with Dad, but on this trip I wanted to get grandpa talking about bandits again. By the time I had all our fishing gear loaded in the station wagon, I could smell bacon, eggs and coffee coming from our kitchen. I saw Grandma and Mom talking and sipping coffee once I walked into the warm room. In winter mom always turned on all four gas burners and lit the toaster oven at the bottom of the stove to heat the room. The day would warm up, but it was still close to forty degrees outside now.

Grandma looked up at me and smiled. "I made some hot cocoa if you want some."

"I sure do Grandma. Thanks, it's still pretty cool outside." Looking at my mom, I asked, "Are Dad and Grandpa up yet?"

"I heard them stirring around a little. I guess they are getting hungry from the bacon and biscuit smells filling the house. I know your sisters are not awake yet. Those girls sure like their sleep time."

I frowned, remembering how hard it was to get my little sister Deb to go to sleep every night. Since my sister Sherry had turned thirteen, my parents thought she needed a little privacy now that she was a *young woman*. "Yea, Debra ought to like sleeping in. I have to trick her into going to sleep every night. She chatters endlessly from her bed across the room until I ask her to *race me to dream land*. She gets all excited and stiffens up like a board, closes her eyes tight and tries *so* hard to beat me."

Grandmother Myrtle laughed so hard I thought she was going to pass out from not taking a breath. When she could talk and had wiped away tears from her brown eyes, she gestured toward me. "I think it's wonderful that you are being the *mature* older brother and letting your *big* sister have her own room. Now come and get your breakfast before your pa and grandpa eat most of it."

I saw Mom looking at my face with a questioning expression. She pretended to be mad, but her amused eyes gave her away. "Yes Buddy, while you're eating you can tell us why your face is so frightful and how you ripped clear through the knees of your new school jeans!"

After breakfast, Dad, Grandpa and I drove off with the Buick loaded with our fishing rods and a large picnic basket mom had packed with sandwiches. We even had an old rusty metal ice chest filled with RC Colas. I was glad my sister Sherry had wanted to go shopping with her friend Judy. My little sister, mom and grandma were going to visit relatives. Any other time they would have been welcome, but I wanted nothing to get in the way of grandpa telling another story. I had to know about his second time in the Army.

After a short stop at a bait store to pick up some worms, we arrived in the area of Mountain Creek Lake. The small lake was in Grand Prairie, but close to the Dallas city boundary line. Dad drove onto a dirt road and after another ten minutes, we arrived at our favorite spot. We would be fishing off of a low, tree covered bank. The spot was shady even on the hottest days, but on this November day, a cool breeze was blowing off the water.

Dad helped me set up my cane pole and attach a red and white bobber to the line. Any fish that took the worm would cause the bobber to dart under water and the fight would begin. By noon we had each caught three fish each. Dad had caught a small bass, a crappie, and a good sized catfish. I had caught two perch and a crappie. Grandpa had pulled in a big bass which weighed at least eight pounds. He caught two smaller catfish, but one fought him for ten minutes before he dragged it onto the bank. My mouth watered at the thought of mom cooking the catfish.

We kept the fish alive staked out on a line in the water. One of my jobs was to check the line every few minutes to make sure a big old turtle or water moccasin was not helping itself to an easy meal. I was most wary of the moccasins. Once I had seen my uncle Herbert hit one of the big snakes with a shovel when it would not budge off the trail we were walking on. The snake had hissed and leaped toward the nearby stream, apparently uninjured by the shovel blow. Dad said moccasins had an attitude unlike most snakes and would not run from a person.

Dad and grandpa had been casting with rod and reels. Dad still thought I was too young to be flipping a fish hook back and forth over our heads. However, it had been my younger sister that had hooked our Aunt Retha while she was trying to learn to cast. My aunt had been caught behind the ear and it took some time to remove the hook from under her skin. That was the last time my aunt had ever gone fishing with us. Besides she was afraid of all things *creepy* and *crawly*. We could chase her around a room with a plastic bug she knew was not real.

Finally we took a break and started eating or sandwiches. I knew this was my chance. I could hardly sit still so filled with anxiety. Though hungry I had to take a chance and bring up the sticky situation about grandpa leaving then rejoining the Army. Trying to sound as indifferent as I could even though my heart was pounding, I asked, "Grandpa, dad said you went back into the Army after getting out. What did you do the second time you were in?" I held my breath and waited. He took so long that I felt he would not answer.

Eventually he sighed and said, "Oh Buddy that was so long ago. I'm not sure your pa wants you hearing about that stuff anyway."

Dad cleared his throat before saying, "Well Pa, Buddy is ten now and I'd like to know what you did myself. I don't believe you've ever told me or John Ray about that second time, or come to think about it, not much about your first enlistment either."

"I guess the wounds hadn't healed much when you were a boy son. As I get older it seems like the old memories and the dead just *refuse* to stay buried." He finished his sandwich and took a long sip of his

RC Cola and settled himself comfortably on a stump. He stared out over the lake following the visible path of Mountain Creek as it fed the lake. I watched his eyes turn misty and wondered if dad saw it too. I knew he was back now, somewhere far in the past…

# CHAPTER 14

## *Back In the Army*

I didn't have much success with my first time back in civilian life. The slow passing of time between May 1915 and January 1916 was a hard time for me. I couldn't find much work. The truth is I didn't hunt very hard and I lost the jobs I did get. Sweeping floors in a dry goods store or digging ditches along dirt roads for the county did not interest me much. I also liked the taste of hard liquor in the evenings. My general disinterest in working and general enjoyment of drinking set hard with my pa. Even though he was gone most of the time preaching all over the Ozarks and East Texas, he would take the time to try and reason with me. Both Ma and Pa did their best, but I just sank deeper into whatever dark pit I had climbed into. They say a man has to strike his lowest bedrock point before he can begin to claw his way up. It just seemed like I could not find the bottom of my hole. It was just that deep.

Then there was the time it nearly came to the point of blows between Pa and me. He had accepted me back home but I had given him plenty of cause to regret it. James Henry Draper always seemed to be full of righteous anger and indignation when it came to his oldest son. Any who knew him would have agreed he had a commanding personality. His piercing blue eyes could make a strong man take a step back and a weaker one run for cover. James Henry was the kind of preacher that *hell fire* and *brimstone* came easily to. He just could *not* abide one of his own sons spending their time drinking and playing in the devil's back yard.

On an autumn day which was threatening rain, he came home from a trip when I had been drinking heavily and had passed out on his back porch. Ma had tried as best she could to get me up and gone knowing pa was expected. On that day even her sad eyes could not budge me from my drunken stupor. Seemingly a moment later he stood over me with his eyes dark and unreadable from under the brim of his black hat. When I first looked up at him his hands were on his hips and his voice rose like he was behind the pulpit during a southern tent revival. I shifted myself intending to stand but his actions froze me where I was.

He clinched his left fist and his right hand beckoned to the heavens as he spoke. He literally trembled with what I took as rage, but may have been the *Holy Spirit* itself. "James Oscar Draper, I don't care *what* you do with *your* life! I have truly given up on your salvation, but someday if you live past this winter, you may be a father. I pray now that your own offspring do not misuse their lives as you have. What God inspired gifts are wasted will be taken back unto *Himself*. I swear an oath to you now, when the day comes that you have children, I claim *all* of their souls for the Lord!"

With his words spent, his shoulders drooped and he shuffled off. I watched him go and suddenly saw him for the old man he was. My stomach tightened and I felt the same darkness of thought and mood pass over me I had experienced after the death of my men in Glenn Springs. I rolled over and retched off the end of the porch. I managed to stand and stumble on trembling legs to the well pump and wash my face. I felt flushed like a fever was coming on but I knew it was the burn of shame.

Straightening my clothes as best I could, I began the long walk into town. Before I had reached the side of the house my ma came out with a sack of food and some extra clothes in a potato sack. My mother, Mary Sue had been born in Ireland and a kinder woman I had never known. "Oscar, take some food and a few clothes I managed to put together for you. Please son, you know that you need to find a better way with your life. I know you're a good man in your heart. God bless you."

I began walking as rain clouds moved in on me. I was not aware of the rain as it began to fall or the cold as a north wind started blowing. I just walked replaying the last year of my life like a theater play and I did not care much for what I was seeing. I still burned with shame and anger at myself. How could I have ended up in this position? I was disgraced in the eyes of my family and myself. My own family should be embarrassed to admit I was their kin. I had worked hard to earn my military rank and the respect of my men. Yet in a few days of weakness I had thrown away friendships with my reckless actions, risking other's lives in the process. The falling rain became a pattern and I thought I heard Captain Cole's voice telling me again that I could reenlist in the Army.

My mind was made and it was clear I had nowhere else to go. At least now I had a plan. I would walk right back into the Army enlistment office I had originally joined at in Atlanta, Texas. This time I would enlist under my first name. If Captain Cole was right, the Army would never know or possible even care. If my fate was to die in a frozen trench in Europe, at least I would belong somewhere with men I respected surrounding me.

"Hey you there on the porch, you can't sleep here!"

I looked up startled at seeing a large man in uniform approaching me. The left sleeve of his uniform was empty and pinned up with the arm missing. I had walked all night and taken shelter on the wooden porch of the Army recruiting office. He wore sergeant strips in a clean freshly ironed uniform. I abruptly came to my feet, blinking against the blinding sun of the morning sunrise that was bathing the covered porch. "Sorry sergeant, I walked through the night to get here. I wanted to join up."

The man chuckled and said, "Mister you must be in a hurry to get to the war. I expect there'll be plenty of fighting left when you get there."

He had a dimpled chin with a neatly trimmed mustache and sideburns. Gray growing in his mustache and hair indicated he had seen many more years than I. Looking deeply into his green eyes I was pleased to see no condemnation, only concern at my disheveled appearance. I saw the lines at the corners of his eyes crinkle as he smiled. He reached out his right hand and I shook it. "My name is Jim Draper. I'm pleased to meet you."

"I'm Nathaniel Hawthorn Jackson. It's mighty nice to make your acquaintance Mr. Draper. I've heard tell of some mighty fine Drapers from around these parts. I only transferred here a few months back. You can call me *Nate*. Let's go in and get some coffee brewing on the stove. The cold and wet mornings are harder on my bones these days. I'll order us some breakfast from Miss Ruth's Diner. You look like a man who has missed a few meals."

As the strong coffee aromas filled the room I suddenly realized how hungry I was. I must have lost my ma's food sack in the night. "I do have a healthy appetite this morning." Not a minute too soon the enticing aroma of the food arrived ahead of the boy that Miss Ruth used for her deliveries. I think it was the first time I had actually drooled over a meal. After we had eaten I sat back full and satisfied. The warmth of the room was like sitting in one of the hot springs in southern Arkansas. After I had dried my clothes by the pot bellied stove and was dressed, Nate produced a pen and enlistment forms. Even though I knew I was going to sign, I made a show of reading the papers thoroughly.

Nate looked at me thoughtfully. "I want you to be sure of this Mr. Draper. Many men are enlisting because jobs are scarce, maybe patriotisms, or just because they want to get in on a fight. The again there are *other* men who appear to be running away from their past." He let the words hang in the air like he was waiting for an admission or statement from me.

"Well Nate, I might be running away, but it isn't from the law if that's what you're thinking." I quickly signed the papers, remembering to use my first and last name only and handed them back to him.

"That's fine then. Welcome to the U.S. Army. Now that you're one of us, I can tell you that we have been recruiting for a new Army division. It'll be made up mostly of Texas boys, with some Arkansas and Oklahomans thrown in too. They're calling it the *Cactus Division.* This division will be assembled from troops left over from other divisions sent to Europe. You'll *not* be training for Europe's war, but for duty down on the Texas and New Mexico border. The bandits led by Poncho Villa and other such outfits are stirring up plenty of trouble down there."

I was stunned by this turn of events. I did not know if I should be excited or afraid. Trying to hide my bewilderment as best I could at the twisted fate involved in my new assignment I said, "That'll be okay with me Sergeant Jackson. I don't care much for bandits or any others that prey on those that are weak and defenseless. Besides, I hear tell the food, drink and women are *real* spicy down there on both sides of the border." Sergeant Jackson was in a high-spirit now. He seemed genuinely keen on the idea and I wondered if he longed to go as well.

"Now think on this Mr. Draper, you might get a chance to see the other side too. President Wilson authorized the Cactus Division to be trained at Camp Wilson, named for the president himself, near San Antonio. You'll be part of the 18th Infantry while training, then commanded by none other than General John J. Pershing. Some of his men call him *Black Jack*, but not to his face I expect. It may either be because he lost his family in a fire at Fort Bliss, Texas which makes him a dark and moody man, or because he was the one time commander of an all Negro division of Buffalo Soldiers. I hear he is tough on his men and *hell* on his enemies. I suspect old Pancho will get some of what's coming to him. I'm betting you'll earn your pay as well. There are rumors that Pershing may chase the bandits all the way to Mexico City if need be. Now *that* would be a lifelong memory. A historic event like that would be impressive to witness and be a part of."

I had to disagree with Nate that chasing bandits over the border into Mexico would be historic. Alex and I may have been the first soldiers in this century, but there were rumors of cowboys or Texas Rangers who had crossed and exacted their own justice before returning. I certainly knew I would never forget my time in Mexico. Nate and I spent the long afternoon playing checkers and talking to the occasional townsfolk who wandered by the office. We ate supper together before I said my goodbyes. He was a kind man and I hoped to see him again.

The Army paid for a night in the little six room hotel across the street from the train station. The next day I would leave on the noon train that would take me to San Antonio. As I lay in my rented bed that night staring at the yellowed ceiling I replayed my time in the Army and how it had all turned out. Even now my face burned with shame at the thought of my dishonorable discharge. I knew my behavior at home over the past few months had been disgraceful as well. Now I had a chance to redeem myself. I thought about the deadly road ahead of me.

I had experienced a small part of what was involved in taking the fight to the bandits in their own land. It would be a real test for the Army. Like the Indians before them, they would know every cliff, valley and canyon. I figured for certain the bandits could disappear like Apache ghost when chased. Every hilltop crested could be an ambush for the pursuing soldiers. I took comfort in the knowledge that I would no longer be commanding men, but rather a follower of some other's orders.

I lay awake long into the night. I was sure I had done the right thing and was finally on the right trail my ma had wished for me. I craved a drink and found it hard to sleep without the too familiar taste of alcohol on my tongue. I bit my lip and tried to harden myself, resolving not to touch hard liquor again. I reckoned I had some unfinished business on the border and in Mexico too. I knew as well that I could have bought myself a ticket to a quick death. I decided to write to my ma and Alex in the morning. Ma would sleep easier knowing I was alright. If Alex was still serving somewhere on border duty the Army would get him the letter. I wanted him to know I would be back in the area as soon as this latest training was behind me.

# CHAPTER 15

## *The Cactus Division*

It was a bright morning and I estimated the temperatures as no colder than fifty. The date was Saturday, January 8th, 1916 and I was getting my first sight of Fort Wilson after two long days traveling on the Union and Pacific railways. My first notion was that the fort looked rougher than an old pioneer outpost of the 1880's. It was mostly a tent city with a few wooden structures used as officer quarters and a somewhat larger building I assumed was headquarters to the 18th Cavalry. I knew that a few miles away was the much more established Fort Sam Houston. However this camp had obviously been formed in a hurry and reminded me of Glen Springs, except there was an uncountable number of Army tents closely grouped over most of the open land I could see.

I moved with several other men toward the largest building, which indeed turned out to be headquarters. A massive-armed master sergeant with intense dark eyes and a hooked nose walked down the wooded porch and told us to fall into formation in a sharp and commanding tone. Without thinking I immediately did as I had done dozens of times over my military career and lined up abreast of the sergeant about five paces away, and stood at attention. The other men looked around in confusion, then lined up to my right and somewhat in alignment with me. I saw the sergeant give me an appraising look. I feared I had given myself away as a former soldier. His gaze moved on to the other men like a lion sizing up a gazelle for a meal.

"My name is Sergeant Arthur Dunbar and I am *not* your mother." A few of the men laughed until a fierce look from the sergeant made them choke off the snickers. "So don't ask me for nothing. You are here to become soldiers and I am *not* here to wipe your asses! My job is to train you so you don't get killed by the first time some bandit takes a shot at you. If you learn to work together you may survive the pending conflicts ahead. Is that understood?"

A few of the men said meekly, "Yes or yes sir."

Again I slipped up and without thinking I responded by shouting, "Yes master sergeant!"

I caught another look directed at me. "When I ask you a question I want an immediate response, loud and with some spirit. Is that understood?"

This time most of the men yelled out, "Yes master sergeant!"

"Also don't call me sir, I am an enlisted man and I *work* for a living. Now who among you has any past military experience?"

I did not say anything, too leery of questions that would uncover my past dishonorable discharge. Nobody else spoke up either.

His voice was sarcastic as he said, "Okay then we'll do this like you're all new born infants who haven't let go of their mommy's teats. Get over to the supply tent and get some uniforms. I'm sickened by the sight of so many civilians in my camp. It's the large tent over there. If you get lost, ask someone." Sergeant Dunbar pointed in the general direction and when many were still milling around he snapped. "Now move it and I'm not talking about tomorrow!"

Along with the others I had turned to run toward the tent when he stopped me with a solid hand on my shoulder.

"Not you soldier." He looked me straight in the eye. What's your name?"

"Private Jim Draper."

"Now that's an interesting answer, but not what I would expect from a man that has never been in the military. Do you think I'm stupid Private Draper?"

I did not have any idea where this was going but I had come too far to cut and run now. "No Master Sergeant Dunbar I do *not* think you're stupid."

"I have been in the Army for close to twenty years. You think I don't know a former military man when he is standing in front of me? The rest of those men would not know a master sergeant from a captain."

Not knowing what I would say I opened my mouth to deny the truth, but as I started to answer he held up a hand that froze the words in my throat.

"I don't give a damn where you served or why you don't want anyone else to know about it. I need someone experienced to help me get these men ready. They are heading down to the border and those bandits will show no mercy. They'll be killed within days of being assigned duty. If you are the type of man I believe you are, I'll give you a stripe now and another one when you leave training. Make your mind up now. It is time to *lead*, *follow*, or *get the hell out of the way* Draper!" Without giving me a chance to answer he said, "Go to the supply tent and tell Corporal Peabody I said to sew on your first stripe. A private first class pay will make a difference if you have folks back home that could use the money."

I was not seeking any extra duty and only wanted to be responsible for myself, but I knew I could not refuse. This man could make my existence here a living nightmare. I was under his command, like it not. Sergeant Dunbar had shown an uncanny ability to read me like a signed military order. I just hoped this new rank would not lead to my discovery. "Thank you Sergeant Dunbar." We shook hands and just like that I was accountable for the well being of soldiers again. This time I hoped to be better prepared and not lose any men. With great trepidation I knew my second chance with the Army had begun once more.

The training was grueling and the next four weeks were spent crawling through the brush, digging foxholes, firing all manner of weapons, and marching. We spent many hours in the saddle learning advanced cavalry formations. I had to admit the Army had learned a few new tricks since I had last been through training. Fort Wilson had two twin seat Curtiss JN-2 Jennies that crisscrossed the skies above us. The Jennies were biplanes with the wingspans of over forty-three feet and weighing in at over a thousand pounds. I could not imagine how flight had advanced from Kitty Hawk in 1903 to a plane used for war in a few short years. What excited me was their speed. A Jennie had a ninety horsepower engine and could fly at speeds of one hundred miles an hour, much faster if diving from high overhead toward an enemy position. The planes were made of canvas and wood and were not yet armed. I assumed they would be used for observation once we were back on the border. On any given day I counted a half dozen observation balloons far above our heads.

Each soldier was given a new-in-the-box 1911 Colt 45 semi-automatics. The Army had originally issued me a single action Colt 45, even though the double action 38 caliber was in common use at the time. The Army equipped the trainees with the 1903 Springfield 30 caliber, clip fed rifles. These rifles were not new, but appeared to be in mint condition and had probably never been fired. The Springfield rifle commonly referred to as the *03*, came with a sturdy knife-style bayonet, replacing the more flimsy rod-type that I had originally been issued in my first enlistment. Last, each trooper was trained on the Browning 30 caliber model 1895 machine gun. I marveled at what one of these deadly machines could have done for me and my men in Glen Springs. The Browning had a firing rate equal to one hundred men.

I had stopped trying to hide my prior experience and had fallen back into the familiar rhythm of a leadership role in the Army. In fact my fellow trainees and Master Sergeant Dunbar had taken notice that I was exceptionally hard on the men. I had watched my men dying around me and was helpless to stop it. I had seen up close what these men faced and felt I was duty-bound to give them every chance of surviving a fierce attack by Villa's raiders.

Nearing our fourth and final week of training, Sergeant Dunbar pulled me aside. By then he had turned over the day-to-day training to me and given me the promotion of the second stripe early. "Corporal Draper, you have been pushing your men harder than I would have believed possible. Don't mistake me they'll need it where they're going. Your trainees will be better prepared than any of the other troops here at Fort Wilson. I've heard a bit of grumbling but in truth I believe the men take pride in being the best at the fort. My point is I could make a comfortable place for you here. It would mean a sergeant stripe on that sleeve of yours."

I thought about it a moment only. "Sergeant you were right about me and my having prior service experience. I have seen men under my command die. It was a horrible thing to watch. Afterwards I took off on my own path chasing retaliation for what had been done. It resulted in me leaving the Army. I know you could force me to stay, but I'm asking that you do not. I have unfinished business on the border. This time I'll do it by the book." I saw a sudden realization in his eyes and knew I had said too much. I should have known that the Glen Springs attack would have been at the center of much conversation around Army camps. My fate was in his hands. If he wanted he could have me locked up immediately and discharged once more.

He hesitated before he spoke. I had never seen him at a loss for words before. He cast his eyes down. Then, apparently with his decision made, he locked his eyes on mine. "I respect your decision Draper and our words today will remain between us. I'd be pleased to shake your hand and good luck."

I let loose a long lungful of air, not realizing I had stopped breathing. I was not sure I could go through another court marshal. I only wanted to undo some of my past mistakes. This time I would do it the Army way and honorably. I stuck out my hand and he shook it warmly before walking away. My stomach was tense and I wondered for the hundredth time if I had made the right decision to return to the Army.

In another week my training would be done and I would receive orders to return to the Texas border, or possibly to New Mexico. There was the probability that I would be crossing back into Mexico as well. It was much rumored that an invasion of Mexico was to be authorized by President Wilson. This time as many as ten thousand soldiers could be assembled for the task. Not surprisingly my old friend Alex had been right when he said we could fight the bandits better *with* the

Army. If only I had listened to him on the day after the battle in May of 1915. That day began the events that had nearly ruined my life.

Graduation day came quickly and our orders were cut. I would be assigned to duty in Columbia New Mexico with the 13th US Cavalry. We were ordered to report at noon to the parade grounds in our dress uniforms, with our Springfield rifles in hand, bayonets attached. I arrived early and was amazed to see hundreds of men on the grounds. Some of the men were issued a white overcoat, me included. I had not seen all the trainees assembled at one time and it made me think the bandits were in for a bad time.

I marveled at President Wilson, who had ridden at a full gallop through all opposition once he was *hell-bent* on accomplishing a goal. Even though he was a former college president and not a military man, he displayed a good grasp of what the Army needed to drive the hated bandits back across the border. Often our commander-in-chief who was always intended to be a civilian authority had no idea of what a standing army needed to be successful. There had been no wars in this century and the country was fresh out of war heroes to elect as president. The president had his plate full with talk of the Germans negotiating treaties with Mexico and sightings of German submarines said to be patrolling off our coastal cities.

I soon found out what the white jackets were for and why all the troops were assembled. We were to be the subjects in a photograph, taken from one of the observation balloons. Barely controlled chaos was the order of this day. Officers and sergeants barked orders to the men. Confused men milled around, not understanding the orders. These men had just been trained to fight, but now were asked to pose for a photograph so some general could hang it on his wall. At the rear of the crowd the words Cactus Division began to take shape with the letters spelled out by men in the white jackets. I was part of a rough outline of a large cactus which was beginning to take form with the spines of the cactus made by grouping the white-jacketed soldiers holding the bayoneted Springfield rifles at the port arms position.

Finally an assembled group of officers and sergeants were put in place to form the base of the cactus. The words and cactus were framed by mounted cavalrymen, which made a rectangle of soldiers and their horses. I longed for one of the horses underneath me. The rifles became heavy. At least the mounted riders could sit until the photographer was satisfied and took the photograph. The minutes ticked by like days and still we stood. The man next to me swore that if the picture was not taken soon he would wet his uniform pants. I had not had breakfast and my stomach was growling something fierce.

I was in a bad mood and wanted to get started to my new post. The troops were stretched over a hundred yard field. Just as the photographer was ready a cloud would cover the area or some of the horses would act up and have to be forced back into line. At one point one of the men passed out from standing in one spot too long. I hoped it was not one of mine. At last more men in white were arranged to form an 18, which I took to mark the division number. If ever anyone was able to recognize me in the photograph I would be looking to my left. Just before the picture was taken, I caught movement and turned my head to see a man being bucked from a very impatient horse. I knew just how that horse felt. At last we were dismissed and I was free to return to the border and my military life.

# CHAPTER 16

## *Return to Glenn Springs*

This time I traveled on the Southwestern Railway train to Marathon, Texas, which took three days, with a day and a half stopover in Del Rio. The train stopped in many small towns along the way. I had lived in Texas most of my life and had never heard of many of the towns, such as Hondo, Uvalde, and Comstock. I passed the time playing Alex's game of solitaire. With practice I was cutting my rolling of a smoke down to an impressive four minutes. Then later I sat next to a cowboy who rolled his cigarettes in under a minute. I met an Englishman who smoked a long-handled curved pipe I had only seen in photographs. He was real friendly, but I had trouble understanding the man through his accent. He had lost a son and nephew in the Great War and was pleased the Americans were now getting into the fight.

It was getting colder as we drew closer to the mountains of the high desert. I was anxious to get to Marathon and on to my new assignment. Before leaving I had sent a telegram to Alex telling him of my approximate arrival date. I hope he had received the message. I would need his help for what I had in mind. Leaning out of the smoking car I could see the beginnings of the desert terrain and the mountains in the distance, looking like a painted canvas instead of the real peaks I knew. The train began to slow and a long whistle sounded from the steam engine as we rolled into town enveloped in a blanketing cloud of steam.

Earlier and not knowing exactly why, I had changed into a fresh, never worn Army dress uniform. It felt stiff and the change in rank made it seem like I was wearing another man's clothes. I knew the rapid desert temperature changes from hot and cold would quickly break in the uniform. As I stepped down from the train I looked to my left and began to turn my head to scan the surrounding faces when I was picked up in a crushing bear hug. Startled I began to struggle to defend myself before I looked down into the smiling face of Alex. The shorter man had me gripped in a death hold with my arms locked to my sides. "Let me go you ugly ox!"

Alex let go abruptly like a scolded child drops a toy. I was jarred to my core. "Okay amigo, but the *ugly* part hurt my feelings. We didn't own any oxen when I was growing up, so I don't know about that part since I have no idea what one looks like." He looked me over with a critical eye. "You've lost weight Oscar and a stripe. Or is it that you've gained back two of the stripes you lost last year." He stuck out his hand and I shook it warmly.

"Times were hard back home and I've just been through some of the toughest training I ever had with the Cactus Division while you were sitting around getting soft." I said this last part while I was rubbing my arms to get the circulation going again from the recent welcome hug. "Also you better get used to calling me Jim. I enlisted under my first and last name this time."

Alex smiled a mischievous wicked grin as he said, "The way I heard it *you* were responsible for the rough training while your master sergeant sat back and let you take over."

I was incredulous. "How in the name of heaven could you possibly know about that Alex?"

"Relax Oscar, ah, I mean Jim. It's common knowledge among the enlisted ranks who you are and that you've returned." With my surprise still frozen on my face Alex continued. "You and I are famous my friend. I guess Captain Cole or his young lieutenant had a big mouth. Like the disciples in the bible I have denied the story of you and me crossing the border at least three times to newspaper reporters who are still sniffing around for a good story."

I felt a rising panic and my chest tightened. "Alex if I'm turned in I'll be court marshaled again. This time I might get worse than just being thrown out. I could be sent to prison for many years."

"I don't think so amigo. Besides, if you believe the rumors the Army will be chasing bandits across the border legally soon. I think the men will keep your identity a secret. Not a lot has changed in the Army since you left. Most of the officers still have their heads so far up their back sides they can't see the sun."

Knowing there was nothing I could do but move forward, I relaxed a little looking Alex over as we began walking to a waiting wagon. "You look sharp wearing those sergeant strips." I smiled before continuing. "You do know you're too damned short to be a sergeant, but those vice-like arms of yours probably stop anyone but me from telling you so. Why don't you fill me in on what has happened since I left?"

Not ignoring my jab he said, "Well, as you can see I outrank you now. My sergeant stripes were awarded by Captain Cole himself before he shipped out for Europe's war. Just like you I've been stationed in Columbia, New Mexico. We're both assigned to the 13th Cavalry, Troop H, at nearby Camp Furlong. All the talk is that we are going to be permitted to cross the border with General *Black Jack* Pershing himself leading us. The general is still at Fort Bliss, but will cross with us or direct the show from Fort Bliss in El Paso. You'll recall it'll be our second time under his command. He's a good man, but I heard the loss of his family in the fire at Fort Bliss hangs over him like a poisonous fog. Some of the men are afraid he could lead us all into a Custer-like massacre if he ever decides he is ready to join his family again. I personally doubt it. I think he will be *all* Army when the time comes."

Trying to digest all that he had said I grew quiet, lost in my own thoughts. Before long we were standing at the wagon. I could see two shovels in the wagon bed and an old canvas tarp. "Thanks for bringing the wagon. I did not want to explain in detail in the telegram. Alex, I'm going after Bill Kubitz. I'll pick up his body in Glenn Springs and ship it to his family back in Fort Worth. I had a carpenter make up a tin coffin liner and arrange a supply of charcoal to cover the body for preservation until reburial."

Alex looked at me in surprise. "I'll help you of course, but when did you become so serious? I feel for his family but the expense alone will be pretty high. You used to spend every nickel on liquor and gambling. Did you hit it big in a winning game lately?"

"No Alex. I stopped drinking hard liquor and haven't been in a game in many weeks. I have the better part of my pay saved since I've reenlisted. I wired the family and they will bury their son when the body arrives. I believe it is the least I can do for one of my friends. His family will be better off knowing where Bill is buried."

We rode out with no more talk for many miles until the town was far behind us. Alex was driving and in days past a silence between us was comfortable, but finally he said, "Damn it all! You know what happened to your men was not your fault. The Army's best scouts back tracked the bandits to the river and calculated we fought off close to a hundred men. Even if the replacements had arrived we would have lost men."

"I know that Alex, but it does not make me feel any less responsible. You're a sergeant now. If you lose men you command you *will* experience what I am feeling now. I don't think it can be explained away by facts or figures."

It was late afternoon when we finished our grim task. Winter or not the temperature had risen to eighty degrees and the work had been hard. Several townsmen greeted us and I was welcomed as an old friend. At last as the sun was fading behind the mountains, I took the white cross the burial detail had used to mark the grave and we loaded Bill's body into the wagon. I looked over the battleground from the viewpoint of the hill. I knew the details of that night would never leave me. Even now it was as if I could hear the shouts and firing of my men and the bandits. The burned ruins of the cook shack were clearly visible in the fading light and seemed to be taunting me. I resisted the impulse to climb down the hill and tear the rest of that deathtrap down.

We were invited to stay the night with George Compton, his wife and two remaining children, Vivian and Little Johnny. Even though I had heard of Johnny's miraculous survival, I was still relieved to see the boy. I messed up his hair and gave him a comb I had been issued by the Army along with a newly minted silver dollar. He smiled a crooked grin and scooted from the room.

Compton, Kenneth Ellis and some of the other townsfolk told a few stories about the bandit raid and included their side of the events. I had to admit I must have been a sight running up that hill as Compton watched from his higher vantage point above. Nobody felt much like laughing due to Mrs. Compton's haunted eyes. She still deeply grieved the loss of her son Jack. She falsely blamed herself for his death believing if she had been there the boy might have been saved. The next morning I thanked Compton for his support on the night of the battle. The comforting sound of that big old .50 caliber Sharps booming cover fire for us throughout the night was still fresh in my memory.

# CHAPTER 17

## *Camp Furlong*

We were more than two hundred miles away from our assignment in Columbus so when we arrived back in Marathon, we purchased train tickets. It was early afternoon when we left the station, but we located the local funeral parlor and made arrangements to see Bill's body safely home. Before we left the parlor and the simple wooden coffin containing our friend's worldly remains, we both took off our hats. I quoted one of my pa's favorite Bible verses I had heard him recite dozens of times at funerals from Psalm 23:4. I was not sure it was appropriate for my Jewish friend, but I knew of no other words. I closed my eyes and recited from memory…

*"Yea, though I walk through the valley of the shadow of death, I will fear no evil, for thou art with me; thy rod and thy staff they comfort me."*

When we had departed and walked outside to look for a hotel, I saw Alex looking at me like I was a stranger. "Amigo, you have become another man I think."

"Don't fret over me Alex. There is still enough of the *old* me left to get us both into trouble again. I admit I've been through a lot in the past year. Now the new year is shaping up to be one for the history books if old Pancho and Pershing meet."

"It may be that you mean when they meet again. Those two old soldiers have already had a sit-down at Fort Bliss in 1914. Photographs of the two men meeting were shown in newspapers all across the country. At that time Villa was allied with the Mexican government backed by us. The story is told that President Wilson at one time supported Villa over Carranza for Mexican President. I'll bet this did not set well with Villa. Either way it went the constant attacks on Americans embarrasses the government of Mexico and may lead to an invasion on our part. Whatever his motivations for striking the United States are, it spells trouble for those living on the border."

The thought of General Pershing hosting Villa the year before he killed my men and innocent citizens made me madder than a stepped on rattler. "I would have shot that old wolf as soon as he showed his ugly face at the fort, or locked him up for a later hanging if I was in a particularly good humor. I don't believe in drinking tea and talking with outlaws or bandits. They will not stop until the last one is dead, or at least their leaders are."

"I agree completely and most soldiers feel the same. I say we leave politics to the politicians. Soldiers like us just follow orders, or we do most of time. Now let's find some food and a hotel. It's been a long day and that train pulls out at 6:00 o'clock sharp. I still have to check on some new arrivals before I get any rest."

After we ate and checked into our hotel, Alex went to locate other soldiers that had come in on the train for assignment at Camp Furlong. He had sold the idea of the Marathon trip to his first sergeant as an excuse to meet me. He told the sergeant he would keep the new recruits out of trouble, and promised they would be on the train to the camp on time and sober. After he had the men settled to his satisfaction, he came and knocked on my door, then entered and began to pace the room cursing in Spanish. I was sitting on the bed and grinning at his obvious discomfort. His mood reminded me more of myself than my usually more relaxed friend. His frustration was obvious but I had no idea why.

Alex, looking disgusted finally said, "I can honestly say I never appreciated how hard your job was just keeping your men in line. These new soldiers are so green they'll probably shoot their own damn selves before they ever see a bandit. Some just want to get drunk and fight, while others are mad because they were not given orders to fight Germans instead of bandits. The rest are missing their wives, girlfriends, or mommas. No wonder you were *so* hard on those trainees. I never asked for these stripes and I was just fine minding my own business and occasionally yours too."

I could not help myself and started laughing at him as he raged on, his face a twisted red mask. Eventually he cooled off and sat heavily on the only chair. "Well you do fit the job description in most outfits Alex. I have had assignments where the sergeant was the toughest and strongest man in the division. I figure you can handle whatever fighting or mothering those men need."

"I'm not mothering a bunch of boys against wild bandits. If they get their fool heads shot off it'll just be *too* bad."

"Welcome to command my friend. Now it'll be my turn to sit back and watch you twist under the glare of an angry captain or young lieutenant who has everything to prove."

"Maybe I can get busted back in rank again. Bill Kubitz used to lose a stripe a year with a different reason every time. I just don't want to get thrown out of the Army for it." He quickly added, looking downcast, "Sorry, I'm sure that's still a touchy subject for you."

"No, now that I'm here I believe I'll vindicate myself. I'd rather that story never gets told, and certainly not to any newspaper reporters still lurking about." After Alex left for his own room, I wrote a letter to my ma. She would be happy to know I would be assigned to a location she could get mail through to. I put most of my remaining pay in the envelope before I sealed it. I did not know when I would be able to send another letter. I knew if we did cross the border into a fight inside Mexico, mail might be a long time coming or going.

The twelve hour train ride was uneventful. Alex and I spent most of our time riding in the Smoking Car. He still favored his little cigars and got into a poker game, winning about fifty dollars. I stayed out of the game, not in the mood for wasting time or money. I paced the car and found I could not sit for long. I was over-anxious to get to Camp Furlong and ready to begin the next chapter in my Army career. Alex had observed changes that had occurred within me, but a deep hatred still burned within me toward the bandits. Although I knew no matter how many I killed it would never bring my men back. This time I would play by Army rules, but I intended to make the bandits pay a heavy price for attacking Americans.

Right on time the train whistle sounded as the old steam workhorse made a smoky entrance into the sleepy village of Columbus, New Mexico. It was the second week of February, 1916 and I was thankful to finally be back on regular duty with the Army. Breathing in the sights and sounds, I was impressed at the contrasting beauty of desert and surrounding snowcapped mountains. The air was clear and I filled my lungs deeply. It felt like I was home again.

I was curious about the Columbus, but for now Alex and I avoided the settlement and headed straight to the mess tent at Camp Furlong for supper. I was impressed at what I saw of the camp. Several wood or adobe structures were two storied and yet rows of tents could be seen over a hundred yards long and half as wide. I saw dozens of heavy trucks with canvas tarps in place to haul supplier or men. This was still a cavalry outfit and I intended to look over the horseflesh as soon as I could. As we ate hungrily, I wanted Alex to fill me in on the town and camp. "How many men are stationed here?"

"There are nearly one hundred and fifty soldiers here, with more coming in every day. As you might expect, up and down the Texas and New Mexico border townsfolk are arming themselves against real or imagined bandit raids. You may not have heard about Villa's bloody attack on Americans last month of men who were in Mexico to work mines for President Carranza's government. He stopped a train in Santa Isabel, Chihuahua, stripped 17 Americans and executed sixteen of them. One man managed to survive by playing dead."

Alex paused to let me take his words in. I had heard rumors during my training and travels but no details. He shook his head sadly at the needless loss of life and continued. "Those men were sacrificed just so Villa could punish Carranza and continue to brew a boiling pot of trouble for his government with the Americans. Now if you can believe it, Columbus residents, all three hundred of them, don't seem to be worried. They falsely believe they are safe since our camp is between them and the border. Of course there are many border crossings depending on seasonal rains. It's a real possibility that the Bandits could attack the town first."

I was horrified at the death of the American miners. I had heard Carranza had sent men to reopen old mines to finance his government's fight against the revolutionary forces. The American miners had the bad luck to be caught between the two powers in their struggle. My hatred and resolve to *dispatch to hell* as many bandits as possible was strengthened by the story. Alex continued his narration. "The original town of Columbus was settled in 1891. Then in 1902 the whole village was moved three miles north to the present location when the El Paso/ Santa Fe Railroad line built a station."

I thought my heart would stop when I felt a strong hand gripping me solidly on the shoulder. Startled I looked up into the eyes of one of my surviving men from Glen Springs. He was now wearing three stripes and grinning at me like he had just discovered a cache of unclaimed diamonds filling his pocket. He was well over six feet tall, solidly built and had momentarily pinned me to my seat. Before I could react he spoke in a loud voice that those eating nearby would easily hear, "Hello soldier, you must be one of the new trainees that came in today. I'm Sergeant Sean Haltom. What's your name mister?"

Vastly relieved, I stood up and shook his hand. "I'm Jim Draper and I'm pleased to meet you Sergeant Haltom."

He winked and lowered his voice so only Alex and I could hear, "I'm glad you're with us. We'll be ready if those bastards want to try us again. We'll march them straight to their maker. Those of us who know you will keep it to ourselves. If it was not for you none of us would have got out of Glen Springs alive." He raised his voice to the more familiar tone of a sergeant. "Get some rest soldier. I've just added you to the duty roster. You'll be on guard duty overnight from midnight until dawn overlooking the border. We can't tolerate sleeping on duty either. All of our lives may depend on the alertness of the night guards." He slapped Alex's on the back and was gone.

I watched his back as he strode away. After he left, I took several full gulps of air to calm my edgy nerves. I have to admit to feeling some pride during his low-spoken words of thanks. I turned to Alex and said, "I wonder how many times I'm going to have to go through a scare like that? I'm pretty damn sure that I picked a bad time to stop drinking whisky."

"I'm thinking by morning anyone who knows you will have word that you're back. News is a scarce thing in these parts and most are hungry for anything to talk about. I would not worry about your past catching up to you here. Anybody who figures out who you are will respect your privacy or get a thrashing and poor assignments from me or Sean. I expect the men will soon be too busy to make a fuss over the likes of you."

"After we eat you better show me where I'll be sleeping. I'm overtired anyway from all the traveling. It'll be good to get back working on Army business." No sooner had I spoke than I heard the sound of distant thunder. Confused I said to Alex, "That's unusual. When we came in here the sky was clear and promised a cool evening in the desert. Now it sounds like there might be rain."

"You ought to know by now that the desert can change weather from calm to storm in an instant. When it rains it usually floods too. Don't worry about drowning though. We built high earthen mounds out by the Rio Grande. You'll get wet and could end up swimming in the deep foxholes dug along the top of the ridgeline, intended to protect against flying bullets. Finish eating and I'll walk you over to the Quartermaster's Office. You'll need some gear. You've got your pretty new Colt 45 and Springfield, but you'll need a rain slicker, ammo, and toiletry items. The rest you'll have to pay for in town. You know the Army will provide the basics, but writing material and such will have to be paid out of your pocket. If you need some cash I can stand you for it."

"No Alex I'm okay, but thanks. I don't spend much money these days and save most of what I earn. It is good to be back serving with friends and once again in the Army. As to being back on the border, I still reserve judgment on that matter. Say, are you still flush with those gold pieces of yours?"

Alex beamed a broad smile. "I have never figured out why you and some of the other boys think I have gold stashed away somewhere.

It's a simple fact that now and again I win a big poker hand. There is no mystery to it." He hesitated a moment and grinned broadly, then added, "Well, just to be on the safe side, search me good if one of those bastard bandits gets me. I'd rather you have my *poker money* rather than some *loco pistolero.*"

Alex set me up with my gear and an assigned Army cot in the same tent as his. These tents were much larger than the ones in Glenn Springs with sleeping cots for two dozen men. Two more cots were arranged at the head of the rows for the sergeant's use. A desk and two chairs were in the sergeant's area for the completion of paperwork. In my head I paced off about 25 feet by 30 feet inside the living area. The walls and high sloping ceiling were thick canvas and seemed tight enough to keep the wind and rain out. I counted four camp stoves that could be used for heat or cooking. Each man was issue an Army-green trunk to stow his gear in that sat at the foot of the bunk. A rolled blankets and a pillow lay on the cot. I normally needed some quiet when I slept, but I fell into the assigned cot and was instantly asleep, trusting Alex to wake me near midnight.

# CHAPTER 18

## *Lightning Strikes*

Seemingly only moments later, Alex shook me awake from a deep dark hole. I turned over suddenly, disoriented and wondering where I was. During the previous year of hard drinking I had awakened in a few strange places. Shrugging off the bad feeling, I accepted a cup of strong black coffee from Alex. I took out my pocket watch and peered at the time in the dim light. I could barely make out the time as a bit past 11:30. This same pocket watch had been given to me by my grandfather. I was ashamed to say I had pawned the timepiece more than once over the last year. After a few swallows of the coffee my head began to clear and I was able to arrange my thought. "Thanks for waking me." I could feel a cool current of air on my face and smell moisture in the air, but could not tell which direction it was coming from since the winds swirled around inside the tents. "It smells like the storm is moving closer."

"I believe it will be a bad one, but it's still up north of us yet. When you finish your coffee I'll walk with you down to the river. I have to check on the men anyway. These new soldiers are as jumpy as a dog-chased rabbit. If I don't call out as I approach they're liable to shoot me dead."

As we drew nearer to the Rio Grande I saw the mounds were twenty feet high and about fifty feet back from the riverbank. The manmade hill had been built into a continuous wall running for a quarter mile or so. Curious I asked, "How many men are on duty up there?"

"Twelve men unless were sure of trouble. There are twenty foxholes which are staggered to allow sentries to walk between them. I leave it to the men to arrange a pattern of patrol. Some men would rather cower down in a hole all night. Others are too nervous or restless to sit and like to wonder from end to end. As long as everyone stays a wake and the men don't set up a pattern I'm fine with it. We don't want any observers to know where the men are at any given time. Your head and shoulders are visible while walking the line, but a foxhole is never far away if the need arrives to dive for cover. I'll be back around at 2:00 A.M. for another duty check. I'll see you then."

Walking on in the darkness for a few more feet I took in deep breaths of the fresh air. I felt stronger and healthier than I had in a long while. It felt good to belong to something bigger than myself again. Knowing you are surrounded by like-minded men who will fight alongside of you even if death may come, cannot be explained or completely understood by those who have not experienced it. As we approached Alex sang out in a clear voice. I saw men pop their heads up like prairie dogs looking for danger. I began the awkward and difficult climb up the steep sides of the mound. On my way up I stumbled twice on the loosely packed earth. Once the crest had been reached I shook hands with a couple of the men. It was too dark to see faces under the thick cloud cover and the wind sound made it hard to talk much.

For the next two hours I volunteered to walk. My mind was, for now, free of guilt and regret. It felt as if I was once again living my life on the right path my ma had said to find. I fell into the rhythm of the night. Walk slowly to the end, turn around and walk slowly back, eyes alert for movement beyond the river. Even though men were around me, I enjoyed a strong feeling of being alive and in my own world. I was not sure even Alex could understand just how good it felt to be back on duty in the Army.

Before I realized it the time had passed and Alex was making his way up the slope toward my position. He was easily recognizable with his short stature and deep chest. How he knew which man was me was a question. I watched him climb the grade with ease. He carried a sack in one hand and climbed with the other. I was thinking there should be steps put in on the opposite side of the river by the time he reached me.

"Take a break amigo. I've brought us some canned peaches."

We walked off to one end and plopped into an empty foxhole. From this angle I could still see any approach from the north or west. Alex brought out the cans and opened both with his knife. He handed one to me and I greedily drank the cool juice. "Thanks Alex. I forgot how good peaches taste. It reminds me of my ma's pies. She makes good fried pies for packing off to work, or baked one for the supper table."

"You're welcome. Just don't expect this every night. It's a good idea to bring something along to help you get through the long night."

Looking around at the discarded cans littered around the foxhole I said, "I figure it must be the standard practice."

Alex scanned the dark skies and said, "The storm is likely to break soon. The rain smells close. There is a charge of electricity in the air. My hair is standing up and every movement brings a spark. I better go give orders to the other men. I don't mind them hunkering down in one of the holes when it hits as long as they keep their heads up and facing west. I don't want the bandits using this storm as cover for an attack. I'll see you tomorrow. Sergeant Haltom will relieve me at 4:00 o'clock in the morning."

When he had gone I ate another can of peaches, before fishing out my raingear and fumbling into it. Now, sure I was ready for whatever nature threw at me, I began patrolling again. No sooner had I thought this than the bottom fell out of the sky. I was engulfed in hard driven rain. Despites Alex's warning about keeping a watch, I could not see five feet in front of me. I did see bright flashes of lightning so bright I would be momentarily blinded by each flash. I was taught as a child that by timing the flash of lightning and the report in second intervals one could calculate how far away the storm was. If that was true, then the other soldiers on the hill, including myself were in real trouble. The lightning was right on top of us. I attempted to peer through the rain, but it was useless as I could see no others. I hoped Alex had made it back to his tent, although it might not be any safer.

The storm raged on endlessly. At some point I head a cry of anguish, far off but distinct. I now understood the saying, there were not any atheist cowering in a foxhole, not in a war or in a storm such as this. I prayed as I never had before. I only thought I had been scared during the battle in Glen Springs. However, at least then there had been an enemy to strike out at. Here there was only helplessness at the whims of nature's terrible wrath.

All through the rest of the night the storm continued, seemingly stalled on top of our position. Eventually I perceived a small break in the wind and rain. I began to see a little further down the line. After another thirty minutes I was sure the storm was losing hold and blowing further east. I finally moved from my position. My intentions were to check on the other men. The storm had turned the path into a muddy muck and the walking was hard.

As I worked my way along the path, men nodded they were okay and I continued to move further down the line. Nearing the south end, one of the men stood up and hollered directly in my ear against the howling wind. Pointing south he said, "Someone is hurt down there! I heard cries hours ago but could not get to him without being blown off the mound."

I motioned for him to follow me. About ten feet further along, I saw two men lying motionless in the bottom of the last foxhole. Knowing nobody could sleep through a storm such as this I jumped in the hole and went to check the nearest man. He was lying face down and as I rolled him over I saw his eyes were wide and staring. The pungent smell of burnt flesh caught my nose. Sudden memories of the Cookhouse rushed at me. I had smelled my own feet burning during my escape. I knew the man was dead and was beyond help. The next man was breathing, but unconscious. By putting my face next to his I could hear his moans. He seemed to be delirious with pain.

Without hesitation, I pulled him up and over my shoulder and started down the hill. I nearly fell many times on the way down. At the bottom I began a shuffling run under the man's weight. Realizing I did not know where the hospital was, I headed for a large building which still had lights on. Inside I could see a civilian in a tipped-back chair reading in front of the fireplace. I kicked at the door until He saw me and rushed over.

Opening the door he looked aghast at me and I knew I must have looked a frightful sight appearing at his door before dawn. "What the hell is going on soldier?"

"I think he's been lightning-struck. Are you the doctor?"

"No son this is the Customs House. Lay him on the table there and I'll fetch him." He moved quickly to throw on a rain slicker and was gone into the dark.

I lay the man down as gently as my strained muscles would allow. I opened his clothes to examine his wounds. I could see severe burn marks on his left side. He was mumbling again but none of it made any sense. Now that my part was done I felt the shakes coming on. Once again I was reminded of pa's much-mentioned miracles. I was truly amazed that any of us made it off that hill alive. Not knowing what else I could do for him, I leaned exhausted against the table to wait.

I lost track of time but suddenly the door burst open and seven men rushed into the room. I recognized Alex and Sean, and the man I had interrupted, but not the other three. A tall man with tiny round glasses, dressed in a nightshirt tucked into his pants took charge and began examining the soldier's injuries. Alex pulled me off to the side and introduced me to Colonel H.J. Slocum, the Commanding Officer of the camp and W.C. Hoover, the Mayor of Columbus. The two men had been drinking coffee in the colonel's office when notified. I snapped to attention and saluted, but the colonel waived me off.

Colonel Slocum appeared to be in his sixties and had the erect posture of a seasoned military man. He wore a thick mustache, heavy leather jacket, trimmed in fur and had his bloused Army pants tucked into his high boots. Mayor Hoover was a portly man wearing high-waist pants, bow tie, white pressed shirt and fedora hat. He reached out and pumped my hand warmly like he was looking for my vote. I noticed the colonel looking me over and was sure he missed no detail of my drowned hound dog appearance. When his inspection was complete he said, "What happened to the man soldier?"

"I think he was struck by lightning sir. It was flashing so much we were near blinded and striking the ground all around us. The wind and rain were so fierce the men closest to him could not reach him until the storm let up a little. I don't know his name sir, but I left another man dead on the mound. I believe they both took shelter in the same foxhole."

All the color drained from Colonel Slocum's face. He quickly recovered however and turned and addressed the two sergeants. "Arrange a detail to retrieve the deceased soldier and bring him here so the doctor can look him over." Turning back to me he said, "I have not seen you before. What's your name son?"

"I'm Corporal Draper sir and please to meet you."

"I understand you carried the man all the way here. We need more men willing to take charge during trouble." He turned away and addressed Sergeant Haltom. "Have the men on guard duty relieved. I think they have been through enough. Also check to make sure there are no other injuries. Sergeant Alejandro, have details inspect the camp for other damage. I don't want the bandits taking advantage of any weaknesses in our defense." After a pause he added, "See to it Corporal Draper gets another stripe. I like the way he takes charge and sets a good example to the men."

Alex gave me a quick wink from behind the colonel's back and left with Sean. I worried about the attention I kept bringing to myself. Somebody at headquarters might see my name and recognize it as a soldier that was court marshaled last year. "Colonel, do you mind if I stay until the man regains consciousness?"

Before he could answer the doctor called out. "Sir, I think he is coming around. He has been burned severely but I don't believe it is life threatening. Colonel Slocum, I imagine with a few weeks in the infirmary he will recover fully. I've read about dizzy spells and nausea associated with the electrical shock. He may have a time of it but he should pull through it."

I slumped into a chair to wait. The colonel paced the room impatiently. In another twenty minutes the other man's body was brought in and laid out on the same table as the wounded man. The doctor, I now knew was Major Herbert Hanson. He immediately stripped the man from the waist up, then stooped over, studying the man's wounds closely. He then motioned and the colonel and I came over to the table. "If you look at his right elbow it is severely burned by the lightning. I believe he was struck there and the bolt traveled across his body and into this man here." He shook his head sadly at the sight. "I would think the poor fellow came to a quick, and I pray a painless end as the current traveled to his heart stopping it instantly."

As Hanson finished speaking, the wounded man started coughing and his eyes flew open, wildly searching the room. Major Hanson washed his face and assured those present that his patient would recover. I excused myself and headed back to my cot. The tent, which seemed so much larger before, was now crowded with men milling about. However, I was in no mood for talking about the previous night's horrors. Now the Army had added another great fear to my life, being struck by lightning had been linked in my mind with burning to death. After facing both of those two horrors in a little over a year, death by a bullet did not frighten me at all. I mentally shook off the dark images in my head and asked myself once more why I had returned to the Army. I was not thinking straight and needed rest. Now that the danger was past I had the shakes so bad I could not have held a coffee cup. Ignoring the hustle and bustle of the camp around me, I lay back on my cot and dropped off instantly into an exhausted and dreamless sleep.

# CHAPTER 19

## *Dad's Plan and Bob*

"Buddy, you've hooked a big fish!" Dad shouting at me and brought me back to myself. I had been so into grandpa's latest story I had forgotten where I was. I had been sitting in a trance-like state on a shallow bank by the creek. I had leaned back against a large overhanging pecan tree and lost myself in the story. When the fish had struck the baited hook it had nearly ripped the cane pole out of my hands. I gripped it tightly and stood to start hauling it in. It was the first time in my life I was upset that I was catching a fish. I knew now that the magic moment was broken and grandpa would probably not finish the story. After a full ten minute struggle the catfish was on the bank. It was not that big, but the largest of the day. All in all it was a great day. We had caught enough keepers for a goodbye fish fry for my grandparents and grandpa had told another story. This time I was glad my dad and I had heard it together.

The next day we saw grandpa and grandma off on their train. Deb was crying into grandma's dress, not wanting her to leave and it made me squeeze out a tear as well. It took six hours to drive to Texarkana and at least eight to get there by train. Mom had packed them plenty of food that had been left over from the fish fry. Grandma had left us some of her pickled black eyed peas and her wonderful homemade peach cobbler. She could preserve just about any type of food if it fit in a mason jar.

Over the next couple of weeks the days came and went quickly with school during the day and chores and homework at night. One day I arrived at school to see my teacher crying openly at her desk.

All the children watched her closely, quickly taking their seats and sitting quietly. I was reminded of my friend Randy's story about the nuns in his school crying over the President Kennedy's assignation. Whatever it was I knew it was not good news. Finally, Mrs. Burnett looked up and seemed to realize for the first time that we were there. After smoothing her hair into place and wiping her eyes she said, "I'm sorry children. We were told this morning that Bob Frazier died of leukemia late last night."

I could not believe her words. Bob had ridden home with me two or three times on the school bus, staying over the weekend. We all knew he had been sick but did not know what he had would kill him. The word *leukemia* seemed evil and I did not understand how he had been here at school two weeks before and now was gone. I did not understand leukemia was all about and I admit to a guilty fear that somehow I could catch it and die too. I took the news home and my mom and I watched a home movie taken during my birthday party the previous October. My whole class had been invited and it was one of my best memories. There was Bob, happily running around with all of his friends. Knowing he had only months to live seemed to crush my heart.

That night I cried myself to sleep. I had thought at ten I was too old for that, but death had always appeared far off, something that happened to others, not those close to you. For days I seemed to drag myself to school and home again. Mom tried to snap me out of it by saying, "Life goes on for the living Buddy. We honor our friends and family who die before us by remembering them and living the best way we can." It was many months before a day went by that I did not think of my lost friend Bob.

Each evening after supper, my mother would help me with the seemingly endlessly assignments from my teachers. History was my best subject, with math as my worst by far. The concept of numbers plainly did not stick with me. I would get frustrated since I could not see any practical use for it. I knew I would never be an accountant like dad, so math seemed useless. It has also been obvious my attitude interfered with my learning. Dad said I had a "closed mind to math."

One night after I had finished working several assigned math problems for class the next day dad checked my answers. "Much improved. You'll be working in my office before you know it." He could tell from my face that making a living with numbers and figures was not on my list of jobs, so he added, "Well maybe there is hope for your sister Sherry. She has already been helping me on some small accounting projects. How about we get down the encyclopedias and read up on Columbus, New Mexico. I'll bet there is plenty written about the bandits crossing the border into Texas and New Mexico."

Now I was excited. My parents had bought the encyclopedias in 1960 and my sister and I had used the books dozens of times to write papers for school. The large, white, simulated leather books were labeled from A to Z and we started with "B" for bandit. Not finding anything there, we next tried "C" for Columbus. After looking through the material relating to Christopher Columbus, we found a story about a large battle that took place in Columbus, New Mexico in March 1916. Dad read some of it aloud, "Estimates ranging as high as five hundred bandits crossed the border and attacked the small village of Columbus, New Mexico."

We exchanged a look before I said excitedly, "Grandpa was down there at that time! Could we mark the place for now? I don't want to read about it until grandpa tells us the story. Then I'll read every word. It's just like a book that becomes a movie. I like to read about it first in case they left something out. This time we can read about it and then read what the encyclopedia says. I want to write grandpa a letter and ask him when he can tell us what happened. I guess I'll have to wait for Christmas."

"Maybe you won't have to son. When I was in the Army stationed in Germany, pa and I wrote letters every week to each other. If my pa is in the mood, maybe we can get him to write it down for us."

I was not sure I liked the idea of reading the story. It might seem like a history lesson from one of my school books. On the other hand, it would be told by grandpa and I liked that part of it. "Okay, I'll write him now."

"Leave the letter open son and I'll put some pictures of our fishing trip inside. Your grandpa will like that, even though you beat us all with that last catch of yours."

I wasted a lot of paper trying to get the letter to grandpa just right. I started by telling him we had all enjoyed his and grandma's visit. Then how proud I was that he had been a part of history that was written about in our encyclopedia. Afraid he might say I should just read about it I closed with a request for *his* story. He had lived it and was there when the actual history was being made by the men involved.

When I had finished I walked into Dad's home office and handed him the letter. He was rocking slightly forward and back as he smoked his pipe. The cherry flavored tobacco filled the room with a cozy aroma. The soft creaking of his old office chair brought a memory of when I was younger and had played under his desk, opening the left side storage area and the cherry pipe smoke scent had drifted out of the opening. Somehow the smoke made me feel safe, as if dad would always be there for me.

He had been studying some accounting figures when I walked in. Dad, always patient with his kids, stopped what he was doing whenever we rushed in and bothered him with whatever was crowding our mind at the time. "Dad, please mail this tomorrow. I can't wait to see what grandpa writes back."

Dad smiled at me. "Okay, I'll drop it in the box tomorrow on my way to work." He pulled out an envelope and removed a five cent 1963 Christmas tree stamp from his circular brass holder and let me lick it for the envelope. He knew I liked the taste of the paste used on stamps. Whenever I went to the Post Office with dad we would pick the design together. This one showed a decorated Christmas tree on the right and the White House in the background on the left. Our usual pick was either a patriotic or historical one. "You better be off to bed now or your mother will clobber us both. She already wanted to know what you were up to."

"What did you tell her?"

"The truth of course, that you were studying *real* history and we had an idea you could find a way to turn it into a class project or something."

I went to bed happy for the first time in weeks. Just knowing I now had something to look forward to in the days ahead. Also I now had grandpa's stories to share between my dad and me. My sister Debra was long asleep before I finally drifted off and dreamed of Camp Furlong during another lightning storm. Like Grandpa had many years before, I could feel the wind and rain hitting my face in waves. In my dream with each flash I saw shadowy figures creeping ever closer to the American border and the village of Columbus, New Mexico.

# CHAPTER 20

## *Grandpa's Letter Arrives*

In the world of a ten year old, two weeks is an eternity. Every day after school I ran from the bus to check the mailbox for a letter from Grandpa. Then I would rush inside and ask my mom if she had brought in the mail. After nine weekdays of this my mom said, "Yes Buddy, I checked the mail. You know your grandpa will write you soon enough."

"But what if he forgot or doesn't want to?"

"Then you'll see him at Christmas and maybe he will be in the mood for another story then. You and your dad ganging up on him or calling and pestering him are not going to make him write any faster. Those stories are interesting and exciting to you Buddy but stop and consider and you'll realize those are grandpa's memories of *bad* times. They probably hurt him to recall them. From what your dad told me some of what happened to him was horrible. Now for some reason he must have a need to tell them. You need to let him tell them at his own pace."

Mom's words made me stop and think about how the stories might actually harm grandpa with the telling. Why now was it coming out when what happened was so long ago? Why were the stories of those battles and death of his friends coming out at this time? Dad had said grandpa never spoke a word about his Army experience when he was growing up. "Sorry mom I never thought about it that way before. I'll try to wait and give grandpa all the time he needs." I felt like the wind had been completely knocked out of me as I returned to my room. I felt confused as if I had forced grandpa to do something he did not want to do.

After homework and dinner that night I watched the television series Gunsmoke with mom and dad. If possible we never missed the show or Bonanza on Sunday night either. It was a family time like dad had said his family did with radio shows when he was growing up. Later I slipped into bed and lay back thinking over what my mom had said earlier about grandpa. I knew she was right. I could sense how during each story the memories haunted him. However there were other moments when a reflective light would shine in his eyes with the remembrance of good friends and his times with them.

Dad came in to say goodnight and he could see I was disappointed. "Don't worry son, grandpa will write soon. I know your mom told you the stories were probably hard on grandpa to share. She is probably right about that, but he didn't tell me anything about his experiences in the Army when I was growing up. Now for some reason known only to my pa he must want to get his stories out in the open. Get some sleep. Good night Buddy."

The next day when I got home from school I avoided the mail box and walked straight inside. I went to the kitchen to make myself a peanut butter and jelly sandwich and sat down to eat it at the table with a glass of chocolate milk. My older sister Sherry was already home and came into the kitchen with our dog Suggs. Our mix breed mutt was not allowed into the house except when the weather outside was freezing. This told me my mom was not home and Sherry was in charge. Or at least I let her think she was. "Where is mom?"

"She took Debra to the doctor. I think she has an ear infection. Oh, there was something mom wanted me to tell you." She was grinning and I knew she was teasing me. "It was real important too. I just can't seem to remember it right now. Maybe if I had someone make me one of those sandwiches I could remember what she said."

I launched myself out of my seat. "Was it about a letter?" When she did not answer, I hurriedly went to the refrigerator and started making her a sandwich. This was the same sister that had fooled me for a week last Easter when she gave me what I thought was a small speckled bird egg and said I should try to hatch it. I had taken the egg and made it a nest, then tucked it under the edge of the refrigerator where warm air blew. After a week the candy egg had melted and I was still mad about the mean trick. I knew what mom had wanted me to know could be anything from cleaning my room to doing my homework before she came home.

Clearly stalling and enjoying my anxiety, Sherry spoke slowly. "Let's see, she said we could split one of her Cokes with our snack. There was something else too. I just can't remember right this minute."

I went to look under the sink cabinet where mom kept her sodas and pulled one of the eight ounce Cokes and started filling two glasses with ice. One of *my* tricks was to put extra ice in Sherry's drink so I would get more. So far it was one of the few things I had ever beaten her with. After all she did have three years more experience on me. I brought the glasses to the table and she supervised me pour the supposedly equal amounts to fill each glass. Last year my *junkyard dog* antics had cost me dearly when I grabbed up what I thought was a glass of orange juice sitting on the kitchen counter and downed it. Unfortunately for me it was really gasoline my dad had been using to clean something in the garage. Mom had made me swallow a raw egg until I puked most of it up. Then mom was mad at dad for a long time over that one, but I knew my junkyard dog behavior made the fault all mine. Ugh, I could still taste that gasoline every time I thought about it or smelled the stuff. Turning and handing Sherry her drink I said, "Okay now tell me. What did mom say?"

"There is a big fat letter on dad's desk. Mom said you should wait until dad gets home and wait until after supper before y'all read it."

I shot out of my chair and down the hall to the office, which was the front spare bedroom. There on the desk was a thick letter with grandpa's handwriting on the envelope. He had addressed it to Vinson and Buddy Draper. I had never received a letter, other than birthday cards with my name on them. I picked it up, actually trembling with the desire to rip it open immediately. Just holding and turning it in my hand made me feel like I would burst with excitement. Finally, I carefully placed it back on the desk as if it were made of fragile glass.

This being Friday, I was sure we would eat supper out somewhere or dad would cook some hamburgers on his grill in the back yard. After the fire had burned down Sherry and I liked to bury a couple of foil-wrapped potatoes in the coals for a bedtime snack. Normally I loved those cookouts, but tonight I wanted nothing more than the meal to be over so I could hear what grandpa had written.

With nothing else to do and the temperature hovering around twenty degrees outside, Sherry and I went out into the backyard to slide on our 2" by 4" piece of lumber. Mom had invented the fun by pouring a bucket of water on the board and propping it up on our back porch. When it was cold enough, the water would freeze instantly and we had our slide. We had a *real* slide on our swing set, but this one was more fun. After about an hour of play it got too cold and we had to go in. I took a last look at the sky and wished for snow. Every time we got enough snow I would fill my mom's turkey baking pan and she would make us snow cream. I could almost taste it. Now that would be something to look forward to.

Later the hours dragged by and it felt like my family was deliberately drawing out the evening to make me wait. Dad did not get home until after 6:00 o'clock and then Debra was crying with her ears hurting. I felt bad for her but everything was taking too long. By the time we got to the Tasty Freeze, one of my dad's accounting clients, it was already dark. Dad liked to order all the hamburgers the same and I was always opening the backseat car door, which turned on the overhead light, much to everyone's annoyance, as I raked off the onions. Dad talked about his day and wanted to know all about our school day. All I wanted was to get home to that letter. I also wanted to complain to mom about Sherry's teasing me earlier, but I figured they would think it was funny. At the thought I glared at Sherry in the backseat knowing she could not see me, which only added to the fun.

When we finally got back to the house I planned on turning another one of Sherry's and my games against her. We would slide our feet across the carpet then shock each other. You could see the spark jump from our fingers as the other person was shocked when the electricity moved from one of us to the victim. However, when you did not know it was coming, it seemed to hurt more. I waited for her to come out of her room and pounced, touching her on the arm. The crackle of the electricity could be heard clearly in the room. She jumped and let out a high screeching sound that was satisfying to my ears, and then the chase was on. The race around the house ended when my mom's frustrated yell came from the bathroom where she was bathing Debra. *"Knock it off!"*

Still catching my breath, I went into dad's office as he was shuffling papers. "Dad when can we read the letter?"

"After your mom gets Debra out of the tub you can get into the bath. We can read it after that." Dad added, "Patients is one thing you should add to your list to work on improving. All good things are worth the wait son."

I had heard that saying many times, but I knew patients, like math were never going to be big in my life. "Dad tomorrow is Saturday. I'm not going anywhere that I have to be clean for. Can't my bath wait until tomorrow night? I'll just get dirty hiking with Randy again anyway. We are heading to the creek in the morning. I'll be filthy when I get home."

"Quit making excuses. There'll be plenty of time to read the letter before your bedtime. I've got a short pile of work to do first anyway."

An hour later I went back into Dad's office and saw him with the letter open before him. I said in panic, "Dad you were supposed to wait for me!"

"Don't worry son. I was just reading about my Ma's garden. She is planning on planting in the spring. She put a short note inside the letter. You know you're mother and her are always passing information back and forth about their gardens and what herbs or crops will do best this year or next."

Relieved I sat down on one of Dad's polished cherry oak wood office chairs. The only light on in the room was Dad's small desk lamp. I sat in semi-darkness by the door. As fidgety as I normally was, I was ready for an hour of sitting in the hard chair until I heard grandpa's latest story. Then if there was time I would read about the battle in our encyclopedias. "How many pages did he write dad?"

Dad shuffled through the sheets and said, "In fact there are several pages son. Your grandpa must have spent hours on this. You must pull a lot of weight with your grandpa because he doesn't write too many letters these days." He began to arrange the pages, smoothed the edges, and began reading in his clear baritone voice. Even though I was watching dad and hearing his voice, it was as if I could hear grandpa's gruffer tone saying the words too, as if they were both reading together. Slowly, the office disappeared and I began to see through grandpa's eyes as he must have all those years ago.

# CHAPTER 21

## *Making Friends in Columbus*

Over the next few weeks I had time to get to know some of the residence of Columbus. Over the course of my military career I had made it a point to get to know the local residents. Now here at the camp we would often have interested and seemingly proud residents of Columbus come out and watch us drill. We had daily training, spending many hours practicing our marksmanship with the Springfield rifles and, to my great disappointment, the French-made Benet-Mercie machine gun. It was well known among the troops that the gun jammed often. I could not understand the Army's use of the inferior automatic when the Browning we had trained on was available. Once again with the responsibilities of a sergeant, I was responsible for supervision and training men. It unnerved me that these men would be counting on the accuracy and dependability of a foreign made gun of poor quality.

Another fight that Alex, Sean and I fought and lost was the chaining and locking up of the men's firearms when they were not on guard duty. The thought was unthinkably absurd to me. As a sergeant I was allowed to keep my 1911 Colt 45 sidearm, but had to turn in my 03 Springfield. The weapons were chained and locked in the armory. Whatever the motivation behind the standing order issued by Colonel Slocum, it was beyond my understanding. If I had not been allowed to keep my 45, I would certainly have bought or traded for one in town. Alex, Sean and I knew the importance of having weapons close to hand.

I spent many of my off duty days walking around the dusty streets of East Boundary, Broadway, Taft and Boulevard Street. The street names amused me since they seemed a bit high-browed and might have been more appropriate for a town larger than three hundred souls. I liked visiting the various shops and sometimes Alex joined me when we could both manage to be off at the same time. The people were friendly and thankful to have the soldiers around for protection. They were happy to watch their little village growing and prospering with the revenue of money spent in town by soldiers.

If there was any darkness to the town, it would be the rumors of some residents supplying guns to the Mexicans who crossed the river to purchase supplies. I had heard the Mexicans paid in gold or cash. No gold was mined nearby. As far as I knew only silver had been mined in the hills across the border. It made a man wonder where a dirt poor peasant-farmer would get gold or cash money.

Most of the whispered accusations centered around the Ravel Brothers Mercantile, located on Boulevard Street. The brothers encouraged Mexican trade, selling everything from cooking utensils, boots, overalls, and various other bolt goods. It was also said they would cheat their *own* mother if a nickel of profit was in it. In fact their younger brother Arthur Ravel had been sent by their mother to learn a trade. However, the older brothers worked the boy without pity for long hours in the store. The townsfolk worried the brothers could be inviting a raid if cash ran low across the border. It was believed obvious prosperity of the business could be traced to selling large quantities of firearms and ammunition to Villa's men. If such claims could be proven it would go hard on the brothers. Also if the Ravel brothers cheated a man such as Villa, their error in judgment could doom the town as well.

I bought various and sundry items from the only grocery store run by James T. Dean, his wife Eleanor, and their son, Edwin who ran errands for his parents. I got to know the town druggist who owed Miller's Drug Store. Charles C. Miller, when not filling prescriptions for townsfolk or soldiers, was usually sitting on his store porch witling tiny figures for the children who played in the streets. The man was a bachelor who lived at the Hoover Hotel, an adobe structure. The other hotel, the Commercial was built of wood. I did not plan on staying in either hotel, but I had an eye out for cover if an attack came. I figured the adobe building would be the place to hole up if under attack.

Two times while I was in town I went to see silent movies at the theater on Taft Street. The first time I saw Roscoe Arbuckle, better known as *Fatty*, in his movie, *Fatty and Mabel's Simple Life.* The second time I saw, Charlie Chaplin's, *The Tramp.* This was a new experience for me and helped me relax and pass the long days. The theatre was cool and dark inside. The piano player was not very good, but made up for it by hammering out lively tunes while playing the background music for the stories.

On my last visit to town I went by the Telephone Office and met a sweet lady named Grace E. Parks. She was the wife of the Columbus Courier editor and the only telephone operator. Mrs. Parks was kind enough to place a call home for me. My pa had recently had a phone installed with the idea of better serving his church community. If ma's letters were any indication, he was getting plenty of use out of the contraption preaching at weddings and funerals. It was the first time I had used a phone and did not know what to expect. After several short rings, indicating they were on a party line, I heard my ma's voice, kind of far off like she was down a well. "Hello, this is Reverend Draper's residence."

"Ma, it's me, Oscar."

"My word son you sound like you're in China instead of New Mexico. Are you alright?"

"Yes ma I'm okay. I just wanted to check on you and Pa. I got your letters last week. They were mailed to Fort Wilson and the Army forwarded them on to me here at Camp Furlong."

"Oh good, I was fretting about that since I did not have your new address."

"Well they arrived. It's best you don't write me for awhile because we may be on the march soon."

"Mercy, where is the Army sending you now?"

"We don't know ma. Wherever Villa is spotted we'll probably pack up and go after him." With more confidence than I actually felt I said, "Don't you worry ma there are over a hundred soldiers here and we are ready for that old bandit if he shows. I'm going to have to get off soon. I just wanted you and pa to know I'm fine. The Army even gave me back my stripes."

"That's good to hear son. You keep your eyes open and don't turn your back to the border. I'll tell your pa you're fine." She hesitated long enough that I thought the connection had been lost. "Oscar, you know your pa is hard on you but he loves you just the same. Oh, and thanks for the money. It was not necessary, but appreciated none the less. Say a prayer Oscar, goodbye."

After I hung up I could not help the lonely feeling that washed over me. The melancholy mood lasted the rest of the day. Thinking about pa I hoped he had forgiven me for most of the hard days I had put him and ma through. If God was behind this second chance I was being given, I sure figured to give it everything I had this time around. I still blushed red out of shame at the memory of my court marshal and dishonorable discharge from the Army. Also now that I was sober uncomfortable memories came back from the days following my discharge. I had known many men who had blackouts after drinking, but I never believed it would happen to me. Now some of those blackout periods were creeping back and refusing to stay gone.

As it happened I was in town on March 8, 1916 when the noon train whistled into the yellow painted wood train station from El Paso. I watched as the train hissed off excess steam, huffing like a giant dragon in the sun. The white steam clouded around the station like a snowstorm. In a sleepy little village like Columbus a train arriving was a big deal, attended by most available townsfolk if they were not tied down somewhere.

I saw that the crowd was unusually large today and I suspected it was due to the nervous nature of the citizens, hungry for news of Villa and the Mexican Revolution. Sure enough the grocer's son Edwin was running fast down Taft Street toward the train. The boy was handed down a large bundle of newspapers. In moments the crowd had gathered in front of Dean's grocery store to look over the latest news from El Paso. The assembled readers began talking in excited and frightened tones.

As I approached the group, I sensed trouble and my mouth went suddenly dry. Les Middleton who owned a meat market up the street, bloody apron still on said accusingly, "Sergeant it says here that the 13th Cavalry expects Villa to attack Palomas, Mexico. He was observed camped fifteen miles west of Palomas Monday and Tuesday. It reports he has three to four hundred well-mounted men with him. Your Colonel Slocum has assured us for months we were safe, but Palomas is just 20 miles from here."

Irritated at the man's tone, I abruptly took the newspaper he was holding out of his hand and quickly read the bold print headlines. *VILLA EXPECTED TO ATTACK PALOMAS!* Not wasting any time I motioned to a young private who was lounging on the steps of the store with a mongrel of a dog curled up at his feet. "Take this to Colonel Slocum immediately. Tell him it just came in on the train from El Paso." Without a reply the young soldier was running with the newspaper tucked under his arm. The black and white spotted mutt was close at his heels. Turning back to face Middleton and the townspeople I said, "I don't know anything about this but I'm sure the colonel will have something to say about it." I saw Mayor Hoover fast walking toward me. I knew someone must have alerted him to the news.

Greeting me by name, which surprised me that he would remember from the night of the lightning storm, he said, "I'll walk a quick pace with you Sergeant Draper." A moment later I discovered he did indeed set a fast pace for a man of his girth. I was a brisk walker myself, but had to step it up to match the man's gait. As we made our way to the colonel's office he said in a panting voice between steps, "I'm-glad-to-see-you're-wearing-another-stripe-son. You-earned-it. Men-know-how-to-take-charge-are-of-true-value."

Not sure how to respond I said, "Thank you mayor." Arriving at Colonel Slocum's office I saw he was already standing outside reading the newspaper and waiting on us. The soldier-runner I had sent was standing nearby. I saluted as soon as I was within ten paces as was Army custom. The colonel returned the salute in a somewhat irritated manner.

He ignored me and directed his words at Mr. Hoover, putting both hands up in a sign of stop. "Now don't start in on me mayor. If I had leaked that to the newspapers in El Paso, you'd see a hundred guns pointing at the border right now. There won't be an attack that close to us. Villa wouldn't dare come within a three mile range of a well-armed American Army outpost. Besides he would not stand a chance against my men and our machine guns. Why we would turn that old bastard and his bandits into dog meat."

The mayor seemed unconvinced and answered in a somewhat shaky voice. I noticed his manner was agitated and he used his hands expressively as he spoke. "I consider you a friend Colonel Slocum, but don't try to sell a load of manure to a politician. I'm not so sure he won't attack. You've said before you have *no* orders to cross over and pursue him. Now you'd have me go back and tell my citizens that they are *not* in danger? If I back you and we are wrong, I'll expect no less than a tar and feathering. I'll be lucky if I don't get strung up from a tall tree. There is a whole passel of food stock here that Palomas has never seen. I hear that Villa's back is to an adobe wall. He is half *loco* and I believe desperate men will act desperately." As he had been speaking, a large crowd of civilians and soldiers had gathered due to the oratory style of the mayor. Whenever he spoke, his voice carried loud and clear. It was as if he was on a stage addressing hundreds. Now those gathered watched worriedly to see if there would be a clash between the two powers in the area.

While the mayor had been speaking, I was looking over Camp Furlong and wondering which direction a Villa attack might come from. I also noticed no alarm had been sounded in the camp. If it were up to me I would have all the men on their post, armed and ready. Even if the attack did not pan out, it would be good practice for the future. Every Texan remembered the Alamo and we would be outmanned if not outgunned. I turned my attention back to the two men waiting for an opportunity to speak up.

I cleared my throat, knowing I was not in a position to be suggesting anything to my commanding officer. "Sir, it would not hurt to arm the troops. I advise having the men take up defensive positions around the camp and within the town. We could post a dozen men inside the village in strategic positions. I think we could even put a few men on rooftops until we're sure Villa is not in the area."

I think he actually considered it for a quick moment. "No need for that sergeant. It would just panic the residents of Columbus. You can see to it that the night guards are briefed and given extra ammo."

"Sir couldn't we at least pass out the Springfield rifles to the men? It will favor our boys considerably if Villa rides in here." Now I could tell by the colonel's posture that I had stepped over his imaginary boundary line. He straightened up and puffed out his chest.

"That will be *all* sergeant."

When I saluted this time he just waved me away dismissively. Confused and angry at my helpless state, I walked slowly back to camp with the private following me a couple of steps behind and his dog trotting along beside him. When I looked over my shoulder, I saw the colonel take the mayor aside to talk in private. I addressed the private. "What's your name and where are you from private?"

He caught up to me and said, "Jessie P. Taylor from Deming, New Mexico. My dog here is just named Spot. He isn't really mine, regulations and all, but he seems to have adopted me. Is there anything else I could do for you right now sergeant?"

"Just sleep with one eye open." Thinking about my barefooted run up the hill with Villa's men firing at me I added, "One more thing private, it would be a good idea to keep your boots on too. If a few of us are ready, it might make a difference." Private Taylor and Spot headed off toward a group of tents where I assumed his bunk was. He looked to be only around seventeen, but strong and capable enough, although he could be years older. The new recruits seemed too young. They all looked with excited and eager eyes to the experienced soldiers to keep them alive. It was a responsibility I took most seriously. I remembered when I was that young and already a soldier too. Now at twenty-two years old I felt like an old man in the company of children-soldiers.

The only thing I could think to do was find Alex and Sean and tell them what I knew.

It took me sometime to round up Alex and Sean. Sean had been inspecting the lookout post where the men and I had suffered through the lightening storm. Alex had been playing poker in one of the larger tents with a group of five other men I did not know. He was some irritated at me when I pulled him out of the game. When we were alone and walking toward the wall to meet Sean he said, "I was winning Oscar! What is so important it has to cost me money? If you'd relax every now and then you could play with us. You are far too serious now and not as much fun anymore amigo."

I just kept walking and did not answer. He fell into step in a noticeably silent huff. I was going over possibilities in my mind as to what we could do, if anything. When we were closer to the lookout I shouted and waved at Sean. He immediately began walking down the steps I had overseen the men building in the last few weeks. "These steps are a great improvement Oscar, or ah Jim. Good thinking on your part there."

I gestured for Alex and Sean to follow me and we walked along the Rio Grande away from the camp. As we walked I filled them both in on everything I knew and what the colonel's reaction had been. I told them about the nervous mood in Columbus and how the mayor had openly challenged the colonel. When I finished the two men were silent as they considered the possibility of an attack. As one we began looking at the camp as only a trained soldier could. If Villa did attack, which direction would he use? How could a few night sentries defend an entire unarmed camp and the town as well?

Finally Alex broke the silence. "If I was not honor bound I'd saddle a horse and ride on out of here. We may have more than a hundred men this time but only a dozen or so on guard duty will be armed. I don't care much for those odds. If we did know hot and heavy he will ride in it would not be so bad. The people in town will be helpless and most of the men will suffer no less due to the colonel's stubbornness in locking up the guns."

Looking at their concerned faces I said, "Even if Alex and I told Slocum who we are and what we've seen it probably would only get us thrown in the stockade."

Sean's eyes brightened as he came upon an idea. "Well he won't throw me in the brig. Unlike you fellows, I did not chase after the bandits into Mexico. If I could get through to him how bad it was in Glenn Springs, maybe he would listen."

"I'm afraid he would just take away one of those strips for arguing against his opinion. I already stepped on his toes and he was plumb full of acid toward me when he abruptly dismissed me. No, you can try if you're of a mind to, but the best I see is we give extra ammo to the guards and stay awake and alert ourselves. Three armed and vengeful sergeants ought to make a small difference if Villa comes here. I just wish I had my rifle too."

Alex, Sean and I started walking back toward the camp before Alex said, "I am in the same tent as Oscar. I'll stay with one of my poker buddies tonight so we can spread out around the camp. If shooting starts I say we meet at the guard house armory and blow that lock off."

We agreed the idea was strong. Once the men were armed we could organize and deal a crippling blow to Villa's forces. I hoped that this time Villa and his men would pay a high price for attacking Americans. If we were wrong and bandits only raided Palomas on the Mexican side, I was sure we would still hear gunfire reports through the quiet desert air. The distance was only three miles. If that happened, we could arm ourselves and surround the town to provide protection.

# CHAPTER 22

## *Villa Raids Columbus*

At this point dad took his glasses off and rubbed his eyes. I had moved to the floor and had been listening intently. I was afraid he was tired, not wanting to continue, before he said, "Your grandpa put in a short side note here to say he could not personally vouch for everything from here on out. He said he put the story together by talking to his fellow soldiers, reports from witnesses, bandit captives, newspapers, and of course from his own vantage point."

"That's okay. Grandpa was there and he'd know more about it than anyone else who only wrote about it afterwards." Dad excused himself and went to say goodnight to Sherry and Deb. I ran down the hall to the bathroom then bolted back to dad's office. I did not want to give him a chance to change his mind about finishing the letter tonight. In less than five minutes he was back at his desk and reading silently until he found his place...

On March 9, 1916, a few minutes before 4:00 A.M., Pancho Villa slowed his horse to a walk on a dark moonless night. He held up a hand for his 600 men to come to a halt. The bandits had skirted Palomas and were now one mile west of the border town. The men were armed with all the weapons they could carry and enough bandoleers of ammo to fight an extended battle. Four men had cans of kerosene tied to their saddles with leather thongs. With a simple slashing gesture by Pancho, two men dismounted and began cutting away a large section of the wire fence that separated the United States from Mexico.

After all the men were through the opening, the bandits traveled at a turtle's pace along an eastern path. At a signal from Villa, the men stopped again. Without a sound shadows moved and three men appeared from the darkness like ghost. Villa had personally handpicked the men for their ability to move quietly and for their skill with a knife. These three bandits had already taken the first lives of the morning by crawling up behind two sentries and killing them. After a few whispered words with their leader, the band of men moved on.

The immediate destination was a six foot deep drainage waterway which ran for more than a hundred feet between the train station and the Customs House. The culvert channeled flashflood waters away from Columbus. Some of the men crawled along no more than two abreast and scattered back along the entire length of the natural runoff trough. Others walked beside their mounts to lessen the chance for noise. In this manner the progress was slow and the minutes turned slowly until the time was near to 4:30 A.M.

The bandits stopped short on the edge of the village and looked cautiously over the edge of the gully and watched a sentry to the west and at least a hundred yards away walking his patrol. As the men watched, the sentry who was guarding the entrance to Camp Furlong came to a stop, slightly cocking his head to listen. The night was too dark to see but the bandits as one, held their breath, worried he might have heard creaking leather or a horse's hoof on stone. After a few moments the man walked on, apparently satisfied that his mind was playing tricks on him.

Now the Villistas bunched closest to the front turned their attention to the village. Columbus was quiet. The two story train station which towered over their heads had a kerosene lamp glowing inside for the station master. The men observed two more lights burning dimly in widows of the Commercial Hotel. In the camp a vast ocean of Army tents seemed to stretch endlessly under the dark shy. A few of the bandits crossed themselves and would have run except for the sure knowledge that Villa himself or his trusted lieutenants would have cut them down without mercy. All was ready and the eyes of every man close enough to see peered through the darkness for Villa's order that would send them to glory and fame or to hell.

Villa was near the front and recognizable by his distinctive off-white sombrero. His eyes could not be seen but with the raising of his arm, the signal, the sentry was killed by a volley of crashing rifles. The night exploded with the wild cries of, "Viva Mexico" and Viva Villa." Pancho Villa and his men struggled up out of the gully in a snaking wave of death and destruction, which enveloped the sleeping village. A killing lust shone in the eyes of the raiders as they fired through windows, crashed through doors and began looting whatever they could carry. The bandits shot down anyone in their path without hesitation. The echo of gunfire alerted the camp and soldiers began running from their tents in various stages of dress and few with any armament.

In the beginning, with the bandit's complete surprise of Columbus and Camp Furlong, the village lay helpless before the raging tide of raiders. Some of the bandits attacked on foot, while others rode their horses in the style of the bygone battles of the Crusades, or the more recent Apaches and Comanche wars. The citizens of Columbus, like their pioneer ancestors from whom they had descended fought bravely, barricading their doors and shooting until their rifles were empty. The scream of women and children could be heard above the roaring din of flame and gunfire.

Dean's grocery store was the first shop destroyed in an inferno of yellow and orange flames. Mr. Dean was seen running madly toward his store in a hopeless attempt to save his livelihood from ruin. He never made it and was cruelly riddled with rifle fire through his body. He stumbled forward two more steps, already dead and sprawled into the dust in front of his store. His final gesture was to stretch out his hands as if reaching for his store. Within minutes, Miller, the druggist was also dead after his own attempt to save his property. His glassy, unseeing eyes were open and reflected the hot blaze consuming what had been his drugstore.

Whether residents were panicking and running into the streets seeking safety, or were coming to the aid of those injured, the outcome remained the same as they were slaughtered in a barrage of bullets. The bandits, still in control of Columbus, swept through the village killing and looting unchallenged. Dr. Henry Hart, William Davidson, and Nate Walker were the next to die, joining the two dead men in the street.

Archibald Frost and his family were startled awake by gunfire coming from the street in front of their furniture store. Their home was attached to the rear of their store and Archibald left his wife, Mary Alice to stay with their baby son Douglas. With a sense of dread he ventured out on his store porch to determine where the firing was coming from. Only a moment passed before he was shot in the right shoulder. Ducking to the floor for cover, he began making his way on hands and knees back into the store. He decided the only hope for him and his family was to attempt an escape in his Dodge truck.

With his wife's help Archibald gathered his son in his arms and the frightened family made it to the car. Bandits were in the street but seemed to ignore the family until it was clear they were trying to escape. With his headlights off to make it harder for a clear shot, he floored the car. Bullets began peppering the car and Archibald said a quick prayer of thanks that the Dodge brothers had made the sturdy light truck with an all steel body. However, seconds later he realized he had been shot again, this time in the left arm. Eventually, risking more gunfire, he was forced to turn on the lights to navigate the curving, potholed road. Finally escaping Columbus but too weak from loss of blood, he asked Mary Alice to drive the rest of the way into Deming, New Mexico.

Over in the Exchange Office near the Hoover House, Grace Parks was showing her true mettle with a determination of mind and spirit as she worked her phones. Like the radio operator on the Titanic four years before, she was at her operator station ignoring her own peril and calmly making calls to Fort Bliss in El Paso, Texas, alerting authorities in Deming, New Mexico, and any other number she could think of to summon assistance for Columbus. Outside bandits were shooting up the street. Grace connected the lines while clutching her baby daughter, who was innocently breast feeding. Mrs. Parks was bleeding from several cuts from flying glass as rifle fire had penetrated the windows and weatherboarding of the office. She never lost her unconquerable resolve even while blood seeping into her eyes made it hard for her to see. Ignoring the fact that her fate might be to die at the hands of lawless men at any moment she stayed at her task throughout the raid until the danger had passed.

Further down the street fire was devouring the wooden structure that had been the Commercial Hotel like a hungry medieval beast. Minutes earlier bandits had burst through the doors of the hotel and shot five guests before fleeing with everything of value that could be carried. Only a few of those present had escaped unharmed. Hotel customers not shot outright were trapped, with the horrible choice of dying in the flames or death in the streets, cut down by raiders intent to kill any man, woman or child that dared show themselves.

At the Ravel Mercantile, the Villistas seemed to intensify their fury. All the windows were shattered and the doors were torn down. Even above the mayhem shouts were heard. "Where is Sam Ravel?" Villa's men began searching every corner of the store. In the back of the Mercantile, Louis Ravel was hiding under a stack of cowhides. He was lying as flat as possible under the last hide. Louis was terrified as he heard the crashing of glass. Then the sounds grew closer as some of the bandits began ripping the cowhides to pieces suspecting one or more of the brothers must be near.

Out near the edge of Camp Furlong in an adobe shack was John Lucas, a young cavalry officer who commanded the Machine Gun Troop. He had been sleeping off a hangover when he was startled awake by the sound of a horse and rider passing by his open window. As luck, good or bad would have it, he had returned on the *drunkard's special* train on March 8th around midnight from his leave in El Paso. When he had returned to his home, he had taken the time to load his 45 caliber revolver before passing out. Now he peered out the window and saw bandits on horseback and on foot creeping by, recognized by their oversized sombreros.

Lucas realized the men must be bandits and he quickly took up a position in the middle of the room where he could cover all three entrances. His intention was to take at least a few with him before he was killed. Trying to think through his throbbing headache, he decided the only way to warn the camp was to start the fight on his own. Before he could put his plan into action, a sentry was killed and the rising shouts of the raiders could be heard through the clear morning air. He used the confusion to slip out the side door and make his was over to the guardhouse to arm himself with more than a revolver. He was unwavering in his determination to join his fellow troopers in an organize offensive against the bandit attack.

At the Camp Furlong cook shack a half dozen men had begun making preparations for an early meal for the sentries when three bandits burst into the shack. Without hesitation the cooks fought back hard with surprising success with what was at hand. To their credit they were credited with dispatching the first bandits of the morning with boiling water, pots and pans, and finally a shotgun which was used to hunt additional meat for meals. On the other side of the camp stable hands were fighting with equal desperation and bravery. The hands had grabbed pitchforks and a supply of baseball bats used for recreation. The makeshift weapons had been stored in a corner of the stable and were put to deadly use.

Before the echoes had faded from the first rifle volley, I was on my feet and running toward the guard house. I admit I had fallen asleep in a chair by the tent entrance. I had been seduced into sleep by the warming glow of the camp stove. Before I had taken up my position I had made a wasted attempt at convincing some of the soldiers in my tent of the danger, but eventually had given up in angry frustration. The men had looked at me with barely concealed skepticism. Soldiers who had not experienced a Villa attack could not believe bandits would dare attack a town guarded by over a hundred troopers.

Now as I ran through the camp I passed new recruits who were initially helpless without leadership. All were unarmed and caught in a shooting gallery that was their tents. Soldiers ran outside in panic while bullets shredded the canvas of their tents from unseen marksman. It was like trying to take cover behind a gust of wind. Not slowing in my head long dash, I shouted orders to troopers I passed to follow me to the Guard House. Some took up the challenge while others remained lost and confused.

When I arrived at the armory, followed by a dozen men, Sean and Alex were already there along with Lieutenant Castleman and a few others who were trying to break down the thick wooden door or defeat the heavy hinges that secured it. The wasted moments were desperate with shouts and screams coming from the town and in the camp around us. We were frantic knowing men were dying with every tick of the clock. Finally the hinges began to weaken and were breached with a screech that put my teeth on edge. The door was literally torn off two of the three hinges then knocked inward. Like a swarming hive of bees we poured into the dark room and began a frenzied search. After someone struck a match, a Benet-Mercier machine gun, rifles and a large cache of ammo were located. We hurriedly gathered up what we could carry and began to run toward the sound of gunfire.

On a fast pace we covered the hundred yard distance toward Columbus and joined forces with Major Tompkins and six others. We needed no further urging, but the cries of anguish, shouts of men and explosions of gunfire drew us faster to the town. One of the troopers I recognized as the private I had sent running to warn Colonel Slocum the previous afternoon. Jessie Taylor was smiling at me. I observed he was in his full uniform. He gestured to his Army issue attire and leaned in toward me to holler in my ear. "I slept with more than my boots on sergeant."

I did not know most of these officers or soldiers, but knew their type and within minutes I respected their nerve in the face of our obviously outnumbered position. With set jaws and like-minded purpose, we marched into the fray firing as we advanced. I threw myself prone and prepared to fire the Benet-Mercier, targeting a group of bandits running toward us. The cursed French made bi-pod machine gun jammed after only one burst of fire. Disgusted, I tossed the useless thing aside. However minutes later Lieutenant John Lucas and his troopers brought forward other Benet-Merciers which performed perfectly, laying down a deadly and accurate rate of fire. Looking down I noticed the lieutenant was barefoot. I could relate completely, remembering my own mad dash with burned and bare feet up the side of the hill in Glen Springs. The memory steeled my resolve to fight on no matter the risk. Citizens were dying and it was our responsibility to stop the bandits no matter the cost.

Beginning with the first of our volleys we began to cut down bandits wherever we located them. The raiders scattered before the relentless onslaught of the machine guns but were riddled by the screaming rounds. With each step we took, more of Villa's men were killed. Approaching from an alley, I recognized Arthur, the youngest of the Ravel brothers by the light reflected off of burning buildings. No more than fifty paces away from our position, the pitiful boy was only wearing his underwear and had a bandit latched on to either side practically dragging him toward his brother's store.

Knowing it was not the time for caution I instantly opened fire along with Alex and Lieutenant Castleman. The two raiders were slammed by the heavy Springfield slugs, tumbling backwards into the dust. Arthur was apparently uninjured but began screaming hysterically and scurried around like a mouse chased by a falcon. The boy was running wildly in the general direction of the darkness on the edge of town. He kept circling, changing his direction every few seconds until he was finally swallowed by the night. The boys screaming was still heard as we advance to the next street and continued to purge the town of the horde of Villa men.

# CHAPTER 23

## *The Villista's Retreat*

The frantic battle had raged on for more than two hours from street to street until just before dawn. I had lost all track of time and was only able to estimate due to the light beginning to filter over the horizon from the east. Then, clearly heard was the distinct sound of a bugler signaling a retreat. The bugler had to be Mexican. We knew there would be no retreat from the soldiers fighting to save the town. Almost immediately the surviving Villa men began a withdrawal back toward the west and the supposed safety of Mexico. Some of the survivors later said Villa himself was seen astride his horse slashing with his saber at his own men attempting to turn the tide of the retreat, before realizing the effort was useless and joining his men as they rode out of the village.

We began a circle of the town to be sure the raiders had actually left. I wanted to do a house by house search to look for wounded and hidden raiders, but runners from the camp summoned us back. Word was sent to mount up for a chase of the retreating bandits that would be led by Major Frank Tompkins. Apparently Colonel Slocum had authorized the pursuit. It angered me to think about how the pompous colonel had not armed his men earlier. If troopers had been posted on roofs or hidden throughout the town the raid might have been short lived. It occurred to me that it would almost be worth another court marshal to knock the smug colonel on his back side.

In less than twenty minutes, I was riding alongside Alex, Sean and twenty others to meet Major Tomkins who had another thirty men riding with him. As we rode out of the camp, I saw Colonel Slocum and Mayor Hoover standing on top of Cootes Hill watching Villa's retreat and our advance. We rode hard to close the gap from Villa's head start. Every cavalry man there drew strength from the powerful mount beneath him. The pounding of the hoofs and the chase were all that mattered. Each man rode with his own thoughts, knowing potential death was ahead. The horses, sensing the urgency charged on without the smallest need to push them.

Within minutes we were taking fire from what was supposed to be a rear guard that Villa had thrown up. While Villa fled toward Palomas the bandits put up a wall of bullets which were zinging over our heads. We were off our horses and with the four machine guns from earlier and every man heavily armed, we laid down a blistering fire that decimated the rear guard. During the battle Major Tomkins had sent a fast rider back to Colonel Slocum to request permission to pursue into Mexico.

After the initial wave of the attack ebbed, the command came down the line to charge. The major certainly had daring and the audacity to lead his men. He was out front on foot charging the bandits firing his semi-automatic Colt 45 as he ran. Soldiers, some mounted, while others ran on foot broke though the bandit lines and literally rode over the rear guard. I was still mounted and began to see dark shapes crumpled in the sand indicating a seemingly uncountable number of bodies seen for the first time in the rising sun. With not a man wounded among us, the major pushed on. About thirty captives were rounded up and six men were assigned to escort them back to the camp. Before I knew it Palomas was behind us and I was once again chasing Villa bandits into Mexico. I doubted permission had been given, since I found it hard to believe a rider could have caught up to us.

An estimate was made that we were fifteen miles into Mexico. With no sign of the main body of Villa's bandits and the horses exhausted, we turned back. From the tracks it appeared that Villa's remaining men had split up into many smaller parties. When we rode back into Columbus the sun was up and revealed a sight I would never have believed. The town was a burnt shell of what it had been. Devastation, death and grief gripped the town. Ten residents including an unidentified woman who had been a guest in the hotel were dead. Trusted and respected shopkeepers, including Dean and Miller had been swept away in an insane attack by a madman, bent on power for his own gain.

Columbus surviving residents, at least for now were too stricken by their losses to muster much anger. I imagined what their state of mind would be if it was later proved the Ravel brothers had been one of the triggers that brought the attack to their village. Whether or not the brothers were guilty would be debated at a future time. One thing that was known for certain was many 30-30 caliber Winchesters were dropped by killed bandits, which indicated *some* Americans had been supplying arms to Pancho Villa and his men.

It now appeared rumors of possible German government involvement in supplying guns to bandits might be true as well. A large quantity of 7mm German Mausers used by bandits had been recovered. The idea was that Germany wanted to keep the American Army and citizens too busy for war in Europe. The German-made Mausers and American-made Winchesters would fuel interesting talk and heated debate around our campfires at the end of each exhausting day ahead.

Details of soldiers were everywhere along with the townsfolk giving aid to the wounded and trying to restore some order to the chaos. I was told by one of my fellow Troop H men that fourteen soldiers had died, including one sergeant, a lieutenant, and a captain. I did not know any of the men in more than a passing way. I was relieved to see Alex and Sean during the day, although there was no time for talk. However it hit me hard when I discovered later that the teenaged Private Taylor had been killed during the fighting in Columbus. I wished I had thought to keep him closer to me. I did not know what I might have done, but I still felt responsible. I remembered his grinning face in the beginning moments of the fight. Playing it over in my mind I could see him nearby firing and reloading among his fellow soldiers. He had stood bravely to his duty as we fought for our lives and the town, then at the end he was gone. I spoke to several men who were close to me during the battle but no man seemed to know when it had happened.

The day ground on endless as I was ordered to pull details of men for the grim task of dragging bodies of the raiders out into the desert a mile east of town for disposal. For the rest of the afternoon we piled the corpses into wagons and carried them into the desert. After an estimated seventy to a hundred bodies were removed from the town and a like amount collected from the battle grounds where Villa's rear guard had made their stand, the bodies were saturated with gasoline and burned. As the fire, smoke, and horrid odor permeated into the air, for me the last thread of hate and a deep lust for revenge ended.

The events which had begun on that night in Glenn Springs that had burned white hot inside me to kill as many bandits as possible went out as suddenly as a snuffed out candle. I would do my duty but I no longer wanted to kill anyone. The sickening stench that lingered on the wind for days would be a reminder of the morning raid.

Near sunset the bodies of the fourteen soldiers that had died defending Columbus and Camp Furlong were buried. Soldiers near exhaustion from the day's activities worked tirelessly to dig deep graves in the hard-packed earth. After the resting places were ready we returned to clean up as best we could. We dressed in our finest uniforms, including high-sided and polished boots. Our dress uniforms included ties, which most tucked into their shirts so the wind would not blow them into our faces.

Without complaint we stood at attention in the heat of the sun each remembering someone he knew and had lost. My memories of soldiers and friends lost went back to the previous year in Glenn Springs. Now I revisited that same helpless feeling. Before I walked away I saw Spot sitting near the grave of his master, his paws resting across the burial mound. I wondered how the dog knew which grave was Private Taylor's. I motioned over a young boy of about ten standing nearby and tossed him a silver dollar to feed Spot and see the dog had water. It was the least I could do for the soldier's sacrifice.

The solemn and respectful military ceremony had been attended by nearly every surviving citizens of the village. Over the next few days the soldiers returned the respect given that day as the dead of the town were laid to rest. Some were buried in family plots by their houses, while others were laid in freshly dug graves in the town cemetery. After the burials several residents of the community packed up what they could carry and walked or drove toward what they believed would be safer towns, farther away from the border. Although the Army was seen as a savior to most in Columbus, we had also been unable to save everyone or the town and faith in our ability to do so had ebbed to the lowest point since I had arrived.

Among the soldiers and townsfolk who remained there was plenty of strong talk and a general desire to hang the bandit captives from the nearest tree. I blamed Colonel Slocum in part for so many deaths in the camp and village. He had many faults as a leader, but he had a well deserved reputation as a no nonsense military man who would never tolerate civil unrest. He was well aware of the burning hate and animosity in the town. Moving to head off any potential clash between citizens of Columbus and the Army, he discussed the situation with Mayor Hoover. Slocum made it clear that fair trails would be held with necessary rapidity, *before* any hangings.

# CHAPTER 24

## *Waiting for Christmas*

Dad finished reading grandpa's letter, took off his glasses and began rubbing his eyes. We just sat together for a few moments in silence. My imagination was reeling while I tried to sort out all the exciting and yet tragic events that my grandpa had been a part of. I had a dozen questions but knew it was getting late and I would have to wait for another time.

Finally Dad said, "I had no idea my *own* pa had been through such a terrible ordeal as that. It explains a lot about the man he is now and why my sisters, brother and I were raised as we were. What that town suffered is almost more that anyone not there at the time could imagine. It just goes to show the fortitude of men and women who could live through a hell on earth like that and manage to go on with their lives. Buddy you had better take some time and read a little of something fun before you go to bed. You're likely to have a nightmare or two after pa's story. I admit I'll probably have a few bad dreams myself. Your mom might skin us both, but me in particular for reading this letter to you." He paused and added a second later, "Get on to bed now, but add your grandpa in your prayers tonight."

To be honest, I did have a couple of nightmares that night. In the first one I was being chased through the streets of Columbus by bandits with red, glowing, murderous eyes. During the second dream I was standing by my grandfather. He was crying as we both watched dirt being thrown onto the coffins of soldiers and townspeople at their burials. I woke up wet with sweat. Remembering the dream I hoped I had not cried out which would have immediately brought Mom or

Dad rushing into my room. Like the night of the scorpion sting, I had yelled plenty. They thought I was having a bad dream until they saw the swelling under my arm. The next night the same creature stung both my parents. Mom always said Dad had slung it on her after he was stung.

Today with the sun rising I lay in bed a little longer to arrange the previous night's letter into my mind. I had never realized how terrible war could be. My only reference had been from television war movies I had watched with Dad. I had thought the excitement and glory of the battle would make all the killing and death somehow okay.

I knew that I would have to wait for Christmas for my next chance at another story. I worried that dad might not allow me to hear anymore stories. I did not want to lie to him, but I also knew he would be watching me for signs I was upset over the contents of grandpa's letter. I spent another few minutes thinking about what my answer would be if dad asked me if I was okay. I decided I would admit to the nightmares, but not to being terrified during my dreams. I felt a new closeness to my dad and grandfather that I had not known before. We now shared this marvelous adventure. I still wanted to follow the exciting story wherever it might lead.

At breakfast dad sat across from me and we ate eagerly. On Saturdays mom usually went all out and made bacon, eggs and pancakes or French toast. I could see in dad's eyes that he had a question for me. When mom stepped out of the room for a few moments he asked, "How did you sleep son?"

"Okay, I did have a nightmare but it was okay." I hurriedly added, "I know what happened was long ago and can't hurt me now."

"Still, I worry that what your grandpa went through is not something a boy should have to think about or could possibly understand at your age."

"I know that. I can always talk to you about anything and ask questions if I don't understand. Before grandpa started telling me stories I never understood how mean some people could be. I also know that there are good people who try to stop bad men. I guess that kind of balances it out in some kind of way."

He looked at me strangely. I did not know if I had said the right thing or not until he finally said, "That's a very good point of view from what you've learned. There are some wars that have to be fought and can't be avoided, but we have to make every effort to avoid fighting if we can. Many mistakes by good and bad men have led us into wars, but there are men who have to be stopped too. Poncho Villa hurt many innocent folks and your grandpa was doing his duty when he helped to stop him." He paused a moment to think, then grinned at me before continuing. "That having been said, I can almost hear your brain wheels churning to get at another story. I'm going to call my brother John Ray today and tell him what we've found out so far about pa's past. I guess I should mail him the letter so he can read it for himself. I'm betting that he will want to be in on the next story at Christmas."

I answered excitedly. "Thanks dad, I would love that. I can't wait to have grandpa tell us what happened after the big battle! I just hope he is not through telling stories yet." As an afterthought I added, "Could you have Uncle John Ray bring the letter at Christmas? I kind of want to save it."

"Sure and I don't think you have to worry about pa not wanting to tell more stories. Once you knock down the door to the barn, all the animals are naturally going to come out."

I did not always understand all of dad's East Texas sayings, but I think his meaning was that there would be more stories coming from grandpa and that was what I most wanted to believe.

Christmas morning finally came and Sherry and I were up at sunrise, unable to sleep anymore. We rushed into the living room to look under our shiny aluminum tree that we had put up for the past few years. My parents always made sure Santa Claus found our house. I was having serious doubts about the big man in the red suit, but mom had said as long as we still believed the extra presents would keep coming. Shining red and new were two new bikes for my older sister and me. The bikes matched and were gifts from Santa. Smaller presents from mom and dad were wrapped and waiting under the tree. With our excited squeals, mom, dad and Debra came into the room rubbing sleep out of their eyes. Dad as usual was filming us with his 8mm camera. We were half blinded by the camera lights as we opened the presents.

It had been raining overnight, but Sherry and I wanted to ride our bikes before we left for Texarkana. With the long ride ahead, we knew we would not get back into town early enough to ride when we got home. It was a four hour trip each way, with lunch and dinner before we could start back. Christmas day was always my favorite day of the year, and my family would gather at grandpa and grandma's house for presents and to eat. Dad filmed our first rides up and down the street in the soft rain. I had strapped on my toy gun, holster and cowboy hat that I had opened moments before. I imagined I was riding a mighty stallion across the dusty desert with grandpa. My cap gun sounded loud in the morning air. Soon I planned on adding playing cards to rub the spokes of my bike like I had seen older boys do. People would hear me come from a block away with the clicking sound it would make. What great adventures I would have on my new bike.

The drive to Texarkana was uneventful and Sherry and I sat in our favorite rear seat that faced backwards in dad's big Buick station wagon. We had car games with us like checkers that had pegs to keep from losing the parts. We also would try to get the eighteen wheelers to honk their air horns by making tugging motions. If the truck driver did honk, it would usually earn us an immediate admonishment from dad. I felt sorry for dad because every time we did one of these day trips to Texarkana he would usually end the day with a headache. He had to drive straight into the eastern rising sun on the way and into the setting western sun on the way home since Interstate 30 ran east and west.

We went to my Aunt Ruth's house first and opened a few presents. I got to spend a little time in my Grandpa Rufus Clark's garden. He gave me a whole dollar when I helped him pull up some peanuts from the sandy soil. Then we headed to Grandpa Oscar's to eat lunch. Grandma meant well, but bought our presents through mail order. They would most often break before we could get them home. My cousins David, Danny and Jon Marc were there. Even though I was the oldest by a couple of years, I looked forward to the one time a year that we could all play together. There would be no train jumping or climbing down into cellars today since we were all in our Sunday best dress clothes. Lunch was delicious and after everyone had eaten their fill, the food was covered with a large table cloth to be reheated later for our supper.

All I could think about during lunch was getting grandpa outside onto the back porch for another story. As much as I was glad to have my dad and uncle now in on the story, it worried me that too many people might make grandpa hesitate to tell about his time in the Army. If grandma, mom or my aunts decided to listen in, I knew grandpa would not tell everything, or might not tell a story at all. Grandma Myrtle would never approve and I was afraid mom might not either. Another hour passed and desserts were finally finished. I caught my dad's eyes across the room. He was looking at me with a small grin. I guess my anxious fidgeting gave me away and he knew what I was thinking. I overheard dad ask his brother John Ray if he wanted to listen in on one of grandpa's stories. I saw him nod his head and now it was up to me to nudge grandpa into a story telling mood.

The weather was cool enough for a jacket but with no wind stirring it was still a pleasant day to sit outdoors on the covered back porch. I went looking for grandpa and found him already outside. I wished I had a more devious mind like some of the older boys in school, but knew I could never trick an adult into anything. He was walking around his back yard and I swallowed hard as I approached him. My throat felt dry and I was again reminded that adults could not be pushed much by children.

"Grandpa, dad and I liked your letter a lot. Dad even wrote Uncle John Ray about the letter. We looked up the battle in Columbus in our encyclopedia and read all about it. I really liked the fact that you were there and knew things that did not make it into the history books. I was hoping to hear what happened after the battle. Dad and John Ray want to hear it too." As usual when I was excited or afraid, I had said everything in a rush without taking a breath. Now I took a deep one and held it until he answered.

He was quiet for awhile as if thinking it over. Then he signed and said, "That was a long time ago Buddy, I don't know why you want to hear about that old stuff anyway. It may seem like a romantic adventure now, but times were harder back then. Folks lived day to day, went hungry and many children died long before they ever reached your age. I think you should be happy to be living in the here and now."

I answered excitedly and hoped I did not sound like I was begging, which I was. "Grandpa I *am* happy to be here now, but *you* were there and saw it with your own eyes. I love reading about history and it is my best subject at school. It's just that a book doesn't make the past come alive the way it does when you tell it. Also dad says they change everything up in a movie to try and make the story better. I like to read stories by Mark Twain and read about the adventures of Jim Bowie and Davy Crocket. Only I'll never meet anyone who knew them."

"Grandpa smiled at me and patted my head, a rare thing for him to do. When he grinned like that it was like looking at my dad, but through older eyes, that seemed a little sad. "So you've got your pa and John Ray interested too. I guess it's only fitting. I don't rightly know why I didn't tell them any of this when they were your age. Likely they weren't as curious as you, or were too busy and tired from chores on the farm and their schooling. I recall life was not easy for those boys and there was little time for listening or telling tales about my past. You know your pa and uncle started working young to help bring in cash money to help out on the farm. I recon I've gone soft in the head in my old age. These stories just seem to have a life of their own like they want to get out." He hesitated and I allowed myself a little hope since he appeared to be considering my request. "Alright, go fetch your pa and uncle. If any of your younger squirming cousins want to listen in I don't mind if it's alright with their folks."

I ran into the house so fast I tripped over the back stoop and crashed to my knees. My right knee stung something awful but I was up and through the screen door in a flash not wanting grandpa to have a chance to change his mind. I found my uncle and dad still talking in the living room. I blurted out excitedly, "Dad, grandpa is going to tell a story on the back porch. I'm going to find Jon Marc, David and Danny and see if they want to listen"

"Okay son, we're right here. We'll be out in a few minutes. Go on and find your cousins." Dad then turned to John Ray and he nodded his approval. Before I ran off dad added in that curious manner that adults do when they talk about you as if you're not in the room. "That boy sure loves to hear his grandpa tell stories. I have to say I wish pa would've told us a few stories when we were boys."

Dad's words, *right here,* meant I was being too loud. I sometimes had to be reminded that my voice got louder and louder when I was excited. In five minutes I had my cousins rounded up and we were assembled on the covered wooded porch. My Uncle Bob, my Aunt Emily's husband came out and sat on the porch with his feet dangling over the edge. Emily was dad's younger sister and the baby of the family. Dad and John Ray were seated in two of the homemade chairs dad had made for his parents. My cousin Danny cleared his throat like he was going to say something and I gave him a sharp look. Jon Mark fidgeted nearby as he usually did. I sat in the partial shade of the porch with my back against a post. Later I lay down on my stomach when I found the post too hard.

Everyone was quiet and I looked at grandpa who was sitting in the porch swing. He was slowly rocking back and forth. I wondered what he was thinking and thought I saw the beginnings of his far off look I had seen before. I wondered if it was like looking through a telescope at the past. At my age I could only remember back a few years. Even those memories seemed only partially formed like I was peering at the sun through rain heavy clouds. Would I ever have memories that anyone would want to hear about? How would I see those memories? Would they be clear like grandpas or vague and fuzzy like our television when the antenna was removed? Before he began I had a twinge of guilt and hoped the stories grandpa told did not hurt him as dad had suggested it might.

Looking at dad and Uncle John Ray, I saw they were both sitting seemingly relaxed in two of the homemade chairs on the porch. Dad had tipped back his chair and was witling on a piece of wood as he liked to do when he was relaxing outside. The grownups were waiting patiently for grandpa to begin his story. John Ray, dad's younger brother was sitting in one of the homemade chairs with it turned backwards. He was leaning on the high back side of the chair. I admired and envied dad and my uncles. Would I ever have their patience or the stories of these men? When John Ray or Bob came to visit they would swap endless tales around the kitchen table late into the night. They never seemed to run out of experiences. I would stay and hang on every word, imagining the places they had seen and things they had seen. Sometimes dad would talk about being in the Army and stationed in Berlin, Germany. He had traveled to England, Paris and some other countries I had never heard of. I listened until my eyes grew heavy and dad would send me off to bed.

Grandpa settled in on the porch swing and sipped a glass of tea grandma brought to him. Grandma had appeared suddenly and I only noticed her when the backdoor screen slammed. She seemed anxious but not mad as she wiped her hands on her apron. She stood looking at the gathering of family waiting to hear the story. Her eyes were bright and touching each person like she was checking a list. I thought she looked pretty with a slight flush to her cheeks from working in the hot house. I watched as she absently tucked a strand of gray hair that had slipped out of place. I worried what she was thinking before her eyes fixed on mine. Now I felt my own face flush with fear that she might halt the story with a cross word to grandpa. Instead there was amusement in her eyes. She then smiled at me and I felt at that moment a silent message had been passed between us that what brings family together cannot be all bad.

# CHAPTER 25

## *Preparing to Invade*

So familiar to me now, grandpa started off slow like he was unsure of what point to continue, or the memories were hard to get at. I pictured a coal miner chipping away with his pick, one layer at a time. Eventually he picked up speed and excitement in his voice. As before I imagined I could see what he did and hung on every word...

In the days and weeks following the Columbus raid we buried the dead with formal ceremony, but life would be a long time in returning to normal in the little village or in Camp Furlong. First off, the town was famous since the battle was written about as far away as New York City. Estimates of the Villa raiders ranged from five hundred to as many as seven hundred bandits. I figured nobody would ever know for certain. Even the soldiers and citizens that were there could not agree about how many raiders had attacked. Since nobody had yet to interview Pancho Villa or any of his men, the mystery might never be solved.

It could not be confirmed that the despicable Pancho Villa was even among the bandits. Although various citizens and soldiers claimed to have seen him fighting a long side his men and I believe he was. The Chief of Police of Columbus did not doubt that Villa had been leading the attack, or was certainly behind it. Not waiting on the Army's response, posters were nailed up around town offering $5,000 for Francisco (Pancho) Villa's arrest. Sean, Alex and I agreed that Pancho would never have trusted such a daring raid to one of his lieutenants.

Newspapers, film and all manner of other journalist-types began to arrive in countless numbers and swarmed over us like locust on a farmer's field. Of course we were forbidden to talk to these men but it never stopped them from trying. Soldiers just naturally left the political arguing to the politicians. Nobody should mistake that we were not paying attention. Troopers followed the newspapers and often had a good laugh at some of the outlandish and fanciful stories they printed.

At least the men now in Camp Furlong were among us and throughout Columbus. Some argued these print and film men would accompany us into Mexico. It was a thorny matter deciding what stories were truth and which ones were boldfaced lies written from the safety of hundreds of miles away, hiding from where the fighting actually happened, or would. We guessed these cowardly journalists had no pang of conscience when selling more papers justified trumping up the truth.

One thing the stories did, good or bad, was to inflame and outrage citizens across the country about the attacks on Columbus and Camp Furlong. Americans had died at the hands of a foreign invader and from the east coast to the west people were united in the demand that President Wilson go after Pancho Villa's head. The message had been received loud and clear in Washington. For now the war in Europe had taken a back seat to the present threat to our own borders. The menace must be stopped whatever the price.

Many were insisting an invasion of Mexico, even if it caused a war was the only solution. President Wilson desperately wanted to avoid fighting a war in Europe and another one so near home on our own continent. Finally buckling under the intense pressure Wilson reluctantly abandoned his longstanding policy of "watchful waiting". He selected General John J. Pershing to lead a force to capture or kill Villa and as many of his bandits as possible. Townsfolk, on the one hand were thankful for the soldier's sacrifices in saving their town, but were now skeptical that we could protect them.

Men in Columbus were seen armed at all times and night guards were posted in case Villa returned. A few of the more frightened townsfolk moved to bigger towns away from the border. I could not blame them and felt like the Army had failed in our mission to protect the town. I was still seething at Colonel Slocum's refusal to arm his men. The added strength of soldiers with rifles at the ready and on their post would have certainly lessoned the deaths of soldiers and civilians alike and given us an instant advantage. When new arrivals came in we began to hear that several towns along the American and Mexican border had followed similar paths with town militias formed and every grown citizen carrying a gun.

It was now said around camp that we would invade Mexico over the protest of Mexican President Carranza with a force that could climb to well over ten thousand soldiers. It filtered down fast that we would be denied any troop movement by Mexico's trains, support from the Carranza government, or the Mexican Army. At this point most of my fellow troopers were just praying we could avoid having to fight against the Mexican Army. Any such action could surely trigger a war with Mexico. Chasing bandits who had been poorly trained and had to depend on raiding towns for supplies was not the same as fighting against a well-equipped army of trained and disciplined soldiers.

In just two days after the battle, camp talk began to ring true when men and supplies began arriving twice a day by train into Columbus. Suddenly Sean, Alex and I were kept busy during most days supervising newly arrived soldiers. We made assignments, issued equipment and arranged tent quarters for the men. When we were not supervising or training the men, we were helping out the quartermasters in inventories of supplies and the mass amount of food and equipment that would follow us by truck. The pack mule was a thing of the past and the mighty cavalry horse would soon fade into the past, no doubt replaced by an armored contraption or other vehicle.

Before long the mass of vehicles took over all open space. I had never seen so many trucks and cars, including Dodge Brothers, Nash and Jeffry four wheel drive automobiles in one place. Some of the cars were armored and made by White Motor Company in Cleveland, Ohio. The armored vehicles weighed over three tons and could reach a speed of almost forty miles an hour with a thirty-seven horsepower engines. The trucks were well ventilated and had three small openings in the front attached to quick closing hinges. Two higher slots were for the driver and passenger, with another lower down, between the wheels. I assumed the lowest firing point would be for a forward-facing, prone gunner.

Most curious of all to arrive by rail were the Jeffery Quad Armored Trucks which had been made in 1915 at the Rock Island Arsenal in Illinois. They weighed six tons with four wheel drive traction and two driver positions. Either the front or rear driver could steer, drive, or stop the forty horsepower engine. I was told the thing could reach a speed of 15 to 20 miles an hour on a paved road, although few roads were paved near or across the border. The Quad looked like a smaller land-based versions of a Civil War ironclad I had seen pictures of. The rolling monsters had twin turrets with firing slots for rifles or pistols, with each turret capable of mounting a machine gun. The five man crew it took to operate the contraption would face the blisteringly hot interior and the desert would make no exception for soldiers. Troopers made wages that the Jeffery's would never see battle and would sink into the sand. I whispered thanks to God right then that I was a cavalryman with a live horse to carry me into the desert.

Camp Furlong exploded in population with more than a thousand tents visible from any location in camp. The parade grounds and all other available space that did not have an Army trucks parked on it were home to uncountable canvas tents. Our parade ground had become the staging area for a seemingly unstoppable invasion of Mexico. There was now no room for doubt that we would be crossing the border. Everyone knew we were only days away, but the date was yet to be confirmed. Only God or President Wilson could stop us now.

Within five days of the attack on Columbus residents saw the arrival by train of eleven pilots and the support of more than eighty enlisted men from the 1st Aero Squadron. I soon met Captain Benjamin Foulois who was in charge of the packing and transporting of the Jenny's by train to Columbus. Their orders had come down on March 11, 1916, just two days after the attack on Columbus. Available planes had been flown to Fort Sam Houston and had their wings removed for transport.

I had now been in the Army for many years and had never seen the government move so swiftly.

Captain Foulois and his Jenny's arrived by train two day later. Alex and I assisted the captain and his crew with work details for the unloading. His men treated each crate of cargo as if it contained explosives and might ignite with the slightest rattle. No sooner were the crates unloaded and the highly trained crew began the tedious task of assembly. Captain Foulois told me his new orders were to fly to *Casa Grandes,* which would be Pershing's first headquarters in Mexico, observing for bandits along the way. The only thing he did not know was the date the operation was scheduled to begin.

Initially I counted three Curtis Jenny bi-planes. The next day more of the biplanes arrived for a total of eight. After they were assembled, citizens and troopers alike would gather to watch the pilots put their Jenny's through countless take offs and landings. Pilots also enjoyed putting their planes through rigorous aerial maneuvers in the skies above the camp and village. Unfortunately the planes had a reputation as *death traps*, but these pilots handled them well. I was not sure if their aerial acrobatics were necessary for the observation roll they were said to be assigned. I guessed their showy antics were more for fun than anything military. Whatever the reason those pilots were good and entertaining to watch. If the 1st Aero Squadron ever fought in Europe, I figured they would stack up well against Kaiser Wilhelm's ace German pilots.

At night when our administrative duties were finally done, Alex, Sean and I would sit around a camp stove and talk. I was deeply thankful that my two closest friends in camp had survived. Tonight, as I often did, I sat polishing Bill Kubitz' Army belt buckle as he would have. Touching the cool brass calmed me and left my mind free to pick through my thoughts more clearly. I wondered if Bill had felt the same as he shined up this same piece of metal.

I watched Alex smoking a cigar while Sean cleaned his rifle. After a few minutes of silence while each man pondered his own thoughts, Alex looked over at me through a perfect smoke ring and said, "Did you write your ma?"

"Yes, the day after the battle. I did not want her reading one of those half-truth stories and worry I was dead. I spoke to her by phone too as soon as the emergency calls were made and I could get a line out. She fears we will be at war with Mexico soon. I hope she is wrong on that count."

Sean finished his cleaning and loaded the Springfield. "Your ma might be more right about that than all those worthless politicians in Washington. I heard the Army down Mexico way is filled with many sympathetic Villa supporters. You have to recall that the Mexican Army conscripted most of those boys right off the farms. Mexican villagers are more likely to support old Poncho since he will occasionally give something back to the local folks. Of course some of those riders with Villa are conscripts too. I also heard talk that there are posters in some of the border towns to recruit Americans who are attracted to the bandit lifestyle and offer of plunder from the raiding."

His spoken thoughts moved me to a sudden furious fit and I jumped to my feet. When I was excited I used my hands and gestured wildly to make my point. "It is a *bad* man that would betray his country for money. I just can't get it to set right in my head that any man would sell out his own country and neighbors for *any* damn reason. I would certainly give *no* quarter to a *gringo* riding with Pancho Villa if I had him in my sights. In my view they would be a lower coyote than a gunrunner." My wrath vented I sat down in disgust.

Putting out his cigar Alex stood up and stretched. A rare dark mood seemed to be upon him and he spoke with unrestrained intensity. "I know if I was still in Mexico I'd not be supporting Villa. He may throw his *dirty* money around to the poor, but only when it suits him. It's like watching a half-starved and whipped dog come back for more in the hope of a dropped morsel of food. Like my father before him, Villa preys on the weak. He only attacked Columbus because he was frantically in need of food and supplies. When we cross the border to capture him, he will hit us hard then fade away into the desert, never staying to engage us in a sustained battle straight on. Not because he is a coward, but because he is cunning like a *lobo* wolf and smart enough to know when he is outnumbered. Villa lives in a violent world and knows no other way. Our crossing into the territory he has claimed as his own will be chaotic at best. I fear some of us will not be returning from Mexico *mi amigos*."

Alex walked out into the night leaving those within ear shot of his words to ponder what he had said. A sudden shiver ran the length of my spine. I wondered if it was the desert chill in the evening air, or like one of my ma's old wives tales about the sensation related to somebody stepping over your grave. I shrugged off the feeling and said to Sean, "Alex was raised across the border. His pa was by all accounts a merciless and cruel outlaw. He's right about the tactics of Villa. He will run us around the desert like fools and only lady luck will save us. It'll be like the British fighting the Colonists. England had the most powerful army in the world, but they found it impossibly hard to hit a target that could blend into the forest and kill from cover, only to strike again just as suddenly. We'll be in his territory where he'll know every rock, gully and water hole to set an ambush from. I don't know about you, but I'm not feeling too lucky."

# CHAPTER 26

## *General Pershing in Command*

At reveille on the morning of March 13, 1916, just as the first rays of dawn were breaking from the east, orders were shouted to assemble all troopers not assigned a fixed post to the available space on the parade ground. We did not know what was going on but we were instructed to attend in our dress uniforms so we knew we were not marching out today. The men hurriedly dressed and began to assemble. I had been looking forward to a breakfast of bacon, eggs and coffee and was not please with the interruption.

I found Alex and Sean and groused my way over to the parade grounds. I was complaining under my breath and thinking how any good soldier knows an army runs best on a full stomach. A grown man needs to eat before being called to duty. Alex looked over at me and laughed. "Hey, what's the matter? Didn't you sleep well?"

Snapping at him in reply I said, "No I just want some coffee and grub."

"Well now, you and everyone else have been wanting news of what, when, and where we are going. I'll wager this is your ticket back to Mexico."

"I would not take that bet from you, you're too dang lucky. I just think dawn is no time for a stiff dress uniform and hurried assembly."

We walked on and the men began searching for standing room among all the parked vehicles and tents covering the grounds. It was impossible for any formal military line up so the men stood around talking in small groups. After about thirty minutes of anxious waiting I began to hear others grumbling about food or coffee. I was about to say something to Sean and Alex when we heard a steady motor sound in the still morning air. All talk ceased around me and I began to listen more intently as the roar of an engine grew louder. Through the low morning mist a dark object began to take the shape of a new car approaching fast toward us.

Waiting like everyone else the seconds ticked off until I finally recognized the automobile as a Dodge Brothers Touring Special. She was a beauty, shining a glossy black as it came into full view. The vehicle was top of the line and could not have been more than a year old. I had seen one like it in Columbus driven by one of the towns more prosperous merchants. There was no doubting that somebody important was heading our way. Alex must be right and we would finally get some straight answers. I shifted my feet with restless impatience to see who was in the automobile.

The sleek lines of the Dodge Brothers auto came to an abrupt stop. The driver had the familiar profile of Colonel Slocum. I was sure the stout passenger in the front seat was Mayor Hoover. I could only make out the partial shapes of two more passengers in the back seat since the leather top was up and the rear windows were small, blocking my view. As the car came to a complete stop followed by a dew soaked cloud of dust, Colonel Slocum and Mayor Hoover got out and waited for the other two men to follow. As the driver side rear door opened, I recognized the tall, straight-postured man in the perfectly tailored uniform as General *Black Jack* Pershing himself. The man moved like a predatory cat with eyes darting back and forth, missing nothing. He was fifty-five, but appeared older than I recalled, with deeper lines in his face. His eyes appeared more sunken and somehow haunted. I then remembered he had lost his family in a fire at Fort Bliss since I had last served under him.

The second man to emerge had an air of arrogance that I immediately took a dislike to. He also flaunted Army regulations with a custom made, non-regulations holster. I recognized the pistol he carried as the model 1876 single action Colt 45 carried on his right side. He looked to be about thirty years old and wore the rank of 2nd lieutenant. The unknown officer was as sharply dressed as was Pershing. His Colt had what appeared to be a bone or ivory handles. I could just make out some sort of fancy gold engraving on one side of the butt of the weapon and the carving of an eagle on the other side. His US belt buckle was highly polished brass inside a circle. I was thinking that all he needed was a sword to complete the dashing officer dress and attitude he displayed. I wondered who he was and why the normally strict General Pershing would let the man dress as he did?

While Slocum and Hoover remained back by the car, the general walked to a position in front of us. He looked us over and nodded to a few of the men he recognized, myself included. On the other hand, the unknown lieutenant assumed a hawk-like stance to Pershing's right and slightly behind the general. The lieutenant inspected us like we were a ragtag group of militiamen who had volunteered from Columbus for weekend military duty. I had no way of knowing what he was thinking, but his posture struck me wrong. It irked me that this young lieutenant seemed to question our abilities. Many of us standing before him had fought back a horde of bandit raiders determined to kill every man, woman and child in the town and camp.

General Pershing, satisfied with what he saw, began to speak in a commanding voice that left no doubt as to who was now in charge at Camp Furlong. "I am General Pershing. Some of you men have served under me before. I want to thank those of you who fought against Pancho Villa and his bandits. You fought bravely and saved many lives in Columbus. The story of your sacrifice has been blasted across America and you men are being mentioned in every house in the United States. Now we have a long dusty path before us. I will need to draw again on your spirit, resilient will, and require fierce loyalty. We must accomplish the difficult task President Wilson and the American people demand of us to ferret out Villa and his confederates. If we cannot capture or kill him, I intend to cut his supply lines and run him to ground. A man such as Villa, ever desperate, can do little harm while he is running for his life. Those of you who know me will testify that my orders are absolute and I will not tolerate being disobeyed."

He looked around as if determining if we had understood him so far. He leveled his gaze on the men closest to his position. Seemingly satisfied with what he observed he continued after a half minute pause. Gesturing toward the lieutenant beside him he said, "My personal aid, Lieutenant George S. Patton Jr. speaks for me in all matters of any importance. He will relay my orders to your commanding officers. I have received reports from Colonel Slocum that the preparations are going well. I expect to cross into Mexico on March 15th or before. We will travel in two columns which will work their way toward my first headquarters in Casa Grande. The Army is my life, but you men are the reason I serve. I need you troopers to never doubt my resolve." He stopped speaking again and clasped his hands behind his back. Dead silence covered the parade ground as we waited. He literally shook with emotion as he said, "Make no mistake troopers, my intentions are to chase Pancho Villa and his Villistas to *hell* if necessary!"

When he had finished what he had come to say, he turned, shook hands with Patton, and returned to the car. Many of the younger men were so excited by the speech that Pershing drove away to the sound of a thousand men cheering. I looked around at Sean and Alex and some of the experience sergeants around us, and saw no cheering. It is not that we were not moved by his words of a man I thought was a truly great leader, just that we knew our way would be brutal and that all of these men would not be coming back.

As Alex, Sean and I walked back to our tent I felt a forlorn sensation creeping up on me. I was thinking that only my ma was certain to miss me if I did not come back. Dying in the vast emptiness of Mexico was not a subject I wanted to consider. As for me, if God granted me one prayer it would be that when death came to my door it would be when I was a bent old man in Texas with a long life behind me. About then my stomach growled at me like an ornery grizzly. I shrugged off my mood as best I could. I found it peculiar that my gloomy thoughts had not dampened my appetite.

# CHAPTER 27

## *Punitive Expedition*

Finally and yet amazingly within a few short days of the battle in Columbus, our anxious waiting and speculation ended. On March 15, 1916, over the threats and objections of the Mexican government, we began our campaign into Mexico. I marveled at the fact that the government had move in such a swift and decisive manner. A tremendous and unyielding pressure must have forced President Wilson's hand. The president had used an old treaty as an excuse, which allowed hot pursuit, across borders. Newspaper reports had stated Wilson did not take the intrusion into another countries sovereign nation lightly. Some reporters had dubbed our pending invasion as the *Mexican Expedition*, while others called it *Punitive*, to bring Villa to account for all the murders and looting he had committed on the American side of the border. I was just pleased to be going along. Riding one of the big and hardy cavalry horses was a treat as well.

I looked out over the desert shielding my eyes against the glare of the noon day sun. Whoever decided an afternoon start was a good idea had not spent much time in the desert. It might still be spring, but summer comes early in the desert. The day would be hot and dry, with thick dust thrown up from the horses and Army vehicles. I had come to think of the desert as a living, breathing beast, beautiful, but hostile. This wild and untamed country in which we rode refused to accept mistakes and gave no quarter. I believed the desert would willingly grasp every opportunity to kill you. A grown man need not just worry about being taken down by a bandit's bullet, but also mountain lion, rattle snake, thirst and hunger. Even the large variety of scorpions could disable or kill outright in this treacherous desert sands.

We set out in two long columns generally in a southern direction, with Apache scouts out front searching for pathways through the coarse and treacherous sand. General Pershing had established an east and west column. I was secretly please when I caught sight of Pershing riding erect and easy in the saddle of a beautiful and powerful mount. It appeared the man could still sit a saddle hours on end, preferring a solid horse beneath him to the new Army automobiles and trucks. The old cavalry man was one of the few men walking the earth that I deeply admired. I marveled at his ability to motivate his men. He was general who was always out front leading, never observing from a safe position in the rear when battle was upon his men. I knew the kind of leadership shown by Pershing could not be taught at West Point.

I felt pride and great excitement rising in my chest like a crusading soldier at the beginning of his quest. I was certain I was witnessing the last great campaign for the horse cavalry. I was a little saddened and yet excited to be looking at the future of the Army. This would be the first use of auto and truck transportation in a military action. The Army had been testing various vehicles since 1910, but now was the time they would prove their worth. Looking back over the mile long columns I once again marveled at the mass assemblage of men and machines in such a short period. I had witnessed nothing like it before and I was betting few others had either. The magnitude of the mobilization of men might be common in Europe where a World War was being fought, but not in America and certainly not in Mexico.

As the day passed, the columns separated with the west column, including Pershing traveling toward Culbertson's Ranch, which was about one hundred miles west of El Paso, Texas and near the New Mexico and Arizona borders. Alex, Sean and I were in the east column riding toward Ascension and Corralitos. Lieutenant Patton was heading our column which would eventually rendezvous at the general's headquarters with each column finding its own way. We had higher ranking officers in our column, but General Pershing had made it clear who was in charge in his absence.

Squinting through the blazing sun I counted more than a dozen Cavalry Regiment banners. Banners included troopers from the 6th, 7th, 13th, 16th, and the famous 10th U.S. which were commonly called Buffalo Soldiers, an all Negro regiment. The Buffalo Soldiers were famous and much envied and admired for their horsemanship. These men could ride all day without rest. The 10th was fiercely loyal to Pershing who had fought valiantly beside the regiment in the Spanish-American War.

By all accounts Pershing had ridden hard up San Juan Hill leading his men. His commander at the time and later President of the United States, Teddy Roosevelt awarded him by promoting the lowly captain to lofty post as brigadier general over the heads of hundreds of officers. Even though that conflict was now eighteen years in the past, a few old Buffalo troopers still served to remind the young soldiers of their glorious past. Pershing was often heard praising the 10th Cavalry fighting ability to officers under his command. I could bear witness as having seen more than a few fights between troopers of the 10th after an unwary soldier had criticized the general in front of his men.

Just as I was swinging back in the saddle to look forward again, a Curtiss Jenny soared overhead no more than twenty feet off the ground. The plane had appeared as if by magic and was over us and past before we could react. My horse shied away from the fast moving plane and reared onto his hind legs. I had to fight him back in line and hang on with everything I had. The craft had momentarily stirred up a dust storm which raced along behind the Jenny. Seeing anything was next to impossible. Through squinted eyes and coughing from the dust I saw other cavalrymen struggling to regain control of their mounts. A couple of riders lost the contest and landed in a heap on their hindquarters. I assumed that the good captain had received his orders.

Oblivious to the carnage caused on the ground, the Jenny wagged its wings in a friendly wave during the flyover and flew on to the southward to complete the reconnaissance mission. I cursed the plane as it flew out of sight and was gone as suddenly as it had appeared. If I had thought it was possible I would have drawn my Springfield and shot the damn thing down myself. I was not sure if there was any chance these new contraptions of war would help us capture or kill Villa, but one thing was for *damn* certain, Pancho, his men, and all of Mexico would know we were coming.

The scorching day drew on into late afternoon. My clothes were soaked and clinging to me. No breeze stirred and not a single cloud appeared to give the slightest relief. My head was pounding from the heat and peering into the blinding sun. Several stops were made to feed and water the horses. Cavalry horses were big and tough animals, but were pampered with good grass and constant grooming. There was little vegetation and no grass at all on the desert trails we traveled. We used rags made of torn clothing to wipe the horse's mouths and rub their bodies down against the dust. Every time we stopped we had to let the horses cool down about ten minutes or more before they could be watered. Every experienced cavalryman knew only a fool would water a hot horse.

Our eventual destination would be Casa Grandes, Chihuahua, which would be one of General Pershing's Mexican headquarters. It was reported that Signal Corpsmen had set up a wireless telegraph from the United States border to the Pershing Headquarters. It was no secret that President Wilson was a *hands-on* president. He wanted first hand reports on how we progressed in our efforts. I had heard that miles of railroad track were being laid toward Casa Grandes to transport supplies to the area. I thought the move was ironic since we were barred from riding the rails ourselves. Looking toward the western sky it was clear by the setting sun that we would not make it the first night and possibly the day after that either. We would have to stop and camp.

As dusk was approaching the scouts led us to a shallow water hole which had been created when infrequent rain water was protected in the shade of stunted trees. We camped with our backs to a crumbling cliff which rose no more than fifty feet from the desert floor. No tents were set up for the night. We were left to sleep in the sand at greater risk to the desert snakes and scorpions. Sean and I supervised the placement of M1905 Howitzers in an outward facing line surrounding all sides of the camp to guard against a night attack. The mass of vehicles were circled in another layer of protection which reminded me of stories my pa had told me of wagon trains during an Indian attack. Troopers were then posted at every thirty paces to complete the inner most of the barriers.

Chinese cooks spread out among the night camp and began preparing the evening meal. Pershing had brought along five hundred twenty-seven Chinese which had been dubbed by the press as, *Pershing's Chinese*. Plenty of supplies were available on this first night, including coffee. As the first day became weeks and turned into months, provisions would need to be brought in or purchased from the locals. After I saw my men settled and gave out assignments, I met with Alex and Sean to share a campfire and bedding spot. I missed my family, but being in the company of men such as Alex and Sean, I never felt lonely knowing they were nearby.

I was not a big believer in destiny, but it still amazed me that I was once again in the Army and assigned duty alongside my friends. I could have looked upon the assignment as luck or a curse. The Army had many post. I could have been sent far away and never been a witness to these important events. I was once again in a foreign land facing armed conflict and constant possibility of death. Now however I was a participant in something much bigger than myself I could take pride in. If there was any truth to fate smiling, she had taken an interest in me this one time if no other.

After supper was finished and we sat around with our bellies full and sipping hot coffee, the talk around the fire turned to the mysterious Lieutenant Patton. Apparently Sergeant Haltom had at one time been stationed with Lieutenant Patton. He looked around the fire at us after someone had asked who the hell the man was and why he was leading us over higher ranking majors and colonels. "Back in 1913 I was attending the Mounted service School at Fort Riley, Kansas. At the same time the young Lieutenant Patton, fresh back from competing in the 1912 Olympics was there. He was given the position of *Master of the Sword*."

I had never heard Sean put together that many words in all the years I had known him. With the urging of the younger soldiers he continued. "I can't say whether he was *that* good or had some sort powerful tug on the higher powers within the Army. The *Master of the Sword* position was very prestigious and usually assigned to an older and higher ranking officer. Patton wasted no time and took it upon himself to create a new, better design of cavalry sword. The Army had been issuing the same saber since 1861 and a new sword was needed. Patton took charge of the design and manufacture. The model 1913 was the result. The Army quickly adopted the superb fighting weapon to bring about uniformity to officer's issue and to replace the Light Cavalry sword. The *Patton*, as some refer to it, has been a prized possession of Army officers who can afford the quality and high price ever since."

A smaller side discussion broke out about how non-commissioned officers, NCO's, were issued a basic, undecorated saber which nobody carried anymore. The younger troopers naturally wanted a shiny sword. The reality was that the dang things were mostly just in the way. Even a fool could see the end of the charging cavalry horse. Mounted troopers thrusting and slashing their way through a horde of enemy soldiers became ineffective with the advent of repeating arms. If not attending a military wedding or other fancy ceremony which called for full military dress, the sabers were left behind at the barracks. By now Sergeant Haltom speaking about Patton had drawn about a dozen men all grouped about our fire. The curiosity was understandable, but I looked around nervously in case the subject of our conversation was to suddenly appear in our midst.

Eventually after more urging about the details of the sword Sean squatted on his haunches and took back up his narrative. "As most of you know, officers buy their own swords and they come in expensive and very different designs. What Patton created in 1913 was a wicked killing design, expertly balanced and beautiful to hold and admire. It started with a black checkered grip with a guard made of sheet steel to protect the hand. Patton's design has a two edge blade designed for thrusting yet dually capable of slashing an enemy. It is thirty-eight inches long and weighs 2 pounds. The blade is made of forged steel, has bloodletting groves on either side and ends in a chiseled point. Lastly the scabbard is made of hickory wood, treated with oil and covered with rawhide. The finishing touch is to waterproof the scabbard by wrapping it in olive drab canvas. The finished saber is a sight to behold."

The men began to break up and return to their own camps. Now that the sun was fully down, a chilled North wind began to blow with earnest across the vast darkness. Troopers not on guard duty huddled in their blankets against the cool air and squirmed deeper into the sand which retained some of the heat of the day. The cooking fires were extinguished as a security precaution. A campfire in the flat desert could be seen for many miles by enemy or friend. We had no known friends looking for us this night. After the long sun-baked day of riding most of the soldiers were exhausted and only craved food and rest. Every man accepted that the campaign would mean many months spent in the saddle, with hard times ahead of scant food, water, or sleep. For now, the men appreciated the respite and on this night at least I heard little grumbling among them.

From some unseen hidden caves or overhanging cliffs bats by the thousands flitted through the air chasing insects around our heads. The bats were unrecognized in the night, but did not seem to be interested in the soldiers. At first the soldiers ducked comically as the dark wings made a distinct sound as they neared our faces. Troopers would duck and swat at the unseen pest. One minute we would be laughing at a man, then find ourselves going through the same motions a moment later. Eventually we realized they would not strike us. Their uncountable multitudes of wings made a humming noise which I had never heard before. The bat invasion lasted until near dawn. I welcomed the nocturnal creatures as the hungry mosquitoes had disappeared, eaten or in hiding.

Nobody slept much that night and I was full awake a dozen times. Just short of dawn I was up and warming myself over one of the early cook fires. Alex and Sean joined me and a cook handed us each a cup of steaming coffee. The hot liquid was strong and black. I was grateful for the warmth and it tasted just as I preferred. I smiled at my two companions. "I could get used to being served coffee and having someone doing the cooking. Back in Glenn Springs when we shared the cooking, you boys burned more meals than not. I lost so much weight my ma didn't recognize me."

Alex sipped at the scalding coffee and said, "Well *Jim*, as I recall I never did hear *Oscar* volunteering to cook or clean up afterwards."

"That's the privilege of rank Alex. Even though we're now all sergeants, I would gladly blacken some food for you two boys."

Sean squatted beside us and grunted. This morning he seemed to have taken up my usual position of being the grumpy one among us. "All I know is it may come to us eating lizards and bats before we see Texas or New Mexico again. I don't think it will matter much who cooks it. I just want a soft bed and warm body to curl up next to. If I survive this mess I think I'll put the Army behind me and find an easier way to make a living. I have a twin brother back in Houston, Texas who runs a saw mill. He will fix me up with a job and I can build a house near the ocean."

Grinning in the flickering firelight Alex spoke sardonically. "I can't believe there are *two* of you on this earth. Texas is a mighty big state, but two Haltom's running around seems like one too many, even for Texas. Furthermore, I can't help you out with the bed, but out here in the desert you might just find a warm body curled up next to you one cool morning. Diamondback rattlers have been known to do just that."

Quick witted as ever Sean quipped a retort, "Then I'll lop off that night crawler's head with my Bowie knife, skin him and toss him into the nearest cooking pot. I hear they taste powerful good on an empty stomach."

# CHAPTER 28

## *Snakes, Spiders and Javelinas*

As the days passed we pushed on through the endless wasteland of Northern Mexico. We entered into the desolate and rough terrain where the Sierra Madre Mountains could be seen in the distance. Some reports said that Villa had a hideout in these same mountains, but without a confederate of Villa's to guide us, we could search a lifetime without success. I marveled at the distance peaks which some climbed up to ten or even twelve thousand feet. We rode into or around deep canyons which could hide any size army. Ambush was always a concern and the men were wary of a sudden attack. Every hour or so Sean, Alex, or myself would ride back or forward of the column to ensure the men were alert and ready for any imminent threat to our current position. We began riding with our Springfield rifles across our saddles. I began to believe the metal skin of an Army truck might be preferable to the exposed position on the back of a horse.

Water was never far from our minds. During most days our Apache scouts were able to find water where none seemingly could exist. I began to know what to look for in the seemingly barren desert of sand and rock. Small oasis of green would indicate a possible source of water. Some days the scouts would dig into the empty river or creek beds and wait for water to seep to the surface. At other times we would drink from springs or find rain water that had been captured in rock crevices or seeped from underground streams.

On the worst days we would stop several times to slice open Barrel Cactus to suck on the moist fruit inside. The fruit was edible, but dehydration made digesting food hard on a man's stomach. On those hated days a man's urine would be bright yellow, which indicated heat stroke was a strong possibility if water was not found soon. One particularly blistering day we had half a dozen troopers rocked right out of the saddle as they passed out from the heat. The men were cooled as best we could and placed in vehicles for transport until we camped.

On those thirsty days we could do nothing for our horses but watch them suffer. If our mounts had been raised wild they would have found water by instinct alone. However these normally pampered and well fed horses had never had to fend for themselves in nature. A man caught without water would last no more than three days in the country we were passing through if not wise to the ways of the desert. I was thankful that General Pershing had the forethought to include the desert-born Apache scouts on the campaign. It could mean the difference in returning home or being buried in the remote sands.

So far I knew of a couple of snake bites of men and one horse. Two of the attacks had been reported as the result of an encounter with a Western Diamondback Rattler. This snake, although giving a warning rattle, was a particularly nasty creature. An experienced desert traveler knew to stop all movement at the first sight or sound of the snake. Troopers would most often cross paths with the rattlers while walking off to seek some private latrine time. The men had survived but spent three days in agony while recovering from the toxin. It had been the better part of a week before the soldiers could return to duty. The horse had been bitten while grazing on the edge of camp. The poor animal had been tethered and incapable of running away. Not wanting to witness the horses suffering the animal had been put down.

One memorable day the scouts led our column to a camp on the shady side of a broken cliff face. The cavalrymen had been in the saddle since first light and were exhausted. The scouts had discovered a place to cool off and sleep near a spring fed water source. The cool liquid was trickling from a fracture in the rock which ran for about ten feet along the bottom of the cliff before disappearing back underground. I was lightly dozing with my back against the cliff when excited shouts of men brought me quickly to my feet and a mad scramble for my rifle.

To my right I saw a dozen troopers running to surround a stunted tree. Rushing over to see what the commotion was all about I was in time to witness one of the strangest sights in nature. A Mexican King Snake was in a deadly face off with a Western Diamondback Rattler. The winner in this contest would not only be victorious, but eat the opponent. Snakes, being cold blooded naturally hid during the heat of the day, usually in crevices or other shaded dens. Some of the men must have disturbed one of the snakes and the other took the opportunity for a meal over concealment or escape.

Now both snakes were near equal in size. I estimated more than five feet in length and thicker than a man's two hands could grasp. The troopers, starved for any type of entertainment immediately began making bets on which snake would take the other. My money was on the non-venomous King but most believed the poisonous rattler would win. The King Snake was a known killer of other snakes and now advanced, quick-like, avoiding the rattler's killing strike. The reptiles struck and retreated, each attempting to outmaneuver the other. The contest lasted over five minutes with no end in sight.

Eventually the King struck suddenly and caught the rattler at the corner of the head, safely out of the way of the deadly fangs. The King hung on for several minutes before beginning the slow process of consuming the rattler. The men who had been cheering one minute had gone silent as the King took a long twenty minutes to swallow the helpless rattler. As snakes do, the rattler's twitching continued to the end as the loser shook the namesake rattle all the way into the King Snake. After the rattler had completely disappeared, the triumphant King slithered away into a small stand of bushes.

That night I felt little comfort in knowing that one rattler which had populated the spring was dead. The presence of water certainly indicated more creatures were nearby or would be coming in for a drink. At near sundown, a family of javelina, a type of wild pig walked right into our camp. The largest one that we could only assume was a male snorted and snuffled along the ground. I reached for my Colt

45 but Alex stopped me with a gesture. Leaning over he whispered, "That big one there has canine-type teeth and it would be tougher than leather to eat." He pointed at the babies and smaller females following the adult male. "The younger ones and females can be eaten. They are mighty tasty roasted over a fire. I wouldn't try that big old male unless I was starving."

He stood slowly and picked up a fist-sized rock, quickly dispatching the nearest javelina with a perfectly aimed throw. The Chinese cooks who had been watching and wondering what to do about the strange creatures followed his lead. Two more of the young ones fell and two of the females went down in a hail storm of thrown rocks. The older male and two others walked right on through the camp and out, obviously not concerned about the unlucky javelina left behind. I looked at Alex in surprise. "I guess those critters are not too strong on family ties. I thought sure the big one would turn and fight."

"Either that or javelina are dumb as cracked mud." Alex was in high spirits. Now he rubbed his hands together in anticipation. "Whatever the explanation, I can guarantee there is a fine treat in store for us tonight."

Within minutes the javelina were gutted and spitted over a fire. Soon the delicious aroma of cooked pork was making all our mouths water in anticipation. Alex was most popular that night and the cooks brought the choice portions of the meat to our fire. We could never understand much of what they said, but it was apparent that Alex had endeared himself in their eyes. Troopers camping in or near us who had benefited from our bonus feast came by our fire to thank Alex in person.

In his typical humble fashion Alex tossed it off as no big deal. "The food walked into camp after all. When I was growing up in Mexico I killed many javelinas as a boy. The advantage to the stalker is they show no fear of people. Javelina breeds in numbers that must make them unconcerned if some of the younger ones or females are taken by hunters, either man or beast. If I had not acted when I did the Chinese would have figured it out. I just did not want a dozen men shooting up our camp." He looked right at me when he added, "You're included in that bunch Jim."

Once again full and contended I lay down on my bedding and enjoyed the stars above. The closeness of the winking heavens and the coolness of the night reinvigorated me after the days spent under the hot sun. I had forgotten my earlier fear of the night crawlers when Alex moving in a blur leaped to his feet from where he had been enjoying a cigar. I thought he had gone loco when I saw his long knife flash in the moonlight. He stabbed near my head and I rolled away to the opposite side beginning to cuss an enthusiastic stream. I was not sure what kind of fit he was having but I wanted to be out of the line of attack. As I turned to face him with a mouth full of hot profanity, my words caught in my throat.

Alex was standing over my bedding with an overlarge spider stuck to his knife, which was still wiggling with his blade sticking out of the innards. He grinned at me before holding up his catch for the men around us to see. "This, *mi amigos* is a Mexican Red Kneed Tarantula. Not a very friendly species this one. Mexican red will crawl into your bedding seeking warmth before biting the owner of the bed when he moves and startles the spider. This type of tarantula has been known to kill a grown man. If you survive, the bite you might pray for death to claim you as the toxins work through your body. Realizing he was scaring some of the men, he began to laugh as he looked into the frightened faces on the younger men. "Maybe you would want me to put a bullet between your eyes to end your suffering?"

I knew he was teasing but some of the inexperienced, baby faced trooper seemed to be considering his offer as genuine. I still marveled at his knowledge of the creatures in the desert. Even though he had grown up near the desert, many men lived near something or other without ever taking notice. It was good to have friends like Alex nearby. In one day he had fed us and saved me a nasty bite. I tucked the corners of my blankets as best I could and covered my head for good measure before sleeping.

# CHAPTER 29

## *Colonel George F. Dodd*

It felt like months as the sweltering days passed slowly. Eventually we camped near a creek fed pond outside the small village of *Ascension.* As the men came and went into the village we finally began to pick up intelligence information from the Mexican citizens themselves. While the locals did not like the *gringos* in general and the army in particular, American cash money was greatly coveted by the poor farmers and peasants of the villages.

The story we heard repeatedly from sources was that after attacking Columbus, Villa had rallied his men and traveled south to the mountain village of *Namiquipa.* Once more displaying audacity and cunning, he attacked and defeated a *Carrancista* garrison of two hundred men. He had once more proven he would not avoid a fight with a military force and would go out of his way to attack. We were a superior army in size, equipment, and training. I doubted he would attack us head on in a pitched battle. Villa was more likely to ambush smaller bands of soldiers perhaps scouting ahead for water or supplies.

Some of the best intelligence had come from Alex as he had made his way throughout the towns speaking to citizens as he walked the town. If Mexican citizens would respond at all to a foreign soldier, it was more likely to be one that had been born in their own country and spoke the language. Even still he had reported more hostile than friendly encounters due to his uniform of what was seen as an invading army. I suspected that the affable good humor and ready spending habits of Alex were as responsible for the information as anything else.

As a sergeant Alex wrote a report about his observations and handed it in to Colonel George F. Dodd who commanded 370 troopers of the 7th Cavalry. We were now loosely under his command for the time being. Alex had deliberately left some non-military information out of his report. He observed widespread abuses of the Army uniform we all wore. Some of the men were drinking heavily and visiting the local *sporting* houses that had sprang up in the advance of the Army. Military commanders had conceded it would be difficult or impossible to keep all the men in camp. Knowing the men would surrender to their basic instincts, someone had made the decision to issue prophylactics to the men for the $2.00 local charge for copulation.

I spent my time in our camp on the edge of the town. I was certainly no saint, but was uncertain of my own willpower. The craving for hard liquor seemed to have left me, but I did not want to tempt my resolve. Alex brought me some rolling papers and local tobacco. When I offered to pay him he grinned mischievously and rolled a gold coin end over end between his fingers. The coin had materialized from nothing as far as I could tell. He also purchased a month supply of little cigars at an exaggerated price more than twice what he usually paid. I looked questioningly at him. "I guess you sat in on a good poker game in town. It's funny how you keep winning the same coins you seem to never run out of."

He ignored me until he finished lighting a cigar. "Only heaven knows why I'm so lucky amigo." He walked off with a self-satisfied smile on his unshaven mug.

The next town we encountered was *Corralitos.* This time Colonel Dodd purposively sent Alex into the village to gather information. He was allowed to wear civilian clothes as he mingled with the townsfolk. Like a clucking hen I worried that Alex could be in more danger this time. A bandit would not hesitate to kill a nosey stranger, but might think twice about killing an American soldier with his troopers all over town. There was every possibility that Villa had posted men in town for the same purpose of obtaining information.

This time I went along as well as Sean, who was looking forward to a hot bath if one could be found. Sean had talked me into the trip to town with the simple words, "You *stink* something awful Jim!" I had been filthy so long I no longer thought much about it. Sean assured me that anyone downwind of me would be thankful if I bathed too. Rinsing off in a muddy river or creek once a week was cooling but did little other than coat your skin with another layer of dirt. Sean and I left Alex to talk to the townsfolk. He would take his time and wonder around talking to everyone until he stumbled onto citizens who were friendly and talkative. There was none better at coaxing a body into something they had not planned on doing Alex. We parted company with Alex on the far edge of town, but agreed to meet back on the opposite north end of town in three hours.

We were directed to find Pablo Castro, the town's only barber at a corner house fronting the only street. Finding the house and Pablo, Sean managed to negotiate with the man in poor Spanish for a hot bath, shave and haircut. Pablo's *casa* was attached at the back of his shop where we would be treated to a hot bath. In fact Pablo, a friendly, thin man with dark straight hair, insisted we bathe before he would touch our dirty and matted hair.

An elderly stoop-shouldered woman of undermined age led us back through the barber shop to a ten by ten adobe room. I suspected the woman was Pablo's mother, but she never spoke, using gestures to indicate what we were supposed to do. She took our uniforms and began to wash them on the back steps while we bathed. There was not much privacy in Pablo's house. The old woman came and went leaving the back door open as well as a curtain which separated the house from the front shop.

To my dismay, another set of intruders was a goat, two chickens, and finally Pablo's twin daughter's which I figured as being about four years old. The pair kept peeking into the room to gawk at the pale white strangers. Sean took no notice of the company and drifted into a deep sleep, immediately relaxed in the hot tub. Since we had to wait for our clothes to air dry there was no reason to hurry the bath. While Sean slept, I was feeling overexposed and vulnerable. Being naked was no way to fight off an attack by bandits. As usual, even when enjoying something this pleasurable, I was unable to relax and kept my Colt 45 nearby. I never stopped watching the door for any real threat.

I was relieved to see that Pablo was good at his trade. After leaving I felt and looked like a new man. Sean and I stopped to admire ourselves in one of the shop windows. I had not felt this good in longer than I could remember. Just smelling the homemade soap in my clothes made remember how hard ma worked for us kids when we were growing up. The clean bodies and fine smelling clothes put us both in a mindset to celebrate. I decided to trust myself to drink a beer in the saloon.

As we walked down the street the tavern structure made me recall the saloon in Boquillas. All at once the recollection gripped me and began to squeeze at my chest like a python had a hold of me. I tried taking deep breaths as we approached, but I now nervous and jumpy inside my own skin. My good frame of mind soon dissolved into unease and apprehension. My stomach soured as I sat with my back to the wall, my eyes never straying far from the door. Sean tried to engage me in small talk as we drank our warm beer. However it would have been clear to a blind man that I was distracted.

Finally unable to contain the question anymore Sean spit out the words like there was a bad taste in his mouth. "What the *hell* is the matter with you Oscar? You're able to swop mindset *snap-quicker* than any man I know. Your mood turned dark faster than a Texas jackrabbit."

I leaned in and said in a low voice. "Don't forget to call me *Jim* okay? It's just that the last time I was in a Mexican saloon Alex and I killed a few of the bandits that attacked us in Glenn Springs." Thinking about the event made me fume again as if it had just happened yesterday.

Curious now and matching my voice level he asked, "How did you know it was the same raiders Jim? It could have been any number of bad men riding on their own or with other bandit parties."

I sighed and peered toward the back of the saloon wondering if there was a way out through a rear door. Finally turning my attention back to Sean I barked a reply, which I had not intended. "Because I took Bill Kubitz US Army bucket off the big ugly one I shot first. It is the same one you've seen me polishing at night."

Ignoring my outburst he said, "Well I can't say I'm sorry the *son of a bitch* is dead. Bill was a good man as well as a friend too. I heard tell you shipped his body home. That was a fine thing to do for his folks. However you and Alex took a big chance going after those hard cases like that. I'd say you are both lucky to be alive." He went quiet for a spell before continuing. "Jim I've got to be honest. After you and Alex took off some of the men questioned whether you two had gone yellow. Some figured y'all had taken off afraid of another attack. I never understood what your reasons might be but I never believed you and Alex for cowards. I knew there had to be a solid reason for your actions, if misguided at the time."

"It was every bit my own *damn* fool idea. I guess Alex tagged along out of loyalty to me. Thinking back on what was going on with me at the time, I imagine that I was not right in the head. I had a powerful lust to destroy every man that had attacked and killed my men. Alex tried to stop me from the beginning but I was seeing red. I just tucked my head down like a mad bull and charged. I paid dearly for my poor judgment and almost cost Alex his career as well. Worse still I could have gotten another friend killed. To tell the truth I would not be alive if Alex had not been with me. Now by fate or happenstance I've been given another chance to right my wrong. I've no desire to kill anybody, but I will do my duty even if it cost me my life."

Before leaving town I bought several pieces of hard candy. I grew up eating the stuff which was brightly colored and tasty. It was a rare occasion when my siblings and I were treated to the candy. I had a sweet tooth for the different flavors that look more like glass than any child's delight. Sean bought some sewing tack to repair a rip in his uniform. We were well a half hour passed the three hour meeting time but Alex was waiting alongside the road as if he had nowhere to go and no time to be there. I handed him a piece of the candy and he tossed his cigar. His eagerness reminded me of an overgrown child as he loudly slurped at the hard candy.

After a few moments of enjoying the candy, he feigned anger as he said, "While you two were relaxing in the suds, I may possibly discovered where Pancho Villa himself is holed up. I know you two are enjoying the hospitality of Mexico, but capturing Villa could get us back across the border."

Shocked by his words I excitedly blurted out, "Where is he?" The words had exploded from me a moment before Sean echoed exactly the same words.

"I think I have sound information from several prominent citizens that Pancho rode to Guerrero after attacking the *Carrancista* garrison in *Namiquipa*. Some of the villagers heard that he was recovering from a gunshot wound from one of his own men. Apparently the bullet shattered his shinbone. Some bandits rode in here a few days ago looking to take the doctor out by force. He was luckily out of town attending a wedding. Pancho was reportedly shot from the rear by one of his *impressed* volunteers. If the information is true it may be our chance to end this expedition and go home."

# CHAPTER 30

## 7ᵗʰ *Cavalry Draws First Blood*

The next morning Colonel Dodd and his famous 7ᵗʰ Cavalry rode out before dawn. I would have much preferred to sleep in and wave at their dust while sipping coffee in the morning. Instead Alex, Sean and I were assigned to ride with the three hundred and seventy officers, sergeants, and men. The colonel's unabashed style had been used to cajole Lieutenant Patton into approving the attempt. Patton undoubtedly realized if the information was genuine it could result in a quick end to the expedition. Over the next fourteen days I had good reason to curse Alex for being able to understand Spanish and for being so damn friendly with the locals. He had become one of the colonel's favorites and we were along for the hellish ride. I had lost track of the days that men of leisure printed on their calendars, but I knew it was 1916 and thought it was still March.

As we traveled fast over the rough terrain I had plenty of time to observe the sixty-three year old Colonel Dodd. Nobody doubted he was tough in the saddle, which many younger men could not hope to duplicate. He chewed nonstop on custom-made large cigars throughout the day. I never saw him actually light them so I supposed it was a nervous trait. He had spent his younger career chasing Indians. The dry and uncomfortable conditions were nothing new to a man that had fought Indians in the American Southwest.

We brought no cooks and had only the food, water and bedroll that each man could carry on his saddle. A couple dozen pack mules were traveling with us, but they were loaded down with ammunition and other military essentials. Colonel Dodd must be a believer in, *travel light and fast.* Our only existence was the saddle and desert that surrounded us as we rode more than twelve hours every day. Our all too short nights were spent in cold camps with barely four or five hours rest. The conditions were difficult and exhausting for men and animals. Within a week we were critically low on rations which had been quickly consumed. There had been no time to hunt and large game was scarce in the barren lands we crossed.

Along the way Colonel Dodd negotiated to hire Mexican *Vaqueros*, or cowboys to guide us to the town of Guerrero. After a few days Alex began to suspect this rough riding bunch might be leading us in a round-about route in order to slow our progress. It was just not possible to be certain of who was enemy or foe in this country. Even if we killed Villa, the vaqueros and other locals would have to exist in Mexico long after we were gone. They would be caught in the unending power struggle between the Mexican Army and bandits or outlaws of one kind or another. Aiding one group over the other could mean a quick passing from this life if the opposing forces gained the upper hand.

Our guides led us through the steep and treacherous pathway in the Sierra Madre Mountains. These peaks soared as high as five thousand feet above sea level, with the trail barely visible at times. Ice formed at the altitude, making the crossing of three hundred and seventy men a precarious proposition. I studied the frightened faces around me and knew my own face must reflect the same fear. Our horses were not mountain bred and labored at the task from the elevation as well as their exhausted state. Our own breath was visible as we exhaled. Unbelievably I found myself longing for the hot desert floor below. Just yesterday I had cursed the desert heat.

At the highest and narrowest point, a mule laden with ammunition slipped on the ice and went down on his belly hard. Before anyone could react the terrified animal began to slide closer to side. One of the handlers dismounted and I saw the flash of his blade as he instantly sliced through the pack string tying the mule to five others. I also dismounted to see what could be done to save the poor beast and our equipment. Before I took two steps the mule rolled over onto its back and went over the edge.

Mules are the offspring of a male donkey and a female horse. They make a unique sound, half horse whinny and half donkey bray. The horrendous braying shriek I heard was unearthly and grated on the nerves like needles in my spine. I wanted to squeeze my eyes shut but was forced to fight my horse as he reared and danced sideways in fear. Still on foot I was nearly knocked over the side myself. I heard rather than saw the mule hit an outcrop about fifty feet down, which abruptly ended the terror-filled braying. Shuddering I knew the animal's last screech would haunt my dreams for some time.

After struggling to regain control of my horse, I took a few moments to catch my breath. I leaned heavily against my saddle, panting in the thin air. Looking across the space that had opened between me and the animal handler, I looked into his stricken eyes and saw unexpected tears. I had felt for the animal's horror and pain myself, but it was just a mule. The man helplessly gestured to the spot where the mule had gone over and said in a broken voice, "I raised Mollie from a foal."

Unable to think of any words of comfort I shakily attempted to climb back on my horse. Unsteady and seemingly without strength to pull myself back in the saddle, I decided to walk the horse until it was safe to mount. Closer to the truth was that I wanted to trust my own legs on the ice. If I went over it would be my own fault, not the misstep of a worn out horse. Others around me must have had the same idea. A dozen or so dismounted and walked the next quarter mile. I would write a commendation for the handler for his quick actions that saved the other five mules and equipment, but it would be of little comfort for his loss.

At last we arrived at *Bachiniva* to buy badly needed supplies. We had ridden the better part of four hundred miles in an unbelievable twelve day. My backside was blistered and I was now mighty unhappy to be in the cavalry. We were sun burnt and jaded from the tortuous trek. Our mounts were worn out, half starved and used up. I hated to see the once powerful beast with their heads hanging and ribs easily counted. No horses were for sale in the small village which meant our horses would have to be used until they dropped from beneath us. I worried I would end my days charging Villa's banditos as an infantrymen.

A sane man would have waited weeks in town to rest the men and arrange for fresh horses if ours could not be saved. Colonel Dodd might not be insane but he was human and therefore fallible. Dodd seemed to be unstoppable and I would not want to be in Villa's boots if the colonel's 7th caught up to him. He appeared more determined than a man had any right to be and expect to keep on living. We camped on the edge of town near a stream for two days while Alex and a few others entered the town to order supplies and ask around for word of Villa.

The colonel insisted the regular troopers not be allowed time off in town. He was a hard man with no taste for alcohol or women. I hated to admit I admired him. He was plenty smart enough to know that in order to maintain discipline; he could not turn a horde of drunken American soldiers loose to tear down the small village. As for me I was content to catch up on my sleep. When awake I would spend hours sitting in the soothingly cool waters by our camp, sucking on a piece of hard candy and soaking my posterior. However I never let my rifle get too far from my grasp.

That night we were allowed only two hours rest before packing up the gear and hitting the trail. We were fifty-five miles from our destination of Guerrero and long in the saddle before dawn. The final push was over unsteady terrain riding horses who were giving every last breath as they responded to the urgency of their riders. In little than six hours we were stopped a hundred yards from town. As we rested the horses for a final charge into the town, the best marksmen took position to cover our approach. It was March 29th and by the sun I estimated it was close to 8:00 o'clock.

Colonel Dodd split his men into three groups with one circling around to the other side of the town. One would stay put and be the first in and the last, around seventy men would be held back in reserve. The signal was two shots from either rife or pistol. The rapid firing had the duel purposes of drawing out the bandits into the open and signaling the charge. Sean was in the reserve company while Alex and I were among the first troop. The men on the other side of town were to wait one minute before coming in. The delay was to allow a surprise for Villa's men and to avoid a crossfire occurring between Army troopers.

With all ready we sat our mounts in anxious anticipation. I had been in battles before but it had always been sudden and unexpected. Now with a fight immediately ahead of me I felt a mixture of fear and excitement. I heard a ringing in my ears and worried I would not hear the signal shots. Blood seemed to be rushing through my body and I could feel my heart beating in my chest. I wondered if it had been the same with the soldiers who followed Alexander the Great or the brave volunteers facing certain death in the Alamo. Home was far from here but never far from my mind. What I was fighting for at this moment I could not say. Even if I had been called on to speak it would have been difficult since my mouth was dry. I was surprised to find I was sweating even as I sat in the cold morning air.

Crack, boom! The signal had been given. We were charging the street. I rode with my Springfield in my right hand and the other grasping the reins. Bandits began to rush into the streets as we rode in a full gallop up the dusty street. Our horses were giving everything they had left urged forward by their riders. I feared it would be impossible to hit anything on the fast moving horse. However my first shot, lucky I am sure, took a man down just as he raised a pistol to fire. He rolled over and was trampled by cavalrymen assuring his end. There was no time for thought, only action and reaction to what surrounded us. As with the Glen Springs battle, only the immediate second mattered. Fear had no part once the battle was joined.

Other bandits were going down in a hail of zinging bullets. A trooper next to me was knocked off his horse but scrambled up and continued to fire, apparently not seriously hurt. The men of the 7th fought with disciplined precision as they decimated the bandits. The troopers fired and reloaded like machines. The concentrated firing reminded me of the machine guns in Columbus. I emptied my rifle and my Colt 45 before jumping off my horse to reload on steady ground. It was a stupid mistake which left me completely vulnerable. While I reloaded a bandit on horseback charged at me as I blocked his path out of town. I managed to load just two rounds in the Colt, and then fired into his body with both rounds. His horse continued past me as he landed dead in a heap at my feet. I tried not to look at him other than to be sure he was dead while I finished reloading both weapons.

Now sporadic rifle fire began to harass us from windows above and level with the street. Other cavalrymen dismounted and poured deadly fire through the windows until all went silent inside. Villa's men now in full panic were running for their horses. Taking care not to hit each other, the bandits were cut down like cattle in a slaughterhouse. A few of the lucky ones may have escaped but most were captured or killed. I estimated that no more than five minutes had passed before the firing stopped, although at the time it seemed endless. We stood in the after-silence half deaf from the reports of our weapons. The only sound was of the men and horses as we panted heavily to catch our breath. The bloody carnage around us was the proof that our attack had been successful.

I counted no more than five wounded troopers, none seriously. The men walked or were carried to the only hotel for treatment. On the other hand fifty-six bandit bodies littered the street, including one of Villa's nameless generals. Two of Villa's men were believed to be expatriates, Americans who had betrayed their own country for financial reward. Another thirty-five had been wounded and captured. I help organize a burial detail for the bandits while Alex was assigned to interrogate the captives for information. I rounded up Sean to help organize the burial detail. The men were stripped of weapons and ammo before being placed in a common grave. After the disastrous decision to burn the bodies outside Columbus, the burial was a favor to the local town.

As for the citizens of Guerrero, nobody had come out to greet or curse us. The townsfolk must be shell shocked from the explosive attack and sudden death of the bandits which had taken harbor in the village. Every structure in the town would have to be searched to ensure no stragglers were hiding, including Villa. The men in

Guerrero would have to be questioned to gain additional information. If the town was a haven for bandits, weapons would be confiscated for our own protection to ensure they would not be used against us at a later date. Whether the town was a Villa supporter or just his pawns was yet to be determined. Nobody had seen Pancho Villa during the fight, but there was no doubt these were his men.

Sean was mighty peeved at being left out of the fight. He fumed at the circumstances which had left him behind in the reserve troop. "Damn it Jim! You, Alex, and the 7th didn't leave squat for the reserves to do but bury the bodies. You could have let the reserves have some scraps at least. That must have been some amazing charge. We could not see a thing from our position. All we heard was a crash of guns. It sounded like one long continuous thunder clap. You boys did not let up on them for some time."

Unable to grasp his mind-set I said, "I would have gladly let you go in my place. I won't lie and say the experience was not exhilarating, but I was scared half out of my wits. It must be another of my pa's miracles that we did not shoot each other. There was so much close-in firing happening all at once and smoke you could hardly see. Don't fret Sean, I'm betting the good colonel will have plenty more in store for us unless we find Villa among the wounded bandits. Next time just stick close to me. With my luck it is a certainty that Sergeant Draper will be included in any action that has somebody shooting in our direction."

# CHAPTER 31

## *Under the Scary House I Go*

Grandpa stopped speaking and I was brought back to awareness. The back screen door had slammed and Grandma Myrtle, mom, and my aunts Ruth, Emily, and Marie had appeared. Grandma was wringing her hands on a pink apron. She looked around and spoke to the assembled group on the porch. "We'll begin heating up the leftovers soon. I'll bet these boys need a break from them old scary stories anyway."

For once I agreed with her and was not upset that grandpa had been interrupted. As everyone began to break up and move around to get the circulation back into their legs, I realized I was near to peeing in my britches. I had been flat on my belly in the same spot for over two hours. It was hard to get up and move again with my bladder full to the bursting point. To make matters worse my right arm was asleep since I had been using it to prop my head up. It was swinging by my side. The stinging sensation of tingling was slowly making its way down my arm. Pushing through the back screen door I saw a line at the only bathroom in the house. Dad caught my eye and immediately guessed my dilemma. He pointed back out the door and mouthed the word, "Bushes."

It would not be the first or last time I would go outside. As long as nobody could see me I thought of it as a kind of adventure. This time it was close to an emergency. I did not want to ride home in clothes reeking of urine. I hobbled as fast as I could to the bushes at the rear which grew along the back fence. I pressed myself in as far as I could go. The thick evergreen ferns mostly enveloped me. Still nervous I looked over my shoulder one last time before giving in to the release.

Finally relieved I began to feel like myself again and went looking for my cousins. Now that I had time to think about grandpa's story it was one of my favorites. Treks over frozen mountains, hunger, thirst, and finally a big battle was all keen adventure. Of course I felt sorry for what grandpa had to endure, but what a life to remember. What had happened was so long ago but he had made it feel like it had been happening right at the moment. Grandpa had gotten so excited while telling his story that his voice had taken on the inflections and stress of the event he was remembering. I marveled at his ability to recall something so clearly that had happened forty-seven years ago. What must that be like? Also when would I have a chance for another story?

At that time I heard my name being called from the back porch, interrupting my thoughts. It was dad with John Ray beside him. I had not broken anything this trip and they had both seemed to enjoy the story, so I was not sure why I was being summoned. It certainly did not take two grownups to call in one boy to wash up and have some dinner. A little fearfully I dutifully walked toward them, shading my eyes against the late afternoon sun to try and read their faces for a clue.

When I was in easy earshot dad said, "Buddy we have a critical mission for you if you think you're up to it."

I could tell from dad's voice and words that he was teasing in his tone and manner. He was teasing me and playing on my craving for adventure at every turn. "What is it dad?"

By now I was standing on the porch before them. John Ray continuing on dad's theme and said in a very serious voice, "Buddy nobody gets to eat tonight unless you can help us with a problem."

More confused and unsure than ever, dad finally let me in on the trouble. "Son, ma's oven is gas and there is a leak in one of the pipes under the house. I need you to crawl under there and tell us which one is leaking. We can talk to you through the wood floor. Once we figure out which pipe it is we can cut a new section and replace it."

Now I had been feeling pretty grown up since my birthday had passed in October, but this was not a small thing to ask. Even at eleven I knew gas was dangerous and could blow up or put you to sleep forever. "That sounds kind of scary dad. Also there might be snakes under the house." I had actually played under the old peer and beam house when I was about six, but that was before I knew enough to know it was risky.

Dad answered reassuringly. "Buddy all snakes hibernate during the winter. Also we'll only turn on the gas a few seconds at a time. Then use your nose to tell us where the pipe is leaking. Once you find the leak knock on the floor and we will be able to find you."

Okay now I understood what they were asking me to do and was thinking I could possibly do this. Then Uncle John Ray added, "You can take a big old rock with you to smash the spiders and scorpions as you go, then leave the rock behind at the spot of the leak and we'll take it from there."

My voice squeaked out a weak, "Okay."

In ten minutes John Ray and dad were leaning over looking under the house. I was squatting and thinking I would like to back out. My only pay off would be dinner and I guessed my dad would not let us starve. I was afraid of scorpions, having been stung before. Spiders did not bother me, but after grandpa's last story, I was looking for the big harry legs of tarantulas. Finally dad, in the way of a push, gave me an old worn out blanket to use when I stopped. I figured the blanket would mean I would have a better chance of seeing what was crawling toward me when I was on the cloth.

So I began my crawl into the semi-darkness underneath grandma and grandpa's house. Every few minutes or so, I would stop and wiggle up onto my blanket. Once I knocked on the floor above dad would turn on the gas. When my nose did not pick up the rotten egg smell of natural gas, I would move on and try again. It occurred to me while I was in the middle of this searching that exciting adventures were much better when over and you were safe. Now nearing the kitchen I stopped again and knocked. Eureka! My head began to swim. I starting coughing hard before I could even begin my frantic knocking to have the gas turned off.

After placing my spider rock down to mark the pipe leak I quick-crawled my way back into the light. Vastly relieved that my part in the drama was done, I was now free to go play. I stood looking myself over for damage to my clothes. As best I could tell I only saw a lot of dirt on my Christmas clothes. I smiled as I thought that this time dad would have to answer for any rips or stains on my clothes. I dusted myself off as best I could and went to look for my cousins.

# CHAPTER 32

## *Hobo (Hotel) Jungle*

I rounded up David, Danny and Jon Mark and we immediately headed to our favorite spot. The train tracks were blocks away and we ran all the way down to the tracks. There was no thought of jumping a train today since we were in good clothes. We loved to watch the trains come and go. Our favorite pastime was to make up stories about where they were going or coming from. Most of the trains carried freight cars but occasionally we would see a fine passenger train. I had ridden trains before but never got to go back to the sleeper. The sights and sounds transported us away to far places and strangers in distant cities. There was always an adventure here even if it was in our own imaginations.

Our parents knowing we often lost track of time, we had been warned to return for supper in an hour. There was little time to waste. The four of us walked along the tracks for about a mile before finding a thick stand of trees. Inside we could smell smoke from a campfire and some unrecognized food cooking. There was a sensation of mysterious discovery mixed with excitement and fear all at once. Ducking into the trees we saw three men sitting around a campfire cooking something in a pot. I was not familiar with the smell and I just hoped it was not a stray cat or dog. It was too late to back out now that we had been seen. The men did not seem to be aggressive so I said in way of greeting, "Hello. Do you live here?"

A tall man in his forties stood up and said in a friendly enough voice, "No sir. We have a lifetime pass to ride the rails for free. We travel all over this here country on a wish and a whim." He indicated his surroundings with a grand gesture. "This here is a hobo hotel. Some local folks call it the *hobo jungle*. I have had the pleasure of stopping here plenty of times when I am over this way."

He had a dark tan and wore three or more shirts over his stocky build. His nose looked like it had been broken more than once. He made me think of pictures of prize fighters I had seen. "What's your name mister?" Before he could answer I said, indicating my cousins who were staying well behind me at the entrance. "I'm Buddy and these are my cousins, David, Danny and Jon Mark."

The men nodded and so did my cousins. "I'm Buster. This younger one here is Rex and my elder friend is Matt."

Rex appeared to be in his late teens with a handsome enough face, although smudged with dirt now. He had an easy smile and I found myself liking him at once. Matt was much older, probable over sixty, with no hair on top. He had a thick scraggly beard covering most of his face. His left eye appeared as if a cloud had settled inside it. I began to believe he might not be able to see from it by the way he turned his head as he spoke. His voice was low and scratchy. "I'm pleased to meet you young gentlemen."

Just as Matt finished speaking I saw a small white head poking up out of his shirt. I was surprised to realize it was a small mongrel dog. My dad would have called the dog a mutt. I could not tell if the animal was a puppy or just a small breed. Matt saw me looking and he said, "This here is Skipper. He dances and will do other tricks for you boys for the low sum of two bits. Now me, I would not want to be charging you boys, but Skipper is *par-tic-u-lar* and only works for hard coin."

Buster scolded him. "Matt these are our guest and you want to charge them." He looked at me and said, "He makes a little money here and there when folks pony-up for the dog show." I noticed his scorn did not reach his eyes and I thought he was joshing me.

I looked over my shoulder at my cousins and said, "I've got a dime. Anyone else have some money?" I knew *two bits* equaled a quarter. Dad did a magic disappearing trick with a quarter which he called it his two bits trick. That was big money to me but I really wanted to see what Skipper could do. My dog Suggs could not do anything special.

I was trying to imagine the possibility of teaching Suggs something new. All three cousins dug into their pockets. We collected two dimes and five pennies. I had to walk back to them since they were still hanging back. The money seemed a small price to pay to see a hobo dog dance and do tricks. However my cousins were looking at me like I was asking for a dollar from each.

Once I had the money in hand I walked over to Matt and handed him the seven coins. He tucked it away inside a tiny snuff tin he kept in an inside pocket. He then let the little white spotted dog out of his shirt, placing him on the hard packed ground. At first nothing happened and I had time to worry what my cousins would say if the man had taken our money for a dog that only knew how to walk around camp. Then Matt brought his hands together with a loud clopping sound. The move startled me because we had all been standing in the silence waiting for something to happen. I now figured Matt had been waiting to build anticipation and had done it well.

Skipper instantly stood up on his tiny hind legs and began to dance by turning in a circle a half dozen times. The little legs bobbed him up and down as he twisted around. It reminded me of a waltzing couple I had seen on the Lawrence Welk Show. With another gesture from Matt the puppy did three back flips paused, then three more. I began laughing out loud and could hear Jon Mark, David and Danny roaring with laughter behind me. All of us in the hobo hotel began clapping in earnest. Skipper seemed to enjoy our excitement and did three more back flips and began yapping excitedly. Delighted I felt like I was watching an episode of the Red Skelton Show on television.

After the show I felt a kind of kinship and was no longer afraid of the men. I wanted to ask a thousand questions starting with why they rode trains and how they found food. However I could see my cousins remained nervous and stayed near the entrance, seemingly ready to run at the first boo. Perhaps I should have been more cautious as well, but my curiosity was stronger than any remaining fear. Not knowing where to begin I said, "Thanks Matt. Skipper is a great dog." Hearing his name the puppy stood again and pawed the air like a stallion as if he were waving at me.

Looking closely at my surroundings I noticed a rope close line rigged between two trees holding drying clothes, a stack of gathered firewood, and not much else. I could not understand how these men lived with so little. The play forts I built in my backyard at home held more items to camp with and these men lived out here. At my aunt Marie's Jon Mark and I had sleeping bags and a pup tent when we camped. Turning now to look in the direction of the fire I asked, "What's in the pot Rex?" I did not normally address adults by their given name, but he was the youngest of the three men. He was sitting crossed-legged on the ground as he tended the fire and whatever he was cooking.

He quit stirring the brew and tasted the dish from what appeared to be a large hand carved spoon. Rex was strongly built like a construction worker but thin like he had missed a few too many meals. Now he smiled broadly. "Well Buddy I call it pot luck stew. I'll even share the secret ingredients with you boys. If we trap a critter, it is *luck* for us and it goes in the *pot*. To celebrate this fine Christmas day we are having fresh possum. Tomorrow night we might be dining on squirrel or even a fat juicy rat. You and your kin are welcome to our fire tonight or any other." He ginned at me before offering me the spoon for a taste.

My face must have shown my distaste for his meal. I had eaten squirrel meat that dad and grandpa had hunted and it was not too bad. I had even heard of my relatives who lived far out in the country eating possum, but never a rat. I hoped he was just teasing me on that one. Trying to be polite I said, "No thank you Rex. We are overdue back at my grandma's house. In fact we better leave soon before we get into trouble for being late." I directed my next question to Buster. "Why do you live out here mister? It seems like fun and I like to camp out but don't you get cold in the winter and soaked when it rains?"

Buster looked around himself as if he was surprised a palace was not surrounding him. "Well it does get cold and wet out here but we make do. I expect there are many reasons why a man becomes a hobo. Some are hurting for work and have nowhere else to live. Others like me want to live free and easy. I think of the road as their home. I can tell you boys for certain that I have seen me some sights in my day. I've been to just about every state in the union and wherever I lay my head is home."

Before I could ask anything else Jon Mark suddenly appeared beside me, his anxiety apparently forgotten for the moment. He took a couple of steps toward Buster and found his voice. He was only eight years old but stood in the middle of the hobo jungle and said, "My cousins and I ride the trains too. We jump on as the trains come through or are parked and ride up to a mile, then walk back." The three men acted as if they were smothering the urge to laugh. I did not understand the joke and looked at each face. I began to think they were humoring us, but the joshing seemed to be in good fun. I realized that to the hobos our exciting adventures must seem pretty tame.

Matt spoke in his rough-as-gravel voice. Jon Mark and I had to lean in to hear him in his low, almost whisper of a voice. "My fellows, we might have some first class hobo recruits in these boys. I recollect a day long before I lived on the rails. I had a ma and pa who took care of me, but I ran away to see the world. After I fought in the First World War and it cost me my eye it was hard to get hired. I guess my looks make folks nervous. Anyway the President of these United States, I don't recall which one, gave me a pension so I get by on my little dab of money and a bit more from little Skipper here. I'm with friends and I have all a body needs."

We left the hobo jungle and hurried back to grandma's house on the run. The hobos had been friendly but we were afraid we were late for supper. I knew my parents would want to get back on the road soon. As we ran I had a thought and stopped my cousins a block from the house. While we caught our breath I said, "What do you think about taking those hobos some food? We have plenty to eat and those men have almost nothing."

Jon Mark was all for the idea but David and Danny argued we would all get into trouble. They might be right but our parents and churches gave to the poor all the time. Shouldn't we do the same given a chance? I figured the only thing mom and dad would object to was that the men might be dangerous. They had not harmed us so far so why would they hurt us now? I knew I would have to get help from at least David and Danny since they were not leaving until tomorrow. My decision made, I hurried the rest of the way to the house.

Fortunately for us we had not been missed. The delay in fixing the pipe had held off the reheating of the food and we were in time to wash up and eat. I felt guilty as I ate my fill from the leftovers. The men in the hobo jungle hotel were near starving. We were having our third meal of the day, if you counted my bowl of Captain Crunch, my favorite new cereal. I did not want to steal food but I was also afraid my parents would not allow me to return by myself. The more I thought about it I decided I had to tell mom and dad. I thought they would agree to feed the strangers and we could go by there on our way out of town.

Then dad announced that we were staying for the night and would leave in the morning. Sherry and I would make pallets on the floor of the living room along with my Aunt Barbara, Uncle John Ray, David and Danny. Now I had to talk dad into going down to the tracks with me. I believed I would be in trouble for playing by the tracks but it did not matter. It would be worth getting grounded for a month if it meant feeding the hobos a good meal.

As the dishes were being cleared I approached dad and asked him to go outside with me. I was sure he was thinking I wanted to talk to him about another story. Once outside it all came out in a rush of words so fast that dad had to stop me twice and have me back up and repeat something I had said. After I finished he was quiet while he thought it over. My dad was not a man to make snap judgments unless it was an emergency. I knew he would sit long hours with fellow church members who were sick. Also we helped collect food for the poor, but this might be risky and I did not know what he would say.

Finally, "You know you are in trouble for going down to the tracks. I never specifically said not to, but you know it is not safe to walk near the tracks. Secondly I'm glad you want to help out those men, but talking to strangers is something your mother and I have told you not to do. You are older than your cousins and I expect you to look out for them. You all could have been hurt or taken. How could we know where to begin looking for you if something had happened? Son there are children who go missing every year. It would kill your mother if she lost one of her children."

I looked at the floor. "I did not know that, but you're right dad. I deserve to be punished going down by the railroad tracks and for talking to strangers. Still, those men need help. Can we take them food? It's Christmas and all they have to eat is wild possum. Dad they have nothing else to eat as far as I could see."

He softened his stance at my plea. "You know John Ray and I used to work as carpenters for the railroad. We were not supposed to encourage riding the rails but we fed a few of the hobos in our days. I never liked to see anybody go to bed with an empty stomach. Let's go see what my ma can put together for your new friends. Your mother will be scared to death at the thought of you talking to the hobos, but I'm sure she will want to feed them too. My ma and your mother never met the person they were willing to have go hungry."

Relieved I followed dad into the kitchen where he began talking to grandma and mom. They both turned and looked at me a couple of times while he was speaking. My mother looked cross. I could not deny I deserved it. Grandma looked concerned and I did not know if it was for me or the hobos. I figured that if they decided to go feed the men it would be my last trek to the train tracks. Now I had not only gotten myself into trouble, but I had for sure dropped my cousins into the frying pan with me. We would all be in a fix together. So far wanting to do the right thing was not working so well for me.

In the next ten minutes the kitchen was a busy place as ham, turkey and all the remaining mashed potatoes, creamed corn, and green beans were loaded up. Grandma even put in a whole pumpkin pie and a jug of her sweet tea. I smiled broadly at the great feast that was being prepared for the hobos. My fear at being in trouble forgotten, grandma, mom, dad and I loaded the food into dad's Buick. As a last minute I asked mom to bring Deb. I wanted her to see Skipper dance. I then asked dad if he had a quarter on him. He nodded and told him I would need it after we got there. I rode up front to guide us to the Hobo Hotel. The dashboard clock read 7:00 o'clock.

I directed dad to drive alongside the tracks until it became too narrow for the wide car. It was not much further and we gathered the food and began to walk. I hurried because the sun was starting to set and it would be hard to see in the trees. When we entered the hobo jungle the fire had been built up against the evening cold and made seeing a little easier. I only saw the fire blazing but the hobos were nowhere in sight. I looked into the thick stand of trees and could not make out anyone. Dad's face was reflected in the light and he said, "I'll bet they are hiding Buddy. Hobos are not too trusting of strangers. Holler out to them son."

Cupping my hands to my mouth I called to them by name. "Buster, Rex, Matt, where are you? This is my family. Come on out okay?"

Silence, then I heard a crack as someone shifted weight or stepped on a branch. A strong cry, followed by an involuntary oath as if someone had been hurt sounded loud from somewhere ahead in the dark. If I had not been with dad I would have turned and run. I knew who was out there, but my imagination conjured up wicked, harry beast who would jump out any second. Finally, uncertainty and worry was clearly heard in a disembodied voice heard coming from the darkness. "Buddy, why did you bring people here? We never did you boys no harm or nothing. We don't want any trouble."

It was Buster's voice, hidden somewhere in the trees. He was now to my right and must have been on the move when we heard him. I saw that dad too was puzzled at the swift unheard movement. The hobos were being stubborn and I decided to tell them why we were here. "It is okay Buster we've brought some food." I stopped to listen, but heard nothing stirring in the dark. Was it possible they had moved away as I was speaking? Raising my voice even louder I made one last attempt. "I know you can get along without help from anybody but today is Christmas. Everyone should have something special on Christmas. Come out please." I thought I heard Deb crying behind me. I knew if they did not come out soon we would have to leave the food and go.

Then I saw Buster, Matt and Rex peeking out from a massive tree trunk of an East Texas Pine Tree. Slowly the men began making their way back to their fire. They walked woodenly and reminded me of wild animals, afraid, but hungry enough to approach humans for food. I noticed Buster was limping. When they stopped before us I introduced the men to my parents, grandma and Deb, who hung back clinging to grandma's dress. The men appeared as shy as my little sister. They acted not at all like the bold hobos I had spoken to earlier.

As the food was unloaded their eyes opened wide as they watched. Grandma had packed one of her homemade quilts to place the food on. Mom had included paper picnic plates, forks and spoons. Buster built up the fire for additional light. He grinned at me, his face reflected in the campfire. "I tripped over a log out there and skinned my knee like a fool. Buddy you gave us a fright a few minutes back. We figured you for Railroad Police or local lawmen."

"Sorry about that Buster." Nodding his head in response, I watched in awe as he woofed down a large amount of turkey and potatoes with enthusiasm. I was not sure he chewed it much either. "Okay I promise not to tell anyone else you are here. My cousins and I just wanted the three of you to have a good meal for Christmas."

Rex said around a piece of ham he was chewing on, "Thank you kindly folks. Now this boy here is a right fine young man. Buddy and his cousins come along the path and as boys do, they stumbled upon us. We had a nice chat but never thought there would be good grub heading our way, this day or any other. I have not eaten anything so tasty since leaving my mamma's house at fifteen. Most folks don't trust strangers and avoid hobos in particular."

While he had been talking Deb had wormed her way to the front no longer afraid. Then I saw why as Skipper was peeking out from the tattered jacket Rex was wearing. I had almost forgotten the pup and turned to dad. "Do you have that quarter dad? I want Deb to see something funny. That is Skipper looking around. He smells food and I'll bet he wants a bite."

Rex poked the food he had been enjoying into his mouth and let Skipper lick his fingers. When dad handed me the coin I tried to give it to Rex but he refused. "No sir, you keep your money. You folks came all the way down here to feed us. I, we are much obliged by your kindness. It has been a passel of years since anyone has been this kind." He gave the signal and Skipper started to dance. Debra dissolved into amazed giggles that were quickly followed by mom, grandma, and dad's laughter.

After skipper performed for us the dog was fed some scraps and Matt began eating again. I saw that his one good eye was crying as he ate. I wanted to cry too but dad saved me with a reassuring squeeze of my shoulder as he sat beside me. We stayed about thirty minutes before slowly walking back to the car. We had exchanged hugs all around, Merry Christmas blessings and friendly goodbyes. I could not help but worry that the men would be cold or hungry tomorrow or the next day. Would anyone else come along to help them?

As we walked I said, "Will they be alright dad? What if nobody else ever comes by to help them? They might die out there. "

"I'm certain they will be fine Buddy. Those men are a hardy bunch. I've met like-minded men before and they are capable of taking care of themselves. It was good for us to help them, but they would have gotten by without it. Most of them have chosen that life and refuse to be boxed in or conform to what we might believe is a normal life. You should think of them like the stories you've read about famous explorers, Gypsies and the like. The only life they know is the sea or the road."

The ride back to the house was quiet, with everyone lost in their own thoughts. In my community food was collected and donated by churches every year to feed the poor, but this was the first time I had seen hunger up close. As dad pulled into the driveway mom said, "Buddy that was a fine thing to do. We are very proud of you for caring about those men. You are still grounded to the yard for a week for going there, but I think you knew that was coming. Now you are aware of what you should be thankful for everyday. There are many poor people who go to bed hungry every night. We may not have a lot, but more than many others. Tonight I think you should include those men and others like them who have little or nothing in your nightly prayers."

All things considered I knew that I had gotten off light. Being grounded to the yard meant I could at least play with my friends until they got bored and went elsewhere. Another type of grounding I hated was to the house. That punishment was the worse and meant I could not leave the house. If it was during the school year I would have to go straight home and go in. I loved to be outside hiking and playing games with my friends. It was gruelingly hard to watch the world going by from the wrong side of a window. "Yes mom, I will."

# CHAPTER 33

## *The Trail to Tomochic*

The next morning grandpa, dad, John Ray and I ate breakfast early. We then walked outside to the front porch. The street was quiet now with most everyone still off work for the holidays. The morning air was fresh and crisp, but the sun was shining. I was wearing a light jacket. For once I was not thinking about a story. My mind was occupied by the hobos in the woods. I hoped they were alright and still had food left over for breakfast. John Ray and his family would be leaving for his long trip back to Florida after lunch. I would miss my cousins until next Christmas. Now I was not sure if I had put them into trouble along with myself.

My mom, grandma, Aunt Barbara, Debra and Sherry were going downtown to the Texarkana Farmer's Market. David and Danny had to go along with their mother to hunt down some underwear and socks at Sears. They were not too happy about it either. Come to think of it they were not happy with me either. Neither had spoken to me since last night when I got us all into trouble.

Before I knew it grandpa was talking about Mexico again. I was surprised that I had nothing to do with it this time. I guessed that once he had opened up the memories they flowed out as readily as butter melted on warm toast. Maybe this time John Ray, dad, or both had asked grandpa to finish his story. After all we were all going home and who knew when we would all be together again. Next Christmas was far away and I might not be able to come again this summer. As much as I had loved grandpa's letter I liked hearing him in person best of all.

After the battle in Guerrero, we rested three days and restocked supplies from the town. I figured Colonel Dodd was not resting his men as much as the horses and mules. The citizens were wary of us but not outright hostile, which was good enough for me. I did not want an angry peasant sticking a pitchfork in my back as I walked down the street. The wounded had been interviewed. So far no new information had been received about the present location of Villa or his men. Our scouts had followed the trail of the escaping bandits for two days without success. Apparently the trail had been lost over a dry rock surface that extended for miles.

On the second day after our liberation of Guerrero I was present during a meeting between Colonel Dodd, the town mayor and other prominent citizens. Alex was there to translate the exchange. The colonel pressed Mayor Estefan Vega for information about Villa. The mayor was a stout man of perhaps forty. He spoke with his hands always moving to make his point. He was a handsome man and not easily pushed around by Colonel Dodd. He was cooperating but not matched wills easily with the colonel. Vega told the colonel through Alex that Pancho Villa had rode out two days before we arrived. He had an estimated one hundred and fifty men riding with him. Two men had slipped into town to warn Villa. The men had attempted not to be seen but in the small town it was not to be. The next morning Villa and his men had fled.

Alex looked at Colonel Dodd who was standing impatiently for the last bit of information to be translated. "I believe him colonel. He seems genuinely grateful to get the bandits out of town or killed. The town was helpless to defend against Villa and his men. The young women were hidden in caves to save them from being violated. He says Pancho Villa believes himself a demagogue, who all Mexicans should honor. Other citizens I have questioned separately tell more or less the same story. Villa's wounded men say he will hide in caves near *Tomochic* until his leg wound heals."

Colonel Dodd shook hands with Mayor Vega and chewed furiously on his cigar as he weighed his next move. "Well, we have a destination at last. Thank you Sergeant Alejandro. Your assistance has been most appreciated." He turned to a young 7th Cavalry lieutenant and snapped an order. Have all the men return to camp as soon as possible. Instruct the troopers we will ride out at dawn." Turning back to Alex he said, "Eleazar, I will see to it that you receive the highest approbation in my next report to General Pershing."

I turned to the door thinking about all the details I would need to attend to in preparation for us breaking camp that early. When Alex joined me a minute later I could not help but tease him. "Oh *Eleazar*, you are so helpful. How would we win the campaign without you? So now you and the colonel are on a first name basis? I guess I'll have to learn to pronounce your first name now that Colonel Dodd will be calling on you every other minute. Also what the hell does *approbation* mean anyway? I've read a book or two and never saw that five dollar word."

He grinned at my sarcasm and said too seriously, "I'm only fulfilling my duties as requested by the esteemed Colonel Dodd. He does use big words, but I think he means to commend me highly to our famous General Pershing."

I responded in mock disgust. "A cavalry soldier needs a commendation like he needs a cup of water when it is raining buckets. I suppose the *good* colonel will issue every man extra blankets when the temperature reaches 110 degrees in the shade. If I didn't know your smugness is not real I'd slug you." Now I was riding hard and added, "I hope you haven't forgotten your native Spanish language got me and Sean into this mess in the first place. I was looking forward to giving you a farewell party and seeing you off from camp. Now my butt has blisters on top of more blisters because of your darn handy usefulness."

He laughed at my complaints. "Ah my friend if I recollect correctly *you* wanted to be back in the Army with your friends on the border. I must remind you that the Army is your home and that home is too often on the back of a horse."

"Well I recollect what was said was that I wanted to be *back* on the border, the *American* border. How far is this jerkwater town of *Tomochic* anyway?"

"*Por nada mi amigo.* It is nothing. It matters only to your horse as he carries your blistered butt there. All you have to do is enjoy the scenery, hang on, and not fall off."

I tried not to smile as I shook my head from side to side. I had always found it hard to stay grumpy around Alex. His sense of humor was contagious. "With friends like you I certainly could do without so many bad men in Mexico trying to kill me? Sometimes I can't tell the difference between my good friends and bad enemies."

Following Colonel Dodd's orders we were back on the trail before dawn. The men were grumpy but ready to be back on the move. Troopers knew that no end to this daily hell would come until Villa was no longer a threat. We could look upon the recent battle as a victory. However being so close to capturing Villa and missing our chance by no more than twenty-four hours tasted bitter in my mouth. Now reliable information indicated Villa was ahead of us near or in Tomochic. We would once again have a chance to engage him or his men.

Colonel Dodd had fired the vaqueros after the suspicion they had deliberately stalled our travel to allow Villa to make good his escape. It was even supposed that the men or confederates may have been the ones who warned Villa. By noon we were far from our previous camp and had been in the saddle for over six hours. We were allowed a thirty minute break to eat a portion of hardtack, which were dry rations every man carried in his saddle bags. The rations were made from flour, water and salt pounded into a hard cracker or biscuit. The only foreseeable benefit was the rations would not spoil while on the trail. I usually ate the hardtack by breaking off a piece and let it soak in my mouth to soften before swallow it.

My stomach growled and I wished I had bought more of the tasty hard candy in Guerrero if some could be had. I began daydreaming of a plump young and tender javelina stumbling into camp tonight when we stopped. Heck, even a tough-as-leather old javelina would be better than hardtack rations. I was sitting on the ground with Sean leaning back on my saddle when Alex dropped down beside us. There was no shade anywhere and we were due to leave in ten more minutes.

I opened one eye slightly and saw him slide a small canvas bag out of his shirt. The aroma hit me immediately as he passed us each a nice sized chunk of some sort of jerky.

After seeing our surprise he said, "Compliments of Mayor Vega, or actually his oldest daughter." He sighed heavily before saying, "Ah Abelinda, her name means beautiful serpent. Her pretty brown eyes burn their way into my soul."

"Thanks Alex. This is a welcome treat. I needed a break from these dry rations. I'll bet they will still be digesting inside me when I'm an old man. It is like chewing on a piece of old boot leather." Savoring the salty taste of jerky as it trickled down my throat, I added, "I don't care if this is buzzard meat, it taste wonderful." Suddenly recalling what else he had said, I remarked, "I'm thinking you didn't spend *all* your time in town translating."

Sean spoke around a big bite. Yea this is a nice surprise. I owe you Alex. So what does Miss Abelinda look like? Are you going to ride back this way some day and raise a half dozen little Alejandros?"

"My friends with the mention of her name I am breathless. She is as fresh as a new colt pony. I am most tempted by her beautiful eyes. Abelinda has a figure a man would gladly die for if only it could be wrapped in her arms. During the Guerrero battle she was shooting from her father's window. She shot two bandits, one out of his saddle and the other as he ran on foot. The first time I saw her she was sighting down the barrel of an old rifle. She took the fleet-footed raider off his feet. It was his last race. While the other women sheltered in caves she refused her father's wishes to hide. Instead she loaded some rifles and joined our fight."

We were quiet for a minute and I tried to envision what the scene must have been like. To die at the hands of a young woman would be the ultimate disgrace for a Villista bandit. Finally Alex said sadly, "Much to my chagrin she is taller than me. I'm thinking she is yet too young as well. Of course this thing may not end for months. Perhaps if I survive this conflict, and she will permit me, I will visit my sweet Abelinda again. She has beguiled me like the masterful serpent in the *Garden of Eden*."

Absolutely stunned by his words I thought the desert was affecting my hearing. "I have never heard you talk like this Alex. I can't believe you did not introduce us while we were in town. That's just rude. She must be some beauty to catch your eye. Let me think about this a moment. She is too young and too tall. Well the way I see it beauty and a crack shot can make a man forget all the rest." Looking at Sean I said, "Did you hear Alex? He is now using bigger words that Colonel Dodd. I think maybe he *is* love sick. Or perhaps he is just feverish from the heat. I guess we had better catch our bandits quickly so Alex can return to claim his young Amazon bride."

Sean could not help himself. "I'm happy for you Alex." All kidding aside, we could all use a good woman to keep us on the right trail." He stopped, grinned broadly and added in a sinister tone, wiggling his right hand in a snake-like motion. "Beware of the serpent's bite. If you don't treat her well she will surely banish you from the garden."

That evening we camped in time to watch the sun slide down in a great fiery ball in the west. I had never seen a sunset this large. It appeared the sun was touching the earth. I envisioned a great battle between the night and the day. The heat we cursed during the day was prayed for before the cold nights ended. Desert sands radiated captured heat long after dark, but on this evening the sun fought mightily to hold onto the day. Shielding my eyes against the last glare it was as if the sun refused to relinquish rule over the day.

On this early evening we were allowed campfires long enough to cook our meals. Men huddled around camp and combined whatever they carried in a communal pot. One man had traded tobacco for wild onions found by one of the scouts. Alex mixed in some of the jerky to flavor the pot, shared by Alex, Sean and me. While eating I began counting campfires which covered easily the length and breadth of a parade ground. I lost count at a hundred. My last thought as I burrowed into the sand for the last remaining heat of the day was that the flickering fires blinking out one after the other appeared as stars suddenly snuffed out like the lives of the innocent Pancho Villa and his men had killed. How many more would die before this crazy hunt was over?

# CHAPTER 34

## *Death Stalks the 7th*

We spent the better part of April in the saddle. The conditions and grub did not improve much. Our eyes burned with the sting of alkaline as we traveled through the desert. Alkaline was found in many of the desert water sources. It dried into crystals and blew with the sand. We were able to see the white alkaline beds from far off, but they were often dry of water. When we did find water in the alkaline beds, even though it was not poisonous, the water was bitter and slippery to the touch. Sometimes a body had to make do with whatever was available.

Eventually we made our way to the country surrounding the town of Tomochic. We had been beaten by blistering days, cold nights, and the harness of the foreign world we traveled through. There had been days with little food and scarce water for the men and horses. On more days than I wanted to remember my urine was bright yellow indicating dehydration. I had taken my belt in a couple of notches as well. Looking into the faces of the men I saw sunken cheeks and gaunt features. We had all lost weight, but the inner strength that I believed every man possessed had seemingly been lost.

It was near noon when we stopped to survey our situation. Three men were sent into town for supplies and to judge the friendliness of the town. The scouts reported the town was a little over a mile away to east of where we had selected to camp. The town could not be seen with the view obscured by a lazy haze lingering from the morning dew. This time Sean was one of the three chosen to enter the town first. He had a rudimentary use of the Spanish language and was the ranking man sent in. Sean, a corporal and a private rode in driving pack mules ahead to fetch supplies.

Alex had ridden off alone in hopes of hunting or trapping down some grub for our empty bellies. I had argued strongly against his lone ride. However he had been insistent upon the need to forage alone to lessen the noise men made while moving about. We would not exactly starve on our rations, but basic animal fat was needed. Alex was familiar with native plants which could be eaten or herbs which were used for injuries. His knowledge was invaluable.

Since returning to serve with my friends on the border and in Mexico, I felt a slight unease when we were separated. During a fight like we encountered in Columbus and Guerrero, it was impossible to know where your friends were at any given moment. However just knowing Sean and Alex were nearby fortified my own will to endure the madness of war and survive it. Few would talk about the grisly details we witnessed or were part of during a battle. Most of us pushed the memories deep down somewhere inside and hammered the door shut. Although, at least for me there were times in my dreams when I would see the faces of the men I had killed. I felt regret for the deaths only in the sense that all of it could have been avoided in a sane world where men did not victimize the weaker among us.

Our scouts were out searching canyons and nearby cliffs for caves or other hiding places where Villa could be. If he still had one hundred and fifty men with him it would take a sizable area to hide the Villistas and their horses. As with many towns or villages in Mexico, *Tomochic* was reported to be small. The resources of the town would probably not support such a force of men unless the bandits stripped it of all available supplies. We were mostly used up, had few supplies, and some of the men had taken a chance on some brackish water found yesterday and were now sick. One of my men told me the date was April 22nd.

While the men set up camp, I observed some slapdash efforts at setting up a security perimeter. Using up the last of my reserves, I angrily cajoled, shouted, and whatever else it took to roust the troopers around me to improve the shoddy work. Our lives depended on being alert and ready for a sudden attack. With Villa said to be in the area, other officers and sergeants were riding and walking about the camp doing likewise. The men were exhausted and had to be prodded to perform every basic duty. As for me, my motivation was the desire to not be buried on this desolate piece of land. Or if nobody was left for a burial, I did not want my bones scattered by predators, or left bleaching in the sand for uncountable years.

By 2:00pm I was feeling satisfied with our defenses and sat down to rest in the partial shade of a Desert Willow. The tree was about ten feet tall and provided enough shade for half a dozen men. Neither Sean nor Alex had returned, with my duties complete I had nothing else to do. Before long I was nodding off under the tree in a propped up position. My Springfield was across my lap and the Colt was comforting weight in my hand. I had slept little in the past weeks and now my head was heavy. I stopped fighting the urge to surrender to my fatigue and slept.

Three shots rang out in quick session and I was on my feet. Was it rifle or pistol? I was sure it had been rifle shots. Did I dream it or…No, others were looking around too. Then shouts were heard and a bugle charge was sounded. I ran for my horse with my saddle slung heavily over my shoulder. Unlike the raw recruits in Columbus, these men of the 7th knew danger was near and had quickly mounted their horses and readying to charge. Once we were mounted up and directed our horses to face toward the town, we were given orders to move out at a steady trot. Even though the horses were underfed and done in they sensed our excitement and wanted to run.

The word came back through the columns that scouts had observed a large Villa band which had approached the town from the east side, opposite our position. The Villistas were said to be a hundred yards out of town and were walking their horses slowly. Where the shots had been fired from was anybody's guess but it had made Villa's men cautious in their approach. We cut the distance to the town quickly with the ground eating pace. With the haze gone, we were throwing up dust that I was sure could be seen on the other side of *Tomochic*. We skirted the main street and circled to the south side. Then we saw them, more than a hundred strong. The bandits had stopped their mounts as if undecided about their next move.

Without orders we charged right among them. Within an instant the killing and dying enveloped us. It was close in, horribly grisly work. I fired five times with the Colt and knew I had hit at least three men. It was poor shooting to miss at such close range. I had no way of knowing if my hits were fatal. This time I remembered not to empty both weapons. I holstered the Colt and drew out the Springfield just as a bandit on horseback charged directly at me. He held a sword high at an angle ready to slice at my head. In desperation I turned my horse sharply, and then ducked until my face was pressing into my reins. I heard the swish of his blade as it missed me by mere inches. I turned in the saddle and shot him at the base of his neck. He slid off his horse, lost in the roaring commotion of shouting men and constant firing.

As before, I was impressed with the accurate and well disciplined fighting of the 7th as they emptied many saddles. Whizzing bullets zinged around us like an angry swarm of hornets. Suddenly I was pitched forward tumbling heavily to the ground, losing a grip on my rife as my mount was hit. Momentarily stunned I frantically fought to recover my footing. As any cavalryman would, I felt helpless on foot and looked around in desperation to find another horse. My own horse was nearby thrashing in pain, eyes wild in panic. Foolishly I took a moment to put the horse down with my Colt. In the next moment as I swung around to address the fighting, I was knocked off my feet once more. This time the impact was so solid it could only have come from the hindquarters of a spinning horse's rump. My Colt was knocked a dozen feet away.

I clawed my way back to my knees, shaking my head in an attempt to clear it. I felt like a punch-drunk fighter and was vulnerable and unarmed. Before I recovered I heard a demented shriek ahead of me. Looking up I was in time to see a bandit on foot rushing right at me. He did not appear to have a weapon I could see. Near panic, I took a moment to look for my weapon or any other. The man was bleeding from a head wound and I was tasting blood in my own mouth. Looking into his insane, hate filled eyes I knew his intention was to kill me with or without a weapon. If I could not recover my wits in the next few seconds I would surely die.

A second later he crashed into me. His momentum tumbled both of us into the dust. He immediately began gouging my eyes. I in turn took a firm grip on his throat. I began squeezing with all my waning strength. He was on top of me and his weight was making it more difficult to maintain my hold on his throat. His fingers blinded me and I saw white stars exploding behind my eyes. I continued to choke him while twisting and straining my neck back and away from his thumbs. I wanted to reach up and pull his hands away to lessen the pain. However the one single thought I could muster was to throttle him until he stopped his attack, either dead or unable to continue his assault.

I feared the man had won. From some unknown reserves of strength, even while my arms burned and ached, I reached down deep and forcibly willed my muscles to toil harder. I kicked upward with my right leg and managed to flip us over. Now on top I added my weight to his neck. He continued to apply pressure on my eyes, although less. The pain was unbearable. The blinding white light began to fade and darkness closed in on me from the outside in. Knowing I was blacking out. My last thought was that it was over for me. I had lost the fight and now was dying.

Pain thundering behind my eyes like a thousand suns woke me. I could not see anything and did not know if it was day or night. My hands were cramping but empty. I heard no sounds of battle. Now the familiar noise of an Army camp began to float to my ears. It was like someone was slowly turning up the volume on a radio. I heard a cup rattle and water or coffee being poured. I smelled campfire smoke with the sound of food sizzling as it broiled. I had heard it said that if you felt pain you knew you were still alive. Doing a quick mental check I felt plenty of aches all over my body. My tongue was swollen and hurt like I had chopped down on it during the fight. My eyes were the worst with a torturous throbbing that matched the rhythm of my heartbeat.

Lost in thought I was startled to hear a familiar voice. "Feel like a drink Oscar?" It was Alex and his voice sounded gloomy.

Was I dying? If that was to be the way of things why did I wake up at all? Why not die before I had to endure this unsighted agony of pain? Rushing the words out in one breath I said, "Alex what's happening? Am I going to die? I can't see a damn thing! Am I blinded for good?" My voice had been rough and cracked when I spoke, my thick tongue made it hard to form the words. Taking several gulps of air I tried to calm myself.

Placing a restraining hand on my shoulder he said, "Slow down Oscar. Let's deal with one question at a time. Take a drink first." He held a cup of cool water to my lips and I took a long drink. I felt a bandage tied around my eyes. It was wet and cool to the touch. "You are not dying and the town doctor does not think you are blinded permanently. He did say it will be a few days or possibly weeks before you are able to see very well."

"What happened in the fight? Did we win? What about the bandit I was fighting with? I felt myself blacking out and figured I was a cooked goose."

"First, nobody will have to worry about him again. You took care of him *real* permanent. We buried him up on Tomochic's Boot Hill hours ago. After the shooting stopped I found you and him still clutching onto each other in the last moments of an unreal dead struggle. I thought you were both dead."

He stopped and gave me another drink. I forced myself to slow down and think. "Were you headed back to camp when the ruckus started, or hear the firing and then join us?"

"I heard the first three shots and rode into the fight right near the beginning. I had been riding back into camp wondering where everyone was when I saw the 7th charge the town. You and that dead bandit sure had yourself a tumbling brawl. His windpipe was broken and both of his thumbs were dislocated from pushing on your leathery eyes. I can't say if you're lucky or just too ornery to die. I think you must have bitten your tongue pretty bad too. I imagine it will be long in mending. You both were covered in blood with no way to know who it belonged to.

"Forgive me if I don't feel too lucky right now."

"We killed about thirty or so of them before they retreated. They had all of the 7th Cavalry that they wanted and more. That old bastard Pancho got away again." He paused and I waited impatiently, wanting to know everything. Finally he finished softly. "Oscar I'm sorry. We took two casualties."

On the last part his voice had dropped to an unnatural pitch that brought me up short. I sat up sharply, the blood rushing to my head. For an instant I thought I was going to pass out again. Alex reached out a restraining hand to push me back down but I resisted. "Where is Sean? Is he okay? He went into town with two other soldiers. I didn't see him during the fight, but it was so sudden, there was not time to look around." I could hear the desperation in my voice even as I said it.

"He is dead Oscar. The three shots we all heard was an ambush. Some of Villa's men were waiting in town. The shots were to be a signal to Pancho and his men to ride in braced for trouble. That was the bandits you and the 7th tangled with. You knew as well as I that it was inevitable that sooner or later we would lose a man. I know it doesn't help but Sean knew the risk as well as the rest of us. I hate the loss of any man. Sean was a good man and close friend. He didn't deserve to die like that."

My pain momentarily forgotten, I said in a weak voice, "What happened in town? Please tell me they got the bandits who killed them."

"It appears Sean, the corporal and a private were loading supplies onto pack mules when rifle fire cut them down. The shots came from a window above the hotel. I'm guessing they never had a chance and it was over quickly. The private, a soldier by the name of Kevin Berg survived, but was shot through the body. I believe the shot missed anything vital. He will be shipped back to recover in the United States. I know the man. He is a good soldier and was one of my trainees when I first made sergeant. I believe he was born over in Kansas, Missouri. I think I can understand what you meant now about feeling responsible for the men under your command. Sometimes I feel like a mother hen clucking over her chicks.

I had heard enough and could not deal with anymore bad news this night. Suddenly I had no more questions. I lay back and curled up on my bedding. I just wanted to sleep and maybe not wake up. If the Lord decided to take me tonight I would look upon it as a blessing. My grief seemed to be like a solid black object. I could reach out and throw a loop on it but not push it away from me. I felt somehow responsible for Sean's death and yet could not think how or what I could have done differently. With deep regret and sorrow thick in my words I said, "Alex I'm tired and need some rest. I lost my Colt and Springfield when my horse was shot out from under me. If you can find replacements tonight would you put them beside me? I can't see anything but it will make me feel better."

"Sure, you want me to fetch you some grub? We have plenty of supplies now. Our scouts backtracked bandits by following the trail to Villa's camp. They had already disappeared, scattering in smaller bands, probably to meet up again later. They scattered like the rats they are, leaving plenty of provisions behind. I was lucky enough to bag us a couple of javelinas on my way back to camp. That is the aroma drifting on the night air. The javelinas are big fat ones and are roasting over the fire as we speak."

"No thanks Alex. Just get me the guns. I need to rest and work this out for myself." Making a feeble attempt at sounding confident I added, "I'll be right as rain in the morning."

Without hesitation he said, "Alright, I'll also save some choice meat for your breakfast. I expect you will be hungry come morning. You'll need to eat to regain your strength and heal those wounds properly." He paused before continuing. "Oscar, I hate to bring this up but I believe it needs to be said. If you do not recover your sight, you'll be forced to return with the other wounded to the American side of the border. I imagine then you will be discharged. I'm not saying it will happen my friend, but I want you to consider the possibility if things take a turn for the worse." He waited and when I did not reply he walked away.

I could hear every soft footfall as he moved off. I counted twelve steps in the sand before he stopped. With no sight I was amazed at my new ability to hear the tiniest noise. It was as if my other senses were standing in for my lack of sight. I waited a few seconds. Then I heard him walk back toward me. I estimated he covered half the distance back toward me before stopping again as if unsure of something. Knowing my old friend as I did, I saw in my mind's eye him shaking his head as if trying to dislodge a disturbing thought.

The blindness made the loud silence unbearable. "Alex I'm not going to kill myself. I didn't let the bandit do it did I? I want to live to see this through. I'm not beaten yet and not ready to quit this fight. You don't even have to load them. I expect just having them nearby will be a comfort. Also get my kit so I can polish Bill's buckle." He did not immediately answer so I added, "One more thing, as for me leaving, it won't happen that way. You and I will finish this dust up together. You can count on that."

# CHAPTER 35

## *Casa Grande at Last*

The next morning I awoke to more aches in more places than I had ever experienced. Thankfully I had not dreamed and relived the previous day of dreadful horror. I wanted to ask Alex if it was true about Sean's death or just a nightmare. Unfortunately I felt the loss inside. My heart weighed heavy with the sorrow. I could hear the early rustling sounds of camp. The aroma of bacon, or more likely javelina, frying in a pan nearby could be heard as well as somehow tasted by my nose. I greatly appreciated the sounds and aroma of life. It was normal to me and what I needed this morning was routine. I was surprised by how hungry I was.

Of a sudden I realized I could see light. That was good news for a soldier. It meant I could keep my vow from the previous evening to Alex and myself. At least I hoped I could. The fact that I could see light indicated I would be able to see again, hopefully as well as before. I felt around by my blanket and found the rifle and pistol left by Alex. Between the weapons Alex had left two boxes of ammo. By touch I was easily able to determine which rounds were for the 03 Springfield and the Colt 45. In the next few minutes I had both loaded and ready. Alex had found my own holster since I could feel my initials carved on the leather. I hated myself this morning for the strong feelings of self-pity I was experiencing. I was wondering just what use a blind dope with loaded guns would be when I heard someone approaching me.

"Don't shoot me Oscar, I'm friendly." Alex had given up calling me Jim figuring nobody cared out here in the middle of smack dab nowhere.

It surprised me how fast we fell back into our accustomed banter. "You better have a plate of pan-fried javelina if you want to come near a *wounded-dog* blind fool with loaded guns."

"I'll take my chances. Yes I've got a plate for you and coffee too. I had to fight off the boys for some scraps of those wild pigs I brought in. You'd think it was brown sugar cured ham the way they fought over it."

He handed me the plate and I tucked into it like I had not eaten for a month of Sundays. The coffee was good too. We had not tasted coffee in weeks of traveling. In my experience coffee was always the first thing to run out on the trail. My tongue hurt with every bite or sip, but I did not let it slow me down. "This is wonderful. I didn't realize how weak I was from yesterday. If this grub was taken from Villa he must be living better than us."

Sarcastically he said, "Well the American Army is opposed to killing innocent folk and taking everything they own. We took a wagon full of grain and flour back to the town as a good will measure. There is no telling where Villa's foragers looted it from. Say, how about those eyes of yours? Any sign of improvement?"

With no real sincerity in my voice I said, "Good news, I'm seeing light and shadows. I'll have the eyes of an eagle in no time at all." Pausing I added, "Actually, to tell you the truth I'm thankful I can see anything. I was mighty fearful I would be blind for good. At the time I was sure that bandit was shoving my eyes back into my brain."

Turning somber he said, "Oscar, if you are staying there are only two choices. You can hitch a ride on one of the wagons we took from Villa's hideout, or ride attached to the mule string."

Both options felt like humiliation. "I'll ride a horse. Find that man who lost his mule over the mountainside. I'd trust him to guide me over the trail. Where are we heading anyway?"

"Casa Grande. We will meet up with General Pershing before receiving new orders."

My eyes ached with a dull throb. If it's up to me, I'd rather ride with anyone but the 7th. Not that I don't respect them, but those boys can be in the saddle before sunup, ride until noon, then fight until dusk. They aren't human."

Laughing he said, "I'm with you Oscar. Maybe we can get back with our own division, or ride with the general."

Thinking a moment I said, "About Sean, did you see him buried well?"

"Yes, with full military honors. We didn't have our fancy dress uniforms, but the boys in the 7th stood up proud. We dusted off our clothes as best we could and buried him proper. Afterwards I hired some local boys to see his grave is well cared for. I'm just sorry we can't send him back to Texas to his folks. That's two Texans now we've buried. The way I figure it Pancho Villa owes us a debt we're not through collecting on."

Within an hour I was back on a horse but being led along behind a mule string. The wagons were abandoned as too cumbersome for hurried movement. Gradually over the next week I regained my sight, but headaches remained a constant daily reminder of my close brush with death. I had discovered my eyes had been almost completely swollen shut which had added to my lack of sight. With the swelling gone I was once again free to ride away from the smelly wrong end of a mule. With time on the trail, I fretted over the past couple of years. I had been through a kind of hell on earth, some of it brought on by my own actions. I was still a young man, but today I felt a deep seated fatigue like my young soul had been drained away and replaced by that of an old man.

Finally arriving in Casa Grande we were amazed at the camp headquarters. Telegraph poles were strung to the camp. It was our first look at true civilization since leaving Columbus. Of more importance to us was the chow line. We were once again being fed by the Chinese cooks and what a difference it made. Our sorry looking underfed horses were turned out to pasture and new mounts were issued. From all accounts General Pershing was displeased that we had failed to capture Villa on two occasions. However he was excited to hear that we had engaged his men twice and won both battles, with great loss to Villa of men and supplies.

The camp was located in a tree lined area, spring fed, with lots of green grass for the horses. We were once again treated to Army cots and tents. To be up off the desert sand was a relief. I was mighty tired of having insects and small critters running across me in the night. I was sleeping well for the first time since leaving Columbus. Colonel Dodd arranged for several days of rest with no assigned duties. We were allowed to relax and recover from our forced march and tend to battle scars. My sight seemed to have returned to normal and the headaches had mostly disappeared.

I spent the lazy days watching Curtis biplanes fly in and out while completing aerial reconnaissance missions. Half had already been lost but the force was proudly calling itself the 1st Provisional Aero Squadron. The pilots not only flew reconnaissance, but carried dispatches to forward units and mail. The planes had run into trouble due to not being able to fly over the ten to 12 thousand foot mountains. Other problems included dust storms which grounded planes for days, and the desert heat damaging wooded propellers. Four planes had crashed while others had been cannibalized for parts to maintain other planes. Somebody had decided the national insignia of the 1st Aero Squadron would be a red star, painted on the rudder and wings. Even with the limited success of airplane operations it probably meant that flight would always be a part of the Army.

There was no place in Mexico where an American soldier could feel safe, but this camp was constantly patrolled on horseback and on foot by sentries. M1905 Howitzers were manned at all times against a surprise charge and set up on all four sides of the camp. If Pancho and his men attacked, they would be cut to pieces by the cannon fire. The Howitzers were sighted in at a one hundred, fifty and twenty-five yards. Any Villistas who braved that initial onslaught and survived would be cut down by machineguns. Mounted patrols were sent out daily to scout the hills and valleys surrounding camp.

We were in the state of Chihuahua. The town of Casa Grande was sleepy by American standards, but the largest we had seen so far on this side of the border. Along with a larger population came the luxuries of great eating and the ability to resupply any essentials we needed. The importance of the town was measured by the railhead which brought in many tons of needed supplies. The supplies were then unloaded by civilian workers. Everything we needed was supplied by the train or the town's citizens. It was obvious that Casa Grande had boomed in population, swelling in size. The easy profits the American forces brought to the area created a type of gold rush.

However, with the *gold rush* mentality of the new citizens of the town arrived debauchery of every sort. Cantinas stayed open all night and the Mexican beer flowed like the fountains I had seen photographs of from Europe. Off duty soldiers gambled, took up with sporting women, and drank until they were basically unfit for duty even into the next day. Alex suspected that Villa's bandits mingled with citizens and soldiers alike. By removing the bandoliers they typical wore, Villistas could walk unnoticed into town at any time. I did not know why the general allowed such depravity, but he either looked the other way or did not care.

I had observed this general lack of moral restraint before. It was possible that General Pershing would have been unable to stop the behavior if he tried. Only moving the troopers deeper in the desert would halt the running toward liquor and women. I did not personally care how a soldier carried on when off duty. My concern was in what kind of sorry jackleg condition the troopers would be in when we next had to fight. No saint myself I had been seldom sober and mostly useless after I was thrown out of the Army. My actions had hurt my family. I had lost all dignity wallowing in self pity. It was a long climb up out of the deep hole I had dug for myself. I had to admit the Army had been a big part of regaining my self-worth. Now I was becoming the man I wanted to be. I had been given the rare gift of a second chance at redemption.

Alex and I enjoyed a few good meals in town. Restaurants blossomed on every corner and from well located homes, now serving wild deer that had run free in town before the soldiers arrived. I began to put the weight back on I had lost on the trail. As usual

Alex made friends easily and discussed politics, religion and the ongoing Mexican Revolution with shopkeepers in his native Spanish. During those times I would sit back and feel about as useless as a knothole on the nearest wall. I knew enough of the language to pick up about one word in each sentence. Usually I could get the drift of the conversation. Alex always took the time to include me afterwards with what had been said.

One thing we both looked forward to was talking to troopers in other divisions. Soldiers would gather on every corner or while in camp swapping personal stories or reports of other divisions. We were not the only troopers who had suffered hardships with little food and water in the hard country we had ridden through. Snakebites, heatstroke, and every conceivable encounter with man or beast was thrown into a pot and stirred in with the genuine and imagined. Many of the tales were so fanciful nobody could take them seriously. However they were probably at one time grounded in fact. Now they were more folly than real, with the retelling and hearsay of drunken braggarts.

One verified story was about Major Robert Howze of the 11th Cavalry. He had led his men and a party of Apache scouts in a horse charge against bandits. The battle took place near a Mexican ranch called *Ojos Azules*. The hard charging cavalrymen attacked with pistols only. The original intent had been to engage machineguns in the fight, but the mules carrying the automatic weapons could not match the speed of the horses. The major and his men galloped straight at ranch house buildings where the bandits had taken shelter. Sixty-one bandits had been killed and, amazingly no casualties for the 11th Cavalry.

One crisp afternoon a northern wind was howling through camp with rain falling in the distance. I was feeling antsy for fear of a lightning storm. Then a Mexican boy of about ten was directed to me by nearby soldiers loafing outside the chow tent. He did not speak English but was waving a letter excitedly. Recognizing the handwriting as my ma's, I tipped the boy a nickel. He ran off as if I had just given him a month's wage. I looked at the letter with a mix of worry and yet was hungry for news of home. I tried not to hurry wanting to savor it a while before I opened it. I had not spoken to ma or had any contact with home since Columbus. It seemed ages ago now. I was hoping the letter would be full of ma telling me about her garden, pa, my siblings, or other various and sundry items, and not some sort of bad news. Finally, no longer able to control my anticipation I carefully slit one end open with my pocket knife. My hands were shaking so bad I took care not to cut myself. Inside was ma's loose script;

*"Oscar, it has been more than two months since we have spoken. I have written a letter a month and hope they are somehow making it through to wherever you are. Folks are well here. You need not worry about us. I have faith that you are well and taking care of yourself. I am so proud and yet fearful that you returned to face the Army once more. I know you will doubt me when I say your pa paces around the place in worry for you. Of course he frets constantly about your soul as well. Your pa is a stubborn man and you two are much alike. He reads every newspaper article for news of the conflict in Mexico. The talk is mostly about war in Europe but we do read awful reports of the horrible acts of Pancho Villa and his men. Other stories tell of dreadful clashes between the Army and bandits. Oscar, please believe that every day end with a prayer for you. Son, you should say a prayer for your own self now and again too. Love, now and in the hereafter."*

She had signed the letter with a simple, *"Ma."* I had tears in my eyes when I finished reading and was greatly relieved that nobody was sick at home. I wondered where the other letters had ended up but tried to be thankful for the one I did receive. I carefully folded the letter and placed it inside my shirt pocket. I planned on reading the letter again tonight just to be sure I had understood everything ma was saying. She was a self-taught woman and read everything she could find. Ma often spoke in riddles where simple words really meant something far different. I would have to study the letter and mull over her words carefully to be sure.

# CHAPTER 36

## *Ezekiel Lazarus (Shave Tail)*

The storm had not amounted to much and blew through without much real damage but plenty of comical drama. The storm spawned a dozen small twisters climbing no more than a dozen feet high, but filled with coarse desert sands. When the undersized tornados roared through camp, men and animals were spooked into instant calamity. Five horses broke free of tethers, their eyes wild and terrified as they thundered through camp knocking over what the wind had missed. I had seen what we call back home, *dirt devils* before, but never so many at one time.

From my vantage point I caught fast movement to my right. Turning to look in that direction I was just in time to see a young lieutenant upended as he ran in a picnic, the fast-swirling twister seemingly chasing him out of camp. He was not hurt but had to endure laughter coming from the hidden interior of a nearby tent. I stood my ground unafraid, relieved by the lack of expected lightning I had believed was coming. The ruckus ended magically when General Pershing appeared from his tent to see what the disturbance was. He had dispatch papers in his hands and wore a scowl on his face. As he looked about the camp the twisters dissipated at once as if they feared the wrath of the powerful man.

That night after the horses had been recovered and the camp returned to order, Alex and I sat long over our empty supper dishes talking. He had been quieter than usual all afternoon and I figured he must be thinking about his Abelinda. Alex went and refilled our coffee cups before sitting back down at the fire, which was nearest to our tent and now deserted but for us. Other troopers had drifted off to town or guard duty. I studied his face and waited knowing he would talk about what was bothering him in his own time. I believed I could read his face about as well as the one I saw in the mirror every day I had one. We sat in silence watching the yellow flames dance and crackle. I relaxed and settled down more comfortably. Off in the dark of the evening I saw fireflies flicker in the distance like small circling stars. I was counting the seconds between flashes when I heard him clear his voice.

"I saw a man I know in town today. He did not recognize me since I was only fifteen when last we met. He must have been a teenager himself when we first met, but was married to my mother's younger sister, Camilla. He was welcomed at our table on many occasions. I think he was no more than twenty when I left."

He paused and I waited. When he did not immediately continue I asked, "Did he know about your father beating your mother before she died?"

Alex reacted as if I had punched him in the stomach. I had not counted on the memory still affecting him after all the passing years. "I assume so. It was common knowledge in the town but women had no rights. Even respected men looked the other way if a man abused his wife. Women were like cattle or other owned property and often treated worse than a man's horse. As you know I wanted to kill my father but was too weak. After no one in town would help me against my father I just ran away. My mother's sister and husband were visiting out of town at the time of the beating. After she died I did not wait for them to return. My father was a known bad man. Most in town feared him. He would have killed anyone who dared to interfere. He traveled with like-minded outlaws who traveled far from home to places they were not known. They took from those who could not defend against them." He shook his head at a bad thought. "I still carry hatred and the heavy burden of shame at not protecting my mother. If she still lived I would not be here, but living near her."

I sat bolt upright astonished at his words. "That is a child's shame Alex! You were a boy and could not be expected to save your mother. The fault is entirely on your pa's shoulders and not of your making."

"I know that in my head, but still feel it in my heart." He thumped his chest to make his point. Aside from that the man's goes by the name of Ezekiel Lazarus Homdahl, an expatriate who married my fell in love with Camilla and stayed. His real first name is Emil and he speaks Spanish as well as I do. I am hungry to hear news of home. I need to know of my father's fate." He hesitated before saying, "Yet I am afraid to approach Ezekiel."

"Bah, if there is a man you fear I have not met him."

"Yes in battle, but I accept as true that often it is wiser to leave alone the demons living within us. There are ghost that should be abandoned to our past."

I nodded unable to argue his reasoning. "I don't know about all that, but his name sounds like something my pa would have named me had he thought about it. Ezekiel and Lazarus are straight out of the bible. Whatever, you decide I will support you my friend. However if it were me, I would want to know what became of your ranch and pa. He may be dead and the ranch yours."

In the firelight his eyes reflected a dreamy state. "Ah, my home was once a beautiful and green oasis seldom seen in the desert. An underground river has been forced up to the surface by some ancient movement of the earth. The water runs deep and cool across the ranch and then disappears suddenly with no trace. The land has natural stands of timber and green meadows for grazing cattle or sheep. It was given to my family as part of a Spanish land grant many generations ago. When I was younger I dreamed of returning to claim the property, but to do so would mean killing my father to regain what is mine by birthright. One of my ancestors named the ranch *San Miguelito*. I will sleep on the decision tonight. Perhaps in the morning I will feel differently and speak with Holmdahl."

With the first rays of the morning sun glowing orange in the east, Alex shook me awake. The new day had brought about a resolution for Alex. He was still nervous but also excited at the prospect of news from his boyhood home. I deduced this by slowly opening one eye. I peered at him from my sleepy state before saying, "If Pancho is not riding over the nearest hill toward us this minute I may shoot you in the leg."

He shifted his weight from one foot to the other like an excited little boy. Either that or he had to make water. "Oscar I need you with me on this one. I'm going to talk to Holmdahl this morning. Breakfast is on me in town. I'm retuning to where I last saw him. Hopefully he has not already left town."

I sat up and began pulling my boots on, after first turning them upside down to check for scorpions. "Alright Alex but you two need to parley in plain English. I don't like to wait for details through translation. Give me ten minutes to scrape my face and comb my hair." Grumbling to myself I shuffled away.

We found Holmdahl easily enough as he sat waiting on his food order in the busiest eating establishment in town. Maria's was attached to the hotel owned by Juan Soto, the largest rancher in the area. Ezekiel Lazarus Holmdahl was a bean pole of a man. He was a couple of inches over six feet tall, with red-brown hair curling around his face. He could have been mistaken for a school teacher except for the pistol on his hip and rifle across his lap. He had quick, darting eyes that scanned the room continuously like he had enemies.

As we approached him he ignored me but his eyes locked onto Alex. Before we reached his table he was out of his seat and walking quickly toward us. If it were not for his grinning face I would have been reaching for my Colt at his fast advance. "Eleazar Alejandro!" The rest was spoken in rapid Spanish. I was unable to follow a single word of it. The two men embraced which ended in a hardy handshake. Both men smiled broadly before Alex turned and indicated me. "Ezekiel, this is my friend Oscar Draper. We have ridden together for many years. I trust him with my life."

Switching to English effortlessly he said, "I'm pleased to meet you Mr. Draper. I am most delighted that fate has brought Eleazar and you to my slice of country. Please, join me for breakfast." We walked over and he made a place for us at his table. "I recommend the *chorizo* and *migas.* They make the dish better than my wife does, but don't tell her I said that."

Seeing the doubt on my face Alex said, "Chorizo is a flavored pork sausage. Migas are made with small pieces of corn tortillas usually served with scrambled eggs mixed in." I nodded and he ordered for us both in Spanish.

Still smiling happily Holmdahl said, "I see that you are both Army. I can only assume you are here for Pancho Villa." He paused and I saw dark thoughts in his eyes. He looked at Alex before continuing. "The Army brought you here but you came to me to know of your family."

Alex nodded before saying, "I thought the past was buried to me but seeing you in town yesterday, dug up many memories. I'm sorry I could not find you and explain why I had to go. Nobody would help me against my father. I knew if I stayed I would have to kill him."

"I figured it must have been something like that. It is the past but I wish I could have taken you in as my own. No one knew where you had gone and I hoped one day you would return."

Amazingly fast the food was served. Everything smelled delicious and looked even better. As the two men dug into their plates, I ignored my growling stomach and took the opportunity to ask a question, "How did you know it was Alex when we first came in?"

"Ah, senior that was easy. Eleazar has his mother and my wife's eye's. I have not set eyes on him since he was fifteen years old, but would know him at any age."

Leaning his elbows on the table Alex asked in a hopeful whisper, "Is Camilla well? I am ashamed to say I have been gone so long and never returned to visit her. I have not written and would not blame her if she refused to acknowledge my existence."

"Camilla frets over her brother daily. She is well and still as pretty as the day we were married. I swear she is ageless. The young men still much admire her. I find it necessary to knock a few heads occasionally just to keep them in their place."

The man was so earnest in his friendly manner and grinned so much I could not tell when he was joshing or serious. Now Alex asked the question I knew had weighed on his mind for many years. "What news is to be had of my father? Does he still live?"

Ezekiel answered in like fashion, sensing how hard this must be for his old friend. "Your pa lives and remains as mean as a rattler. It's a mystery why some men soften with age yet others grow bitter, raging through the day as if they were at war with life itself. It's a marvel I haven't shot him myself. He finds me useful and leaves me alone. I assure you he leaves Camilla and our children alone as well. Camilla would shoot him without hesitation if he harmed the children."

"Is he still living at San Miguelito?"

"Yes but the place is not as it was. To feed my family in hard times, I've taken work there myself. The ranch has seen finer days. I worked many a day from dawn to dusk to repair and replace but to no avail. Your pa continues to ride with outlaws. I must tell you he gives aid and shelter to Pancho Villa and his men. I recently heard that one of Villa's generals is hiding out at the ranch. It is said that his wife meets him there."

Before Alex could ask I said, "Which general and how many men does he have with him?" Suddenly believing I had spoken out of turn, I realized this was not about Pancho but Alex coming to terms with his pa. I waited to see what he would say next. If he was not interested in Villa's men I would remain silent on the matter as well, for now.

Finally he spoke. "It is as I expected. I knew that if my father lived he would harbor such a man as Villa." He lowered his voice before continuing. "Your familiarity with the set up at the ranch is valuable my friend but dangerous knowledge as well. As an Army sergeant I must report what you have said. You may stay and receive a reward for your information. Or if you prefer you could ride away. I will keep your name from the Army if you request it. You will have to live in Mexico after we are gone. I fear for you and Camilla's safety if you help us." He looked around suspiciously before saying, "There could be Villa men in town or the next table. Somehow the word would get around that you have aided the Army."

We both waited for a full minute as he used a piece of bread to sop up the last of his eggs. While he thought over the offer, I was thinking the decision would cause him much trouble in the land he now called home. He did not appear to be a man that rushed a decision or was easily pushed around. Citizens of Mexico both hated or loved Villa depending on which town was raided or harbored him.

At last his decision made he leaned in with a spark in his eyes, of what I could not tell. "Villa is a devil! He has killed many innocent men and women in Mexico and America. Until he is dead there will be no peace in my adopted country or yours. I will not take a reward for turning in the general and Villa's men. I will accept a fee for my guide services. Of course Alex could guide them, but perhaps it is unwise to have it known who you are related to."

"It is true that I risk my Army career. If it were known I am the son of one who harbors Villa's men, trust in me could be lost. Have you any news of my father's movements? Will he be at the ranch if we raid it?"

"There is no way of knowing. I have not been on the ranch in weeks. Your father comes and disappears as he pleases. For a man pushing sixty he can still remain long in the saddle. If he is there he may chose to fight with the Villista's. Only heaven knows what will happen then. I warn you the general and his men will not surrender. Also the ranch naturally fortified and will not be easily taken. You must understand that your actions might be responsible for ending your father's life. Eleazar I ask you to consider carefully before you decide."

"No! My father has drawn this to his own door. He has shamed our family name for decades. It broke my grandfather's heart to die knowing he had spawned a monster. My own personal hell was watching my mother die at the hands of the man. I had suffered many beatings at his hands as well, but only my mother's safety worried me. After the last beating she just withered to nothing and was gone. At fifteen I was helpless to stop his attack or my mother's death. Father wanted me to be like him. He took me on his raids and I witnessed his cruelty many times in villages hundreds of miles away. There was no revolution, no excuse, but for a man's greed, and not wanting to labor honestly for his wages."

Feeling urgency was warranted, I callously ignored my friend's torment. Knowing my own mother would not approve of my outburst, I pushed myself into the exchange. In total exasperation I said, "Ezekiel who is the general?" I knew there was no dancing around a major dust up if we raided the ranch. We needed to return to camp and deliver Holmdahl's words to General Pershing. Then the Army brass could choose the best path to follow. We had missed our opportunities before and now was the time to strike.

"General Julio Cardenas was reportedly at the ranch as late as a week ago. He is one of Villa's personal bodyguards. There are some reports that say he is a colonel, but he now wears the rank of general. I have seen him at the ranch many times. He may have left but will surely return as long as his wife remains on the ranch."

There it was, spoken out loud and no way to take it back in. Alex had to inform General Pershing and let the Army machine do as it would. No trooper wanted to spend one day longer than was necessary in Mexico. If there was a way to end the conflict sooner, we should act on that hope. If Cardenas could be captured alive he could lead us right to Pancho Villa's front gate, or I reasoned, whatever cave he was hiding in.

It was decided that Alex would talk to Pershing and suggest that Holmdahl guide the Army to San Miguelito. The fact that the ranch and land belonged to the Alejandro family would be left omitted from the report unless it became necessary to disclose it. Alex would say he had merely overheard Ezekiel talking to others and questioned him about the ranch and Villa's men. I decided to wait in camp and not follow Alex in like I had done is Guerrero. I wanted to be as far away from the fireworks in the headquarters as possible. I had no idea if the reports of General Cardenas would be trusted and acted upon or disregarded as hearsay.

I said a quiet prayer the Colonel Dodd was out of camp and not looking for another fight. I had seen all of the hard riding colonel I wanted. Thinking about my own suffering while under the command of Dodd, I suddenly remembered that Sean and others had given much more. Thinking about it now, I wished I had asked how far the ranch was from Casa Grande. As I waited I made ready harness and saddle in preparation for riding out. I was now fit for duty and did not want to be left behind. I would rather take my chances riding with Alex and whoever was chosen for command.

As the minutes dragged into more than an hour I began to wonder what could possibly be taking so damn long. Cardenas could be riding away as they endlessly debated the matter. We had missed Villa by scant days before. As late morning became noon I began to hear raised voices over toward the headquarters tent. I imagined it had to be a disagreement between officers. No enlisted man would dare risk raising his voice in the presence of the general. Either way I took it to mean that some kind of a plan was being hammered out. Indecision and inaction was not in my nature and lately I had tasted a plate full of both.

Finally after another half hour I saw Holmdahl and Alex emerged from the headquarters tent. They began walking fast in the direction of the shade tree where I waited. I stood and stretched in anticipation. From the look on the two men's faces I was glad I had written my ma and mailed it already. They wore twin expressions of determination and purpose. Neither man would look as they did if we were in for a lazy evening in camp. If it were not for the seriousness of the situation I would have laughed at the two men. Alex short and stocky and Ezekiel tall and thin made quite a sight.

As soon as Alex was in speaking distance he said without preamble, "Pack your gear Oscar. We're leaving tonight. We'll be traveling by automobile this time and will be led by Lieutenant Patton."

I thought myself ready for any turn of events, but this was not what was expected. "Alex we are cavalrymen. What do we know of fighting from automobiles?"

"I expect we will travel by vehicle then attack on foot. We can move much faster and further. Ezekiel says the sand is swept clear by winds for most of the way. By car we can make it in two days as opposed to nearly a week by horses. The decision was Patton's who argued long and hard for the right to lead. The lieutenant is an old cavalryman too, but the general and all ranking officers agreed this is the way to approach the raid on the ranch.

I groaned loudly. "You and I have seen action twice since we left Columbus. Good men have been killed already in this campaign. Now we have a chance to capture one of Pancho's bodyguards and the Army wants to abandon known tactics for an untried strategy. I think Patton's itch for glory could get us all killed in a hurry."

Alex shrugged in defeat. I knew he shared my concerns. "General Pershing has faith in him and we'll just have to trust his judgment."

"I do trust his judgment. I just wish Pershing was leading us instead.

Alex looked at Holmdahl and smiled wickedly. "The general said Ezekiel is unproven and unknown. I had to vouch for him. Pershing actually used the words, *shave tail*, just like when they shave an untrained mule's tail so the handlers can tell the difference."

Holmdahl spoke up in his own defense. "Yes he has no faith in me yet. I must prove myself in his eyes. I told him I had been a vaquero and fought bandits and outlaws before. No rancher in this country can take his family's safety for granted. We will see who the shave tail is when the bullets start flying."

# CHAPTER 37

## *Hell's Unpaved Highway*

The only thing I knew for sure about Patton was that when he had a plan, time is not wasted on further discussion. Almost immediately the camp was a flurry of movement. Handpicked men were assembled and vehicles were loaded in preparation for travel. For better or worse Alex had vouched for Holmdahl and requested me to be assigned as well with a fighter's bird's eye seat to history. I was sure that never before had a vehicle assault been attempted by American military forces. There were even rumors some of the vehicles were armored. True or not I could not tell the difference by casual observation.

Alex and I were of little help, not knowing what preparation an automobile needed. We stowed our gear in our assigned transport vehicle, then mostly just stayed out of the way. Lieutenant Patton was everywhere barking orders in his brusque manner. A civilian merchant made the mistake of attempting to argue with Patton. The man complained that the last minute request was unreasonable. The lieutenant badgered the man until he was near teas and ran to complete the order. Patton was a hands-on leader, leaving nothing to chance. He tolerated no slipshod or errant military discipline. The only time he stopped moving was to pause in midstride and relight a curved wooded pipe. Smoking such a pipe was an unusual habit for a man of his age. I thought if he was copying his obvious role model General Pershing.

We would travel in three open touring motor cars which would carry about fifteen men to the ranch. The handpicked troopers were from the 6th Infantry Regiment. Alex and I did not know any of the men. However they looked solid and had an excellent reputation as fighters. With the Dodge Touring Cars packed and ready, we pulled out near midnight. It was crowded in the back seat but I found the rocking motion soothing. Before we were on the road an hour Alex was asleep next to me. Slouching further down in the seat I leaned back and closed my eyes. I was bone-weary from the long day of activity. My last thought before surrendering to exhaustion was that I could get used to this new Army travel.

We stopped a few times throughout the night to relieve our bladders and change drivers. I was not asked to drive and was fine with the decision. At times there were no roads and we drove three abreast where the desert would allow. The maneuver cut down on the dust being swallowed by every occupant except the lead car which held Patton. The man had no quit in him and I marveled at how he had tolerated horses for so long. The lieutenant possessed no smidgen of patience and would have ridden horses to their death to get at the enemy.

As the sun rose a short camp was made for coffee and breakfast. We were approaching the *hacienda* from the west and the rising sun glared blindingly into our faces. In under an hour we were again traveling across the windswept desert. The desert was not as smooth now and the car dipped and banged along as it drove over pitted and an uneven surface. Alex leaned over and shouted in my ear. "We will not be able to continue much further at this pace. The desert becomes more broken. We could lose half of a car in a hole."

"Cupping my hands to be heard I said, "How much longer until we have to slow down? I think my back is busted from the bouncing."

"I think not much further now. It is hard to judge since I last traveled this way by horse. I hope the right decision was made to attack *San Miguelito*. The closer we get the more dread I feel that it will go badly."

"Let's hope if it does go poorly it is for the Villistas and not us. I'm still counting on returning to Texas with all my limbs and still breathing to boot." After a moment I added, "Of course having friends like you I'm lucky to still be alive at all." Sarcastically I added, "Thanks again amigo for getting me invited to the party."

"Por nada amigo, it is nothing. It was the least I could do after you led us into the first fight in Mexico with bandits. You should take comfort in the knowledge that we should not have survived that time either. Yet here we are, alive to perhaps die another day."

Smiling in spite of myself I said, "Alex somehow those comforting words make me want to run screeching into the night like that boy in Columbus."

True to his words in the next ten minutes our speed was reduced to a less jarring rate. Alex estimated we had covered over half the distance to the ranch. It was estimated we could arrive as early as the next morning. With our slower speed conversation became easier. Our current driver was a twenty-two year old infantryman from Kentucky named Rolland Phelps. He held the rank of sergeant and had a wiry build with blond hair, now coated with red dust. He spoke over his shoulder addressing Alex since he was aware he had brought in the original information. "If you are thinking about riding straight up to the ranch and jumping out into a fight, forget it. Lieutenant Patton may have never seen combat before this but he is a careful man. The man is well-read and studies history and battle tactics."

"Are you saying he won't attack right away?"

"Exactly, he will sit a spell somewhere that he can watch and reconnoiter the area. He will send men out and gather more intelligence that way. Eventually when he believes all is ready he will strike like a snake, swift and sure. I know whoever is at that ranch had better say their prayers. I believe there is no mercy in him."

I sat up and leaned forward. "How could you know all that if he is untested in battle?"

"I served under him at Fort Riley, Kansas. We had yearly mock-battles or war games some called them. Patton, a west point graduate would spend days on the ground planning for every contingency like a master chess player. As the games began he would maneuver his men into a win every time. I expect no less when the shooting is real. Also you can bet he will be in the thick of it. He is no man to wait in camp and be told what occurred later. No sir, not Patton. Have you seen his binoculars or that fancy carved Colt 45? The binoculars were a gift from his father after he graduated from West Point, and he special-ordered the pistol."

"It would have been hard to miss the pistol. Are those his initials on the stock?"

"Yes, on the binocular case too. G.S.P stands for George Smith Patton. He is a junior, named after his grandfather, a colonel in the Confederate Army.

Alex was quiet and I did not know if I should feel better or not. I was all for careful but not to the point of inaction. Sometimes a man or Army just naturally had to charge into the teeth of the opposing force. Unlike Patton I had not studied ancient battles at West Point. I did not believe I knew more than the educated leaders in the Army. However I had seen fighting close up and personal. I believed a certain amount of experience counted for much. No man really knew for sure how they would react when the targets were shooting back. I had seen men fold up in a heap and cry. Still others became like some kind of war machine when under fire as if some prehistoric beast had been awakened.

After a full day in the car, we finally made camp near a broken cliff, which we put at our back. This was a dry camp except for what water we carried. No fires were lit and each man made do with whatever was brought. My supper was a handful of beef jerky and dessert was a piece of hard rock candy. It was not too filling but better than hard tact crackers. Holmdahl had told Patton we were too close for fires as night riders moving under cover of darkness would see any campfires and report our presence. The automobiles were placed between us and any possible approach.

Arranging shifts for night guards, Alex and I would be taking the last period before daylight. At about 4:00 o'clock Sergeant Phelps shook me awake. The moon was up and a man could see out over long distances. Alex was already up pulling on his uniform. Rolland handed us each a cup of steaming coffee. Apparently my voice had not woken up yet because when I tried to speak it came out in a whispered croak. "How can we have hot coffee if we can't have a fire?"

"To Patton cooked food is not important, but he likes a hot cup first thing in the morning. We dug a two foot pit and put a couple of pots on. We then blocked the fire with the cars and some scrub brush."

"Well I like hot cocoa every morning. Alex enjoys a cup of steaming tea too," I joked. I don't suppose any bacon and eggs could be scrambled up on that hidden flame of yours?"

"Sorry, as far as I know we aren't taking time for a cooked breakfast."

After Rolland walked over to his bedding we armed ourselves and made our way to the outer edge of camp, just beyond the cars. Surprisingly I was enjoying the cool morning air and the coffee had put me in a fine mood. Speaking in a low whisper I asked, "Alex, how close are we to your home?"

Lowering his voice so that I had to take a step closer to hear his words he said, "I recognized this cliff as a landmark I used when hunting as a boy. We will draw near to the ranch by 10:00 o'clock or so. I'm certain Ezekiel will lead us to a glen of trees positioned on a hill that overlooks the ranch. It is too far away for an attack but close enough for field glasses. I'd suggest only one or two men at a time should watch. The rest should stay hidden below in a shallow valley. If Villa's men are there they will surely be out scouting or watching all approaches from the ranch."

"It must be hard on you after all this time. Coming home under the circumstances and still carrying the hatred for your pa." I studied the moon awhile before continuing. "Alex whatever happens, don't let the past cloud your mind. Your father *will* shoot you even if he knows it is you, especially with that uniform on. Of that I am certain."

"You are right of course, but I may not be able to fulfill my youthful promise that I would surely kill him if ever we met again. I have aged and no longer the impulsive child my father last abused. If you are close by at the moment of decision and I hesitate, kill him quickly as if he is a rabid dog. No one else need die at his hands." After those words he drifted away circling the camp. Even with the full moon he instantly faded into shadow and was lost to my eyes.

As I moved about the edge of the camp, I tried to imagine what Alex must be thinking? He was coming home, but not as a son, but a soldier, part of an army against his kin. Thinking of my pa, I knew no matter how angry I had been at him, I could not have taken his life. If I could not do it after the whipping for drinking, I supposed I never could. Ending the life of your own father was a horrible prospect. I truly hoped that turn of events was not in my friend's future.

Thinking of home made me vow that if I did make it through this conflict alive I intended to return home and try to patch things up with my pa. He was not a forgiving man, not unlike his son. Suddenly I realized what ma had meant in her letter. Between pa and me it was as if we were fighting ourselves. We were so much alike there would always be trouble between father and son. When we looked at each other we saw what we hated most in ourselves. My pa saw me as irresponsible and undisciplined. Certainly I had to admit that at times both had been true. I saw him as the restraints people wanted to impose on others, especially when pushing their own beliefs. I hated the idea of becoming like him, but as I aged, I saw more of him in me every day.

Pa is a God-fearing man and I believe he practices most of what he preaches. The trouble was he tilted heavily toward the *hellfire* and *damnation* style religion. Pa believed in the time-honored traditional of Old Testament values. To pa, his sermons centered a constant theme of *an eye for an eye*, as his golden rule. He would never strive to resemble the more forgiving God of the New Testament. *Turn the other cheek* was not in my pa's character. Understanding this, I could either embrace him the way he was or stay out of his way. Ma knew this and accepted it as a matter of fact that we would never get along.

# CHAPTER 38

## *Strategy for San Miguelito*

Before the sun was fully up over the horizon we were once again on the move. We traveled slower now in the real anticipation of meeting a Villa patrol or making too much noise and announcing our arrival. Every man was on edge and had weapons loaded and at the ready. I had fired from a horse before but was not sure of aiming from a sitting position deep in the automobile. I supposed the metal skin of the car would provide some protection from pistol fire but probably not stop a rifle slug.

As Alex had predicted we began to slow and then stop when the sun indicated it was near to 10:00 o'clock. It was May 12th by my count. I recognized the tree-covered hill Alex had spoken of as we unloaded from the vehicle. We were on the backside of the outcropping and not in view of *San Miguelito*. It appeared some ancient and powerful earth event had forced the knoll up out of the surrounding desert. I saw no similar projections anywhere in sight. I longed to see the ranch for myself but knew the time was not now. The stand of trees resembled some sort of pine tree and was a welcome change from the broken and barren desert. I found myself missing the Arkansas Ozarks I had ridden through as a child with my pa.

Ezekiel and Alex took off on foot joined by two infantry troopers who were skilled trackers. I was pleased to see Patton had stayed behind to organize the camp and not followed the more experienced men to spy on the ranch. I felt a slight and begrudging admiration for the lieutenant bubbling up in me at his command decisions that had gotten us this far. I reserved the right to change my opinion later when the shooting began. I had no problem with a stern officer as long as the man remained in one frame of mind. I had served under higher ranking officers whose moods swung hither and yon like the breeze.

In under an hour Alex was back down the hill and heading in the direction of Patton. I meandered in the general direction hoping to catch a few words that would give me a clue as to what we were up against. When Alex reached the lieutenant he saluted and Patton waved him off impatiently. He squatted and taking his knife out began to draw in the sand. I knew that unless he was detailing bandit positions Alex could have drawn the ranch before he ventured up into the trees.

Now Patton was also on his haunches studying the crude drawing intently. He had drawn the rough outline of a dozen building. One or two were marked with an "X", indicating some importance. In front of the buildings was a large yard or cattle pen. Then there was a long corridor I took for an entrance. As I approached Alex was touching up the crude sketch. "Here is out problem lieutenant. This approach is the only way into the ranch. If it were me I'd have sighted in rifle distances. It would be suicide to approach the ranch from the front."

Alex, Lieutenant Patton and some others were standing nearby. They studied his drawing to imagine flaws or other options for approach and attack. Finally Alex leaned back indicating locations with the point of his knife. "We might be able to belly-up on all sides through the grass for a few well-aimed pot shots, but we don't have enough men for a sustained fire."

Patton immediately seized on the idea and expanded it. I remembered Rolland saying he had studied battle tactics. "I see what you mean sergeant. We might be able to flush them out by making them think we are a larger force. The best sharpshooters could fire, move, then fire from new locations. It is not important if the troopers score a hit only that it spooks them into fleeing straight into our guns which will be concentrated at the gate. Are you sure there is no way to sneak out the back? I don't want a single trooper taking a full charge solo."

"Sir, there is no other way out. I'm sure of it. This could work. Do you want me to arrange shifts for all the men to rotate up onto the hill?"

"No, not everyone should be used. Select only those you feel can move quietly. Keep field glass use to a minimum and only when the sun is at your backs. No smoking and of course no fires anywhere. The smell of smoke can travel a goodly distance. If we advertise our presence we could lose our advantage. If we can capture one of the bandits alive, he could lead to Villa. That is the ideal scenario, but I don't want to lose a man to accomplish it."

Alex selected Sergeant Phelps, me, and two others who had woodsman or hunting experience. I would be climbing the hill at near sunset. As a boy of twelve I had moved through the woods hunting small game to add to the supper table. I had imagined myself an Indian and practiced moving quietly through the think pine trees that soared thirty to forty feet above. I hunted the woods with a .22 caliber single shot rife. My pa trusted me with six bullets each time. He expected six animals in return on his investment and I seldom missed. Sometimes I brought home squirrels, rabbits, possum, and even turtles. There was almost no meat that was shunned at our table.

Over the next twenty-four hours we watched and waited. At no time did anyone see bandits enter or leave the ranch. The ranch appeared almost deserted except for minimal movement to feed or water cattle and horses. Ranch hands stayed close to the river rock house which was centered among the outlying buildings. The very lack of movement was suspicious in itself. Ranch hands had to complete chores outside of the main gates.

On the early morning of May 14th I was on my belly watching the house and yard through the field glasses. I heard a slight whisper of movement to my right. It was no more than a field mouse might make in the grass. I knew Ezekiel was observing the ranch from the opposite face of the hill. He could not have approached on my right without climbing down the opposite side risking loose rock and certainly much noise. He then would have to make his way back up. That made no kind of sense and Holmdahl was a practical man.

The hair on the back of my neck stiffened like a porcupine's quills. I felt my heart thumping in my chest. I began to slide one hand toward my Colt. Before I got close to the 45 I froze when the morning's first gray light shown on a well-polished, high leather riding boot positioned less than a foot from my head. Either the man had stolen the boots or they belonged to a cavalryman.

Patton sat back casually on his heels. He said in his usual no-nonsense and direct manner, "What have you observed this morning Sergeant Draper?"

There was no question that the man's sudden appearance had startled me. I thanked the heavens I had not been asleep. Trying to keep my voice even I said, "Not much sir. Somebody threw out what I assumed were chamber pots a few minutes ago."

The next words he spoke worried me more than his sudden arrival. "I know who you are Draper. It was not hard to figure out. Even in El Paso I heard the story of a sergeant and his loyal Mexican-American corporal who chased bandits into Mexico. The way I heard it from Dave Allison, a Texas Ranger friend of mine, you and then Corporal Alejandro killed a few of the bastards that attacked Glen Springs, killing citizens and troopers under your command. The official report states your small garrison fought bravely against as many as three hundred bandits. I admire that. I expect your fellow Texans who died at the Alamo were no less brave."

I had not denied his words but did not have any idea what he would do with the knowledge he now possessed. "Thank you sir but it was a stupid mistake crossing into Mexico. I paid dearly for it and could have gotten Alex and I killed for our trouble." Realizing that he might think I was speaking in the present tense I added, "Without orders I mean."

He chuckled under his breath. "I too have been known to flaunt the rules when it suits me. The key is to know when to shine so those in charge will keep you around. Sadly the Army must, by necessity operates on rules and regulation if discipline is to be maintained. Tell me, is it true you recovered a trophy stolen by the bandits from one of your men?"

"Yes sir, the US belt buckle I wear. I took it from the first bandit I killed in *Boquillas*. It was a foolish act but I was not in my right mind when I took off on impulse. My men and townsfolk were dead, nothing would bring them back. I should have been back in Glen Springs working to restore order to the camp and town. Somehow it worked out and now I am here. I have much regret at my past actions."

Quietly considering my words he said, "Regret is for civilians and old men safely retired to a life of contemplation, not soldiers. The past cannot be changed and only weighs us down." I could not argue his point. Continuing he comment he added, "I am a curious man who will undoubtedly spend his life in the Army. Tell me sergeant; did taking the life of your enemy cause you distress?"

"Perhaps it should have. He was the first to die by my actions. At least he was the first I witnessed dying. There must have been others in Glen Springs. However firing at enemies in the dark is not the same as looking in a man's eyes as he dies by your hand. Then and every time I've killed since I believed either they would die or I would."

He stood up and said, "Thank you soldier. I can't say I approve of what you and Sergeant Alejandro did, but I envy you the experience. Sergeant Draper your secret is safe with me. I find it ironic that fate, if you believe in such, has mocked you by returning you to the same country. You and Alejandro are once more chasing bandits in this damnable foreign land." As if suddenly remembering another point he said, "Ah, and our valuable Sergeant Alejandro has returned to his boyhood home pursuing much more than bandits. I believe he seeks answers from his troubled youth and has come home for answers."

Shocked at his words I said, "Sir how could you know this was his home?"

"It was the only obvious conclusion. On the trail I noticed a yearning in him that only home could satisfy. However he was not looking back but ahead. I have observed the way he looks over the land and speaks of it lovingly, as if the ranch is a beautiful woman. Do not misunderstand; I am interested in his and your past only as a mental diversion. The here and now is foremost in my mind. I trust you will both do your duty and not let past grievances dictate your actions."

"Yes sir, certainly." I was vastly relieved by his words and excited by his timeline of attack. We had few supplies and the desert provided little for an extended stay in the area. If a raid had been delayed much longer we would have been forced to restock in the nearest town of *Rubio*. To enter the village would surely tip Villa's confederates of our presence in the area. Spending days spying on the ranch was not my idea of a soldier's duty.

I got to my feet brushing the grass and pine needles off my uniform. I turned feeling the impulse to shake his hand in thanks. However the spot where he had stood was empty. He had moved off as quietly as he arrived. I peered into the shadow of the trees and could neither see nor hear anything. I now knew I was not the only boy stalking game in the woods when growing up. Lieutenant Patton was a mystery man. Alex was not going to believe this most recent turn of the card."

# CHAPTER 39

## *Patton's 1ˢᵗ Battle*

As it turned out I would not have a chance to speak with Alex before our assault on the hacienda grounds. I was disappointed when relieved of duty at eight o'clock and returned to camp, but Alex was not there. I was told he was out scouting the ranch with Ezekiel. My nerves were jittery due to the upcoming fight. It was always the case when I knew a fight was coming. Sometimes it was easier for the worry and anxiety if the attack was sudden and unplanned. My stomach was twisted into a tight knot. I forced myself to eat and drink two cups of coffee. The wind was blowing from the east into our faces and I reasoned that was why Patton had allowed a fire for cooking a much needed hot meal. None of us expected an easy day and knew we would need all the energy we could muster.

The hustle and bustle of the camp made me hurry my meal to join in the preparation. We would travel by automobile to the ranch, skirting the hill and approaching along the main road. Troopers would be in position before the arrival of the main party for the assault. Once we turned onto the road leading to the main gate our presence would be known. Anything could happen at that point. If General Cardenas and his men were inside they would be desperate and not inclined to surrender.

By 11:30AM on May 14ᵗʰ the motor cars were loaded and waiting for Lieutenant Patton's signal to advance. He was in the first vehicle calmly writing in a small notebook he always carried. For a man of thirty he was extremely self-confident and some would say cocky and arrogant. Those qualities had also best observed in George Armstrong

Custer, most notably, who had not been served well by the attributes. Lieutenant Patton on the other hand had the ability to make a man want to trust and follow him. Again I decided to wait and see how the lieutenant handled himself in the impending fracas. No sane man went into battle unafraid, but each man reacted differently under the stress of killing or being killed.

Fifteen minutes later we waited back off the road that leads to the gate. Patton was in the lead car and I sat in the third. Each man was armed with his 03 Springfield rifles. Some carried semi-automatics, or revolvers. Sergeant Phelps had told me Patton was carrying his fancy designed single action Colt 45. He was said to load the traditional five rounds in his Colt with the hammer resting on an empty chamber for safety. He had a Springfield propped next to him. The tension was as thick as a morning fog in the Ozarks. Every man knew the shooting would begin at any moment. Cardenas and his men were not about to walk out with their hands in the air and surrender. I believed we were as ready as a small troop could be against an unknown sized force. Nobody wanted a fight less than me but the waiting around was not my strong suit.

At exactly noon intermitted firing began from our concealed marksman. The crack of rifles were heard two or three at a time, then silence as they crawled to previously selected firing positions. If I had not known there were four troopers firing I would not have been able to estimate. If the plan was working those inside would be confused by the number as well. With a jolt and flying dust we were on the move at break neck speed.

In less than a minute we were in sight of the gate. Before the vehicle came to a stop Patton had climbed out onto the side runners. He launched himself off of the lead vehicle. He was running and had his engraved ivory stocked peacemaker in his right hand and Springfield in the other. A moment later our car stopped and I saw why Patton had taken up a position by the gate. He was shouting for three armed horsemen to stop. My first thought was he would be killed. A second thought was that our marksman plan to startle the bandits had worked. The bandits had been spooked alright, but showed no sign of stopping.

They urged their horses into a full charge whipping them as they rode toward the gate.

Upon seeing Patton near the gate the bandits redirected their horses toward him and charged on. The lead rider could be seen tugging his rifle from the scabbard on his saddle. Unbelievably Patton stood his ground. He took careful aim like a soldier at firing practice and fired all five loaded rounds from his Colt at the rapidly advancing bandits. The men were still sixty feet away with the distance closing fast. He scored a hit on the lead Villista. The impact on the man's arm was clearly seen. His arm swung uselessly at his side. Patton took a step back, pausing to reload. The wounded bandit went off the side of his horse. Instantly recovering his balance he sprang to his feet, and then sprinted for the partial cover of some stunted trees.

By now I was surrounded by four other troopers but we could not risk firing at the bandits for fear of hitting Patton. The second bandit frantically seeking escape rode swiftly toward Patton's position. As one man we aimed but Patton was between us and the fleeing bandits. As the second one rapidly approached the lieutenant calmly aimed at the man's horse and fired one round that brought the bandit and horse tumbling to the ground. He had skidded off to one side. We now had a target but the man was momentarily trapped under his horse.

We looked to Patton to see what his actions would be, mercy or instant death while helpless. The lieutenant aimed his pistol but waited, showing a knight's chivalry as the man struggled out from under his horse. However, once free he opened fire and our rifles answered needlessly. Patton had instantly shot him with deadly accuracy through the center of his chest. The man fell back like a chopped tree not far from his dead horse. We then concentrated our fire on the third bandit. The man was literally riddled through the body with multiple slugs from our .30 caliber Springfield rifles.

The firing stopped abruptly. Everyone began to reload and continuously scanned the area for additional threats. We knew the first bandit was somewhere under cover. Nobody wanted to follow him into the scrub brush, even with his one arm shot up. We were standing in the open exposed to his hidden fire. I was thinking we should move back toward the cover of the automobiles, but Patton motioned for us to begin circling toward the tree line.

Before we could obey his orders the missing bandit foolishly rushed from cover firing hastily in the direction of Patton. He was rapid firing a pump-action .35 caliber rifle. He carried it with the stock low by his hip. When the rifle was empty he dropped it and pulled out a revolver. He was crouched and running hard in waist high grass and hard to get a bead on. In the next instant Ezekiel Lazarus Holmdahl rose up from his hidden position in the grass. His sudden appearance stirred a memory of the Lazarus pa preached about from the New Testament. He was a good thirty feet away and fired one time with his pistol. The bandit's momentum pitched him forward on his face. He twitched once but was dead instantly.

After the dust settled we slowly walked over to the body and, kicking the revolver aside we turned him over. He had a perfectly round .32 caliber hole in the middle of his forehead. There was no doubt of who had killed him. The only one of us that carried such a weapon was Ezekiel. Patton looked at the bandit and said, "I've seen him in photographs. That is Colonel Cardenas and the reports were true. He *is* wearing the rank of a general and not that of a colonel."

Holmdahl said, "Yes sir. I've seen him, um, around the town. I expect his *newly* widowed wife might be up at the ranch house."

Patton smiled, obviously relieved to have his first fight behind him and delighted at the outcome. He stuck out his hand and Holmdahl shook it. "I suppose you saved my ass back there. I did not see him coming. I guess you earned your money and an apology for that *shave tail* remark. You were most helpful on this campaign. I would hire you anytime. Are there others we need to round up?"

Ezekiel said, "Your troopers are entering the ranch to check. We killed another one over by the ranch house. He fell off his horse and made a run on foot before the boys started firing up here. He wears the rank of a private in Villa's Revolutionary Army, for whatever that's worth. I don't recognize him."

Patton looked pleased and rubbed his hands together like a man ready to tuck in for a fine meal. "It is a shame we failed to capture one alive but this was a thunderously good success. Have Sergeant Alejandro interview civilians at the ranch. They might know something of use."

As they talked we were walking to inspect the other two bodies. The first was a private. Ezekiel identified him as Juan Garza, a local man who grew up in the area. The second wore the rank of captain. The captain had fallen with his arm across his face. Patton leaned over the man to remove his arm. He said, "I presume this one must be Captain Isador Lopez. He tugged on the man's sleeve and his arm fell back, exposing an older version of a face I knew well. I heard Ezekiel take in a quick breath and curse under his breath. I looked at the man and saw horror in his eyes. He motioned with a slight tilt of his head for me to walk with him.

Leaving Patton and the others to check the bodies we walked a ways back to one of the automobiles. As soon as we were out of earshot of the others he said what I had feared. "That may be Captain Lopez, but he is also Isador Alejandro, Eleazar's father. He must have been using his mother's last name. There were rumors of a ruthless captain, but I never suspected this or saw Isador in that uniform. It figures he would want to be part of Pancho Villa's mystic. Playing at being a revolutionary finally got him killed. I can't say I'm sorry. He has been deserving of a hard death for a long while. I would have shot him myself if Camilla had not stopped me. When we returned and found Camilla's sister dead at his hands, I went into a boiling rage. It would have resulted in one of us killing the other if not for my wife's intervention."

I scratched my head while thinking it through. "I don't give a tinker's damn about the man. I only care about how Alex will react. He may hate him but the man was his pa in any case."

Looking over my shoulder I saw Patton instructing troopers to tie ropes to the corpse's feet. I was aghast but believed he had intentions of hauling them back with us to Casa Grande. I had only a minute to decide my course of action. "Ezekiel, find Alex and get that private's body up here double time."

"Oscar what can you do. Patton is more stubborn than you if that is possible."

"I plan on talking Patton into a trade. It may be like asking a storm to rain elsewhere, but I have to try. He is going to experience a *mutiny of one* if he tries to take that body off this ranch. Alex deserves the opportunity to bury his pa. Hurry up now. Please, as quickly as you can."

As I returned to Patton's side he was looking at the general who had died with his hand near an ornate, richly carved sword. I imagined he would have charged us with the saber even against numerous rifles. Patton reached down, pulled the sword free and turned it over in his hands admiring it from every angle. Cardenas's body rested near his dead horse. We both looked at the shiny, highly polished silver-studded saddle on the back of the horse. I saw the general also wore silver spurs and the new-appearing revolver he had died holding was where we had kicked it to the side. I had never seen anything like the .35 caliber Remington pump rifle he had been rapid-firing at Patton. Smoke was still slowly curling up from the hot barrel.

Patton instructed the saddle, sword, spurs, revolver, and rifle to be removed and placed in his Dodge. I did not fault him the trophies. It was a common enough practice and had been around as long as conflict between men existed. My pa would have said something of a religious nature such as when Cain killed Able he took his brother's property as his own. I mouthed the words to myself, "T*o the victor belong the spoils*."

Patton spun toward me quick as a panther. He had a frown on his face as if he had read my mind. For a second I thought I had spoken out loud. "You don't approve sergeant?" Gesturing to my belt he added, "If I recall your own words that US buckle was taken from the first man you killed."

His intuition was so sharp. For a second I thought he would strike me. "Sir I was taking back the buckle from a bandit who stole it." I quickly added, "I assure you my intention is not to judge your actions. You are my lieutenant and I respect that. However if you would allow me, I do have a request. The captain over there is not who he appears.

The last name was an alias, or at least it was his mother's name. He is Sergeant Alejandro's father. Holmdahl tells me his real name is Isador Lopez-Alejandro."

I observed that Patton would be a fearsome poker player. He covered his surprise effortlessly, and then asked suspiciously, "Did Sergeant Alejandro know his father was one of Villa's most trusted men?"

His heated tone made it clear he was not happy at the thought of one of his men being somehow aligned with bandits. "No sir. Only that his pa was a bad man and might be harboring bandits. He was not even sure his father still lived. Alejandro ran away at fifteen and had not returned to *San Miguelito* until we all arrived."

The lieutenant wrinkled his nose as if he smelled something rotten. "Sergeant as distasteful as it is we must bring the bodies back. Proof of our success will put fear into our enemies. Victory is what drives positive citizen support. Without that support no conflict is won. There are politics to be considered in any war. War is driven by politics and ran by politicians."

"Sir, I don't dispute what you say but could we perhaps switch bodies with that of the captain and the dead private down by the ranch? Even with politics considered, is it possible that one body less would make that much of a difference?"

He was quiet so long I wondered what my next move would be. I did not want to go against my commanding officer's wishes. However this was for my friend and not a personal request for me. Finally I opened my mouth and said, "Sir. I had no idea what else to say but he cut me off with a gesture. I felt my face redden at his callous disregard of the death of a father of one of his men. I realized he was not looking at me but over my shoulder. Two troopers had returned with additional rope to tie the feet of the captain.

Abruptly he said, "No, not this one. Leave him awhile longer. Take the cars back to where we stopped before the raid. Wait for me there. I'll join you shortly."

"Yes sir." The troopers snapped to attention responding to his sharp tone. They scurried off to follow his orders.

Without preamble he said, "Get Alejandro up here and switch out the corpses. He took out a gold pocket watch and it opened with a soft click. It is near to 2:00 o'clock now. We will wait down in camp until 5:00pm precisely, and no longer. Bring the private's body down by one of the ranch horses dressed in the captain's clothes. This property may belong to Alejandro, but for now your butts belong to the Army and to me. I expect to see you both in camp and on time. Make haste man or there will be the devil to pay." As I turned quickly away he said, "Do not make me regret this Sergeant Draper. Also get Holmdahl to ride into Rubio and pick up supplies. You and Alejandro can bring them with you." He handed me a dozen silver dollars.

Vastly relieved I said, "Thank you sir." It was all I could think to say. Looking around I saw Ezekiel and Alex walking toward us. They led a pony with a body across the back. From the way Alex walked I knew he had been told what this was all about. He had dread written all over him. I longed to be anywhere but here and wished I could leave as Patton had just done. However a friend was there in times of celebration and also when family members were buried.

As soon as he was close enough I said, "Alex I'm sorry. We had no way of knowing."

With a long sigh he said, "It was as expected. Given a choice I would have liked to confront him with my return. I will change his clothes with the private. Then I will bury my father myself. I must carry him a spell. He does not deserve burial next to my mother in her flower garden. I will meet you both at the house in an hour."

"Alex you don't have to do this alone. Also we have to be back in camp by 5:00pm or there will be big trouble with Patton."

"Ah, the lieutenant, he may have no mercy toward his enemies, but he is a compassionate man all the same. Do not worry Oscar; I'll be back in plenty of time. We will meet Patton's deadline with time to spare. "

Holmdahl and I honored his wishes and walked to the house. He had much to do and saddled horses and pack mules to fetch the supplies. As he worked he said, "Eleazar intends to sign a paper giving me and his aunt power of attorney and control of San Miguelito. I expect he will return one day after his Army enlistment is up. I just pray he survives this conflict. Your road is long and this mess is far from over. Please watch over him Oscar so that my wife and children sees his return. There is no other family except his sister and our four children. They will be excited to know they have an uncle.

"Fighting in Mexico being what it is I cannot promise anything, but I will certainly try. Alex and I look after each other as soldiers and friends." Suddenly remembering the friends I had already lost, I added, "Take good care of the ranch. I will do my best to see Alex returns to the beauty of this place.

As we talked we both heard the unmistakable sound of a fast-running horse. We both raised our rifles as a white stallion charged away from us. I was attempting to align my sights on the back of the rider as he rode over the uneven ground. Before I could fire Holmdahl pushed down my rifle barrel. He shook his head before saying, "Oscar don't shoot. It's the general's wife. She is no threat to us."

I had no taste for killing a woman but said in concern, "What if she brings more bandits here? It could mean trouble for you and your family after we've gone."

"Don't worry about that. She hated him and would have eventually stabbed him in his sleep. She will only return home. His bride was stolen from a village many miles to the north. Like Villa himself, if a woman refused him she'd die." He climbed into the saddle and looked longingly at the house. I knew he dearly ached to see his family, but one last chore stood between them. "Oscar go to the house and meet my family. I'll be along as soon as I'm finished."

At the house I met Camilla and her children. I could see the resemblance between her and Alex. The children were a cross between Ezekiel and Camilla. I fell in love with their beautiful three year old daughter Eva. It was mutual love as she climbed immediately into my lap the minute I sat down. She was adorable. Eva opened a longing inside me for a family of my own I had not known existed. Every few minutes I would put her out of my lap to pace the floor in anxious anticipation of meeting Patton's deadline. Each time Eva followed in my footsteps like a tiny shadow. When I stopped so did she. At one point she held up tiny arms and wiggled her fingers to be picked up. Now my pacing was joined with the fresh smell of the weightless child in my arms. If for no other reason than the innocent child I held, I wanted men such as Pancho Villa and men like him to be stopped.

At last Alex walked through the door sweat-covered and dirty from his grim task. Ignoring the manner of dress and cleanliness, Camilla rushed over to him. The way she clinched him in a long hug brought unwelcome tears to the eyes of every adult in the room. Finally pulling free she inspected him closely as if counting bullet holes. Finally satisfied with what she saw she said, "Eleazar you have become a handsome man I think. You must wash and I will prepare a meal fit for an honorable and brave warrior. It is good that you have become your own man and not like your father." She paused suddenly remembering he had just buried his father. "Do not grieve for him. Isador's death will save many more helpless victims from his despicable ways. Go clean up and then meet my children. I will prepare a quick meal. The children will be pleased to know they have a living uncle."

Alex looked at me and noticed my constant companion for the first time. His amused expression was unreadable. I expected he would razz me later for holding the child like a city dwelling civilian. I said, "Eva this is your Uncle Alejandro." The girl squirmed in my arms and shied away from the unknown man before her. "Maybe she will like you better when you don't smell like old sweat and dirt." He shrugged and left to clean up as best he could. I looked over at an old grandfather clock against the wall and noted the time as 3:30. We had one and a half hours to make our deadline. I began to pace again. From one end of the room to the other I went, much to the delight of Eva who seemed to enjoy the walking.

Within thirty minutes we were eating an early supper at a cloth-covered table like civilized men, women, and children. It was hard to believe that a short time ago most of us were involved in a kill or be killed conflict. I had not realized how much I had missed family gatherings since rejoining the Army. I felt guilty at enjoying such a fine meal while my fellow soldiers waited in camp. However the feeling disappeared as soon as I tasted Camilla's cooking. Alex had washed and combed his hair back and was no longer the grimy apparition that had scared Eva. She was now sitting in his lap, apparently over her infatuation with the gringo. Camilla served a meal any king would be envious of. Alex had killed a calf and we were dining on beef-filled tortillas, fresh potatoes, and corn grown on the ranch.

Alex leaned his left elbow on the table. He reached over and covered Camilla's small hand with his own. He then placed a small leather sack into her hand. She had to use her other hand to support the weight. Her face wore a questioning look. "Camilla there is enough gold in there to keep the ranch running until I return. God only knows when that might be, or not at all. Don't flash more than a nugget or two in the same place. Ezekiel should ride to outlying towns and buy what you need."

She opened the sack slowly and peered inside suspiciously as if an ugly rodent might pop up and bite her. Instant concern crossed her face. "What is this Eleazar?" The soft spoken woman had disappeared and a wildcat now sat in her place. Her eyes flashed angrily and she spoke with strong conviction. "If this is money that Isador stole I won't touch it. I'd rather my children starve than profit from stolen money."

We all stared at Alex in silence. He surrounded both of her hands with his for a moment, then smiled and leaned back. "No, Camilla that is another reason for spending the gold in small amounts and in different villages. When I was about twelve I met an old miner who explained panning for gold to me. I tried it on the river that runs through the ranch and saw good color. I would take small amounts, a nugget or two and my mother would use the money for supplies. Father often left us with nothing for months while he was off on the outlaw trails. I knew there would be those in town that would believe the gold had been stolen, but that was preferable to greedy claim grabbers who might force us off the ranch or begin digging on the land."

Well you could have tipped my chair over with a feather. I had always suspected Alex of having a stash of money somewhere, but I never suspected he had access to real gold. Camilla stood and hugged him fiercely before sitting back down. "Thank you Eleazar, your mother would be proud of her son. We will be fine until your return, but please return soon. This trouble cannot last forever."

"Save any grub for me?" Ezekiel was smiling broadly at his wife and children. I've surely missed Camilla's cooking."

We all looked at the door where he had suddenly appeared. His children rushed from the table to greet their pa. Camilla too stood and hugged her husband before saying through happy tears, "My husband is a fine man. He will take care of your hacienda as he has all these years. *San Miguelito* is yours now."

Later, after we said our long goodbyes, we were riding ranch horses back to camp. We had two pack mules in tow loaded with supplies Ezekiel had obtained in town. My curiosity I asked, "Is it true what you said about the gold?"

It is but I left out a detail or two. I do not want to have anyone pressure my sister and Ezekiel for information about gold. What I did not tell then is that I spent days back tracking the gold to the source and found a small vein. It is a crumbling rock face. The one inch wide vein of gold will last my lifetime if used sparingly. It is true that if the river is panned you will find small dust or an occasional nugget."

"You never cease to amaze me Alex. So you went off alone, buried your pa then retrieved more gold. I always knew you had a secret stash somewhere."

"That is exactly what I did, but I haven't touched the gold since I was a boy. I left home and came across to America and never went back until we all did. I'm just lucky at cards and you aren't. Even that ruby ring you won was because if I won all the time nobody would play with me anymore. Now you are the only other man alive who knows the whole story. I am counting on one of us surviving to return. If it is you, I need you to write a letter or visit my family to pass on the good news."

We rode on in silence. I was thinking about recent events at the ranch. Alex must have been thinking along the same lines because a mischievous expression suddenly lit up his face. Leaning over in his saddle he doffed his hat and slapped my shoulder with it. Dust flew up from my clothes and I looked at him in surprise. Finally unable to contain himself any longer he said, "I'm sure *Eva* would welcome your return. She sure is fond of her *Uncle* Oscar."

I gave him a hard look before saying, "My friend, if you want to live past today you had best keep your sweet niece between the two of us."

"Well I guess I had better pray one of us lives to return with the truth to *San Miguelito*. I would prefer it be me, but I wish you luck as just the same." His smirk told me he was joking but the dangers the troopers faced this side of the border were all too real. This mess was not over by a long and dusty mile.

As we rode along little Eva was never far from my thoughts. When Alex and I were trying to leave she had cried and clung to my pant leg. Her small dark curls and tearful eyes tugged at my heart as we were leaving. There had been few times in my life that I had been around children. I never expected to be affected so easily. Even now I could hear Eva's mournful wails in my head. I marveled at how fast a child loves. Even the recent memories of violence had been dampened by her innocent smile. Someday there would be children of my own. I figured all I had to do was make it out of Mexico alive. Then I would find a good woman who could tolerate my moody temperament and homespun looks. Should be easy enough I expect.

# CHAPTER 40

## *Mad Dash to Fame*

We made our deadline and the last body was loaded onto the middle automobile Alex and I would follow back to Casa Grande. The tied down bodies reminded me of dead deer after a hunt. The order to return the bodies to Pershing's headquarters did not set well with me or Alex. I believed killing another in self defense or war was sometimes a necessary action, but displaying them like a trophy elk was a distasteful practice. Lieutenant Patton had been all business when we rode in but was pleased by the provisions Ezekiel had obtained and the food Camilla had packed for the men. Alex let the horses and mules free. He assured me they would find their own way back to the ranch.

Heeding Ezekiel's warning about transporting our strange cargo across Mexico. We set off at a pace that would have killed horses in under a day. None of the men seemed to consider it strange that the body we brought in was younger and thinner than Captain Lopez. Either Patton had said something or the men just did not care. The mission had been a roaring success. Lieutenant Patton was pleased and so too would be General Pershing and I imagined President Wilson as well when informed of the outcome. When those of power who lead were in good spirits their men would usually benefit from the good cheer as well. We could all hope for some well deserved rest at Casa Grande. I was looking forward to eating well again back at the headquarters before riding out again on whatever mission I was assigned to.

Hour after hour the miles fell behind us. Scenery changed gradually from flat open desert to hilly dunes and even small stands of woods. We stopped only for quick breaks and to make coffee. This time I took a turn driving and actually enjoyed the control of such a powerful and responsive machine. The new actions of gas, brake, and clutch were foreign to me. With practice I stopped grinding the gears, stalling the powerful engine, and moved us forward. I had graduated from the simple use of reins and my knees to guide a horse to maneuvering a ton of machinery across the desert. As much as I loved horses, the assault on San Miguelito had proven the era of horses in war was quickly fading. As we bounced along I concentrated only on getting us back to camp without rolling the Dodge automobile over and killing us all.

The last of the fuel we carried was rapidly being used in the mad dash back to Casa Grande. If we did not arrive soon we would be walking back. At a few places we passed peasant farmers who openly stared at the human cargo we carried. I was glad the three bodies had been divided between Patton and the other Dodge Touring Car. I was in the rear car and could still smell the rotting corpses. I tied a handkerchief around my face like an old west outlaw. The effort only helped a little. Before long the Mexican desert would claim Patton's prized freight before he could return it to Pershing's headquarters.

As the sun slipped over the horizon on the second day I noticed the three troopers in the back appeared to be sleeping. I stole glances at Alex occasionally who was riding in the front seat. He had his hat pulled low over his eyes but I could tell he was not asleep. His arms were folded across his chest indicating he probably did not want to talk. Since our return to the road he had become quiet. With time to think he had slipped into an uncharacteristic moodiness. Whenever we stopped for fuel or to change drivers he would separate himself from the others. Much had happened that affected him deeply. I had no doubt his return to the ranch and the death of his pa had dredged up bad memories he had kept buried for years. So far I had not had an opportunity to speak with him since we were never alone.

Finally he looked over his shoulder into the back seat. Satisfied the men were asleep he said, "I'm not getting any handsomer. Why do you keep looking at my ugly mug?"

"I think you know why. Ever since your return to *San Miguelito* and your father's death, you've tried to act like it doesn't bother you. Perhaps you still have not accepted the man you hated is dead. Despise him or not he was your pa and that means he is the only father you ever knew. I have felt something similar with my own pa. There were times I wished I could kill him myself, but I could not have done it. I'm sure I will grieve when he does pass."

"I *am* glad he is dead and equally thankful that I was not the one to take his life. He was a *bad* man. Many suffered at his hands, my mother for one and me for another. I would have liked to confront him with his evil deeds. For him to see a son he drove from home as a boy return as a man would have been very satisfying to me. I have let go of my hate and anger."

I looked over at him to judge his sincerity. I saw no trace of doubt or uncertainty. "Well if your father's abuse and death are behind you, what is bothering you?"

Alex leaned his head back and gathered in his thoughts. I let him think, knowing he would answer eventually. It was more than ten minutes before he said, "I appreciate your concern, Oscar, but I buried my father years before I actually dug the hole and dump him into it. It is that now there is the reality of knowing I have a place to return to and family waiting for me. If I had died before it would have mattered only to a few others. My passing would have been no more than a small ripple in a pond, soon faded. Now there are others counting on me. It is not my own safety but that of others that concerns me."

We were quiet for awhile as I thought about his words. I had made a sure-fire mess of my own life. However, I had always been able to distinguish other's problems with more clarity. Finally I said, "Alex I believe your father would have been surprised at the man you have become. You hated him so much and never were able to confront him. I'm glad it was resolved. Your aunt, her children and family are proud of the man you are. You are a respected, brave, and indispensable soldier. I've read about self-made men who grew rich. Newspapers brag of their wealth and charitable deeds. You my friend are self-made, have saved many. You have killed wicked men who prey on the innocent. I'd say you have made a fine man of yourself."

He sat up straight thinking over what I had said. "Thank you. Before returning to *San Miguelito* I was cocksure of my importance and proud of what I had accomplished with the Army. I know some believe self-pride is a sin, but confidence in one's abilities is a handy thing to have as a career soldier. I guess I had forgotten how that felt. Returning to the place of one's birth can make a man feel small. It must have brought back a way of thinking akin to when I was a helpless boy. Back then I was unable to stop my father from hurting my mother and me. All I could do was run away and start somewhere new."

"You're not a helpless boy now. You might want to rethink that career soldier idea. You are forgetting about that sweet mayor's daughter who would love to raise some little Alejandro children on your ranch. Why such a woman would want a poor soldier like you I just can't say."

"Mm Abelinda," he said with a soft sigh. She is another reason I must return from this conflict. It was much simpler when I only had to look after your leather hide. Now I have this lovely young woman, an aunt, brother-in-law, and their four children counting on me to return. All at once I'm exploding with family."

"Just remember Alex I'm a grown man. You just worry about yourself. Stay alive and return to your family. When this conflict ends I plan on finding a nice safe Army camp somewhere to spend the rest of my career. I believe I have proved to myself what I'm worth. There is no sense spending my time getting shot at any longer than I have to. Someday I will return home to Texas and make a family of my own."

"Ha, you have never played it safe since the doctor spanked your behind. You'd probably die of boredom pushing papers around a desk."

"I was born at home thank you. There was not a doctor in the county that would have ridden all the way out to our house. I don't expect pa could have paid him with anything but a bartered chicken or a wedding or funeral ceremony anyway."

I drove on through the night while Alex slept. At about 4:00 o'clock in the morning he took over and I settled into the passenger seat and pulled my field jacket over me to fend off the cool night air. I was instantly asleep. In a dream I relived the battle at San Miguelito. I saw the vivid colors and every detail was crisp as a winter morning in the Ozarks. This time Lieutenant Patton was killed when Ezekiel never rose up and shot the charging bandit. I saw the Villista swing his rifle toward me and advance on my position rapidly shooting as he came on. The man wore a demon's smile. I heard no sound but saw puffs of smoke from the barrel each time he fired. My guns were empty. I frantically tried to reload but kept dropping the cartridges as if my hands were numb. Then I felt bullets tearing into my flesh with white hot searing pain.

A rough hand gripped my shoulder and shook me awake. Confused I sat up in the seat and looked around. The rising sun quickly flushed away the dream. I recognized stretch of desert we were crossing. I figured we were only an hour out of Casa Grande. "Hell how many dreams like that am I going to have before I can trust myself to sleep easy again?"

"I don't know Oscar but it seems to me that dark thoughts are most awake when we are not. I have experienced these dreams myself. You were thrashing around so much it was easy to guess you were in a *bad* place." He gestured at the land around us. "We will be back in camp in less than an hour."

"That's a good thing. Those three rotting bodies are enough to make any man have nightmares. I hope Pershing appreciates what we had to go through to bring them back. We are mighty lucky we were not lynched by locals along the way."

"Speaking of the bodies, Ezekiel told me you were not going to let Patton leave with my father's body. Oscar I know how much returning to the Army meant to you. The fact that you were willing to disobey an order from a lieutenant for me is not something I will ever forget. I appreciate you speaking up on my behalf."

"As you say, it was nothing. I respect Patton's ability to lead. He does not hesitate to risk himself in a fight, but he was wrong. I don't know what I would have done had he ordered me to load your pa's body. Patton surprised me with his decision to let us switch bodies. I thought he was all business. Also he wanted the corpses to count coup with the general and President Wilson. He said proof we were winning was needed. He may be right but soldiers should not have to play politics. Besides, you're as close as a brother to me. My pa always said *family* comes *before* anything else. I expect what he really meant was any one of my brothers, sisters, ma, or any *other* family but me."

In another half hour we began to pass horses and vehicles heading to or away from the headquarters. Our arrival must have been trumpeted in advance because it appeared the whole camp was out to greet us. A mob of soldiers were crowding around Pershing. Like he had at the beginning of the battle at *San Miguelito* Patton climbed out onto the running board and jumped off his car before it came to a sudden stop before Pershing's tent. Alex and the other driver rolled in close by and parked. The immediate area was dust covered and nothing could be seen for a full minute. By the time the sand had settled Patton and Pershing were exchanging hardy handshakes and backslaps.

Anyone present could see the relief in Pershing at the prospect of having his star lieutenant back at headquarters. The assembled group included newspapermen and photographers. The crowd closed in with everyone talking at once. Finally after Pershing had congratulated Patton he turned his attention to the grim cargo strapped to the hoods of two of the Dodge automobiles. I think he actually gagged as the stench reached his nose. The horrid sight and odor of the three bloated and black bodies was not what he expected. Pershing had certainly seen death close up before but not in this way.

Alex and I leaned against the car and watched. I had no idea if the general would be pleased or dress down Patton for bringing back the dead men. I was surprised when he singled out Alex and me and ordered us to arrange an immediate burial detail far outside of camp. We both snapped to attention and started picking men at random to cut the men down. Sometimes I loathed being a sergeant again, but at least I would not be digging the holes.

Before we set off for our task Patton walked over and offered a rare smile. "Tonight all the men involved in the raid will dine with General Pershing in his tent. He wants to hear about the fight from every man. After you finish the burial detail go into town and have your uniforms cleaned and ironed." Just as quickly as it had appeared the smile was gone and his icy eyes fixed us to the spot. He then made a face like his stomach had just turned sour before saying, "We could all use a bath too." He started to turn away then added in a confidential manner, "I trust our slight deception in the favor of Sergeant Alejandro will go unreported?" With that he walked away in his usual brisk manner.

I looked at Alex. "Now I've seen everything a soldier could in this man's Army. When enlisted men are invited to sit down for a fancy meal with officers, I guess it's possible the sun could go down in the east tonight."

He shrugged. "It's okay by me. I wanted a bath in the worse way. Think about it Oscar, Pershing and Patton will be dining *far* better than anything we could scare up. You are a man who likes his grub hot and plentiful and that meal will fit the bill perfectly. Now, let's get this detail over with."

A wagon was hitched and loaded with the bodies. Nobody wanted the smell to get trapped in the bed of one of the trucks. As it was we might have to burn the wagon to rid it of the smell. The burial was not a very respectful affair and reminded me of the Columbus burials all over again. We had the men dig one long trench and all three bodies were dumped in and the dirt thrown back. These men had been my enemy. I searched inside myself but could not find room for sympathy for the dead Villista's. If it were not these men it could have been any of the troopers, including myself. Our burial would have probably been more in line with a scattering of our bones by vultures or other scavengers.

With the distasteful labor accomplished, I was looking forward to a long soak in a hot bath. Not for the first time I regretted giving up hard liquor. I needed something to dull memories of the last couple of years of my life. It was as if the putrid odor of the recently covered had slipped inside me. I felt that given two lifetimes I would still not be able to forget what I had seen and done in Mexico. The dead may be buried but their faces haunted me every night and sometimes even when awake. I did not regret the death of the bad men, only that they died for Villa's cause.

That night Alex and I were dressed in our newly cleaned and creased uniforms. We had no dress uniforms but neither did anyone else. I had not been this clean in weeks. Drink and food were plentiful. It was a temptation to overindulge in both. Pershing did not drink but was happy as a sober man could be. He was keen on the idea that a major figure in Villa's army had been killed. He kept slapping Patton on the back and calling him his, "little bandito." General Cardenas' weapons, saddle, and spurs were passed around for everyone to examine. The *spoils* were given to Patton as mementos.

As the battle particulars were told the journalist wrote furiously. Dozens of photographs were taken of Patton and Pershing. Already stories of the raid on the ranch had been telegraphed across America. I was sure by now Lieutenant Patton was fast becoming a household name. I wondered if my ma and pa would read about the battle. Of course there would have been no mention of the enlisted trooper's names. That was just as well. I would never speak of it to ma anyway. The less she knew the better. I was not sure if pa would believe me if I told him the story. Pa had a mighty low expectation of what I would become. Despite this recent success we had little to show for our months in Mexico. The country was hungry for news. How much longer would we fight in Mexico? Would we ever capture of kill Pancho Villa?

I tuned back to the celebration as one of the newspapermen asked Patton why he had shot the horse as the bandit charged at him. "Because a Texas Ranger friend of mine I met in El Paso told me to do just that if I ever found myself on the wrong end of a charging horse. Dave Allison would say it is hard to miss a horse, but a man makes a poor target bent low over his saddle. Stop the horse and the man will tumble down too. Cardenas was trapped under his horse for a spell but came up shooting when he got free. I plan on buying a large caliber revolver like Cardenas carried to add to my holster rig. I almost bought it while I was reloading. I could hear bullets whipping past me like an angry swarm of hornets."

One of the men laughed and dubbed Patton a "Bandit Killer". The newsmen liked the sound of that and said that would make for a good headline. Patton beamed and obviously enjoyed the attention. He sat in the center of the men and relit his pipe on a burning twig he fished from the campfire. Patton and Pershing were both in high spirits. Then some newsman mistakenly asked to see his pearl handled six shooter. A flash of anger burst free in an instant and he jumped up pulling his pistol out and held it near the man's face. "See this? It's a single action Colt .45 caliber pistol. It has hand carved ivory handles. You need to get the facts right in your story if you are going to write about me. Only a tin horned pimp would put pearl handles on a fine gun like this."

The confronted man was so scared his loss of color was obvious even in the campfire light surrounding the circle of men. Patton sat back down but did not holster his Colt. He pulled his knife and carved two small notches close together on the left underside of the stock. He held it up proudly and said, "Now, there were three bandits killed. I figure I only contributed to killing two of them." Nervous laughter was heard but nobody relaxed until he returned the pistol to his holster. The man was a mystery. Lieutenant Patton had a blistering fire burning inside him. I thought again about Custer and his last stand. I was sure there would be many more battles ahead for Patton. He was a restless warrior who would always seek battles to fight. I was sure Patton was not a man who would die safely retired at home in his own bed.

# CHAPTER 41

## *Playing Troopers and Bandits*

The tinny sound of the front chain link fence gate clanging open brought me back to myself. Mom and grandma were smiling at us gathered on the porch. Grandpa had stopped talking as soon as the gate had sounded a warning. My head was in a fog and both my hands were asleep from propping myself up on the porch for so long. I looked at my new Timex watch I had received for Christmas from grandma and grandpa. We had been on the porch for over two hours. The story had been the best so far. Of course it had been violent. Death and hardship for the soldiers had been everywhere. Grandpa's story was more exciting than any Gun Smoke episode or western I had ever seen at the movies. Grandpa had been through so much and I felt the loss of his friends when they died. Was he done or would there be more stories?

Those gathered on the porch stood and stretched. Suddenly remembering the last time, I took off in a sprint for the bathroom. I knew we would get on the road soon to return home. That meant I could not ask dad about grandpa's story until later, after we were home. After finishing in the bathroom, I walked back inside. Dad and John Ray were talking to grandpa. I scooted up to listen in case they were discussing the story. John Ray was saying, "Pa why did you wait so long to tell us you had met Patton. We read all about him becoming one heck of a famous general in World War II."

Dad added, "Can you write down another story and send it by mail? We all need to know what you and Sergeant Alejandro did the rest of your time in Mexico." He noticed me and added, "I'll bet Buddy wants another ear full too."

"We'll see. I expect I could get a letter out sometime after New Years." He jostled my hair and said, "Buddy got this whole thing started and now I can't seem to stop. Those were hard years, but I had good friends." A lonely look of sadness took over his face. "I'm sad to say most of them are gone now. I don't really know why I could not talk about it before."

I was really happy that dad and John Ray were now in on the stories, but I missed having grandpa to myself sometimes. What had begun as simple story time had become more of a family event. I tried to understand what dad and Uncle John Ray felt. If dad had experienced anything like what grandpa had I would want to know too. As it was I pestered dad all the time for stories of his time stationed in Germany after World War II. He had told me that in the fifties the Berlin Wall had been a simple barbed wire fence. Soldiers stationed in West Berlin were armed with a semi-automatic Colt 45 and an M-1 rifle. On the other side of the wire Russian tanks patrolled daily. Dad had said that sometimes a line of tanks would charge the fence in mock invasions. At the last possible minute they would turn and run along the inside of the fence. He said a lone soldier looking down the barrel of a Russian tank was enough to make some men wet themselves in fear.

On the way home I shared with Sherry some of the highlights of the last story. For once she seemed interested. We were sitting in the rear seat of the Buick station wagon and I kept my voice low. Sherry had studied in history class about Patton when he was a general in World War II, but had never read about him before the war. She was surprised that our own grandpa had known such an important man when Patton was just a lieutenant. I planned on reading everything I could about Patton in our encyclopedias when I got home. I would ask dad to take me to the downtown library. Or maybe I could find something in the school library when school started up after the holidays.

Suddenly remembering I was grounded, I thought I would have plenty of time to read while hanging out in the house. Today was the 26th and a Thursday. I would have to stay inside the rest of my

Christmas holiday thanks to my stunt of talking to the hobos. I was not completely sure if I was in trouble only for talking to strangers, or for going down by the railroad tracks. Still it all seemed worth it to know my new friends had been fed. The first time I had really wanted to help others had bit me like a mean dog off his chain. Eventually the slight rocking motion of the car put everyone in the car asleep but dad. I felt sorry for dad since he always had to drive. Someday when I was older I promised myself I would help him drive.

I fell into a dream of grandpa. It seemed so real as if I was one of the troopers looking on in Mexico. Grandpa was young and handsome with unruly hair, but he seemed downcast and troubled. He sat near a campfire staring sadly into a coffee cup. Lazy smoke wafted up from the cup as he tasted the hot liquid. Nearby there were many tents and sturdy horses cropping at the green grass. A strong-appearing Mexican in an Army uniform smiled down at him, then clapped him on the back and sat down next to him. I was sure it had to be Alejandro. I was happy that they were together and grandpa was no longer alone. Yet the man drinking coffee was not my grandpa, but Oscar. He put down his cup and began polishing a US Army belt buckle until it sparkled like gold.

Slowly I drifted back awake. An Elvis Presley song, *Devil in Disguise* was playing softly on Sherry's transistor radio. That excited me because it meant we were near home or she would not be able to pick up the station. I looked outside trying to figure out where we were. Mom broke into my thoughts as she spoke from the front seat, "Sherry would you turn that up a little? I like that song." After that I could hear mom singing along softly.

Dad always listened to Country and Western music performers. He liked Johnny Cash, Jim Reeves, and Marty Robbins. Mom listened to Elvis Presley, Jerry Lee Lewis, and Roy Orbinson. Mom and my Aunt Ruth had met Elvis at the Louisiana Hayride and got his autograph when she and dad used to go there. They had seen Hank Williams, Johnny Cash, Elvis, and many other singers that were just starting out. Mom and dad's records were played often by Sherry and me on the family's big RCA player in the living room. Then last Christmas

Sherry had gotten her own portable record player and she sometimes let me borrow it. It came in a red and white case and could be easily moved from her room to mine.

As we pulled into the driveway I saw Randy, his brothers and a couple of his sisters playing down the street. I literally ached to join them. Mom must have sensed my misery. She looked over at dad. He nodded like a baseball pitcher I had seen on television agreeing to his catcher's pitch choice. I marveled at their ability to read each other's minds. This I would never figure out. Mom said, "I guess you can start your grounding after the holidays. We have all been cooped up in the car for hours. Besides, you can't ride your new bike in the house. I'll have something thrown together for supper in about two hours. Do *not* be late Buddy."

"Thank you," I shouted over my shoulder as I was out of the car and down the street so fast I never heard a reply if there was one. When I met up with Randy, we walked to a local store where we sometimes stocked sodas and beer in the hottest part of the summer. We did it more for the coolness of the walk in coolers than the dollar we got to share for the hour's work. After spending time in the cooler it felt good to walk back outside under the hot Texas sun. Old man Miller had a bad back and was friendly enough. We enjoyed helping him out. As we cut through the field behind our house, I told Randy about the latest war story from grandpa. I told him every detail of meeting the three hobos and their dog. I ended by telling him about my grounding that would begin after the holidays.

Randy had an infectious chuckle that always made me smile. "Buddy you manage to get into trouble even when I'm *not* with you. I'll bet those bums were neat to talk to."

"I don't think they like being called bums, but they were fun to talk to. Imagine traveling all over the country riding on a train. Of course my dad told me there are Railroad Police who try to keep the hobos from riding for free."

"Buddy how long is your grounding for this time?"

"Two long weeks and I start after the holidays. If you remember I got a month after the trouble we got into last year over going up in the attic to see the church bell?"

"Yea, after Sunday school and before church started we went up to take a look. Then the singing started while we were up there. We could not get down or out without being seen."

"Dad called the police and everyone in my family went out looking for us. The whole time we were sitting up there listening to the sermon. We sweated buckets waiting for the preacher to wrap up that message. He was on a roll and did not finish for awhile. I tried to tell dad and mom afterwards that I had not missed a word, but somehow that did not help much."

Today we bought R.C. Colas and peanuts, putting the peanuts into our sodas. One time we had put the contents of a candy-powdered straw into our drinks. When the drinks overflowed we were thrown out of the store, but not before we had to mop the floor. We were walking directly on the rails and could walk a mile without falling off. The tracks ran near the end of Royal. There had never been a chance to jump and ride a train here. The trains never slowed down near our houses. As we walked we looked for soda bottles. We could cash them in for three cents each.

I thought of another time I had made my dad madder than I had ever seen him. "Randy do you remember when that poor lady and her car were hit by the train over by the Sears and Roebuck store?"

"Yes, her car stalled right on the tracks. I believe she made it out safely too. Then for some crazy reason she ran back like she had forgotten something. Her daughter stood in horror and watched her mom get hit. The daughter was holding her baby. She thought her mom had run back in a panic thinking the baby was still in the car."

"Uh huh, it took almost a mile before the train came to a stop right in front of Royal. You picked up some keys and I took home the car windshield inspection sticker. We found the stuff after the police had left. Dad was so angry. If he ever says, *damn* or *hell*, it's bad. He said we had disrespected the woman who had died. Dad called the police. We had to give the stuff back and apologize. Parents are always big on apologizing. Do you remember the time my mom made me tell that little girl who lived across the street I was sorry for saying she had cooties? Her mom got mad and called my mom. How was I to know that cooties were a real thing? That invisible bug got me in deep trouble with mom."

"Hey, do you want to stay over at my house tonight? We can make chili after dad and his friends finish playing poker. I think Channel 11 is running holiday movies all night. There won't be any Hercules movies but it'll be okay. You might as well have some fun until you start your grounding. If you keep getting in trouble I'll have to get a new best friend to hang out with."

"Sure, I'll ask my mom after we finish playing." Randy and I took turns spending the night at each other's houses. His dad Paul and his mom Vickie were great fun and always nice to me. Paul liked to play poker and we would sometimes watch, but our favorite thing to do was make homemade chili. We put whatever we could find in the pantry in it. As long as we cleaned up our mess our mom's did not mind. What a day this had been. Now there was more to come.

For the next two hours we played war, one of my favorite games. Randy was one of eight kids of which five were old enough to play. Randy and I were the oldest boys so we were always on opposite teams and planned strategy for our groups. We divided into two teams with Rory and Roxanne on my team. Rory was the funniest of the Cruz children. He made me laugh constantly with wisecracks and jokes. Randy took Ronny and Carla. I noticed Jo Ann was not around for some reason. During the game we would run, duck and hide with our stick guns or plastic toy ones.

At one point Randy's next door neighbor, Mrs. Black yelled at us to quiet down. She was a widow lady. I sometimes did chores for her, but she was also the crankiest lady on the street. The chores were mom's idea to help the lady out. Mrs. Black had often gotten me into trouble by tattling to mom. Naturally today I was pretending I was grandpa fighting bandits in Mexico. I was having a great time. At one point I darted for cover between Randy's house and his garage. Caught in the ten feet of open space between the house and garage a sudden ambush burst from the corner of the house. I was shot full of imaginary holes by the bandits.

In the tradition of *To Hell and Back,* my favorite Audie Murphy war movie, I died trying for a leaping slow-motion death like I had seen in a dozen movies. I landed hard and rolled over. When I came to a stop I realized I was really bleeding. Blood was pouring from beneath my left knee. My dress jeans were ripped. In spite of the blood I was more worried about what mom would say about the big hole in my jeans. Just as I was about to inspect the damage to the jeans, Randy and his *bandits* arrived to capture me and gloat over their victory.

Randy literally skidded to a quick stop dead in his tracks when he saw all the blood. He stood completely still and pointed at my left leg like a trained hunting dog. "Buddy, look at your leg."

Everyone gathered around me in stunned silence staring in amazement at my leg. I could not imagine what was wrong with them. Sure I was bleeding but I had been cut and scarred before this. In fact my family was kind of use to me coming in bruised, bloody or both. Then I took a close look at my left leg and pulled it up as close to my chest as it would go. Just under the knee and slightly to the left was a two inch triangular piece of glass from a soda pop bottle. I must have landed on it and drove it deep into my leg. Funny thing is I felt no pain and reached down and withdrew the glass as if I was picking up an interesting bug to examine.

Pain hit me like a fireplace poker that had just been removed from hours in flames. My head swam a lap around the pool. I thought I would pass out. Gritting my teeth I refused to black out in front of my friends or cry over the agony in my leg. Randy's mom Vicky came outside to see what all the fuss was about and immediately took charge. She was like my second mother and her calm helped me quiet. Randy, you, Ronny and Rory carry him to his house. Lu Ann, run on ahead and tell his parents." The three of them half carried, half dragged me down the street to my house.

When we were in front of my door I asked them to put me down. "Randy, get my dad." As he disappeared into my front door, we never knocked at each other's houses, I shouted after him, "Have someone bring a towel to wrap my leg up in. A moment later Lu Ann came outside carrying a large towel. Dad was with her and had his car keys already in his hand."

Within a minute they had me loaded into the Buick for the ride to the hospital. He invited Randy to come along, probably to keep my mind off the pain. Despite the towel I had wrapped around my leg I was bleeding all over the floorboard of dad's car. Blood was pooling on the floor and I was lightheaded. Through clinched teeth I told dad what had happened. He looked both tired and worried. I felt bad for him since he had just driven for six hours to get us home. Getting hurt was not a reason to be in trouble with dad. He figured it was just boys doing what boys do. However it did seem like I got hurt more than most of my friends.

The next thing I recalled was coming to in a hospital bed. At first everything was blurry and nothing made sense. Slowly I began to make out details in the room. First, there was Randy sitting close by in a chair by the bed. Then I saw mom and dad standing by the bed looking terribly worried. Mom was crying and I wondered what had happened. Who was sick? Oh, then I remembered. It was me who had been hurt. I began to call to mind small bits and pieces. "Mom, how did you get down here? Did you ride with us? I don't think you did."

She was hugging me one handed and wiping her eyes with the other. "No Shirley Gage drove me down. How are you feeling Buddy?"

"Puny, why don't I remember getting here? Are they going to give me stitches?"

"You feinted in the car. Look at your leg. They finished already. You've been out for about thirty minutes."

Mom pulled back the covers and I could see my leg was wrapped in bandages below the knee. "Well then let's go home."

Dad spoke up. "Oh no Buddy, you're too weak to go home now. You'll have to stay the night at least. Your momma will stay with you. I'll take Randy home when I go."

"What hospital is this?"

"You're at Great Southwest Hospital," dad said.

At that moment Jo Ann walked into the room. She was Randy's older sister but only a few months older than me. I thought she looked real cute in her Candy Striper uniform. I had forgotten she had talked about her volunteer job at a local hospital. I blushed as she came over and tucked the covers in around me. Jo Ann looked directly at me with a mischievous smile like I was her personal patient. "I'll take good care of him Mr. and Mrs. Draper." Mom and dad both smiled at Jo Ann. She and I teased each other all the time at school, but this was not lunch or after class. My friends and I still thought girls were yucky, but Jo Ann was okay-yucky.

Eventually dad and Randy said goodbye. Jo Ann was getting off work too so dad took her home as well. When mom and I were alone I said, "I'm sorry about the jeans mom."

"That doesn't matter, only that you are okay. I know boys are supposed to be rough and tumble but could you at least *try* to keep from slicing yourself up? I guess I should be thankful you have not ever broken a bone yet." She stopped for a second as we always did when we said something we did not want to come true. Then she knocked a couple of time on the nearby wood of the window sill. "You just try to be more careful young man. You scared me half out of my wits. I couldn't stand the loss of a child."

My mom's grandmother had been half Cherokee and like her grandmother, mom sometimes got a sense when something bad was about to happen, but not with me. I guess I just wore out her extra talent for seeing the future with too much activity on my part. Dad teasingly called mom his little *"witch"*. The little part was because she was 5'2". Mom weighed less than a hundred pounds. We always laughed when dad called her that. "Mom I don't want to stay here. I want to go home and sleep in my own bed."

"Buddy you know we only have one car. Besides Doctor Weiner absolutely forbid us to take you home until tomorrow. He said you need to rest now. Loss of blood makes you tired and sleeping will help heal you."

I yawned and felt my eyes drooping. I could see the concern on mom's face as she watched me. I shook my head still fighting the exhaustion closing in on me. In a tinny voice that sounded far off I said, "Mom where will you sleep?"

"They are bringing me in a roll-a-way bed. I'll be fine. Now go to sleep. I'll be here if you wake and need anything."

"Okay I am so sleepy." After a pause I said weakly from the floating edge of sleep, "Mom, I passed out I did not feint. Feinting is what girls do...

This time I did not dream. It was like falling into a dark bottomless cave, lacking light or sound. I was floating in the emptiness with no feelings for a very long time. Eventually a slight rhythmic squeaking noise came to my ears. Squeak, pause, and squeak again. What was that noise? Try as I might I could not identify it. Then, bright December sunlight was flooding into my eyes. I sat up suddenly with no idea of where I was. Across the room Jo Ann had just finished raising the heavy blinds on the window. She turned around and studied me from across the room. I could not read her expression and wondered if I would ever understand the mystery of girls? A full six seconds passed before she finally awarded me to a dazzling smile showing even white teeth.

"How is my star patient this morning?" I fell back onto the bed with the room swirling around me at a dizzying speed. I was afraid I would pass out again, or worse still, throw up in front of Jo Ann. By the time the room settled into a slight rocking motion Jo Ann and mom were by my bed. Jo Ann turned to mom before saying in alarm, "I'm so sorry. He sat up too quickly. Before I could stop him he got dizzy." To me she said, "Silly, don't sit up so fast like that again. You scared me."

Mom looked at me and said in mock anger, "You wait until the one minute I step out to get a cup of coffee and then you try to hurt yourself again." She sighed in mock exasperation. "What am I going to do with you?"

"Sorry mom. I didn't know where I was. My head feels light. Why am I so dizzy?"

At That moment Dr. Weiner walked into the room. He was round-bellied and had been our family doctor as long as I could remember.

He answered my question with a concerned smile. "Because Buddy you lost too much blood. It will take a few days before you feel like yourself."

"When can I go home?"

He ignored me and I knew what would come next. Every time he had to stitch me up he would always lectured me on being more careful. "Buddy before you're grown, if you live to grow up that is, you will look like Frankenstein's monster with all the stitch scars on you."

"Okay, I'm sorry and I'll be more careful, but when can I go home?"

"I heard that a few times from you Buddy, but in a few weeks or months here we are again. This time you managed to make it into the hospital instead of just my office. I'll bet I've put two dozen stitches in you over your short life. I know your dad works hard for his money. Are you trying to drive your family to the poor house?"

Mom interrupted us with the question I most wanted to know. "When can I take Buddy home doctor?"

"I expect we can release him this morning. Let's see if he can hold down some breakfast and walk around a bit without falling first."

He left to make other rounds. Mom looked around the room and, not seeing a telephone said, "I'm going to step down the hall to the lobby and call your dad. Don't get up. I will be right back. Watch him for me Jo Ann."

After she left I listened for awhile. Not hearing anyone in the hall I said, "Help me to sit up okay? If I get dizzy again I'll lay back down."

She looked nervously at the door. "Buddy are you *trying* to get me in trouble? This is not school. I'm only eleven and had to lie about my age to work at this hospital job."

"Volunteer job you mean. I just want to sit up." She came around to the left side of the bed and took my hand and pulled. Her hand was warm and soft. My face flushed again but I liked the feeling this time. Once I was up she held onto my hand for an extra second. At the moment we both noticed it she let go abruptly. At eleven years old I did not know what to think about girls but I figured I must have a crush on Jo Ann. She was my friend's sister and for some reason that seemed like a problem. Also none of my friends admitted they liked girls yet.

"Now her face seemed red too. She tucked an extra pillow behind my back to prop me up. "Buddy I have got to go see other patients. I can't just babysit you all day. You know you're not the *only* helpless person in here."

"Yes but you are worried about *me*. Admit it. I won't tell anyone." I grinned, easily slipping into our familiar teasing banter. "Besides, you can't leave until my mom comes back. You're stuck with me." She opened her mouth to retort, but mom walked back in carrying my food tray. Jo Ann beat a hasty retreat out the door and disappeared.

Mom watched her go suspiciously, and then turned her attention back to me. She studied my face. From her scrutiny I felt like I had done something wrong, but had no idea what it could be. Finally mom crossed her arms over her chest and said, "Buddy now that I've had time to think about it some more, maybe you *should* keep playing games with Randy and the other *boys* in the neighborhood. I guess even if it means you get hurt every now and again, it is just boys being boys." She ran her fingers through my wavy hair looking worried. Parents always seemed to be upset over things and yet would not explain what it was. Sometimes my parents were harder to understand than girls were.

We had to return to school on January 2nd, a Thursday, so we were excited about the short week. Living in Grand Prairie, but also in Tarrant County, we were bused almost twenty miles to C.E. Dunn Elementary School in Arlington. We had to wait on the bus one street over from our own. The Cruz bunch along with Sherry and I cut through an alley and waited shivering in the sudden cold front that had visited last night. The temperature was thirty-five degrees but felt much colder. The wind was howling up the alley and cut through our coats making the day more miserable than ever. Randy, his brothers, sisters, and Sherry and I were huddled in a group against the cold. By mutual agreement every few minutes we would rotate a few of us to the outside to shield those inside.

Nothing really helped. I wiggled my little toes, afraid they might be frozen. As far as I knew those little toes were not needed for much, but I still preferred not to lose one of them. Jo Ann was standing near me. She smiled shyly every time I looked in her direction. I thought it must have something to do with what happened at the hospital but was not sure. With that thought, I reached down and felt my leg where the stitches had recently been removed. It still hurt every time I put weight on it. I had begged to return to school to be with my friends. Knowing I was grounded to the house as soon as I returned home made school seem more appealing. At least I could play outside during recess period. Every day I had noticed that if I walked too much on my leg it would be swollen and throbbing with pain. Of course I ignored it and packed as much play time into school as I could.

Jo Ann was close enough now that I could smell whatever soap she used. Was she cold or did she *want* to stand close to me? Suddenly a gust of wind hit us so hard it almost knocked the group down. We shared a silly group stagger before regaining our balance. Giggles broke out in the circle, but I was distracted by a thought. As if the wind had suddenly blown the answer to me, I finally realized what mom had been so upset about. She thought that if I began to like girls, her son would no longer be her little boy. I had to admit I was starting to think about girls more, but I was still not ready to admit it to them or my friends. With the moon-eyes I was getting from Jo Ann and a pretty, freckle-faced red-headed girl named Drew Baldwin at school, I might have to make a decision about girls before I wanted to.

Finally the bus arrived and we were crowded inside where some of us had to stand because the seats were full. I had once seen an uncle open a can of sardines. The tiny smelly fish were packed so close; I thought that was how we must look. The days of my grounding dragged on and finally the two weeks ended. I had spent many hours reading library books about grandpa's Lieutenant Patton. He had become a great general and had fought in both World Wars. I found interesting storied about General Pershing there too. He had fought bravely in the First World War. I read that he had become a general by being promoted all the way from the rank of captain by Teddy

Roosevelt, which caused a big stir at the time. It was exciting to know my grandpa had known both men. Even dad had been amazed that his own father had known these men, and yet never shared it with him or his brother and sisters.

After missing so much play time it was glorious to hike or play with friends every day after school. I had to admit to looking for Jo Ann every time I went outside to play. She was on my mind more that I would admit to anyone. I had almost forgotten about grandpa's promise to write another letter. Then just like last time the letter arrived on a Friday. There it was thick and inviting, sitting on dad's desk. I picked it up and my heart beat faster. I turned it over slowly and examined it from every side. I imagined the thrilling adventures within the words were whispering to me through the envelope. I put it back on the desk with a little pat. Excitedly I shouted, "Mom, what time will dad be home?"

# CHAPTER 42

## *Pershing's Informant*

It was not quite like the last time. Dad was as anxious to read the letter as I was. Him and I set up the backyard grill and had the coals beginning to turn white less than thirty minutes after he came through the door. Sherry helped mom in the kitchen slice lettuce, tomatoes, and onions for dad. I wanted sliced pickles too, fresh from my Uncle Herbert's pickle plant in Texarkana. He always gave me a jar every time I visited. I usually ate the whole jar by myself over a couple of months. I would store the pickle jar under my bed. I even drank all the pickle juice once the jar was empty. This time I had sacrificed a big fat one for the hamburger cookout. Mom and I had traded two of her Cokes, one each for Sherry and me, for the pickle. I would have given it anyway, but it was a nice trade.

The Gage family, Shirley, Bobby, and their children, Diane, Pam, and Paula, joined us from next door. Mrs. Gage was pregnant, due at any time. Mom had said she was having a girl by the way she was carrying the baby. I was in a great mood and the extra guest just added to the feeling of having a party. Dad always liked to have Fritos with his hamburger and mom made her special onion dip to go with it. By 6:30 we were eating and having a great time. Mr. Gage was a mechanic and sometimes worked on the family Buick. One time when we were late to church and the engine would not start, he opened the Buick hood, touched a couple of things, and then gave the engine a scowl. It started right up.

Mr. Gage sometimes let me mow his yard. However, he had thrown so many metal parts into the grass it was a risky job. I usually avoided the task unless I was saving for something special. Then I would pull the lawnmower backwards to look for bolts, sparkplugs, or any other potential metal missiles hiding in the grass of his yard. Dad let me use his mower if I replaced the gas. Then there was the time I put kerosene in the tank by mistake and ruined the mower. Our garage was dark and I picked up the wrong can by accident. The lawn mower ran perfectly the whole time but afterwards dad said the metal parts of the engine were fused together. Even Mr. Gage could not save that engine. The mistake was costly. I had to pay for it out of my earnings from washing cars and mowing in the neighborhood. I took almost any odd job to pay dad back. However, Randy's dad Paul helped us build a nice go cart with the mower wheels.

That night after we had eaten dad placed a fat water melon on our backyard pick nick table. He took a long kitchen knife and cut slices of the yellow-inside water melon. We did not usually get the yellow ones so it was a rare treat. Everyone ate without spoons and some of us added salt. Dad always carved slices off with the knife for himself. Mom would usually worry about him cutting himself since he kept his knives razor sharp. Afterwards I took the garden hose and washed the table down as Sherry gathered the rinds to throw into the metal garbage can. I thought it was funny that the seeds would plants themselves in our yard, but never grow a watermelon big enough for us to eat. Suggs ran about the yard yapping at me happily thinking I was playing with the water hose.

Mom and Shirley sat in the living room talking and dad invited Bobby to listen to the letter. He explained some of what we had heard or read already. Bobby was interested and we went into dad's office. There were two hard wooden office chairs. I took one and Bobby the other. Dad sat behind his desk and took out a blue plastic letter opener he had received from one of his accounting clients. He carefully sliced open the end of the letter. I took in a big breath in anticipation. The feeling was similar to when I was about to watch a movie I was excited about, but much stronger. I had heard other adults refer to dad as a perfectionist. He could not be rushed and was careful about every thought and action.

At first dad read to himself and I knew it must be family news that grandpa had put in the letter. Having experienced this before I held my tongue and waited for him to finish. After a minute or so he began reading out loud in his strong voice. As before it seemed like I could hear grandpa's gruffer voice laid over dad's…

The weeks dragged on with patrols scouting south and north by Jenny bi-plane, mounted troopers and vehicle. As for Alex and I we were back in a saddle twelve hours a day. For the most part I loved the freedom of it all. I had witnessed the future of the Army and the vehicles that would replace my horse. It was easy to predict that the end of the cavalry life was coming. Yet that knowledge made me hang on tighter to the past. Alex and I went out on separate missions and together. We usually returned the same night. At other times we made it back within three to five days to *Casa Grande*.

It filtered down that Patton was now a first Lieutenant, promoted after his success at killing three of Villa's top men. He had indeed become a national figure. My ma had even mentioned Patton by name in a letter. She wanted to know if I knew him. I wrote back that I had seen him around camp, but nothing about my involvement in the battle at *San Miguelito*. She would have been terrified for my safety. Newspaper reports had played up the event to make Patton a hero, which he was, or would be someday. He was still young and reckless and could get himself killed first. When I thought about *San Miguelito* I knew most of us had fought worse battles and many times more bandits than the four we had killed there. I had been in more danger in Glen Springs or Columbus than during our attack on the ranch at *San Miguelito*.

General Pershing had a hoard of hungry peasants feeding him supposed leads as to the whereabouts of Pancho Villa. We were no longer dining with Pershing, but the word was that the general was frustrated by restrictions placed on him by President Wilson. Apparently Mexican President Carranza was putting up one awful stink over our invasion. President Wilson had been repeatedly assured that Pancho Villa was dead and we should withdrawal immediately from Mexico. If that were true it made no sense that raids were still occurring on the border between the United States and Mexico. Our leaving border towns unprotected had opened a window that other bandits were pouring through. In fact President Wilson had ordered the activation of 75,000 National Guardsmen into service for patrol of the borders of Texas and New Mexico.

The general had other pressing matters to deal with too. As the blood lust for Villa's head ebbed away, the boredom and endless routine of camp life, fueled by alcohol exploded. Drunken gunfights between Mexican citizens in town and troopers became a daily fact of life. When I was not on duty, I made short trips to town to get necessary items, and then hotfooted it back to camp. I did not want to get shot by angry citizens or have to kill a soldier either. Pershing studied the matter and solved the problems through his usually tactic. He imposed rigid training maneuvers to keep us busy. If we were not on patrol we would complete endless cavalry drills. We spent days combing the desert on horseback searching for any sign of Villa, then spent hours back in the saddle around camp practicing to ride a horse. I suspected the general was actually preparing us for fighting in Europe if the war overseas dragged on.

I had somewhat lost track of the days, but sometime passed the middle of June, 1916 one of Pershing's informants rode into camp with a report of Villa's whereabouts. I was in camp with Alex and he was called in to translate for the general. The man was so dirty it was impossible to tell what race he was. Secondly he had a rat-like appearance that set me on edge immediately. My ma would not have approved of my instant dislike of a man I did not know. However I had no desire to ride into a trap set by Villa. There were nearly one hundred men in camp at the time. We stood around listening while Alex translated the man's words. If he was Mexican or not I was not sure, but he spit out the language like a native. Alex told Pershing the man's name was Acalan and he was a Mexican-Indian.

It was easy to see that General Pershing was taking Acalan's story with what my ma would have called a *healthy dose* of skepticism. The man told Pershing that Pancho had been observed along with his Revolutionary Army moving around the town of Carrizal, Chihuahua.

The village was northwest of our position, in Chihuahua. Over the next three days the same story was told by other citizens who rode into camp. Excitement ripped through camp like a forest wildfire. Every man wanted to return home. If not home than at least get back over on the American side of the border. Any chance to accomplish this was exciting news. It seemed this might be our chance to end our invasion.

Elements of the 7th Cavalry and the 10th, composed of Buffalo Soldiers were assembled for the trip to Carrizal. Alex and I were once again detailed to the 7th. We rode out a hundred strong on June 18th to scout the area for Villistas. The ride took two days before we neared the town. It was impossible to keep our presence a secret. There were no known canyons or other places to hide the men and horses. Acalan was sent into Carrizal to assess the situation. I had argued that Alex should be sent in with him. I did not trust Acalan and believed he should not have been allowed to accompany us. Alex must have felt the same because he told Acalan he would shoot him dead if he betrayed us. The words sounded worse in Spanish, but the message was received. Acalan did not look like a happy man when he rode out.

The captain decided against general opinion that Acalan would go in alone and report back to the group. The Army was not a democracy, but some commanders listened to seasoned veterans more than others. We set up camp on June 20th and the men were spread out. Picket lines were set out for the horses. Wanting to travel light, we had brought no artillery. Cannons would have been a comfort. The horses were used as an outer shield against an attack after darkness fell.

Alex and I went about assigning night guards before we trudged back our bedrolls. Alex stopped to talk to a couple of the men and the three of them shared cigars. I was not feeling sociable and walked on in a surly mood with no real reason I could point a finger at. I was sure there would be no sleeping for me this night. The breeze was warm, but the wind carried a faint smell of rain from the far off mountains. I could see lightning further off to the north which probably accounted for my unease.

The sun had set more than two hours back and it was plenty dark with no moon. I heard someone approaching and recognized Alex by the sound of his steps. My hearing had vastly improved after my recent experience with blindness. "I know what you're thinking Oscar."

"Maybe I was thinking I should shoot any Mexican sneaking up on me in the dark."

I could not see his face but heard his laugh clearly. "No, you're wondering if that storm will come down on us. It won't. It's just the heat of the day slamming into the cold air of the mountains. If it rains it'll be miles from here. You'll be safe unless you shelter in a dry river. Flash floods can come at you quick."

"I know your *smart-butt* grew up in Mexico, but if that storm comes through here, I'll hold you responsible. I've seen all the lightning I want. For now I'm more worried about Villa riding in here with five-hundred men. He wouldn't have to shoot a one of us. He could just stampede these horses right over us. We can't defend ourselves in the dark."

"Well I hope he isn't as smart as you. Anyway, they can't ride in here without us hearing them. A rock falling off a crumbling cliff can carry for miles out here in the desert."

"I guess you're right. Still, even if we hear a large force on the march we have no cover out here in the open. What do you think about that sorry excuse for a man Acalan?"

"His name is from the old Aztec. Most native Indians never associated with the Spanish and their blood is considered pure."

Sarcastically I said, "I'm happy for him but that doesn't mean we can trust him. Some men earn their living through a life of grifting. Greed is a hard demon to put down. Also hunger is a powerful motivator with times hard on both sides of the border."

I heard Alex shrug in the darkness. "That is true. Maybe he just wants us out of his country. Most Indians don't like the Mexican Army or any form of government. They stay to themselves mostly and have no reason to like us either."

Whatever I was about to say was lost to me. We heard a lone horse walking gingerly. If it was Acalan, he was careful not to get shot by the night guards. Alex and I moved further out from the horses. I placed a restraining hand on the shoulder of one of the troopers. The man was tracking the soft sounds with his rifle. I whispered, "Wait. Don't shoot until you know who is out there. It might be Pershing's informant." Then I added, "Don't shoot me either soldier."

Alex and I moved out and separated with our Springfield rifles at the ready. When the rider was thirty feet from camp he stopped and sat his horse. Alex from far off to my left spoke in Spanish to the rider. I could not catch any of the exchange but the rider's words with Alex seemed excited. I thought it sounded like Acalan. Alex turned and shouted to the night guards. "Let him pass he says he has word of Villa."

Ten minutes later at around 11:00 o'clock, a dozen of us were sitting around a small fire with Acalan, Lieutenant Henry Adair and Captain Francis Boyd. Both men were unfamiliar to me but seemed capable enough. Adair was wiry, thin and nervous in his movements. Boyd was stocky and wore a permanent frown on his face. His one expression made it hard to read the man. Acalan drank coffee as he shifted his position every few seconds. The captain spoke now in a low voice to Alex. "What does he say? I can tell he has news by the way he keeps fidgeting. Either that or he is about to piss his pants."

Alex spoke to Acalan and most of us strained to discern any information, but had to settle for the translation. "He says Villa is in town with two dozen men. They are drinking hard and will be useless in we attack by morning. Their camp is a little north of the town and as exposed as ours. If we ride through town, then turn north it is a short trail to their camp. He says it is no more than a half mile north from town."

Boyd did not change his frown but he fell quit as he thought about the prospect of ending our search. Eagerness shown in his eyes, either from the possibility of promotion, glory, or returning home was upon him. Sweat popped out on my forehead. I admit I was frightened. This could be excellent news or a trap. Was it to be victory and home, or death waiting?

"Finally Captain Boyd asked, "Sergeant Alejandro ask him again about their defensive position. I need to know all of it?""

Alex spoke again and after Acalan answered, he stepped away from the fire indicating the captain to follow. Over my shoulder I heard the whispered words of the captain and Alex. "It sounds too good sir. He says they are camped in the open and will be passed out drunk and easily taken. I don't trust him captain. The man is hiding something, what I can't say."

Yes, I agree. Pancho would never let all his men get drunk. Someone has to be on watch. Either that or it is a trap. That old bastard has not lived this long by being careless. He may act in desperation, such as attacking Columbus, but a hunted man cannot afford to be slapdash about his security. If our Mr. Acalan is leading us into the lion's mouth he will be the first to die. I want you to see to it personally that he is out in front of us when we move out."

"Sir, I could take a few men and scout the town. We could check the camp while it is still dark. It would be better to know something about the layout before we go charging in."

"Sorry I can't risk a stumble in the dark alerting them. We will have to find our way in the daylight." Captain Boyd returned to the fire but did not sit back down. "Lieutenant Adair I want you to have the men up and assembled an hour before dawn. Every man needs a hot meal in his belly and be armed to the teeth. By my recollection tomorrow is June 21st. We will ride out at first light." He looked at the men around him. "If Pancho Villa is over there I intend to bring him back to Pershing trussed up like a Christmas goose. He can ride *in* the saddle or *over* it. The choice is his to make."

Surprisingly I returned to my bedding and slept soundly for about two hours, then relieved one of the troopers to rest. Alex did the same. I was alone with my thoughts in total darkness. The wind was stirring but no creature movement was heard. I was getting used to the now familiar sensation of anxiety, but this time I felt something new. I felt like a worn out old man. The fatigue went straight down to the bone. The life of a trooper was hard. A soldier who had lost all taste for fighting was not worth much to the Army. If I did not gather my wits about me I would not be ready for the upcoming fight. I was not weary from the travel or the months of patrols, but the whole prospect of fighting a ghost like Pancho Villa. It seemed my plans for a career in the Army might not be in the cards or what I now wanted.

I thought of Patton's words, "War is driven by politics and ran by politicians." I no longer wanted to kill or die here in this cursed desert either. Villa was as much at home in the Mexican desert as a rattler, whereas we were the interlopers here. I now believed If Pancho, his men, or lawless others of like mind crossed the Rio Grande into the United States again, we should give them the smoking death they had coming. I just did not believe in all this nonsense of chasing bandits round the bushes. However it had been my experience that sergeants were rarely asked for their opinion.

# CHAPTER 43

## *The Carrizal Affair*

Not knowing exactly where we were in Mexico, I only had a rough estimated of being northwest of Casa Grande. We were mounted and ready for a charge or whatever the captain ordered. Each man prepared himself in his own way. Buffalo Soldiers from the 10th were up front eager to be the first into the fray. The 10th were serious-minded fighters. As far as I was concerned they had nothing to prove, but maybe they thought otherwise. It occurred to me that if Villa was in or around Carrizal, there might not be enough of him left to haul back to General Pershing. As the old saying went, these men *rode for the brand*. That *brand* was Pershing. These Buffalo Soldiers would ride through Hades and back for their general.

The previous evening Alex had reminded Boyd that in Mexico it was hard to tell friend from foe. In some parts Pancho was a hero and might be defended by townsfolk. The captain stubbornly refused offers by Alex to go into town and talk to citizens to get the lay of the land. I was reminded that as impulsive as Patton was, he planned every angle before an attack. For better or worse we were riding into the unknown, feeling our way along like a blind man who has dropped his cane.

Pancho could be dead drunk with his men or have hundreds of Villistas hidden in a canyon ready to spring into the attack. If Captain Boyd had a date with destiny then we were along for the ride. I reminded myself that nobody had forced me into the Army either time. A soldier's place was to follow orders. Every trooper had a

302    J. Michael Beck

commander, but on the field of battle, the only man that mattered was the brass leading your troop.

I caught sight of Lieutenant Adair up front, whereas Captain Boyd was nearby and about six feet ahead of where Alex and I sat our horses. Speaking in a whisper I said to Alex, "Do not act like you have to win this fight by yourself. Remember, you are a man with a family and a ranch waiting for you."

He grinned at me, perfectly as ease opposed to my own anxiety. "Do not worry my friend; my destiny is to die surrounded by my children and grandchildren generations from now. Oscar Take care of your own backside and stay in the saddle this time. Then we will ride out of Mexico together."

Acalan, per the captain's orders was directly ahead of Alex. Most of the men eyed him with suspicion. The man sat quietly on his horse. To most he seemed outwardly calm, but sweat rolled down his face. That was most unusual in the cool morning air. I looked over at Alex and saw he was watching the man carefully. Feeling my eyes on him, Alex turned and a wordless thought passed between us. I knew my friend had seen it too.

At that moment I caught sight of movement toward the front of the column. There would be no warison or bugle call to attack. A silent hand gesture from the captain to move out had been seen by all the men in the beginning light of the day. Just as the sun was breaking over the horizon the men at the front of the columns began to edge their horses forward at a slow trot. This time we did not skirt the town but rode right down the center of the street. We were two hundred strong and our columns stretched past either end of Carrizal. I saw few citizens out moving at the early hour and no alarm was raised. A sleepy shopkeeper sweeping his porch looked at us in shocked disbelief. An old woman sat on a porch rocking slowing. Her eyes seemed glassy and I thought she might be blind. He head cocked slightly and her nostrils flared with the smell of horses. An old mongrel dog rolled over but failed to offer even a feeble bark.

As before I pulled my rifle out of my scabbard and pointed it down and across my saddle. If I had need of the 03 I wanted to use it first before going to the 45. At that moment my eyes began to throb reminding me of my near death in battle. I vowed to keep a death grip on at least one of my weapons if I was thrown again. In my mind I changed the phrase *death grip* to just hanging onto the gun. A thousand worries crowded my mind when I should have been concentrating on the matter at hand. Would my horse panic when the shooting began? Would I be wounded again or fall dead here in Mexico? How would my ma hear of my death? I mentally shook myself to focus my attention.

We were turning now as we rode through Carrizal and turned north. The ground began a gradual incline as we trotted toward nothing we could see from the middle of the line. I glanced at Acalan and saw he was positively beside himself with fear. The man reminded me of a caged wild animal. He looked around nervously as if he would be shot from the saddle at any moment. If he had set a trap for us he might discover his fear was real enough. I had no doubt that the captain or Alex would do what they intended. He would be killed without hesitation. Alex was not the sort of man who would normally shoot a man from behind. However our own survival might depend on his actions. We could not risk a traitor escaping to bring Villa's men raining down on us from ambush.

At the head of the column the crack of rifle fire was heard and the battle was joined. I could feel the column surge forward as if we were swept away on the tide. Horses were not machines, but living animals with training and emotions. At the first sights and sounds of a fight the animals would either panic or excitedly speed into the heart of the action. My horse chose to break into a gallop without a command from me. Shouts and more rifle volleys came crashing to my ears. Then the confusion of men and dust were joined. Visibility from the dust dropped to almost nothing as we rode ahead following those in front. It maddened me to not be able to see what was ahead. The distinctive sound of the Springfield rifles were followed instantly by barrage of fire from unrecognized rifles. Uniformed soldiers on foot and horseback rushed our position. We now fought for our lives against a larger, if not superior force.

After the first shots had rang out Acalan made a quick attempt to break to his right. Alex, anticipating the move made a fast maneuver to position himself between Acalan and the outside open space beyond the columns. By plan the man had deliberately been given a smaller horse. The larger mount Alex rode easily forced the slighter animal back in line. I rode into a position on the man's left to box him in. The panic rising in him was plain to see. Acalan wanted to be free of us in the worst way. Whether it was from fear of the battle itself or a sign of betrayal I did not know.

In the next moment I was into the scrap and had no more time to waste on Acalan. Riders and footed soldiers charged at us from two sides. I fired my Springfield four times and knocked two men from the saddle and another I hit as he ran toward me with a sword poised to run me or my horse through. Firing was all around me and in the thick of the dust and smoke I lost sight of Alex and the captain. The soldiers wore uniforms but it was impossible to tell what kind. Most of Villa's men wore a Mexican Revolutionary Army of sorts. However in some part of my mind I noticed the rhythm of the fighting seemed different. These men were well trained and fought with well ordered discipline, not the insane rage of bandits I had faced before. I put aside my doubts and fought on.

It was obvious we had encountered a better trained and equipped force than expected. These men did not fight like drunken bandits, but sober and disciplined soldiers. I swore out loud in hopes that Alex or Captain Boyd killed the son-of-a-bitch that sent us into this mess. By now I was down to my Colt with no chance to reload as I rode. I clubbed a soldier off his horse with the Springfield's stock, and then slid the bloody rifle back into the scabbard.

My horse responded beautifully to the commands I gave him with my knees when my hands were full. At that instant I felt a shot run the length of my scalp. With my hat taken with the bullet blood flowed immediately down over my face and into my eyes. The top of my head burned like molten lava. I did not think the wound was serious or I would be unconscious or too injured to care. I wiped my face in time to see a rider raising a rifle to shoot me. As if with a mind of its own, I felt the 45 in my hand buck twice. The man was swept over backwards. He left his horse as if he had ridden into a low tree branch at a full gallop.

Again wiping my face I frantically looked around me for any new threats. Before I could decide what to do about the wound or reload, the retreat bugle sounded. Relief washed over me as troopers immediately swung west back toward our camp. Through the coursing blood stinging my eyes I could make out bodies on the ground. If the wounded or dead were friend or enemy I could not tell. My heart weighed heavily in my chest as I rode ahead following the troopers ahead from the area. The firing was becoming sporadic as we put the battlefield behind us. With no pursuit immediately following, we needed to regroup in camp and assess our position. Was Alex captured or killed? Either way I vowed to return no matter the cost.

It felt wrong, like I was trapped in a nightmare that would not release me. There had been no clear victory or defeat. Judging from the sun the clash between the two armies had lasted no more than twenty minutes. It had been sudden and brief but costly. I was back in camp and a soldier was washing my wound. As I had thought the bullet had passed along my hairline and was not serious. I had lost a lot of blood and felt weak. Whether from the after affects of the battle or loss of blood I could not tell. No one had seen Alex since the fighting began and there were over thirty-five troopers missing, including the young Lieutenant Adair.

If not for orders I would have ridden out as soon as my wound was cleaned and the bleeding stopped. I was impatient for action. The thought of leaving Alex unburied or captured by bandits was unthinkable. I listened intently to troopers who were involved in the initial moments of the battle. It was said that as we peaked out on the rise a large camp was indeed in the open. However there had been possibly three hundred soldiers spread out in large tented camps. Immediately those in camp who had been alerted by the sound of our horses began firing at the troopers. Lieutenant Adair urged his horse forward in an insane charge. His men watched in stricken horror as he was shot from the saddle by numerous rifle strikes. Adair was the first man lost to the blistering fire.

In turn, most of the first shooters in the opposing camp were struck down under the return fire from the 10th. After that initial burst of firing the battle was lost in the confusion of men, horses, and dust that I had experienced. The troopers agreed that our arrival had been a surprise, but the camp had not been manned by a couple dozen drunken bandits sleeping off a night in the town. The general agreement was that we had encountered a superior force in numbers, well trained and too professional to be Villa's usual bandits.

Most of those soldiers who had been at the front believed we had killed more than forty on their side. Whatever the cost in lives, we were still in danger if we were attacked again. We had less than 180 men in camp and no artillery. With my head wound cleaned and a bandage applied, I was trying to think of a way to slip out of camp and look for Alex. Before I could form a plan, riders were heard coming from the direction of the town. Not a full army but a smaller group, at least the smaller group were approaching first. I was hoping to see Alex and some of the troopers returning. Some men dropped to a prone defensive position, including me, while others ran for their horses.

Six soldiers rode to the edge of camp. At least one was wearing the rank of captain. I did not recognize the uniform immediately, but a sickening feeling washed over me. These men were Carranzistas, so named for the Mexican president. It had been regular army soldiers we had attacked. The Mexican Federals carried a white flag and waited patiently for our commander to address them. In the stunned silence, Captain Boyd rose from the ground and approached the men. He walked with his only remaining officer, Lieutenant Joshua Morey a few steps behind.

Captain Boyd stood, back straight, but when he walked forward it made me think of a man walking to the gallows. He did not fear the men before him, but the mistake that had been made. His career would be altered or even ended by the events of today. We would all have to live with ourselves after today's actions. Boyd carried a rifle but had the barrel pointed at the dirt. About halfway to the point where the Mexican soldiers waited he faltered in his steps. Turning slightly he looked over his shoulder and said, "Lieutenant Morey, I will be in need of somebody to translate."

"There will be no need captain, I speak English well enough. I have traveled extensively in your beautiful country." The Mexican Army Captain that had spoken moved his horse forward a few paces. He was dark complexioned and had a scar across his face from his nose to the corner of his lip. I could not say the scar made him appear as the dashing officer of stories, but the sword wound gave him instant respect in the eyes of the men before him. Know he had seen battle and survived had weight with soldiers of any race. Now he sat proudly on his mount, but grief was etched into his face. He let silence settle around him before he spoke again. "I am Captain Antonio Castillo of the Federal Army of Mexico. I assume you are the captain who, along with your men attacked our camp this morning."

Our captain spoke slowly with great formality. "Sir I am Captain Boyd. On behalf of my men and myself, I apologize for our inadvertent error. We had what we believed was a reliable informant. Our intentions and orders were to capture Pancho Villa, not assault the proud and noble Mexican Army. The mistake is most regrettable."

Captain Castillo sat quietly as he considered Boyd's words. "I believe it was inevitable that when two mighty armies are both in pursuit of the same devil, mistakes would be made. Captain you and I are military men. Our actions and their effects are not entirely in our control. However I fear there will be grave consequences for both of our governments because of the loss of life today. My commander and personal mentor, General Felix Gomez was killed in the battle along with forty-five of my men."

If Captain Boyd was shocked he hid it well. "I too am missing men. The rough count is that we are missing thirty-seven troopers. I am truly sorry for the loss of your men and the general. May we recover our dead?"

"Yes certainly. Also we are holding twenty-three of your men. I assure you those wounded are being cared for. Your famous Buffalo

Soldiers rode in without fear of death. I suggest an exchange quickly, before word reaches the capitol. My superiors may not be so generous. Political forces beyond my rank may demand the retention of your men." He paused and spoke again. "Ah, another suggestion captain, you might consider a hasty retreat from Carrizal for the safety of your command. When the general's replacement arrives you may be hunted."

Before Captain Boyd could respond the sound of horses walking was heard. Every man present reacted swiftly. Soldiers were much alike no matter what country they called home. Both sides readied weapons fearing further betrayal. Fingers tightened on triggers, including my own. Nerves were on edge with dozens of rifles tracking the sound as the riders neared. With or without orders shooting could start at any instant. A creak of a saddle or a popped knuckle could as easily set it off as a fired shot.

Then I heard Alex hail the camp in a clear voice, shouted out so everyone could hear. "Settle down boys. It's just a friendly soldier and our old *friend* Acalan." He then repeated what he had said in Spanish for our guest. Alex rode into view leading Acalan's horse. The man's hands were tied to the pommel. Alex looked questioningly at all the guns trained on him and Acalan. The troopers visibly relaxed. However the Mexican soldiers, though they lowered their weapons, watched the new arrivals warily.

I was vastly relieved at seeing my old friend, seemingly uninjured. I next turned my attention to Acalan. I studied the man through hate-filled eyes. He looked used up, no more than an outer shell of the man he had been. Acalan did not have a mark on him. It was just that that he appeared to have had all the moisture sucked out of him. The man was more frightened than the last time I had seen him. In fact he looked terrified. I believed he had good reason too. Both sides of this affair had good reason to want him dead.

In an instant Captain Castillo's calm exploded into anger. As soon as Acalan was close enough to recognize, the captain drew out a long-barreled pistol. Cocking it, he pointed the weapon at Acalan's head. We were all startled by the Mexican officer's sudden action. Alex, using his knees only urged his horse out of the line of fire. Captain Castillo demanded, "Is this the traitor who guided you to our camp?"

Boyd answered in a perplexed tone, "Yes it is. The man has supplied reliable information to General Pershing in the past. I do not ask you to excuse our actions, but we did not trust him. Unfortunately that mistrust was ignored. I take full responsibility. The fault is mine. I allowed Acalan to lead us to your camp." Looking at Alex he said, "We should have scouted your camp last night. Do you recognize him Captain Castillo?"

"He is a known Villa confederate and has been seen spying on our camp for weeks. Forgive me captain but I must alter the terms of our agreement. I'm sure you can appreciate that my men will be in search of a scapegoat for the losses of their beloved general and fellow Carranzistas. Those of us who faithfully follow President Carranza often face condemnation from our own families and friends. As you have discovered sometimes it is difficult to know friend from foe. The Mexican Revolution has divided the country much like your own Civil War did in the United States. I believe Acalan will do nicely as a sacrificial lamb."

Captain Boyd took only a short moment to make his decision. He nodded at Alex and shrugged. Alex began the motion of handing over the reins to one of the Mexican soldiers. Before he could complete the act a lariat was looped suddenly over the man. As the rope tightened pinning his arms to his body, he grunted. His eyes were wildly flickering around in panic as he was roughly pulled from the horse. Acalan's screams seemed to echo in my head as he was dragged away. Searching myself for regret or remorse I could find none. Acalan had created his own bad luck. He was delivered to death's door, sealing his end by his own hand. A traitor's greed had cost him his life.

The exchange of our men and the recovery of our dead troopers were completed within the hour. The dead were tied across saddles for the two day trip back to Casa Grande. There would be no fancy banquettes and cheers when we returned this time. Captain Boyd's bold plan to deliver Pancho Villa to General Pershing had been dashed. There would only be the funerals of lost friends to attend to.

The mood among the men was gloomy. Our hopes for a swift end to this campaign were lost as well.

Thinking about Acalan I realized if he had returned with us to Casa Grande, I was not sure his fate would have been much different than the one he now endured. Maybe he would not have been tortured, but the general would not doubt have hung the man from the nearest tree. I would not soon forget my short time in Carrizal. The further I could put the town behind me the better. The sour taste in my mouth would not go away overnight.

I knew there were many soldiers who rode for the glory and patriotism. The thrill of battle was embedded in their soul as if they were descended from some great warrior race. Still there were others who simple looked to the Army for a job or became career soldiers. On this day there had been no glory or pride in the taking or loss of soldier's lives in this unfortunate battle. There were not only the deaths on both sides to consider, but the political repercussions. Captain Boyd's career was surely ruined.

Trying to lift my mood with a more pleasant memory, I thought about the ideal moment when Alex had appeared. That made me smile. I had been so relieved to see Alex ride up I was near to busting a gut. I had wiped my eyes more than once as some specks of dust irritated them. Now as we rode the trail back the men were quiet, most likely thinking about the day of tragedy. Our horses made little sound in the soft dust of the trail. Wherever history judged the blame, it would fall on others to decide.

There had been no time for explanations before. Now my curiosity got the better of me. Turning to Alex I said, "The first thing you should know is you scared ten years off my life when you disappeared. During the fight, I had blood running into my eyes from a scalp wound. I could not even see if you were among the dead on the battlefield. What the *hell* happened back there with Acalan?"

"Thanks for the concern my friend. There was little chance to think about my actions. I just reacted to Acalan's efforts to escape. He tried to bolt just as the fighting started. I forced him back inside with my larger horse. I saw you box him in as well. Then he saw his chance as a trooper's horse went down in front of him. I had him in my sights, but was unable to shoot him in the back. So, cursing myself for a fool I chased him down. I achcd to stay and get into the fight. I knew you and the other troopers needed my help."

I lost my temper thinking about how the little weasel Acalan's actions had almost cost us our lives. Also I had killed Mexican soldiers who did not deserve to die. Like us they were just doing their duty. It made me lash out at Alex, which I immediately regretted. "Why didn't you just let the *bastard* go? We were facing an unknown force much larger than our own. Yes he betrayed us, but surely one man could not have mattered that much?"

Ignoring my anger he said, "Believe me Oscar I wanted to, but Captain Boyd had given me personal orders. I was not to let Acalan get away unless I wanted to lose two of my three strips. As it turned out I'm glad. I would have hated to kill Mexican soldiers. They were not attacking us, but merely defending themselves from out attack. We would have done the same under similar circumstances."

Lowering my voice I said, "Well it felt a lot like an attack to me. They sure were not walking through the motions. I'll have another scar to remember their non-attack by." Despite my outburst, the reality of his words struck me hard. Mexico, its soldiers, and citizens were not our enemy. Now through a disastrous set of circumstances many of my fellow troopers and me had taken the lives of Mexican soldiers. I would have to live with that remorse the rest of my days.

In a faltering voice I said, "I truly wish I could say I had not taken any lives on this day Alex. There was so much confusion, dust and dying on both sides. We could see uniforms, but not what kind. Soldiers we thought were bandits responded to our attacked with equal violence to our own. Both sides fought desperately to defend themselves. I could not be more ashamed if we had attacked and killed our own men in some bizarre twist of misunderstanding."

He sighed deeply. His tone was sad as he spoke. "Oscar it was a mistake, not your fault. We follow orders and if Captain Boyd had let me scout the camp last night it might have turned out differently. Any fool could have seen the camp was too orderly for bandits, even in the dark. Besides that it was a larger force. We are fortunate to have escaped torture and starvation deaths in a Mexican prison. Perhaps General Pershing could have negotiated a release eventually. However we would have been broken in mind and body before that occurred. The captain used poor judgment, but if any blame is to be assigned for the today's tragedy the blood is on Acalan's hands. His fate is a certainty and probably fatal by now."

"I know you're right but it does not make the pill taste any less bitter. I had best begin looking forward instead of back or else I'll go insane with guilt. Just don't scare me like that again. Although, I don't know why I should worry? I keep getting busted up and you haven't had so much as a scratch."

# CHAPTER 44

## *January 1917 Withdrawal*

For the rest of 1916 Alex and I rode out on dozens of overnight missions. Sometimes we rode together and other time apart. About half of the scouting rides into the desert were one to two week-long campaigns. One mission sent us as far south as *Parral*. Those citizens we spoke with had seen nothing of the bandits. It seemed they were holed up. Our orders never changed. We were to kill or capture Pancho Villa and his Villistas. Yet time and again soldiers returned empty handed, exhausted and dispirited. Soldiers were conditioned to follow most orders without question, but we were not dim-witted. We had every reason to believe our scouting parties were a fool's folly. Our Indian scouts could track a mouse across a rock, yet Villa was hiding anywhere but the places we were searching.

We were now restricted from the northern deserts and villages by President Wilson's orders. We believed it was likely that Villa was being protected by the Mexican government, or that he was hiding north of Casa Grande. If the last part was true, the Mexican government intended to capture him themselves. There were no more victories to celebrate over bandits. We had little or nothing to lift our spirits. Men were disgruntled. Thoughts of returning home invaded every waking moment, and most of our dreams. As word of the fighting in Europe reached us, it became clear our president wanted to avoid a war on two fronts. With the fierce bite missing from troopers, we were no more dangerous than a toothless wolf. Morale reached a new low not previously seen.

I kept in touch with my ma throughout my time in Mexico. I would write letters at night, and then post them whenever I returned to *Casa Grande*. The letters were exchanged as time permitted. Sometimes there would be a letter included inside from one of my brothers. I would send a letter and get three back before she answered the one I had sent. The mail was not reliable but arrived eventually. One of subjects written about was my inability to put aside the rough times between pa and me. I would no longer abide his disapproval of me. I made it clear that I would not be coming home straight away when I left Mexico. I saw no immediate future for me in the Atlanta, Texas area.

Ma was some upset by the gap between father and son, but accepted my decision. She knew her husband and son, being much alike, were never going to get along. We were both stubborn and naturally dug in our heels when pushed. I hated to hurt ma in any way. I could still feel pa's critical eyes watching his wayward son in a drunken stupor on his porch. I was not ready to forget the beating I took at his hands when I had come home drunk as a boy. I knew I was to blame, but it did not ease the pain. Maybe at some future date we would come together. For now I was not strong enough to see further disappointment in his eyes. No matter what I accomplished it would never be enough for my pa.

Ma and I had an ongoing joke between us. She good-naturedly called me her "*broken* son". The first time she said I was "*broke*"; I thought she meant I was always penniless. Later I understood she intended to say I was somehow different. My older brother Joe drove an ice truck. He was very reliable, married with children. My younger brothers, Isaac and Nobel were well on their way to being settled and living normal lives. As for me, I was always on the move and so far had been a big disappointment to pa. However, ma loved all her children without judgment or reservations.

Unexpectedly our last night in camp came sooner than any of us could have imagined. The general called together all men who were not on guard duty to address us. He raised his voice so everyone could hear. "Men, tomorrow has been a long time coming for us. I know it felt like our existence here and the hardships we've faced were eternal. Each of you has given of yourselves as I knew you would. We leave behind our blood and sweat on foreign soil. Sadly we have buried our dead here as well. I say now to future critics that the *Punitive Expedition* was a *roaring* good success." A long chorus of cheers burst from the men assembled. Pershing waited for the excitement to die down, smiling a rare smile. We continued to shout out approval of his words.

The grins and general good mood in the crowd was like a solid object we could touch and taste. Finally he waved for us to quiet down. "We killed or wounded many of Villa's men. Numerous more deserted him as pressure mounted on the bandits. Even old Pancho himself was gravely wounded. President Wilson has praised our efforts as responsible for all but stopping raids along the border. Villa was too busy running and hiding to plunder our country. I will *never* forget your sacrifice and dedication." He paused and took a long look at the group of men before him. It appeared as if he was committing the moment to memory.

A hush fell over us as we waited to hear the words we were aching for. "Tomorrow we return to Columbus and the on to El Paso. There will be no train rides home. We will ride our mounts like the cavalrymen we are. I want every town we pass through and every citizen we see to remember the men who pursued Pancho Villa into Mexican territory." Cheers drowned out any further words. The roaring lasted for some time. I was sure the old general wiped away tears at our response.

Finally on January 27th, 1917 Alex and I were among the first 10,690 troopers to ride out of Casa Grande for Columbus, New Mexico. General Pershing was leading the columns. As before, it made me mighty proud to see him riding a spirited mount. Watching the general riding proudly in his dress uniform gave me a lump in my throat and tears to my eyes. Every man knew this would be the last ride for the proud U.S. Cavalry. We might be an obsolete way of engaging the enemy, but nobody could take away our pride, or claim our memories. I was as excited as a school boy as I stood in my stirrups and watched the mass of men and horses moving ever nearer to our own border.

Alex was riding on my right and grinning despite the sadness he tried to hide. His leaving Mexico was hard on him now. I knew that every mile we put behind us and his true home caused him anxiety. Before we had crossed into Mexico the second time I was sure Alex would retire someday to one of the border towns on the United States side. Now I was certain that when his enlistment was done he would return to his beloved Abelinda and take her to *San Miguelito*. He now owned a beautiful hacienda and had family in Mexico. With work his ranch could be a successful operation. If Villa and other bandits were ever defeated the country surrounding the ranch could be a peaceful place to raise a family.

Our return to Columbus was a pleasurable event. The townsfolk treated us as heroes. There had been no further attacks during our time in Mexico and the citizens believed our efforts had contributed to their safety. There were all day pick nicks in the town and enough speeches to wear out a politician. I reconnected with friends made during my previous time in the village. However the general was in a hurry to return to Fort Bliss, El Paso, so our stay was just three days. Alex and I had been assigned to Fort Bliss under General Pershing before and would be again. I was looking forward to the posting. However the war in Europe weighed on every soldier's mind. The very real possibility was that we may have survived the invasion of one country just to die in another.

Elements of the Georgia National Guard and the 1st Kentucky Infantry were stationed in Columbus so we camped in the open wherever space could be found. Small detachments of Texas Rangers were also using Camp Furlong as their temporary headquarters. The small village appeared to be prospering. Every hotel room and boardinghouse room was filled. The town had successfully rebuilt over our absence. New buildings were evident on every corner. It was hard to imagine the shattered town we had left the previous year. New arrivals that were somehow not aware of the vicious bandit attack would find little evidence that Villa and his bandits had nearly burned the town out of existence. After we were dismissed, Alex and I walked to the town cemetery. We wanted to visit the graves of those we knew as our way of honoring those lost to Villa's terrible raid.

At the graveyard I looked at the new stones and cursed under my breath. "If there has been any good that resulted from the Mexican Revolution I can't see it."

Alex knelt and rearranged some flowers on a grave. "We have lost many friends to the man. His reign of terror is not over I think. Someday he will pay for what he has done."

"If not in this life then certainly the next is what my pa would say. As for me I would like to see him suffer in this life. Villa's fate in eternity after death is not as satisfying to those of us who have witnessed his cruelty in person."

Alex spoke with strong emotion. "I agree but our past need for vengeance resulted in your discharge from the Army. As for me if I ever find myself in the same square mile as Villa, one of us will be facing our maker."

"Thanks for including me in the need for vengeance, but we both know it was my decision. I could have got us both killed. If I had listened to you it would have saved me from a dishonorable discharge from the Army and a lost stripe for you."

"I'm dry behind the ears Oscar and a grown man. Nobody made be follow you to Mexico. Besides, I was thirsty for a beer and wanted to see some pretty senoritas."

General Pershing spent his time in Columbus meeting with New Mexico officials. He also wired ahead to a couple of Congressmen to meet with him. His purpose was the safety of over five-hundred Chinese refugees that had accompanied us into Mexico. Their assistance to the expedition was touted as *invaluable* by Pershing to newspapers that interviewed him. The headlines called the refugees, *"Pershing's Chinese"*. At the time of our arrival back in New Mexico there was a ban on Chinese immigration due to the Federal Chinese Exclusion Act. His popularity and recognition gave him power with the public. He used his esteem to pressure Congress to pass Public Resolution 29, which allowed the Chinese to stay in the United States.

318  J. Michael Beck

On our last evening in Columbus, Alex and I were invited to eat supper with several townsfolk. Not-so-old war stories were exchanged about the night of Villa's raid on the town. We toasted friends lost that fateful night. Folks on both sides of the border had suffered at the hands of Villa. Of course we were asked about our experiences in Mexico. I was not in a talkative mood, but Alex dazzled those present with tales of explosive gunfights, dangerous battles, and wicked betrayal. By the time we said our goodbyes and turned in for the night, I believed Alex could have run for mayor and beaten W. C. Hoover or any other opponents easily.

The next day Columbus fell behind us before the sun was fully upon us. I would be hard pressed to say why, but I felt like leaving Columbus was like departing my second home. A soldier tended to put down roots quickly, or not at all. I would miss many of the folks who lived there. I had every intentions of returning some day. However I knew life had a way of getting in the way. As we rode on through New Mexico and into Texas, crowds gathered to watch the army that had engaged Pancho Villa in Mexico. Troopers were given gifts of food or hand-made tokens wherever we rode. Most of us had supposed that by not capturing or killing Villa, our return would be more akin to a whipped dog slipping back into the house unnoticed.

It felt in some way that I had finally overcome the demons that had resulted in my dishonorable discharge. My continuing fall from humanity that followed my discharge seemed much further behind me. I realized I was feeling a warm satisfaction at returning to Fort Bliss. No man in the Army who had traveled to Mexico could be pleased with all that had happened while in Mexico. What was most important to me was that I had done my duty. I admit to fairly beaming with delight. I had met every challenge head on, proving myself as my own man.

After more than a week we rode into El Paso, Texas, which is situated next to the New Mexico border. It felt wonderful to be at the long journey's end. The sight before us was one those present would never been forget. Thousands of people cheered us as we rode toward Fort Bliss. We were astounded by the sight of so many well wishers.

Every man rode straighter in the saddle. It was a proud moment for us all. I looked out over the crowds and realized Genera Pershing had placed the vehicles in the rear to follow the horses. It might be the end for the mighty U.S. Cavalry, but we were all savoring this last ride into camp.

# CHAPTER 45

## *Brass Knuckles*

Dad stopped reading out loud, but read on silently for a few moments more. Bobby looked at Dad and said in an awestruck tone, "That was amazing! Is there more to the story?"

"Not as much. Pa goes on to talk about his leave and adjusting to life at Fort Bliss."

Bobby stood up and stretched. "I'd like to hear the rest tomorrow if that's okay. I had no idea that all happened. You should be proud of your dad. For some reason they skipped over that bit of history when I was in school. I do remember General Pershing from World War I and of course General Patton from World War II. I had no idea Patton served down Mexico way."

"Yes, well until Pa started telling some of his experiences to Buddy, he had never talked about any of this before. My brother and sisters and I knew he was stationed down on the border, but nothing about what he did."

I got up to go to the bathroom as Bobby said his goodbyes. "I'd better round up Shirley and the girls and get on home. It's getting late. Shirley and Charlene enjoy their time together. Thanks for letting me sit in on the letter reading. It was great entertainment, better than television."

To me Dad said, "How about we finish this tomorrow Buddy?"

"Okay Dad, fine with me. Tomorrow though, you promise?"

"Yep, I have some errands to run in the morning. You can tag along if you don't have any odd jobs lined up. We can finish up after supper tomorrow."

Dad had been raised during the Depression and approved of his children earning their own money. "No, I'll go with you. I'll bet I can talk you into an ice cream cone before we get home."

The next morning after breakfast, dad and I left to visit some of his accounting clients. During the school week, I usually ate oak meal or a quick bowl of Cap'n Crunch, while my dad would stick with his boring Corn Flakes. However, on the weekends mom had time to fix us eggs, bacon, and buttered toast. We both had full stomach and were in high spirits when we set out. Dad went to his drycleaner's account first and on to two service stations near downtown Grand Prairie. Then we went to the post office and the bank.

By that time it was near noon and we ended with dad's last client and my favorite. Webber's Root Beer Stand was a hamburger joint, not fancy but tasty. Since I had just had a burger the night before, I ordered a chilidog and their homemade French fries. Afterwards I got my ice cream cone. As I was stuffing the last of the cone in my mouth I told Dad, "I want to work here someday. I'll bet I could learn to make their food as well as anyone."

Without hesitation he answered, "I'll bet you could. I could arrange that when you're older. Mrs. Mayberry is the manager and she'd hire you. Only thing is you need to be fourteen in Texas to work, and then only part time. I don't think your mother would approve of you working too soon."

"Neat. I like her. She told me to call her May. Dad I already work all over the neighborhood."

"That's not the same thing. If you have homework, you can put off mowing a yard or washing a car. On the other hand, if you're scheduled to work at a real job you have to be there, and on time. No allowance is made for homework. Maybe in a few more years you can work during the summer or on weekends."

"Oh, that will be great. I'll have money all the time like Sherry. She babysits a lot."

"Yes and she earns every penny too. Some kids are not so nice to keep. Sherry manages them well, but comes home exhausted. I worry she might not want children after chasing those brats all evening. Or it could go the other way and Sherry might become a teacher so she can have kids around all day."

On the way home I asked, "Dad, why did Grandpa and his father not get along?"

He thought about it awhile, probably deciding how much to tell me. "Well your great Grandpa James Henry was a pious man." When he saw I did not understand he added, "He was very religious, but sometimes his faith made him critical of others. He passed away in 1945 when I was fourteen. Frankly he scared me too, but he loved his community and did a lot to help folks. He was a rather stern man at home but known in Atlanta, Texas area as a kind and giving man. You know he is the man in the portrait in our hall. You'll inherit it when you turn eighteen along with the family coat of arms. That's because you're the oldest son and a 4th generation James."

"So if I have a son I'll have to name him James too so he can inherit?"

"That is only if you want to. I did not start the tradition, my grandfather did. You're free to do what you want. Nobody will force it on you. In fact neither of us uses our first names anyway." Despite his words, I thought the tradition was important to him.

Before I could ask if my grandpa and his father ever made up, we arrived home and I forgot all about it. I went inside and asked mom what time supper was. Then I took off down the street to see what the Cruz bunch was up to. I planned on asking Randy if he wanted to listen to the rest of grandpa's story. His dad Paul told me he was with his mom visiting his grandpa Mr. Vasquez in Dallas. Darn I thought; Mr. Vasquez had a daughter named Cynthia who was as pretty a girl as I had ever seen. I would not have minded going along.

Rats, I thought as I walked away. At that moment I saw some kids playing on the far end of the street. I knew some of them slightly but figured it would be a good time to make a new friend. Walking their way I saw a blond boy about my age shooting a bb gun at a bird's nest high in a tree. He was taller than me and heavier. I had heard his name was Donald. His younger brother I thought was named Steve was watching him. I anxiously wanted a turn at shooting. Donald had a reputation of getting into trouble of a bad sort. I did not know if it was true. Dad had told his children often that we should relate to people the way they were with us, not by what others said about them. I just hoped he would let me shoot his gun. Dad had taught Sherry and me to shoot. I wanted to show off a little for these new kids.

"What are you shooting at?"

Donald and Steve looked at me and they both grinned. "We're trying to shoot that old bird's nest out of the tree. Want to give it a try?"

Steve grunted a protest but Donald elbowed him in the ribs. He handed me the bb gun and I took careful aim at the nest and hit it with my first shot. I had a second to feel good about myself before an eerie screech rang out. A bird tried to fly up from the nest but flew instead in circles like a crazed bat before falling near my feet. The bird was dying and I felt awful. "Why didn't you tell me there was a bird in the nest?"

Donald looked at me strangely. "I didn't know the bird was home and you didn't ask."

I handed him the bb gun and started walking home dejectedly. As if I did not feel bad enough, I could see Mrs. Black leaning against her fence with an, *I'm going to tell you mother* expression planted on her face. I was about to break into a run to get home and tell mom and dad myself when someone grabbed me from behind. I was roughly pulled off my feet and something hard hit me in the eye. I saw a bright flash of light explode behind my eyes. I was stunned and ended up flat on my back. I shook my head trying to clear it of the light. I then felt a great weight on my chest and another impact to my face. This time the blow had been to my mouth. I tasted blood from a split lip.

I heard a commotion above me but could not see well enough to make out any details. The next thing I knew Donald was helping me up. I asked in a shaky voice, "Why did you hit me?"

"It wasn't me. I just pulled the kid off you. I think he lives a few blocks over and I don't know his name. How bad are you hurt?"

I was beginning to see well enough to look around me. "My head, eye and lips hurt badly. I think I hear a ringing in my ears. What did he hit me with? It felt like a baseball bat."

"It might as well have been. He held out a brass object. I had never seen anything like it before. "They are called brass knuckles. They fit over your fist and make it harder."

"Oh man. I think, yea, I'm going to throw up!" My stomach lurched and out came my lunch.

Eventually Donald asked, "Do you need me to send Steve after your parents?"

When I could speak again I said weakly, "No, but come over to my house. Bring those brass things and show them to my dad. If he thinks I started a fight he'll be mad."

I slowly made my way home with Donald and Steve trailing behind. At my house I looked down at myself and saw blood on my shirt. "Boy, if I have to go to the hospital again for stitches my folks will drive me to that boy's house and let him finish killing me."

Inside mom and dad took over. Dad talked to Donald and Steve and took the brass knuckles to take to the kid's parents. Mom rushed me off to the bathroom to see how bad I was hurt. It did not appear as bad as it felt. Once I was cleaned up a little I returned to the living room where dad, Donald and Steve waited. "How do you feel Buddy?"

"About like a freight train sideswiped me. At least it does not look like I'll need to get stitched up this time. My head hurts and I'm going to have a big shiner on my eye. I never even saw this boy. I was walking home and felt a tug from behind. The next minute was all jumbled up and lost in bright lights."

Dad looked over at Steve and Donald, "Thank you boys for walking him home. I'm going to try and find that boy's parents. If that fails I'll either call the police or contact the principle at school and report this. If Donald had not happened along that boy might have killed you. Mrs. Black called and said she saw the whole thing."

After Dad left to go talk to Mom, I walked Donald and Steve to the door. "Thanks for pulling him off me. Will you point him out the next time we see him. I wish my dad would just drop it, but I know he won't. I'd like to have that kid try to hit me again when I can see it coming."

Steve spoke suddenly. I'm not so sure that's a good idea Buddy. That kid is a head taller than you or I. He won't bother you again with Donald around. He knocked him on his butt."

So now I had two new friends. "Thanks guys. See y'all on the bus Monday."

# CHAPTER 46

## *Fort Bliss and Alex's Goodbye*

That night Mom made a fuss over me. She made pot roast, mashed potatoes, and even baked a pecan pie. Those were my favorites. I ate everything on my plate and asked for seconds. I was extra-hungry since I had lost my lunch. After supper Mom gave me aspirin which helped.

Dad looked at me with concern. "You are really banged up Buddy. Do you want to read the rest of your grandpa's story another time?"

"No please. I want to close my eyes and hear another story, not think about brass knuckles."

"Okay, let's see, where was I? Oh, here it is, they had just arrived at Fort Bliss, Texas…"

Alex and I had a few friends at Fort Bliss and we looked them up first. Then, after we were granted a month-long leave, we headed out to a favorite fishing hole on the Rio Grande. We had skipped out on several fancy banquets sponsored by the City of El Paso. We were sitting at our favorite spot shaded by a stunted tree. It felt good to relax and soak up the sun. Although it was January, the day was warm this far west. I was feeling a new energy just knowing I had no responsibilities at the moment. I noticed Alex was looking longingly out into Mexico toward the southwest. He had been quiet for some time and I figured he was thinking about *San Miguelito*. Probably Abelinda played on his mind as well.

We had braced our poles into the dirt of the river bank. I was witling on a stick and thinking about nothing more than frying up some fish if we could catch any. Then the silence started eating at me and invaded my thoughts. Any other time Alex and I could sit for a good spell in amiable silence, but this time I knew something was bothering him. I put down the stick and started rolling a smoke which helped me arrange my thoughts. Finally breaking into the quiet I said, "I'll wager that with a swift horse you would have time to ride back to visit Abelinda. Or, if you're planning on living in Mexico eventually, I suppose you could simply *not* return."

He shook his head at the idea. "No, I would never leave before my enlistment is up. We may be needed yet to fight in Europe. My hitch will end in December. That gives me eleven months to settle on a plan."

"Your dedication is admirable. However why risk your life for a country that will *not* be your home at some point? Now me I don't have anyone except ma who frets about me returning. If I end my days in a blown up foxhole there won't be many who will care. You have family waiting and a home to return to."

He laughed at my feeble efforts to roll the cigarette and reached inside his shirt for a cigar. "I may return to live in Mexico, but this country will always have my loyalty. I became a man here. America gave me opportunity to learn and prosper. For that I will always be grateful."

From the Mexican side of the river, we watched as a small rowboat began crossing about fifty feet downstream from where we sat. I reached for my Colt which was wrapped inside a small burlap sack I carried for supplies. I tucked the 45 under my right leg. Alex had his rifle leaning against the tree. I counted two men, a woman and a child in the boat. Upon reaching the United States side of the border, one of the men, the woman and the child who appeared to be about four stepped off onto the bank. The man in the boat accepted a coin and then immediately began rowing back to Mexico.

Now alone with what we believed was his family, the man put his arm around his wife protectively. The woman clung to her daughter's hand as her husband looked around warily. They hesitated, momentarily frozen to the spot as if not sure of which direction to take. We were in deep shadows. By sitting still I knew we would not be visible without a close study of where we sat. Alex and I had tethered our horses on a stand of grass on the far side of the hill behind us. We were not in uniform and by rights should not have been armed. The days of hostile Indians roaming the area was long past, but the border was still a dangerous place.

With a sudden movement Alex was on his feet and gave me a *wait here* gesture. I was startled by his actions, not perceiving any threat in the man and woman. He started walking toward the new arrivals, leaving his rifle behind. The man saw him at once and actually cowered back a step, keeping his family behind him. I could not see Alex smiling but knew he would be now that I understood his intentions. He approached with hands open in a friendly manner. Other than a pocket knife he carried, Alex was not armed. I was not so trusting and stood up with the Colt behind my back. As he neared a rapid exchange of Spanish whipped back and forth between Alex and the man.

During the conversation the child peeked out from behind her mother's leg. The woman mostly looked at the ground shyly. As the conversation ended Alex reached into his pants pocket and pressed a couple of coins into the man's hand. More excited conversation between all parties came next. Even the child grinned at Alex, who patted the young boy on the head, who looked to be about six. Then the three travelers began walking toward the direction of El Paso. They seemed to march away with more strength of purpose than when they arrived.

As Alex approached I said excitedly, "What did they say?"

He dropped back down next to me before he said, "Nice family. I told my new friend's Ronaldo and Lupe Rios they could find work at the Hotel Paso del Norte in the city. I know the owner, Zack T. White. He is a good man and will give them work. Lupe is going to have another child and they are hard-pressed for money."

"Isn't the Hotel Paso del Norte pretty fancy? I heard even Black Jack Pershing stays there when he entertains military brass or other dignitaries. I don't remember you ever staying there."

Yes it was built with all the finery in 1912. I heard he spent more than a million dollars constructing his palace. I have played poker there a few times. On occasions I have taken some of Zack's wealth home with me. He likes to play on the high terrace outside. Sometimes the games last around the clock."

"You amaze me Alex. Don't think I didn't see those twenty dollar gold eagles you gave that family. I suppose the money will help them along their way too."

"It was nothing. Folks helped me when I came here. I actually crossed near this very spot."

Alex was embarrassed when anyone mentioned his generosity. "Like your sister Camilla said, you have become your own man, and nothing like your father." I paused as a thought struck me. "My pa would say God just *slapped* me. The fish aren't biting and it's over three miles to town. Our horses can easily handle the extra weight of three hitchhikers."

He held out a hand to help me up. "That would be an excellent way to begin our leave. I'll even buy you a fat juicy steak at the Hotel Paso del Norte. Their cooking is better than ours anyway."

We rounded up the trio. Alex loaned his horse to Ronaldo and Lupe, while we doubled up on my mount. The boy, whose name was also Ronaldo, was called Rondo to avoid confusion. He rode in his father's lap. At the hotel Alex introduced us to Mr. White who insisted we call him Zack. Looking at the opulence, I felt decidedly underdressed. However Zack would hear none of it and seated us at his best table. We were surrounded by gentleman and ladies in fancy evening wear who looked at us in amazement at the treatment we received from the owner.

After Zack had left to attend to other guest I asked in a stage whisper, "Okay why is Zack being so nice to us?"

"Maybe he intends to entice me back to his poker table. He may want a chance to win back some of the money he has lost to me. He hates to lose a penny at cards, but will turn around and give away a fortune to those in need."

"I know you are a skilled player Alex but looking around this mansion I think the man can afford to lose a few dollars."

"It's not the amount that matters to men of his status, but the thrill of winning."

Alex began talking to Ronaldo and Lupe to ease their obvious discomfort at their new found surroundings. I rummaged around in my bag and brought out a piece of hard candy for the boy. I looked at his mother who nodded her approval before I handed it to Rondo. He squealed his delight. My ma would not approve but I was too hungry to worry about ruining my supper. After a pause in the conversation I asked Alex, "Do you think Zack will hire them?"

"I'm sure of it. They will be fine in this country if they wish to stay. Their baby is due in September and the baby will be named after me if it's a boy. I am honored by their decision."

"You are becoming quite the family man lately." Then the food arrived. The time for talking had ended. My earlier dream of a fish frying over a campfire was forgotten. Being pampered was nice. My t-bone steak weighed at least a pound. I tucked in with gusto. That night I had dishes I did not even recognize. It had been a long time since any meal tasted that good.

In April of 1917 Congress approved what they called the Purple Heart. It was supposed to be for soldiers wounded in the line-of-duty from the point it was created. However, in August I received one for the battle in *Tomochic* where I almost lost my sight. More important to me was the loss of my friend Sean Haltom during the same fight. His body left behind in Mexico still troubled me. In the same ceremony all the men who had served across the border in the Punitive Expedition received the Mexican Service Badge.

The months of 1917 dragged on without Alex and I being shipped overseas. From all accounts the war was losing steam. We had heard Patton was now a captain. Talk of some sort of an armistice was spoken of hopefully at Fort Bliss and the El Paso city streets. Lupe had a beautiful baby boy and named him Eleazar. The child was healthy and a joy to watch. Alex and I visited the family of four once a week for supper at their rented boardinghouse.

I was assigned to a fusty old office in the basement of a stone building. It was a clerical job, not something a sergeant should do. So many were clustered on the border I was not needed for patrol. This was what I had feared would be in store for me if I stayed too long in the Army. In October Alex received his 4th stripe. I doubted it would change his mind about leaving the Army. The thought of his leaving left my mouth dry. I hated to lose any friend. I had missed him terribly when discharged before. Now it would happen again. Mexico was far away from East Texas where I intended to eventually live. I figured with the passing of time we would never see one another again. I was closer to Alex than any of my brothers. I hoped that would change when I went home. Other than ma, Alex was the only one I felt close to.

The night before he would leave the troopers gave him a good send off. I wanted to get drunk and not think about tomorrow, but somehow fought off the temptation. General Pershing and Patton were off fighting in Europe. Every officer we knew showed up to pay their respects. Alex was well liked and would be missed. Even Colonel Dodd, soon to ship overseas, came by to convince him he was too valuable to the Army. I knew his way was set.

The next morning we both rode by so he could say goodbye to little Eleazar, Ronaldo, Lupe, and Rondo. Lupe and Rondo began to cry. I wanted to sit down with them and weep too. Later we rode away from Fort Bliss. We sat our horses looking across the Rio Grande to the southwest. "Alex I know your home is over there, but it won't be the same around here."

"You'll do fine Oscar. You have been the best friend I ever had, but my trail is…over there. Stay in touch mi amigo. I don't expect the Army will hold you much longer. Old cavalrymen like us were never intended to ride a desk. Vaya con Dios."

"Goodbye my friend. Take care of yourself." We shook hands and I watched as he rode away. I sat a long while thinking about my own path. It felt like an anvil was crushing my chest. When I could no longer see his silhouette I returned to camp, feeling very much alone. As lonesome mood crept upon up on me like a cold desert wind, I realized the sensation was one I had not felt since rejoining the Army. It was not a welcome arrival.

# CHAPTER 47

## Discharge and Riding the Rails

As Alex had predicted the Army would not hold me for long. However I had always believed the decision would be mine to make. World War I ended officially at the eleventh hour, on the eleventh day, of the eleventh month of 1918. Thousands of soldiers began returning to the states. As it turned out, I had no more say over my second discharge than the first one. I received my discharge papers in January 1919. I would receive a pension of $85.00 a month and was happy to have it. I was now considered *surplus,* no different than excessive war artillery or Cavalry horses. Uncountable younger soldiers were ready and eager to fill my boots, many with fighting experience in the European war.

I came to believe my departure from Fort Bliss was fortunate timing. A serious flu epidemic was beginning to take lives at military post around the country. It had first been reported at Fort Riley, Kansas. Most believed the flu had been brought back by soldiers from Spain, and therefore it was often called the Spanish Flu. One idea tossed about was that the close quarters of men and beast during the war was to blame for the rapid spread of the contagious infection. In the United States reports put the hospitalized number at one million. Deaths rose tragically and were listed at 44,000 and climbing. Whatever the original source, folks were beginning to die in large numbers around the world. Nothing I had ever heard of besides the bubonic plague had killed so many. Any cough or sneeze brought immediate apprehension of falling victim to the often fatal flu. I was thankfully spared from the illness. However everyone knew someone who was sick and others that had died.

The country was suffering through changes, some good, but mostly bad. America was gearing down from a world war which had fueled industry and created jobs in communities. Now mass unemployment resulted in millions of hungry souls competing for work. Every slim opportunity for work brought about dozens of men jostling for the same job. Only sure that I would eventually settle in East Texas, I began to travel around the country by train. I rode in paid seats when money was to be had. More often than not I jumped aboard and rode the rails in boxcars when my pockets were empty.

Sometimes weeks would pass without my having two nickels to rub together in my pockets. My frequent poverty put me in the sights of Railroad *Dicks*. Officially these men were Railroad Detectives. The railroads hired them as policemen, but they were more often bully than lawmen. Originally they were used to prevent train robberies in the days after the Civil War. Now they seemed to enjoy their work of searching for vagabonds like me and my fellow hobos. We were called *tramps* by the Dicks. If caught we were kicked off the train forcefully and painfully, while the train was moving if possible.

Hobo jungles, which were small communities along the railroad tracks, became my boardinghouse on numerous cold and dreadful nights. My worldly possessions could all be held in my burlap sack. In the hobo slang it was called a *bindle;* however mine had straps for carrying over the shoulder instead of cloth looped through a stick as I saw others do. I traveled with few possessions, including a US Army issued bedroll, two sets of clothes, and a pocket watch bought in Columbus. Too many days were spent huddled, hungry and shivering near small campfires.

I lost a dozen pounds due to missing many meals. Sometimes three days or more would pass with no more than two sparse meals gratefully obtained. I dreamed about my mother's cooking. There were other days where I longed for some of the hard tack I had complained about while in the Army. Just thinking about dropping some hard tack into a soup to soften it would actually make my mouth water. The mostly-regular meals I had enjoyed while in the Army were long distant. I was often so hungry that I believed if I had been allowed to take my horse with me when I was discharged, I would have eaten the animal months ago. These days I carried a small container of salt instead of rock candy. I discovered the ingredient was welcomed at every campfire pot luck supper. Any man with food contributed to the pot and was invited to eat.

Occasionally kind folks would feed us. There was an accepted manner of begging for those who rode the rails. It began with a polite knock on the back door of houses which were close to the tracks. Then a hungry man would ask for a meal. I hated myself every time I was reduced to asking for a meal. I often asked instead if there were chores to do to earn my supper. Chopping wood or mending a fence was honest work and kept me warm besides. The begging had the unexpected benefit of giving me a direction.

I began to get paid in cash money if my employer had it to pay for a day's labor. I took odd jobs wherever I could find them. Discovering a knack for carpentry, I found enjoyment in working with my hands. After that, I naturally drifted toward small building projects. One day it might be repairing a chicken coop. The next week it might be building a back porch or adding a fireplace to a ramshackle house. Of course there were other days when I would labor from *can't see to can't see,* and then be paid with a single meal.

I would soon come to realize that cash money was a rare thing once outside the cities. Country folks more often used a workable bartering system instead of silver coin or folding money. This was not a new idea and had been used in America for as long as people had lived here. My pa had often bartered his ministry skills in marrying folks, and then been paid in livestock. Ma sometimes knitted socks or sweaters, then sold them or traded the items for whatever she needed. Being offered a home cooked meal I had no problem with, but dragging around a goat or herding a cow would make it impossible to hop a train.

Most men I met were just like me, homeless vagabonds who lead a life of no responsibility, accountable to no man. We had few ties to a more civilized community. As with any group of men there will always be those who prey on those they perceived as weaker. Twice I had to fight to save my few possessions from theft. During one of these times, I was threatened at knifepoint to turn over my bindle. It might have been stupid, but I was more mad than scared. I began to use my bag as a club. The result was knocking two teeth from the head of my attacker. When I heard the satisfying *clunk* sound, I remembered Bill's US belt buckle inside the bindle. I had carefully buttoned the buckle into one of my shirt pockets. Word traveled faster through the hobo community than the U.S. mail. After that night I was left alone.

During my wandering I passed through El Paso every few months. I would pick up mail and visit friends. Alex and Abelinda were married three months after he left the Army. They now lived at *San Miguelito*. I was pleased to read Abelinda had a baby boy, in January 1919. The child had naturally been named after his papa. Little Alex was healthy and strong. It was hard to believe my old friend was now a daddy. If I thought there was work to be had anywhere in Mexico, I would have walked all the way to *San Miguelito* to visit the family.

His niece, Eva was now five and wrote letters to me which Alex included with his own. Her childish writing was improving, but still hard to make out. Considering she was learning to write in both Spanish and English, I thought it was pretty good. Her art work was better and once she sent me a drawing of a soldier riding a big horse. The letter said it was me and that made me proud. Eva asked each time when I would visit again. I was pleased that she even remembered me. In her young world there must be more interesting pursuits than writing an ex-soldier she had met when she was barely three years old.

Onetime there was a letter from Josephine Leigh. That pleased me. The letter had been postmarked on several military camps, including Casa Grande. How the letter made it to me I will never know. Josephine was settled back in New York and doing fine. She was working as a photographer's apprentice in the city. She was considering a move to Savanna, Georgia, where she had friends. I sat down and wrote her back. I brought her up to date on Alex and myself. I left out my first discharge from the Army after Alex and I had dropped her off. My last line asked her to write again, but that it might be a long while before I could write back. She was a fine woman. It still made me smile to think of how we had met with her dressed as a man.

During the summer of 1919, disturbing news came from Alex about the present situation concerning Pancho Villa and some of his men. Shortly after our withdrawal in January 1917, Villa had been soundly beaten by Federalist soldiers near Torreon. This part I knew about from newspaper reports. With most of his Revolutionary Army either wiped out, or deserting him, he changed tactic to a more ambush style of fighting. The much smaller bandit bands could not attack large forces directly, but dogged them at every turn.

He continued to raid and clashed with federal troops at Buena Vista, *San Bernardino* Canyon, and struck near the town of *La Gruilla*, Texas. The last known Villa attack was just across the border near El Paso in June 1919. What concerned me most was that he had raided on two occasions at *San Miguelito*. Perhaps he attacked the hacienda out of retaliation for the death of Cardenas and his men. So far nobody had been hurt, but Mexican authorities were not concerned with one ranch outside a small village. Alex and Holmdahl had to keep additional loyal men at the ranch house to protect their families and property. Some of the men had ridden with Villa as young men attracted by excitement, but now hated him for his cruelty.

As I read on I felt a mixture of relief and anger at the actions of the Mexican government, under new President Benito Juarez. President Juarez granted complete amnesty to Villa in exchange for disbanding his remaining bandits. He was given 25,000 acres of ranch land near Parral, Chihuahua. I recalled that when in Mexico, Pershing petitioned President Wilson for permission to attack the state of Chihuahua and wipe out Villa for good. The request had been promptly denied by the president. Villa was allowed the security of fifty bodyguards. The ranks were filled with his most trusted men. The Mexican government paid for these bodyguards, known as *Dorados*. Pancho Villa now lived the life of a rich land owner and rancher. His days were spent enjoying cockfighting and bedding as many women as he could find.

The government left him alone so long as he avoided any connection to Mexican politics.

The way I figured it, if Villa had actually retired, then San Miguelito should be safe, and therefore Alex and his family would be left alone. Still, those that had fought or suffered from the man's brutality would seethe at his life of leisure and comfort. Was it possible Villa could quit his bandit ways? Past behavior of seizing whatever he desired as his own or destroying it made it unlikely. I closed my letter by asking he keep me informed of new developments. Whatever Alex needed of me, he had only to ask. I owed him too much to ever refuse.

I had no desire to fight in Mexico again, but the news was as abrasive as a desert sandstorm to know that Villa was still alive. I was a civilian and wondered what one man could do, other than fret over the circumstances. Villa was living like a king in a castle even after all his evil deeds. The man walked on the graves of the men and women he had ruined or killed. He needed a large dose of justice to fall on his neck like the French Revolution's guillotine wiped out French royalty. I would wager that the king and queen of France had thought themselves above the citizens. They had supposed they would be untouched by the French Revolution.

I was certain the whole matter in Mexico was coming to an ugly conclusion. However I did not for a moment believe the outcome would affect me. I will admit there is more to the Mexico story concerning Pancho Villa. Forgive me if I'm reluctant to share the particulars of the events now. I promise to write or speak of it at a later time. For today the recollection must remain locked within me. It is an ugly memory, yet I'm not ready to let go of it just now.

# CHAPTER 48

## *Oscar and His Myrtle*

I could not contain myself and blurted out as soon as Dad stopped reading, "Why won't he tell us what happened?"

"Buddy you have to respect his wishes. You need to *slow-your-pony* a minute and think about how hard this must be on your grandpa. These stories might be big adventures to you, but he has been reliving some dreadful times in his life. He'll tell us when he is in a mood to. If that day never comes we'll have to live with his decision. The fact he has shared so much with us already is pretty amazing."

"I know. I guess I'll have to wait. Dad is there more?"

"Yes there is. He writes about returning home. Do you still want me to read it tonight?"

"Oh yes, what else does Grandpa say?"

Dad shuffled a few pages and adjusted his glasses. I can tell you this; my brother, sisters and I have never heard much about the time before my parents met, except rumors. This has been an interesting family history lesson for me. I'll have to send this letter on to John Ray. To get to hear it from pa himself has been a real eye opener." Dad got a quizzical look on his face as if he had just been studying one of his crossword puzzles. "By the way Buddy, this Josephine Leigh, have you heard your grandpa mention her before?"

"Yes, I told you. She dressed as a man and took guns to Mexico to sell to the bandits. Grandpa caught her and took the guns to his captain. Alex gave her money and they let her go. Then grandpa was kicked out of the Army. Grandpa told me that stormy night in his cellar."

"Well that explains another family mystery. There was one time when we were kids that pa helped out a woman who was having a hard time of it. Pa never would say where he met her. Ma was so mad that she did not speak to him for a week. I'll bet it was Josephine Leigh."

"I don't know. Maybe there will be something about her later. Dad, grandma already told me how she met grandpa. Just like grandpa she acted like she was lost in the memory. She even sounded different, kind of dreamy and younger. I still want to hear grandpa's side of it."

Dad shook his head in wonder. "I am in *pure* shock at how much you know about my ma and pa that I don't. We are going to have to swap notes after Pa finishes his storytelling."

I settled back closing my eyes again as Dad began reading. I was ready to be gently tugged back in time to wherever Grandpa was now. His stories wrapped themselves around me. It was a familiar sensation now like when I would heat my blanket in front of our gas stove before diving into a cold bed…

What I do want to write about now is my return to East Texas and meeting Myrtle. Somehow the time slipped by. Seasons arrived, past, and then came again. There were good years and bad. In the summer of 1925 I found myself in East Texas. During the months of June and July I had been working steady to rebuild a house in Shreveport, Louisiana. Now I was riding in a comfortable paid seat headed for promised work in Fort Worth, Texas. It was not a planned thing, but I realized the train would stop in Texarkana. On an impulse I decided to hitch a ride to Atlanta, Texas not more than fifty miles away. I figured on staying a few days with my folks, then drifting on.

During the years of 1923 and 1924 I had seen some surprising success as I traveled about the country like a gypsy hunting work. Gratefully I met generous friends who fed me along the way when in times when I had nothing. A few slipped me a few dollars if they had it. At other times I lucked into work here or there. I heard it said somewhere that the harder you work, the luckier you get. It seemed to be true with me. I was employed for the better part of a year as a night watchman at the Mayo Clinic in Rochester, Minnesota, but I discovered quickly that it was too blasted cold up there. I suffered through temperatures lower than zero. Minus zero was a cold unheard of in Texas. Transient workers shared drafty ramshackle shacks along the Zumbro River. You could not gather enough wood to keep the shivers out all night. For me the severe cold was not worth the regular pay.

Before too much time had passed I had a powerful yearning for a southern state to warm up in. By keeping an ear to the ground, and making friends with folks who were rambling like me, I heard rumors of work being passed around. I give much credit to others for the fortunate circumstances I found myself in. Now in June of 1925 I was not what anyone would call prosperous, but I was wearing clean work clothes and had sturdy boots. I had a little money saved against further hard times and coin in my pocket. The only thing missing in my life was a good woman and a family. I could not think of anything else a man could wish for.

As apprehensive as I was about seeing my pa, I had a strong need to talk to my mother. I was now thirty years old. Counting up the years I realized my folks were aging. Nobody knows how long a soul has to walk the earth. I figured I had better make my peace while they were both still around? The thought of Ma's delicious cooking was a strong motivator as well. I had dreamed about her grub ever since leaving home the last time. Just thinking about tucking into supper at her table made me lightheaded. There had been many days of hunger on the road that I thought I smelled the tantalizing aroma of her biscuits fresh out of the stove.

When the train whistled into Texarkana, I got off and walked out of the station. I took in a deep breath and tasted pine in the air. It had been a long time but the smell was one I still believed of as home. The Eastern side of Texas was heavily forested from Houston to Texarkana. Now with my boots back in Bowie County, it sounded and smelled prosperous. Everywhere I looked was new buildings. I could hear the sound of hammers and saws over the steam engine puffing. The smell of sawdust drifted on the slight breeze. That raw smell of cedar, pine, and oak was one I had always loved. I was thinking I could do a lot worse than staying right here and finding work.

An inner compass directed my steps as I began walking in the direction of Atlanta. However before I got more than a dozen footfalls from the train station, I saw a blinding flash of lightning cross the otherwise clear sky. The lightning was followed immediately by the crack of the thunder. The short hairs on the back of my neck stood up and my anxiety level soared. I spoke out loud in exclamation. "Oh damn it! Welcome to Texas Oscar." As I looked on in disbelief angry dark clouds rolled in from a northern direction. Wind was picking up and had a surprising chill for summer. My pa had always said that if you did not like the Texas weather, wait a minute and it'll change.

In a heartbeat I lost my taste for walking to Atlanta and began looking around for a place to stay the night. Sleeping outside in a thunder storm was more of a fearful possibility than just about any suffering I had ever experienced. I began a hurried pace toward the only hotel I saw in quick walking distance. The Cosmopolitan was a grand hotel. It looked like it was far out of my price range for certain. However I was quick stepping to get out of the pending storm. If I had time and courage to dally about, I could ask around and find a boardinghouse a common laborer could afford. Resigned to spending a month's wage on a dry bed, I made my way into the lobby.

The hotel was stately. I had not seen anything so fancy since the Hotel Paso del Norte. The hotel was old but well maintained. I thought of the hotel as a female. She was like a classy lady who had aged well. I walked up to the desk and asked for a room. The price was $5.00 a night. They might as well have pointed a gun at me in the lobby because the price was daylight robbery. I would have to work more than a week to earn back the money. Including supper tonight, the one night at the hotel was going to cut deep into my tentative prosperity.

Resigned to my fate, I paid the clerk and then refused to hand my bag to a bellhop. The young man looked like he had not used a razor yet. He insisted on showing me to my room even after I protested. He said his name was Jed Rawlings. When we reached the second floor of the hotel Jed showed me to a room with fancy brass numbers reading *277* on the door. I thanked him and he moved off without a tip. As I was fumbling with the lock, an attractive woman came out of the room two doors down from mine. She was wearing a black maid's uniform, and had apparently been cleaning the room before I walked up.

Before she noticed me I had time to observe her straight black hair. She was pretty. I saw that her cheeks were flushed crimson from her labor. When she looked up and saw me, her eyes quickly averted to the floor. I could not think of anything to say. Every possibility that crossed my mind was rejected as flimsy. She seemed familiar in some way. As far as I knew I did not know anyone in Texarkana. With the lock opened, the moment passed and I stepped inside and closed the door. I had scant practice at talking to women. I had purposely avoided any relationship successfully to this point.

Once in the safety of my room, a dozen words came to mind. I chided myself for not saying something to her. I spoke out loud. "What is your name? Mine is Oscar. Where can a hungry man find a good meal?" Maybe I could have said a simple *hello*. There was no doubt I had been alone too long. While I stood in the middle of the room muttering to myself like an escaped lunatic, I saw another flash of lightning through the open window, followed by a boom that shook the hotel. I crossed the room and slammed it shut, closing the curtains as I did. The storm chose that moment to let go. Torrents of rain slammed down on Texarkana. Well at least I was inside and dry. I peered fearfully at the window and wondered if lightning could come through the glass. Not taking any chances, I moved away and lay on the bed.

That night I cleaned myself up and slicked back my hair before going down to the lobby to ask about supper. I admit that I was looking around for the pretty maid, but she was not around. I was pleased to discover there was a diner in the hotel. The rain was still coming down in waves. I had not been looking forward to stepping outside into the downpour. I ordered a meal of pheasant. The bird was tender and served with black eyed peas, spinach, and a whole loaf of bread. I paid a dollar, which was often more than I made in a day. I was in an unusually optimistic mood for a change. I sat long over the meal sipping strong black coffee.

I was pleased when the maid from earlier came in. She had changed into a flowered print dress. She went to a corner and seated herself. A woman eating alone was unusual, but she was an employee. Before long the waitress was talking to her in friendly tones. After the waitress left she reached into a large bag and pulled out a book. Flipping through until she found her place she began reading. I studied her face trying to remember where I might have met her before. Was it possible? Or more likely she just reminded me of someone else? Since I had been raised less than fifty miles from here, perhaps I knew her family? Then it slapped me in the face like a beaver's tail smacking water.

In an instant, before I could think or talk myself out of it, I was out of my seat and crossing the room. As my shadow fell across her face, she looked up startled at my sudden appearance. If she recognized me from earlier or before that, I saw none of it in her pretty face. Her hand flew up to her face and she tried to look past me to see if anyone was nearby in case she needed help. Without preamble I blurted out, "I know you Myrtle Wheelington." It had come out as more of an accusation, which was not my intention. I was just excited because I had finally placed her.

I can't recall what she said, if anything. Seeing the confusion and a little fear in her eyes, I added hurriedly, "I'm James Oscar Draper. We both grew up in Atlanta. My pa is the reverend around those parts. You and your folks lived down the dirt road from our home. We went to school together in that drafty one room school house."

Recovering her earlier shock at my approach, she said, "Now that I see you up close, I know you too Oscar. Do you still tease little girls mercilessly and give your parents gray hair?"

Her voice was soft but her words were harsh. I did not know if I should turn and make a swift retreat or stay and assure her I had grown up a little. Then I saw her smile. She was having a little fun at my expense. The teasing gave me courage. "Yes you know what they say about the preacher's children. May I sit down Miss Myrtle?"

"Okay but you can stop calling me *Miss*; it makes me sound like a youngster, which I'm not."

I watched her eat and marveled at the dainty way of her. I ordered more coffee just to have something to do with my hands. I had never courted a woman and had no idea if I was doing it correctly or stumbling down the stairs. With each minute that passed and she had not order me away from her table, I figured I was fairing tolerable. The supper and coffee lasted for an hour. I tried to pay for her meal when the waitress returned. She refused my offer.

Myrtle had left her folk's farm to help out with cash money. She stayed over in the hotel during her work week and returned home to Atlanta on her days off. Eventually she asked, "What about you Oscar? Where have you been since leaving home?"

I was flattered that any woman would care where I had been. I told her a little about my days in the Army and my drifting throughout the country. I left out Mexico or my first hitch in the service. "It's no secret back home that I don't get on with my pa. He is a good man but a hard one as well. I have kept in touch with my ma. We write letters when time allows."

After the meal I walked her to room *101* on the first floor. She was sharing the room with one other maid. At her door I asked, "Do you suppose I could see you again Myrtle? I can't say when I'll get back this way, but I'll make it as soon as possible."

She thought about it longer than I would have liked. Finally she said, "Oscar as I said before, I'm not a young girl. I know how men folk are. You say you'll be back, but you will more likely lose track of time and drift back through here months or even years from now. I don't know how long I'll be here and I'm not getting any younger."

I protested, "I'm planning on visiting my folks, then doing some work in Fort Worth. I intend to settle somewhere close by. I will be back. I'll just need to find steady work hereabouts."

Again she paused as she thought about what I had said. "We'll see. Just don't expect to find me sitting around wondering when you might find your way back this way."

"It's settled then. If it's alright with you, I'll look for you tomorrow. Goodnight Myrtle."

"Good night Oscar." She held out her hand and I shook it. The formality of our actions made us both smile. It was a good thing Alex was not here to tease me with one of his snarky comments. We had given him plenty of sass when he had fallen hard for Abelinda. Was I smitten by Myrtle or just a lonely man? I fell asleep that night thinking about her sweet smile and soft brown eyes.

The next morning I ate breakfast in the hotel diner. I was spending money like I was a man of leisure. I ate slowly and knew what I was really doing was stalling until I saw Myrtle again. There was no place in a wondering man's life for courting, but most times complicated matters had a way of working themselves out. With my meal finished, I got up and made my way to the front of the hotel. I could not search every floor for Myrtle. Indecision froze me at the front door. I was anxious to get started home and should just walk away, yet some powerful sensation said to wait.

Finally I opened the front door. I then looked over my shoulder and saw her standing on the second floor balcony looking at me. Her face was unreadable, but in another moment I would have been gone. Would she have cried out? Probably not, but I reversed direction and ran up the stairs skipping every other step like an excited school boy until I made the landing. Looking around and not seeing anyone nearby I approached her before I saying, "I was afraid I would have to wait until returning to see you again."

She looked at me sternly before saying, "I suppose you think my day would have been ruined if you had not climbed up those stairs?"

I had noticed the night before that she sometimes said one thing while her eyes and smile said another. She smiled now. I was thinking she was happy I had found her. Suddenly tongue tied, I stood without saying anything for a dozen beats of my heart. Finally when I began to speak I rushed out the words in rapid-fire form. "Okay then. I have a long way to walk and had best go. I enjoyed our talk last night. It was a pleasure to see someone from back home and I hope to see you soon. If you'll let me I want to take you to supper when I return. We could see a picture show if you like."

"Okay that'll be fine. Goodbye Oscar. I expect you will find me here or in Atlanta. Don't let the time slip away from you though."

"I won't. Goodbye Myrtle." I walked outside and started off. I discovered there was a new bounce in my step. Myrtle was a mighty fine woman. My head was buzzing like I had just taken a long pull on potent local corn liquor. I had almost given up finding a woman who could tolerate my rough country raising. Now I had met a girl from Atlanta. She was a hometown girl who seemed ready to accept me for who I was. It pleased me that a good woman such as Myrtle would give a chance to a homely drifter such as me. I remembered her ma and pa. They were solid country folk. I breathed deep of the East Texas air and continued walking west.

# CHAPTER 49

## *The Fort Worth Chief's House*

The rain was long gone. The sun felt good on my face. I put Texarkana six miles behind me, maintaining a steady pace. Before I realized it, a dusty black 1915 Ford Model T truck stopped along the rough road just in front of me. The truck was some beat up, with farm or ranch equipment in the bed. As I approached the Ford I saw a handsome man with coal black hair combed back. He was deeply tanned from working in the sun. He waved me forward.

I ran up and jumped in after he said, "Hop in mister." His smile was friendly as he stuck out his hand. "I'm Rufus Jefferson Clark. I'm pleased to meet you. You can call me Rufus."

His grip was firm. "Oscar Draper, I thank you kindly for stopping. I was so lost in thought I had plumb forgotten to stick out a thumb."

"I could surely see that. You were *long-striding* with a purpose. The war has been over awhile now. Where were you marching off to *young man*?"

Nobody had called me a young man in a few years. I took a closer look at Rufus and saw he could not be more than two years older than me. I was sure he had native Indian blood in him. "In fact I am a former soldier. I don't think I was marching since I was a cavalryman. I was in the Army during the war but never shipped overseas. I'm heading home to my parent's in Atlanta. I came in on the train from Shreveport yesterday afternoon. I've been gone a good long while. I'd be pleased for a ride in that direction."

He put the car in first gear and maneuvered us back onto the blacktop road. "That'll be fine. I could use the company. I'm driving to Dallas to pick up drilling equipment. I intend to drill a new water well on my farm. I also need to throw up a new chicken coop. My old one is about to fall in. Any night critter can slip in and gobble up my chickens. Anyway I expect I can get you a few miles closer to home."

"Oh damn, I have work waiting in Fort Worth. Isn't Dallas only thirty miles or so east of Fort Worth? I was surely looking forward to sitting at my ma's table a spell. If you don't mind could I hitch all the way to Dallas? Then when I'm done there I'll make my way here back this way. If you still need help, I can build you a coop. I don't know anything about drilling wells, but I've been doing simple carpentry jobs across twenty states since I left the service.

"That'll be fine. I can pay you steady for a bit with plenty of repair projects. I suspect some of the surrounding farms could use your help too. I lost my wife and pa to the flu in 1920. Ever since then I've been working myself day and night trying to keep up the farm. The flu killed so many that farm workers have been hard to come by. Then there were others who moved to town to take work."

"I'm sorry to hear that about your wife and pa. Many good folks I knew died as well. I'd appreciate the work. I'm probably going to need a week or more to finish in Fort Worth. I was heading further west but now that I see there might be work close to home, I might as well stick around awhile. Also I met a special lady in Texarkana that I intend on courting when I get back up there. Atlanta is home and I always expected to settle here eventually. I've found there are usually opportunities wherever a man looks. In my experience you just have to flip over enough rocks to scare up a meal or a paying job." My feet were aching from walking in my heavy work boots. As I settled back in the seat, I thought about how good it would have been to have my feet under my ma's table once more.

I fell asleep and dreamed of Mexico. I slept hard and woke up confused. I expected to see Alex driving one of the Dodge Town Cars. Mr. Clark was pulling into a filling station in Sulfur Springs. As much as I missed Alex, I was relieved to see I was not still in Mexico. Old Pancho Villa was dead anyway. I had best leave his soul alone to burn in hell. "Sorry Rufus I must have been tuckered out. Do you want me to take a turn at driving? It has been a few years but I suppose I could keep your truck on the road."

"Yes I would. I started this day at 5:30. I could use a nap myself. We should be there in two more hours unless we get stuck behind some big trucks. This old blacktop road is mighty narrow to pass safely on."

I steered the Ford back onto the road grinding a few gears along the way. The civilian truck was not as big and powerful as the Dodge Brothers Army trucks. After a few miles I began to get a feel for the lighter vehicle. Left alone with my thoughts, I was chapped at missing a chance to see my ma. It would have been good to wake up in my old bed to the sound of roosters crowing. That *cock-a-doodle-do* noise might even be pleasant now. However, when I was growing up, it irritated me no end. It meant it was time to get up and begin the chores. More than once I had thought about killing pa's prize rooster. Come to think of it, the Army's morning bugle reveille had not been any less annoying.

As it turned out Rufus let me tag along and help him load the drilling equipment, then he drove me all the way to an address on the north side of Fort Worth. It was after six o'clock and I was hoping to get some work done before dark. I was being paid good money to reinforce and repair a frame. Standing before the house it looked about ready to tumble into the dirt. The roof was in bad shape and the porch was leaning low on the right side. Rufus stood beside me scratching his head. "Are you sure you don't want to ride back with me? If I had the time I could help you fix this jumbled mess. She looks like a collapse is coming at any moment."

"I appreciate that. I agree with your observation though. I hope you're wrong about it falling in anytime soon. I'll be sleeping inside."

He shrugged. "Well I expect she might stand another few days. I guess the family has moved off somewhere safe until you fix her up a bit."

"Yep. The owner bought this disaster because he was born and grew up here. As you can see the land is on a pretty hill. The view makes this a nice spot for a house. He wants to live here again with his family."

"Gosh dog it! I think he should tear it down and start over."

"Me too, there is no wonder he included room and board with the job. Anyway, I hope to get back your way when this job is done. I'll hitch a ride to Atlanta, and then look you up. I plan on seeing the nice lady I met in Texarkana too."

"You do that Oscar. If you can right this here wreak, I can surely help you find work with the farmers around my parts."

We shook hands. I walked closer to the shack as he waved and drove away. The door was covered with a rough-cut piece of board hammered across the entrance. I shuddered as I pried the lumber off and peered inside. It was dark, wet and smelled like old mildew. The floors appeared to be moving with roaches or other critters. What they were feeding on was a mystery. I looked around outside and saw a large oak tree. That would be my camp with dirt for a bed and gathered rocks for a stove. As a man who is often alone will do, I addressed myself out loud. "Well Oscar, your pa taught you not to be a quitter before you've even begun." It would not be the first night I had slept outside. Thinking again about the soft bed at ma's house made me want to chase Rufus down.

The next morning I set about repairing the house. The first task was opening the shack and getting some air inside. Once I could see, I realized the floors were rotted and would have to be replaced. The walls would stand and the porch could be fixed with shoring up. As I worked thoughts of home and Myrtle alternated through my head. It passed the time. About noon I saw a shiny new 1925 Essex two door sedan pull onto the property. I had been working since first light and looked forward to any company and a chance for a break.

The sun was hot and I estimated the temperature to be in the upper eighties. A well-dressed man and woman stepped out of the sedan as soon as it came to a halt. The man was in his early fifties and the woman perhaps ten years younger. They waved and I walked over, putting my shirt back on as I walked. "Hello, I'm Oscar draper. Are you Mister Ferguson?"

"Yes, I see you've begun work on the old homestead." He stuck out a hand and I shook it.

His handshake was hardened by solid muscle. He dressed like a banker, but had the arms and chest of longshoremen I had met in coastal cities. My thoughts were that calling the ramshackle building behind me a *homestead* was being entirely too generous. Gesturing toward the house I said, "She is in poor shape Mister Ferguson. I understand you grew up here, but I could as easy build you a new home as fix this one."

"Please, call me Standifer. This is my wife May."

I nodded to May and said, "It is my pleasure." On closer inspection Standifer was lean and fit for his age. He was energetic, tanned from working outdoors and what women would call ruggedly handsome. His eyes seemed to be constantly on the move, evaluating, missing nothing. Mrs. May Ferguson had red-brown hair and was petite and graceful in her movements. I thought she was rather pale, as she avoided the direct sun with a small, brightly colored umbrella.

I turned my attention back to Ferguson. He gestured to the shack. "I know she is a pitiful sight, but she was home once. Also in the tragic fire of April 1909 on the south side of the city, it became obvious that building so close to others was not the wisest course for a home location. Our children are grown and we will not need as much room. I am aware it will be a chore to restore the house, but I want to live in her again. The view from the hill is breathtaking. Don't you think so Mr. Draper?"

"As for my name, Oscar will do. Yes, it is rather nice up here. The constant breeze will help with the heat of the day. I will fix her up if you can get the supplies ordered and delivered up here? I can do a lot of preparing, but I'll need the lumber, nails, and shingles before I get very much further."

Of course May and I brought you a hardy meal. I'm sure you're hungry. We've brought enough supplies for fourteen days. I'll be around at least once a week if you need anything."

"That will be fine. I thank you. I had not realized how isolated I would be out here. I'm a good walker and figured on walking out for meals or cooking over a camp fire. I expect many more folks will move out this way eventually."

As I ate May bragged about her husband in a soft voice. Mr. Ferguson protested, but he had a right to be proud of his accomplishments. He had been one of the original paid firemen in the city in 1893. Then in 1919 he had been appointed as chief. "Standifer was riding Company Number 1 Panther Engine on April 3, 1909 when the *Great South Side Fire started*. At least twenty square miles of the city south of downtown was destroyed. Only one person lost his life, but if not for the efforts of firemen like Standifer the whole of downtown would have been lost. It was obviously not as horrific as the Chicago fire, but firemen saved many lives that day."

Ferguson spoke up and added, "After that tragic day horse drawn fire engines were replaced with motorized vehicles. The fires were so hot that day our hoses melted and were useless. In the panic to get to the fire, one horse was killed; another broke a leg and had to be put down. It was a terrible event but we learned much from our mistakes."

Standifer and May left in the early afternoon. I got back to work ripping out windows and later the floors. Over the next six weeks the shack began to resemble a home once more. I gave letters to mail to Standifer whenever he visited. He had kindly let me use his address for return mail. I wrote to ma and Alex. With each letter to Alex I included short notes to Eva. I figured she must be about twelve by now. Letters sent to Myrtle where sent in care of the hotel. I did not tell my ma I was coming home. I wanted it to be a surprise and I did not want to disappoint her if I was waylaid again. I would sit around my campfire each night and read through several times the letters from friends and family. It was my only entertainment. With the money from this job I would be set for the winter if work became scarce.

Finally the summer ended and the house was finished. I had been sleeping inside the house for the better part of a month on the floor. Today I bathed in the no name creek running through the property, which was fed by the Trinity River. I was dressed and waiting when Standifer and May arrived. She had not been inside in over a month and was in for a shock. I felt she had been apprehensive after seeing the old house. It was her husband's dream and he was asking her to share it with him. My job was not to paint or pretty the house up. Standifer had hired others for that. The painters had worked around my efforts while I made the house structurally sound. My pa would have said pride was a sin. However I was mighty pleased to see what I had shaped with my hands. Now the old house would stand for many years.

After walking inside with some trepidation, May burst into tears. Once she recovered from her initial surprise, she dabbed at her eyes as she walked around the house. May admired the view by looking through every window. The house faced toward the south. The city's downtown area could easily been seen from the high hill. The wraparound porch circled three sides of the house. The porch had deviled me for days as I struggled to support the sagging beams. I appreciated the cleverness of the original designer who had arranged the porch to catch breezes from whichever direction the wind was blowing.

May's inspection complete, she came to hug her husband and then myself. She was too emotional for words. That night the couple invited me to one the city's best diners. They fed me a one pound steak at the Star Café down near the old stockyards. It was the best steak I had ever eaten. That night I stayed with Standifer and May at their present home in town. The feel of a soft bed was mighty comfortable at first, however after much tossing about; I ended the night sleeping on the floor. The next morning Standifer generously paid my wages and threw in a train ticket on the Texas and Pacific Railroad back to Texarkana.

# CHAPTER 50

## *Courting and Home*

Just as the summer had begun, I was once again headed home. Feeling a bit selfish I planned on courting Myrtle first if she still agreed to it. It was a Friday morning, the first week of September. With a self-satisfied sigh, I settled into my seat for a nap. It had been an exhaustingly hot summer. Each twelve-plus hour day had been worked in scorching heat, followed by equally sweltering nights. Then I would face another brutal day. Throughout the summer I had not taken a single day of leisure. Now I told myself, other than a single night out with Myrtle, I needed to quit stalling and go home.

After a relaxing nap and fine meal in the dining car, I began to fret about the ruby ring I had won in the poker game all those years ago in Glenn Springs. I knew it was somewhere in my bindle, although I had not looked on it in a couple of years. I began to search the sack from corner to corner. I emptied out the contents onto the empty seat next to me. Any observer would have thought my mind had slipped out my ears as I frantically tossed my belongings about. Finally, I found the ruby ring ticked into a small snuff can I had carried for years. The can had been safely inside the pocket of an old stained shirt I only wore for the dirtiest jobs.

Once the ring was found, I began to wonder what has possessed me. What was I thinking of doing with the ring? What right had I to assume Myrtle would even have me? I had only had one meal with her. Thinking about it I realized she was the only one eating. I had not even been invited to that. Either way I was somehow sure the ring would be on her hand someday. I put the ring in the bottom end of the watch pocket in my jeans. I was as nervous as a rabbit who wonders across an Army firing range.

At near six o'clock the train whistled our arrival in Texarkana. We were coming in from the opposite end of town. I was mentally placing the hotel in my mind. Before the train had stopped moving I was off the train and headed to the Cosmopolitan Hotel. Myrtle's return letters had been friendly, but vague, holding no promise of a warm welcome when I returned. I was in a hurry to catch her in case she was heading home to Atlanta. I did not want to see her at home. Too many folks would know us there. My reputation would not be the best in the small town where everything is known about every citizen.

My plan was to check in at the hotel if she was working and buy her dinner if she would let me. By 6:15 I was in the lobby and inquiring about Myrtle. The snooty clerk did not want to give me any information about staff. Turning away I went and knocked on her door. I heard movement inside and hoped it was her and not the roommate. She opened the door and was dressed for traveling. My smile was wide at seeing her. I must have looked like the village fool but I could not stop smiling. "Hi Myrtle, were you going home for the weekend?"

"Yes, I was about to do just that. I suppose you could have written or called to tell me you'd be coming in today."

"First, there are no phones where I was working and second, I did not know I would finish up on a Thursday. Could we sit in the lobby for awhile?"

"No, I don't care much for Mr. Hodges. He is too nosey and annoying for my taste. Let's walk outside in the back. There is a table and chairs for hotel staff to take their breaks."

As we walked I asked her, "Do you think you could stay in town tonight? I wanted to take you to a fancy supper and a picture show. I *was* going home too, but first I wanted to see you."

She looked at me like she was trying to determine if I was drunk or a lunatic. I figured my country ways might make me seem less than sincere. After we were seated outside she said, "I don't have any idea what you are thinking in that head of yours, but you have been roaming all over the country for years. In my experience once a man gets itchy feet he can't stay in one place very long. I have no interest in a man that will always be gone." She shook her head sadly and added. "When I last spoke with you Atlanta and home was your direction. Then I get letters from Fort Worth."

Now I was forced to examine my own motivation. I could understand her hesitation. In her eyes I was not ready to settle down. In fact the life on the road had lost all appeal. I somehow knew this was the moment to set her mind at ease or lose any chance at seeing her again. "Myrtle, I am ready to move back home. I want a home, wife and family. After I left here a nice man gave me a ride all the way to Fort Worth. He says he has work for me and knows others who can hire me as well.

Seeing nobody else around, I took both of her hands in mine. I was pleased when she did not pull away. I did not go home after I left here because I could not pass up a ride to Dallas. I told you I had work waiting down that way. I was just planning on staying a couple of days with my folks. Then I met you and everything changed. Stay tonight and we will have a big night on the town. I've been working hard all summer without a break. Daydreaming about seeing you again got me through."

I was quiet for a while letting her think. If she said no, I would just start walking or hitching a ride home. She smiled now which made my heartbeat faster. Slipping back into her teasing tone she said, "The part about thinking about me all summer was a nice touch Oscar. Okay. I'll stay tonight. Go check in and I'll wait for you here. I suppose I'm as dressed as I can be. See you in a few minutes. There is a diner I've been pining to try here in town and a picture show I want to see."

I let go of her hands and started for the front desk in a hurry. Smiling over my shoulder before I disappeared into the interior of the hotel I said, "Don't change your mind Myrtle."

I wish I could say the night could not have gone better. We still managed to get to know each other better and managed to have a good time. The fault for any mishaps was all my doing. We had a delicious supper. Then I took her to a fancy picture show. It was a fancy building called the Saenger Theatre. It took an hour to eat, and then we walked to the theatre. The problem came about because of the movie. Myrtle had read some book about the story and we saw *The Big Parade*. It was a war story. As the battles began I began to squirm in my seat. I realized I was sweating heavily. Nobody else appeared to be hot. I was overheated like someone was holding my feet to a fire. It was not a physical pain, but uncomfortable to be sure. I excused myself and walked out into the grand lobby. I found a toilet and rinsed my face in cool water. The toilet was so ritzy that it had an attendant. The man looked at me with some concern and asked, "Are you okay mister?"

I squeaked out, "Yea, it must have been something I had for supper. I'll be fine." In fact my hands were shaking and my stomach began to lurch. I held on tightly not wanting to lose my high-dollar meal. Eventually after about tem minutes I had recovered some balance. Peeking inside the theatre I saw that the battle had ended. I slid back into my seat. I began to think the picture show had stirred up memories of my times in Mexico. I wanted to forget, not relive those days. Why would anyone make a drama about the horrible times in World War I? I had missed the war and had been glad of it. I finally decided that there were those who wanted to see the war for themselves. Just as I was feeling normal, the sensation was stirred up again when another battle was shown. Myrtle tossed me a look of concern as I got up again. I patted her hand and smiled reassurance I did not feel.

I waited in the lobby this time. When Myrtle came out I was sure she would be upset. Instead she took my arm and we walked back to the hotel. She was in a good mood and chatted happily. Myrtle did not seem interested in whatever problem had made me leave the theatre. That was just as well because I did not want to talk about Mexico. Also I did not understand what had happened anyway.

At the hotel I walked her to her room. We stood at the door and talked a minute more. With my previous anxiety forgotten I said, "There is only *one* chance to get a first kiss right." If she had slammed the door in my face, I would have taken that as a no. Instead she waited and I kissed her. The next day I took her out again. We shared lunch and another supper. On Sunday we rode with a friend of hers to Atlanta. We were dropped off on the main street. Taking in the town I told her, "I never expected to meet anyone from home that I liked. The past two days have been a pleasure. I will look for work then come see you."

She leaned forward and looked at me sternly. "See that you do. I'm not introducing you to my folks until you have steady employment. I'm afraid with your reputation they might disown me just for speaking to you." She smiled then and I hoped she had been joshing.

We parted ways to walk to our folk's homes. For my part, I circled the town to come up to my folk's house from the opposite direction of Myrtle. Her pa was about as stern as mine. He might shoot me on sight after he found out I was courting his daughter. As I walked the ruby ring lay heavy on my mind. I touched the ring through the material of my pants. My decision was made and it felt good. The next time I saw Myrtle I was going to give it to her if she would have me. I was now thirty-one and reflected that a man should not put off having a family when the time seemed right. I figured if I waited much longer I would be too wedged into my ways to ever settle down. I had traveled about as far as a man could and still find his way back. It was time for a wife, family, and a home.

Arriving at my ma and pa's house I walked to the back of the property where the hand water pump was. I looked around and did not see many changes. The place had not prospered but had not suffered either as far as I could see. Pa could do most of the work himself if he was not on the road. There were others he could call on who owed him for preaching or just wanted to help out the minister. Neighbors in Atlanta were generous by nature and would help out anybody in need. They were a touch suspicious of outsiders, but would feed and employ them all the same.

I looked at the pump remembering the well was deep and the water was always cold no matter the time of year. I began cranking the pump to wash my face and taste the freshness of home. The pump creaked and groaned before the cool liquid finally shot out with good force splashing my clothes. I was cupping my hands to drink when Ma appeared in the back door. She was flushed with excitement and older than I had imagined she would be.

She ran at a good pace across the yard to gather me into her arms. The hug lasted a good while. I hugged her back gently. Ma seemed somehow fragile. I was afraid I would hurt her if I returned the affection as strongly as I was receiving it. I was standing there feeling awful ashamed of myself for being so long gone. Ma was crying and trying to talk through her tears. Finally, between sobs she managed, "Oscar, I knew it was you when I heard the old pump creak. Pa thought I was crazy and said so, but I knew my boy had returned."

Eventually she pulled away to inspect me. I looked over her shoulder and saw Pa standing in the back doorway. He never smiled much and mostly had two moods. He was either fiery, like when he was preaching, or quiet when he was mad. He was not smiling now and his aged face exaggerated the look. Ma looked fearfully back and forth at our faces. I knew I would leave again before arguing with pa. Ma had always been the peacekeeper between us. I walked to the back porch where he stood. I never knew what to expect from Pa from one moment to the next. That held true now. All I said was, "Hi Pa." Then I stuck out my hand.

He still did not smile and left my hand outstretched for a awkward moment. Finally he shook it and said, "Hello Oscar. You look fit. I expect you must be hungry. Your ma has some vittles on the table. She always cooks plenty. We best eat before it gets cold."

Dad stopped reading. He took off his glasses, wiping his eyes. I had never seen my dad cry and I sat quietly. A dozen questions raced in my head, but I waited a while longer. "Dad Rufus Clark, who gave Grandpa a ride, is Mom's dad, my Grandpa Rufus. Is that all there is? What else happened between my grandparents? When did he ask her to marry him?"

"That was news to me about your mom's dad. I had no idea they met that early on. The story on my folks is that the third time Pa went courting he gave her the ring and asked her to marry him. We always heard the ruby ring had come from a poker game. I never thought it was true. My folks were married June 7th, 1926 at the Oak Lawn

Baptist Church in Piney Grove, Texas. That was thirty-eight years ago this June. Pa was thirty-two at the time and ma was twenty-six when they married."

"I have heard whispers ever since I was little that Grandpa Draper not a good man when he was younger. Now I know what he went through. I guess it was Grandpa's mamma that brought him and his pa together again. Do you think it was Grandma Myrtle who settled Grandpa down? He never stirs up trouble like he did when he was younger."

"That is probably true, but there one other story about the change that came over my pa. It centered around me so I took a particular interest in it. I pieced together some of it from my brother and sisters. Ma had my older sister Marie in 1927, then me in 1929, and later John Ray, Ruth, and Emily. I turned thirteen in 1942 and got real sick when my appendix ruptured. Nobody really knew what was wrong with me. I was running high fever and hurting bad. Folks didn't much go to the hospital back then. I suffered at home more than a day. Eventually, fearing he would lose me, pa took me to an Atlanta hospital."

I was excited now. Yes Dad, Aunt Marie told me you almost died."

"Yes, Ma was sick with worry and the doctor confirmed her worst fears. My folks were told that I had appendicitis. They said it was too late and I would die before morning. Apparently when the appendix ruptures poison is released throughout the body. That poison was the reason for the fever and it had been too long. I believe my pa always knew God was real, but had never embraced the belief himself. I think it was partly a rebellion against his own pa. As I said before, James Henry was an unyielding man. He and Pa were both stubborn and always rubbed each other wrong."

Dad sat a moment putting together the story before continuing. "After hearing the doctor's words, my father went to the hospital courtyard and hit his knees to pray. Nobody knew what to do and left him alone. After a couple of hours James Henry arrived and walked out to the courtyard. He put an arm on his son's shoulder and knelt beside him. They prayed like that all night. The next morning the fever was gone, along with all trace of the appendicitis. It was a miracle

Buddy. That night ended the feud for good. Now your grandfather is a Christian and has surely mellowed."

I shook my head and said doubtfully, "Is that even possible Dad?"

"Don't forget son that Matthew 17:20 reads that with faith as *small* as a mustard seed, we can tell the mountain to move from *here* to *there* and it will."

# CHAPTER 51

## *Little Brother and Grandpa's Last Visit*

It saddened me to think that with this last letter grandpa might be done with storytelling. He still owed me the promised tale of whatever it was that happened in 1923. However I knew he could be pressed on the matter. I began working more odd jobs and had to stop spending weeks during the summer with relatives in Texarkana. I missed those visits, but had gotten a taste of having money in my pocket. I liked it too. Of course I still saw grandpa at Christmas and at a few other family occasions. The experience of sharing in his stories had brought us closer than ever. As much as I wanted to ask, I never bothered him about his missing story.

On December 28th, 1965 my baby brother was born. I had finally got my big Christmas wish and had a little brother. Dad had called home as soon as mom had the baby. When I asked excitedly if the baby was a boy or girl Dad began asking if we were okay and minding Sherry, who was babysitting us. Then he starts talking about chores. I knew he was stalling and playing with us. Sherry and Deb were shouting in my ear and jumping up and down to hear the news. We all kept saying, "Dad what did Mom have?" This was one time my dad's sense of humor was *not* funny.

Finally he stopped torturing us and said we had a nine pound baby brother named Gary Joel. When I relayed the news, Debra started crying. She had been holding out for a baby sister. I was too excited to feel sorry for her. Dad, always the accountant, called Gary his *little tax deduction*, since he was able to claim him on his taxes for the entire year of 1965. I had been only six when Debra was born so having a baby in the house was great fun. Gary was a big hit with my friends as well. He was a chubby, happy baby who grew so quickly we were amazed. We could play with him on the floor for hours. Randy and Rory made him laugh so hard he could not catch his breath. He was a bundle of energy and Mom was glad when we entertained him.

Our next door neighbor Shirley had her fourth daughter six months before Mom. Her oldest was Diane, next there was Pam, then Paula and finally the baby girl named Susie. It was love at first sight between Susie and Gary. Even before he could stand on his own he would hang onto our chain link fence gurgling as he tried to talk to Susie on the other side. For Gary's first Christmas in 1966 I spent a month of pay on his presents. Each time I thought the perfect gift was in my hand, I would see something else I wanted him to have.

In 1967 when I was fourteen, Dad got me hired at Webber's Root Beer Stand just like he had promised he would. I worked every job in the hamburger joint, including fountain boy, french-fry boy, onion ring maker, and even car hop. I hated taking orders to cars because I believed it was a girl's job. That was the one job I avoided successfully unless someone called in sick.

After getting bitten by the working bug, I worked at other fast-food restaurants, including What-A-Burger, Dairy Queen and McDonalds. At some of the jobs Randy worked with me too. I enjoyed working and the money that came with it. I dreamed of the day when I would graduate and get to work full time.

Jo Ann and I kept our flirtation to just friendship. Eventually I started liking her Aunt Cynthia, the youngest sister of Randy and Jo Ann's mother Vickie. Cynthia had been born late in the life of her mom. Cindy was a few months older than me and my first true girlfriend. She attended junior high in Dallas. I only saw her during summers or on weekends when her older brother Sonny would visit their sister's house. Mom was not thrilled that her oldest son had a girlfriend.

In the summer of 1970 I got my driver's license. Dad helped out by selling me the family 1967 model Volkswagen Beetle. Dad usually drove Buicks, but had bought the bug as an extra family car when it was new. Dad and Sherry had both wreaked it at one time. Mom would not drive it because of the stick shift. I had saved five-hundred dollars from my earnings and wanted the car more than anything. Yet when I had been driving only two weeks, a big new Cadillac ran a red light and the car was totaled. I took the insurance money and bought a 1965 Dodge Dart. The car was not as new, but it had imitation wood panel inside and out, plus a 273 V-8 engine. I felt like I was king of the road with the three-speed shift on the column. Dad said I had a lead foot. Some local police officers agreed with him. After a few speeding tickets, replaced tires and a clutch or two, I learned to slow down a little.

That same summer I heard my grandparents would be coming for a visit. It had been a few years and I figured I knew why. A few months before their house had burned down. I selfishly thought how much I would miss that house. I reminded myself how my grandparents had lost everything and would have to figure out what to do next. Since the fire they had been staying with my Aunt Ruth and Uncle Herbert in Texarkana.

I felt bad about my their terrible loss, but could not help but be thrilled that this might be the time I would hear what I had begun to think of as the *missing story*. Of course by then I had many other interest, like my new girlfriend Sally, drama class, R.O.T.C., collecting coins, and driving around endlessly with my friends when I was not working. Even with my other interest, the fact that Grandpa was visiting made me as excited as when I was ten years old.

When I asked Dad what the visit was about he said, "I'm not sure Buddy. They've had a rough patch lately and may just need a change of pace. However, when I told him you had your driver's license he asked if you could drive him somewhere during the visit."

"I'd be happy to, but what could that be all about? Does he know anyone around here"?

"Not that I ever heard of. I know you Buddy. You're thinking he wants to tell you that last story. That may be so, but you have to wait for him to bring it up."

"I will, but is it possible he forgot about it all together? He might never tell us?"

"I can't say. Even if that *is* the case, we must accept it. Pa said he would tell us when he was ready to let go of the memory. Remember he said it was a *bad* one. No, he said *ugly*."

"It's been so long. That was five years ago when I was only eleven."

"Yes that's about right. I know you don't have any patients, but my pa is seventy-six now. You can't push him. I think you know your grandpa won't budge until he is ready. Also drive carefully. Your grandpa does not like cars much. If he is willing to ride with a new young driver it must be important."

"I know Dad, but it is really hard not to. You know I'll take him wherever he wants to go."

On a Saturday, at exactly noon in August 1970, I was with Dad, Mom, Debra and Gary when the train came into the station in Grand Prairie. That summer we had moved to Arlington, the next town over, but this was still the closest train station. The last time I had been here I was ten or eleven. Now I was driving the rather large Buick family station wagon. Dad still owned at three seat wagon. We had brought the car so everyone would fit comfortably. Sherry was now married and in Illinois with her husband. He was in the Air Force going through Technical School. Debra and Mom had ridden in the back seat with Gary, who was now four and a half. Due to rough and rowdy ways, he was already getting hurt more often than I ever did. I often told Dad that Gary's *fear* button was disconnected.

When Grandpa and Grandma stepped down from the train, I was shocked at how much they had both aged. I had just seen them both at Christmas, but hey seemed to have aged ten years. Grandpa was seventy-six, but Grandma was younger at seventy. A lot of the spring had left their step. I felt fear for them in the pit of my stomach. The only close family member I had lost was a favorite uncles, but no grandparents since I was old enough to remember. My mom's mother, Donie Zoe had died when I was six months old. If my parent's noticed it, they were quick to cover it up. Hugs all around and much happy chatter followed.

Dad treated us all to lunch at Wyatt's Cafeteria, which was near the train station. Grandma was quieter than I remembered. I noticed Grandpa was more serious as well. Gary brightened the mood with his antics. I think he had more food on his face and the floor than he ever actually ate. Afterwards we headed home. Now I was nervous. Driving with so much responsibility scared me. It was one thing to risk yourself stupidly by speeding and reckless driving, but now most of my family were relying on me to drive carefully. Once home we sat outside and enjoyed the early evening. The talk was light and the subject of the fire was avoided. After Debra and Gary were off to bed, I expected to stay up late enjoying the conversation like the adults had done when I was a boy. Now I could easily stay up until midnight and was ready to hear all the talk.

I was disappointed when at about ten o'clock Grandma said she was tired and Grandpa got up and said goodnight as well. "Mom walked them to their room and I was left alone with Dad at the dining table. "I did not expect to get a story tonight, but y'all used to sit up talking late into the night. I was looking forward to that."

"Buddy my folks are not so young anymore. Also they have been through a lot. I saw your face when they first stepped off the train. This year has been rough on them. Imagine how you would feel if we lost everything in this house."

"I know. I guess that old house went up pretty quick. I'm just glad they got out. All those photographs are gone too. One time Jon Marc and I found some tintype photographs under Grandma's bed. She told us who everyone was, but I don't remember anyone now."

"Don't kick yourself too hard Buddy. I saw those photographs when I was growing up and never took an interest in them. I only know they did not actually make them from tin and that they were used as early as the Civil War. I guess that family history is lost for good."

Dad looked over my shoulder at something and I turned to see Grandpa walking slowly toward the back of my chair. It was more of a shuffle and he wore a beaten hound dog expression. It alarmed me and I came quickly to my feet in case he needed help. He stopped a few feet away as if he had run out of energy. "Grandpa, did you need something?"

He stood a minute putting together his thoughts. "Buddy, if you're able to, I need you to drive me somewhere tomorrow."

Without hesitation I answered. "Sure thing Grandpa, just tell me what time and where?"

"Ten will be about right. Can we get to an address in Fort Worth by 11:00?"

"Yes, we can. If you have the address we'll look it up on Dad's map he keeps in the station wagon. But we'll take my Dodge Dart."

"Okay that'll be fine. Goodnight then." He turned around and headed back to Sherry's bedroom where they were sleeping."

I turned back to Dad with a questioning look. He just shrugged. "Dad I don't know what is going on with Grandpa, but I'm worried about him. He seems to have a lot on his mind. I need to get up early and call my manager at McDonalds. I'm supposed to be in at 8:00 a.m."

"I offered to take him. I know how you hate to miss work, but I think he wants you to do it. I can't help but feel you two have unfinished business to attend to."

"That's okay Dad. I want to take him. I just hope everything is okay. Then anticipating his concern I added, I won't bother him for a story and I'll take good care of him Dad." It took me a long time to fall asleep that night. I felt like my grandparents were slipping away. It just made me want to hang on that much tighter. I finally rolled over and hoped tomorrow would bring answers.

I awoke at 7:00 a.m. and heard as well as smelled the sounds and aroma of breakfast cooking. I was taken back to the morning of Thanksgiving in 1963. Before I opened my eyes it was easy to believe I was eleven again. Life was so much simpler then. I had wanted to grow up so bad then. Now I had harder school work, responsibilities at work, car expenses, and a girlfriend I was still struggling to figure out. As much as I enjoyed being with her it was hard to find time with all the demands placed on me. How had the time passed so swiftly? Pushing my silly worries aside my stomach growled which got me up and moving. I took a quick bath. In less than twenty minutes I had called in sick and was eating a plate of eggs and bacon. I still did not like coffee but loved orange juice or Tang if the fresh stuff was not available.

Grandpa was also dressed and eating. He was not very talkative and mostly pushed his food around his plate. I know he loved my mom's cooking so his actions heightened my worry. Dad had taken off to visit his clients. Debra was still sleeping and Gary was watching cartoons in den. I did not see grandma and knew it was not like her to sleep in. Mom, reading my thoughts said, "Your grandma is not feeling well. Your dad left his map in the living room." Looking at Grandpa she added, "Oscar do you want me to pack you two a lunch or will you boys make it back for lunch?"

His mood was much improved over last night and he even appeared younger. "Oh, I guess if we aren't back I can buy Buddy some catfish."

"You should let your grandson buy you lunch. He works too much and has plenty of money. McDonalds is even considering him for Swing Manager. He works twenty-five hours during the week and ten more on weekends. It's a wonder he hasn't lost that girlfriend of his."

"I would be happy to buy Grandpa some lunch. Zeke's Fish and Chips in Fort Worth has great catfish. As for Sally, she loves me. I work days on weekends so we have lots of time for dating." To Grandpa I said, "Do you have the address where we're going? I'll go look it up."

He reached into the pockets of his jeans and fished out a piece of crumpled paper off a yellow notepad. An address on South Main in Fort Worth was written out carefully in pencil. I took it and went to look for the map. I recognized the address as south of downtown near a group of hospitals. I thought it could be found without too much trouble. I returned to the kitchen and said, "I can find it Grandpa. Whenever you're ready we can go."

I saw Mom looking at me. Before she could say it I beat her to it. "I'll be careful." I saw her glance at Grandpa as he tasted his breakfast without eating much. I guess she was using her mental powers on me, because it was the first time I had been able to read *her* thoughts. She was not worried about me but my grandpa.

Grandpa pushed himself to his feet. "I'm going to check on Myrtle, and then we can go."

"Okay I'll start my car." After he left I said, "I don't know what this is all about, just that it's important to him." Then Debra was in the doorway. She was now eleven and cute as a picture.

Along the way I talked about the sights along the way. The General Motors plant, Six Flags Over Texas, and then the Fort Worth skyline. Grandpa did not say much. I noticed he kept touching something solid in his right front pocket. Finally exiting off of Interstate-30 onto South Main, it seemed a good time to get more information about our destination. "Grandpa we can't be more than a couple of miles away. What will I be looking for?"

As if he was somewhere far away, his eyes slowly focused before he said, "It's a cemetery Buddy. We are meeting an old friend. Then I need to pay my respects to another old friend."

Cemeteries were everywhere around the hospital district, so I began watching street signs for the block numbers. Eventually I saw the huge John Peter Smith Hospital building on my right up ahead. The cemetery was practically in the shadow of the hospital just to the south. I saw a foreboding black painted iron gate with large words in white which read *Hebrew Rest*. Underneath were three equally large white letters with the initials, *E.H.R.* A distinguished Hispanic man was standing rod-straight near the gate waiting. His hair was combed back, thick and silver. He had a short but stocky build which made me think of a retired boxer.

Grandpa was more animated now than I had seen him in years. He was clearly excited. He rolled the passenger side window down and waved at the man. Now I was wound-up as well, without really knowing why. I quickly parked across the street, fearing if I did not do so fast grandpa might launch himself from my moving car. As it was I had barely brought the Dodge Dart to a stop before he was out of the car and rushing across the street. In my mind's eye I saw him getting hit by a car and my parents disowning me, but he made it safely. I had never seen grandpa move so swiftly. In the next instant I saw the two men shake hands, and then hug for some time. Stopping to read

370    J. Michael Beck

a historical marker to give them a little time, I read the *E* stood for Emanuel. The land was donated by John Peter Smith in 1879 when the cemetery began.

I made my way much slower to where they were standing. I now had an idea who the man was. I wondered if the hammering of my heart could be heard as I approached. It felt as if I was about to meet one of the legends of my childhood. I could not have been more thrilled if Patton, Pershing, or Wyatt Earp was standing before me. Grandpa broke free of the man and turned toward me. "Alex, this is Buddy, my grandson. He coaxed most of our adventures out of me. I admit it felt good to get some of the poison out of my head." To me he said, "Buddy, this is Eleazar Alejandro, my *truest* friend and fellow U.S. Army Cavalryman."

We shook hands. Alex had a grip like a gorilla and a grin just like I had imagined when I was ten. He looked to be in his early seventies, but I could not be sure. He inspected me now. "What do think Oscar? Is he Army material?"

"He is, but I don't think he will join the Army. Buddy takes Air Force ROTC. I expect he'll end up as one of them fly boys we hated back on the border."

I managed to get out, "Nice to meet you Mr. Alejandro." I had so many questions running through my head that my thoughts were a blur. Reminding myself this reunion was not for my benefit, I waited to find out more about why we were here.

Turning suddenly serious grandpa said, "I'm so glad you're here Alex. Let's go see Bill?"

Alex refused to have his mood dampened. "To give *you* a hard time again will make it worth the trip. I see your hair is thinner than I remember, although the color is expected at our age."

"Well you are a might more *fleshy* than I remember. It must be Abelinda's cooking and too many grandchildren to do your heavy lifting these days."

Both men laughed at their old banter. Grandpa put his arm around the shorter man and they opened the gate to enter. I had been by this old cemetery a dozen times, yet grandpa had never mentioned he had a friend buried here. A friend named Bill. Was his buddy in Glenn Springs named Bill? Bill something; I could not recall the last name. I did remember that when grandpa had returned, he recovered Bill's body and shipped the remains to his family. Then we were standing in front of Bill Kubitz' grave. The stone read, William *Kubitz, Died May 15, 1915.*

It was a family plot with six other graves. The whole cemetery was well-maintained and cared for. Grandpa was standing next to Alex. His head was down as if he were praying or crying. This time Alex reached up and placed a hand on his shoulder. The two men stood like that for what seemed five minutes. Finally Alex said, "Oscar, one of the finest things you ever did was pay for his body to be returned to his folks. All these years since dying in Glenn Springs he has laid beside family, loved and looked after. Following your example, I had Sean removed from that lonesome boot hill in Tomochic and sent home to his family in Kansas City, Missouri."

"Yes, I was glad to do it. Thank you Alex, you taking care of Sean has let me rest easier about leaving him behind. Bill's family sent me postcards of thanks every year until they passed."

Grandpa put his hand in his pocket like I had seen him do before. This time he brought something out. I was standing slightly behind and could not clearly see what it was, only that it was some sort of shiny metal. He handed it to Alex, who inspected it briefly, turning it slowly over in his hand, before handing it back. Grandpa then stepped forward, placing it on Bill's tombstone. When he backed up I saw it clearly. It was the brass US belt buckle that Bill Kubitz had owned before he was killed. Now it was my turn to get weepy eyes. The buckle had meant so much to grandpa, but now he had given it back to the original owner.

After a few minutes more we turned and began walking silently back to the gate. Stopping to place a hand on the gate grandpa said to me, "Buddy don't ever turn your back on your family or friends in life or death. Now, since *life* is for the *living,* let's find that catfish place."

# CHAPTER 52

## *Then It Was Too Late*

Despite grandpa's words about family, I spent the next year and a half self-centered, involved in my own world of high school, working, dating, and having fun. I used work as an excuse to not visit any of my relatives in Texarkana, including my grandparents. I even missed Christmas, using the excuse I would have to work early on the 26th. It was not just my grandparents who I neglected, but all family. I knew grandpa and grandma's health was failing, but there always seemed like there would be time for a visit later.

I had put the last, *missing story* long out of my mind. Either grandpa had forgotten, or he still did not want to tell me. I told myself I could visit and sit around for years waiting for him to get around to it. Even when I heard grandpa was in the hospital I put off thinking about it. My mother's dad had been hospitalized a couple of times and always recovered. I had bigger things on my plate, including being a Swing Manager at McDonalds, and Randy and I joining the Air Force after graduation. Dad and mom tried to convince me to visit, but I dodged all their efforts to reason with me.

Then it was too late. I got the news at work from mom at about 10:00 o'clock. It was a Saturday and I was working the 8:00 a.m. to 5:00 p.m. shift. She never called me at work. I knew it had to be important and probably bad news. Fear tightened my throat and I forced myself to take long deep breaths. My hands were shaking as I was handed the phone in the back office. Grandpa had passed away early in the morning. I was rocked back on my heels by the news. For once I did not think about my job or girlfriend. I just told Mike Elliott, my manager, I would need the next two days off. I then drove straight home. Mom, Sherry, and Debra were packing. The plan was to leave Sunday morning for a possible funeral on Monday. Sherry's husband was stationed with the Air Force in Thailand, so she had moved back home until his return.

Nobody had reached dad even though mom had left messages at all of the client business accounts he usually stopped at on Saturdays. Now that I was home it felt like a python had wrapped itself around my chest. I had only lost one uncle who I was close to and did not know what to do with myself. Thinking about dad not even knowing about the loss of his father weighed on my mind. Dad was a strong man, but this was his pa. To even imagine losing my own dad was devastating.

I sat in the living room in stunned silence. If slapping myself would have waked me from this terrible dream, I would have gladly taken a Muhammad Ali punch. I was not too happy with myself. Images of grandpa came to mind. I could almost hear him reliving-in-the-telling of his stories as I eagerly listened on the floor, porch outside, or rested on the pallet in his storm cellar. Yet I could not bring his face to mind. It escaped me completely. I could have looked at any number of photographs we had in the home, yet I somehow needed to reclaim the memory from whatever hole it had slipped into. No matter what I tried grandpa's face stayed just beyond my reach.

Sometime around 2:30 p.m. mom made tuna fish sandwiches, usually one of my favorite lunches. Today nobody had much of an appetite. We kept watching the door and listening for dad's car outside. Our usual joke was to stop eating when dad came home late and say we had waited on him. He would always look at our half-eaten plates of food and play along by saying, "Yes, I can see that." Today was not a good day for humor.

The talk at the table had centered around how grandma had been sick a lot lately. The family had been worried about her, but grandpa had seemed fine. At a little after 3:00 dad walked in. Of course we had heard his car, but nobody seemed anxious to rush outside with the news. We were still gathered around the table. When no one made the joke dad began studying our faces in turn. Mom stood up and walked over and hugged him. I could see dad counting his children over her shoulder. All four of his kids were present. Nobody was bleeding so that seemed to relax him a little.

Finally he pulled mom back and said, "What's wrong Charlene?"

"It's your father. I'm sorry but he's gone."

"Gone? Gone where honey?"

"I mean he died early this morning."

He did not react as I would have suspected. He went straight to the phone and began calling his brother John Ray and then his sisters. My motives were pure cowardice, but I decided it would be a good time to take Gary and Debra for ice cream. The tension in the house was thick with grief. I was not ready to cope with it. We slipped outside where the March air was fresh and crisp. Instead of driving I decided we would walk to the plaza a few blocks away. Gary had boundless energy and the walk would take us through Hillcrest Park down the street. I was reminded of taking the same route in early December of 1970 to pick out a Christmas tree. Dad, Sherry, Debra and I had made the walk carefully due to icy patches. It had been our first December in the house. Mom had kept Gary home due to the chilly night air and ice. He protested, putting up quite a fuss, but mom stood her ground.

Debra had turned eleven on May 9th and Gary would be five this coming December 28th. They were good kids. I enjoyed being with them. I scolded myself mentally at never spending enough time with them. How hard would it be to take them along for movies or picnics in the Fort Worth Botanic Gardens with Sally and I? Grandpa's words at the cemetery haunted me. I had been too busy and full of myself to find time for my younger siblings. Also I had turned my back on grandpa during most of his last two years of life. That was a mistake I could not undo. Now all I had left was honoring him in death.

The trip was long and tiring. Dad had wanted to leave that night so he could visit more with family. We were on the road by 5:00 p.m. and ran smack into traffic leaving a football game at the Dallas Cotton Bowl. It was after seven o'clock before we found lighter traffic on the east side of Dallas. Dad knew it would be after ten before we made it to Texarkana, so we stopped at Kentucky Fried Chicken before pushing on. I knew dad had been up since before seven, so I talked him into letting me drive the rest of the way. I had only driven to Texarkana one other time. However I knew if I stayed on I-30 East I could not get lost.

We headed to my Aunt Ruth and Uncle Herbert's house to stay the night. Ruth was my dad's sister and had been my mom's best friend when they were growing up together. She had made extra food for us and reheated it when we arrived. Nobody ever went hungry in Ruth's house. The talk was muted as her younger son Jeffery and my Grandpa Clark were already asleep. Debra and Gary were also out cold, having fallen asleep in the car. Sometimes I missed the non-responsibility of being younger.

I had been up as long as dad and was feeling the effects of it now. After I ate a piece of pecan pie, I excused myself and walked zombie-like to the living room couch where I had slept many times as a child. Ruth had left sheets and a blanket on the open hide-a-bed. I fell across it face down and thought I would be instantly asleep. After a few minutes of breathing into the sheets I realized my mind had other ideas.

Random thoughts began to bounce around my head. I saw images of childhood all associated with Texarkana. There was the shooting of the window in this very living room with a bb gun when the house was being built. I had wreaked my Uncle Herbert's car driving too fast on a gravel road. I saw myself helping Grandpa Clark, who was two years older than Grandpa Draper feed his chickens or plant peanuts in his garden. There was the time I drove Brenda's scooter while being chased by a whole pack of stray dogs. Finally there were Grandpa Draper's thrilling stories of his adventures.

There had been so many great summers spent with my grandparents, aunts, uncles, and cousins, yet I had not visited them in more than a year and a half. No excuses held any weight in the jail, created by myself, that I was locked in. I tried once more time to recall Grandpa Draper's features. No matter how hard I tried to sweep away the fog from his face it would not come. I finally gave up and made myself a promise not to take family or friends for granted ever again. Sometime afterwards I fell into a bottomless well, but found the sleep troubled.

The next morning I was awakened by the pleasant smell of bacon, coffee, and the single resident rooster. Grandpa Clark liked to rise early and start breakfast. His usual bedtime of 8:00 p.m. and he would wake before dawn on most mornings. I was reminded of when I was a child and would get up early with him and watch him cook. He would usually make me a biscuit with thick pancake syrup to hold me until everything was ready. I made my way into the kitchen and squinted into the bright lights. Nobody else was up. "Hi grandpa, this reminds me of when I was young and used to visit for a week or so."

He looked at me funny. "Buddy, I'm eighty years old. From where I'm standing you are still *young*. I'm sorry about your Grandpa Oscar. He was a bit grumpy, but a good man all the same. I always called him *old man* even though I was two years older than Oscar."

"Thanks grandpa. He told me he met you in 1925 when you picked him up hitchhiking."

"That is so. I had forgotten about that. You know your ma and pa say you favor him. Not only in looks but that you're *too* serious. I'm sure you're hurt over your grandpa's death, but what else has you unsettled Buddy?"

Grandpa had asked me that same question as long as I could remember. He always knew when one of his grandchildren was upset. When we were little we would sit on his lap and cry out whatever it was that had stung, bruised, bit, or otherwise turned our normally happy world upside down. "It is not just the loss of Grandpa Oscar, but that I have not been here in a long time. I only made time for me, myself, and I. I've been selfish, putting *me* ahead of family."

Grandpa looked surprised at my admission. "Well I have seen you, but then I rode home with your folks last December and stayed a week. Come to think of it you were not home much that week." He looked at my beaten-down hound dog expression and added, "Buddy you turn eighteen this year. You need to give yourself a little slack. At your age you want to think of yourself as a man. You started naturally becoming independent of your folks."

"I guess so, but the last thing I remember Grandpa Oscar saying to me was to never turn my back on family and friends."

Whatever else he would have said was lost when mom, dad, and my aunt and uncle came in. After I ate I walked outside and looked around. Grandpa Clark's chicken coop was gone, cited by the city and torn down. The place was no longer in the country and new regulations prohibited a coop full of chickens. Memories were everywhere. The apple trees where Sherry and I had eaten so many green apples we were sick for two days. Grandpa Clark had warned us with, "Here now, here!" His *here* always came out with two syllables. He smiled and kept walking with the knowledge we would find out he was right in short order. I sat in his garden where he still grew corn, potatoes, and peanuts. Sandy East Texas soil would grow anything.

Sunday was spent visiting the various cemeteries around Texarkana to pay respect to family that had passed. We ate lunch at Grandpa Oscar's favorite catfish place. Intended to honor him, it just reminded me of the last catfish meal I had shared with him. The funeral was set for 10:00 a.m. on Monday at the Texarkana Funeral Home. Grandma Myrtle was sick and neither her or Uncle John Ray could attend. John Ray was frozen in up in Colorado where he had been in training. Grandma had been sick awhile, yet her husband of forty-six years had died first.

The ushers put immediate family up front and to the left. I was asked to be a pall bearer. It was my first time. I understood it was supposed to be an honor to be asked. The church was mostly full. I did not know who all these people were, but figured most were members of Ruth's church where my grandparents were also members. I was sitting with the other pall bearers and sat on the right side.

During the funeral I tried again to recall grandpa's face without success. I had read somewhere that people often block images or memories that do not want to remember. I wanted to remember his face and could not understand why I could not do it. The family were scheduled to view the body last, so the pallbearers were first to go. I had remained detached and unemotional during the funeral, so now I stood with the others and made my way to the casket. Jon Marc, also a pallbearer, was on my right and followed behind me.

When I looked down on grandpa's face it hit me like dump truck dropping bricks. Every moment with him instantly became a flooded river rapid after a dam had burst. I felt my knees weaken and feared I would fall. Seeing my distress, Jon Marc nudged me with his arm. I recovered enough to stumble away and return to my seat. My hands felt like ice. The church suddenly seemed close and confining. I had trouble drawing a full breath. While the others paid their respects, I battled to regain control. I could not remember crying since I was eight and told myself now was not the time. Later in private I could let go of my composure.

After another thirty minutes I was feeling better. We loaded grandpa's body up and began the twenty mile trip to the cemetery. The car caravan stretched back over a mile. The graveside service was short. At the end the pallbearers placed their carnations on the casket before it was lowered. With my responsibilities completed, I walked away and found Dad. I had slipped out of the habit of hugging him, but I did so now. As I pulled away I saw Mr. Alejandro, dressed in a fine-cut suit dropping a handful of dirt into Grandpa's grave.

He was with an attractive woman of about sixty, but she wore the age well. She had long hair styled in fashionable curls. Gray had invaded the dark hair but it complimented her looks. Her dress was black and classy. At first I thought it might be Abelinda, but she was obviously not Hispanic. Dad started to turn away, but I stopped him. I wanted him to meet his father's life-long friend. "Dad that's Mr. Alejandro, I mean Alex, Grandpa Oscar's army friend!"

Alex waved when he saw me. I rushed ahead and dad followed a few steps behind. When I arrived in front of the couple, I impulsively hugged him. He said, "Buddy I'm sorry about your grandpa. He loved you very much. I hope you know that."

"I do, and he thought you were one of the best men he ever met. He said he never had a *truer friend*. How did you know he had died?"

"I didn't, my timing is bad. I was coming to visit him. He wrote and said he had been sick."

I felt Dad's presence at my shoulder and said, "Mr. Alejandro, this is my dad, James Draper. He has heard some of Grandpa Oscar's stories. I told him a few more."

They shook hands before Alex said, "It is a pleasure to meet you. Oscar was proud of his children. You and Buddy favor Oscar." He grinned broadly before saying, although if Oscar was here, I'd say that is *too* bad. He always thought he was homely and I teased him every chance I got." He then turned to the woman. "If Oscar told Buddy all of the stories, I'll bet he mentioned Ms. Josephine Leigh. We met in Mexico where Oscar and I helped her out."

Just like that I was ten years old again. I tried to picture Josephine Leigh dressed as Joe Leigh, the gunrunner. My eyes lit up. It felt like Alex and Josephine were family. I longed to have hours talking with them about the stories Grandpa had shared with me and Dad. "Oh my, it's great to meet you. I feel like we are old friends already through the stories. Grandpa said he kept in touch with you for years. Thanks for coming. I just wish you could have visited him sooner."

She had pretty brown eyes just as I had imagined she would. Josephine shook hands with my dad and hugged me. Never great with math, I calculated she had to actually be over seventy. She smiled radiantly. "Alex is being modest. He and Oscar saved my life in Mexico. Then years later Oscar helped me once more when I was hired at the Red River Arsenal here in Texarkana. I stayed a few years until I got back on my feet, then I moved back to Savanna."

"We are going to my aunt's house for lunch. Please join us? I have so many questions."

Dad echoed my sentiments, but Alex looked at Josephine. "I'm sorry. Thanks you for the invite, but I have a ranch to run. Ms. Leigh has to get started back too." He smiled broadly. "If I stay gone too long my grandchildren will take over and put me out to beg in the streets."

I was crushed but accepted their decision. Remembering Dad always had a pen on him I borrowed it and got both of their addresses. "I'm joining the U.S. Air Force after I graduate. I hope both of you will write me and keep in touch." They assured me they would. This had been a roller coaster day. Spending time with one of my childhood heroes made today even more memorable.

Dad excused himself and Alex pulled me aside. "Buddy your grandpa wrote me about something important he left you. I'm no longer a young man. Promise me you'll not share what you find outside of your family until I've passed on. After that it won't matter."

How could I say no? "I don't understand, but of course I'll do as you say."

I was very disappointed that Alex and Josephine had not been able to return to my aunt's house. Only their joint assurance that they would write helped me put the matter from my mind. It had been the second time I had met Alex. I still had so many questions about Grandpa and their life in the army. Church members had prepared food for the family at Aunt Ruth's house. After two hours of polite conversations and stories about when we were younger, we went to the hospital to visit grandma.

As anyone would imagine the visit was sad. All anyone could think to say was that Oscar had been a good man and that his loss would be felt by many. After we returned to Ruth's she pulled me aside and said, "Buddy, you know your grandparents lost just about everything they owned in the fire."

"I know it was a terrible thing." I was at a complete loss as to where all this was going. I still believed my parents, aunts and uncles still believed I was a child. Now my aunt was telling me stuff like I was an adult. It was an unfamiliar feeling. I did not know if I should embrace it or run the other way.

"Your Grandpa Oscar and Myrtle were thankfully able to escape without injury. However, Oscar grabbed one item from the burning house. It was an old metal box and must have been very important to him. He only said it held a few *various and sundry items*. He asks me to look after it for him. After he got back from his visit to your parent's house he told me he wanted you to have the keepsakes inside the box after he passed. I tried to argue with him to tell you personally. I kidded him that he was too ornery to ever die. However his stubborn mind was set. In fact he acted very mysterious about the whole thing.

He said something about it being real important to you and I shouldn't make jokes."

She motioned for me to follow to her bedroom. She pulled down a gray box about six inches deep and a foot square. The box was old, scarred, and missing a lot of paint from years of constant shuffling from one shelf to another. The container had a small metal handle on the top and a simple hasp. The lock was secured by a small but sturdy looking padlock. Ruth handed me a key and left the room. I just looked at the box too afraid to open it. It made no sane sense. The box seemed to hold promise and yet warning that if I tampered with Grandpa's belongings he would somehow be angered. It occurred to me that this was one of those crucial moments you hear about that defines you as a man.

Possibly my first adult decision was to decide manhood would have to wait for another time to exert itself. I would not open the box without my dad. He and I had not started this journey at the same time, but we would finish it together. I left it on the bed but slipped the key into my pocket before going to get Dad. I found him talking to my Uncle Herbert and Grandpa Clark. I waited impatiently until there was a break in the conversation. "Dad, can you come with me? I need to show you something." He looked at me questioningly I am sure he could see in my eyes it was something that needed his attention now. Our parent's always seemed to know when we needed them.

When we had walked away from the others he said, "Okay I see something is on your mind. What is this all about? What's going on Buddy?"

Dad had always been able to read his children easily with a quick glance. "It's in Ruth's bedroom. You have to see this." He followed me to her door where I knocked. Hearing no answer, I stepped inside. I walked over to the bed and asked, "Have you ever seen this before?"

His eyes lit up. "Of course, it's pa's *box-of-secrets*. He's had it as far back as I can remember. John Ray and I used to get it down from the closet and try to pick the lock. We even asked our ma about it. She just shrugged. She either did not know or did not want to answer. I had forgotten all about this old container. Truthfully if I had remembered it I would have believed it had been lost in the fire."

"It would have been too. It was the only thing Grandpa rescued from the house before everything else was lost. Ruth just gave me the key and said Grandpa left whatever is in there to me. I didn't feel right opening it without you. What do you think he left me? Aunt Ruth said he did this after his last visit to our house. Do you think it could be the answers to what he did in 1923?"

"I guess we will find out. My pa turned out to be much more of a mystery man than any of his children knew. I just wish John Ray was here instead of frozen in up in Colorado."

I tried to hand dad the key but he nodded for me to open it. I fumbled and could not get it open with my suddenly cold and shaking hands. Every time I was upset, scared or mad, my hands turned to ice. Now it felt like my fingers were frozen chunks. Finally I managed to get the lock unlatched and opened the lid as if snakes would leap out. Dad leaned in to look. Inside was Grandpa's wooden box with his playing cards, Purple Heart, Mexican Campaign Medal, his pocket watch and a pocket knife. I saw an interesting piece of shiny metal. It was heavy and misshapen. I placed it into the playing card box to look at later. Next there were yellowed papers with U.S. Army logos on them.

Dad lifted the papers carefully and began to reading them. His eyebrows lifted up in surprise. "These are both of Pa's enlistment and discharge papers from the Army."

I looked passed him to where a much newer envelope. It was oversized with the sides bulging with promise. It had been placed under the military papers. I reached inside and lovingly picked up the letter. Undoing the small metal clasp I slid a letter of several pages into my hand. On the outside of the envelope was one word written in Grandpa's scrawling hand, *Buddy*. I was so excited I wanted to shout from the highest tree in East Texas for everyone to hear. Instead my words came out in a croaking whisper. "Grandpa didn't forget. He promised me and he kept his word."

Dad's eyes were wet and I realized mine were too. We were like two children who had just opened a treasure chest. "Your grandpa did just as he said he would. You should consider how hard it was on him the last two years of his life. Even with the fire that destroyed their house and Myrtle sick he took time to write this letter for you. Ever since you and I started sharing your Grandpa Oscar's stories I've discovered he was full of surprises and more than a few secrets."

"I know. Alex told me at the funeral that Grandpa had written him about something important that had been left for me. He was very mysterious about it and asked me not to share what I found outside the family as long as he lived. Dad what in the world could be *so* bad that neither Grandpa or Alex wanted it known until they passed away?"

"There is only one way to find out son. I know you're anxious to read the letter, but we should seal it back and take it home tomorrow. This is the final one we'll get to share from your Grandpa Oscar. He addressed it to you so this time you can read this one to me."

It was late afternoon before we got home on Tuesday. I called in for another day off from work. Grandpa's last letter had never been far from my mind. Surprisingly I was not anxious to immediately read it as soon as we got home. I wanted to savor it awhile, knowing it would be the last letter. I believed that had been on dad's mind when he said we should take it home before reading it. I called Randy to talk about the letter but he was off at the Fort Worth Zoo with his girlfriend Melissa. It was one of our favorite dating spots. Since we would be joining the service after graduation, we had both been trying to spend as much time with our girlfriends as possible. Neither of our girlfriends Melissa or Sally was excited about us joining.

Loafing around the house I was lost as to what to do with my free time. I rarely had any time at the house anymore. I had left the letter in Dad's office, which was now in the front room of the Arlington house. The area had been a carport until dad remodeled it. I walked in now to check on the letter. Dad was sitting at his desk, but was not working. He was gently rocking back in his chair. The soft squeaking noise it made was a comfortable sound I had heard many times as a child. He usually listened to gospel music when he worked. However today he had his radio off. That was a sure sign he was deep in thought. "Hello Buddy, did you want to read the letter now?"

"No that's okay Dad. I was just feeling restless. We can wait until after supper. It almost feels like when I read it I'll have to say goodbye to Grandpa forever. Maybe I should just put it on a shelf like a trophy and look at it every day."

"Son that letter was written and given to you to read. Besides you should think of your grandpa as always being with you. I believe if you love someone you will always carry a piece of them with you. All he ever did for you, even the stories, they are a part of who you are now."

"That sounds like a good way of looking at it. If it is okay with you we'll read it tonight. After we are done, I guess we should mail it to Uncle John Ray. I know he will mail it back to me."

"He will after he makes a copy. Was your uncle the reason you chose the Air Force?"

"In part it was. He has a good career and I don't want to stay in food service. For now college is not right for me. The army paid for your education and the service will pay for mine. I know that's why Randy is joining too. Besides, I like the U.S. Air Force uniform best."

"Well you'll be joining in 1973. We are still in Vietnam, but at least you won't be crawling around the jungle. Your mom is not pleased about you enlisting. The draft is over and I think she'd rather have you stay at McDonald's than go into the service. At least she'll be comforted that if you go over you'll be on a base."

"Yea, if I get myself shot I'll be guarding a jet. The Vietcong will be the one crawling in the jungle. Not much comfort but better than some will have it."

# CHAPTER 53

## *Return to Mexico and San Miguelito*

After supper Dad and I went into his office. I sat across from him on the left end of his desk in one of the comfortable chairs he used for income tax customers. It had been many years since we had read one of Grandpa's letters. This would be the last. Dad took the letter off his desk and handed it to me along with his old blue letter opener. I cut a clean slice along the top. Taking a full breath I reached inside and pulled out several folded sheets of paper. There were not as many pages as some of his long letters, but enough to wet my appetite. I looked at Dad and he nodded. It felt like a torch-passing moment and I was ready this time. I felt something like pride stir inside me. I leaned back, propping my feet on the side of his desk. Then I began to read Grandpa Oscar's words…

I won't make apology for not writing this letter sooner. There were reasons why I could not share it before. Outside the family I doubt anybody will take it seriously anyway, but still I felt it best if I waited. The year of 1923 started out with promise. I had been working steady and had more than a few coins in my pocket, hidden in my shoes, hat, and even sewn into the lining of my clothes. Robbery on the road was a common event on the hobo trail I rode or walked. Eating regular was a luxury I could now afford. Tomorrow it might not be as true. A man's fortunes were surely not a certainty when traveling about seeking work like a gypsy.

Like I wrote before, I had been keeping in touch with a few friends by passing through El Paso once or twice a year. It was late March when I received a letter from Alex that rocked me back on my heels.

Officially Pancho Villa had been given a full pardon and retired to his 25,000 acre government-given hacienda in *Parral*, Chihuahua since 1920. However, unofficially he still had bandits who, under his orders made raids on villages and haciendas far away from the eyes of Mexican authorities. Two such raids had been made on *San Miguelito* before 1919.

In January 1923 Villa's men raided again. The news and outcome of the raid devastated me. Alex, Abelinda, their son Little Alex, Holmdahl and his wife and three children were living on the ranch. Holmdahl's daughter Eva, now nine years old had been blinded in both eyes from flying glass. In the confusion, Ezekiel and Camilla Holmdahl's oldest son Emil, who had been twelve, took up a rifle. The boy was killed, along with two ranch hands. It had been the most brutal assault on *San Miguelito* yet. The hacienda was now fortified by necessity.

I stopped reading and sat where I was until I could catch my breath. It was as if some drunk had just sucker punched me in the gut. All of my old hatred and desire for killing boiled up in me. An innocent girl had been maimed and her brother killed. I ached for the family. How would Eva cope with the loss of her budding artistic ability? She had the added grief of losing her brother who was just defending his home. Villa's trail of destructive violence appeared to be without end. The attacks on innocent folk had to be stopped. Pancho Villa could now pull the strings from a safe distance. I had lost close friends and come close to losing my own life as a result of Villa's madness. How many families on both sides of the border had lost everything to the man's greed and evil? My entire body shook with helpless rage.

When I regained some control over my emotions, I began to read again. Alex was asking me to come to *San Miguelito* to help. His instructions included a train schedule that would take me from El Paso, Texas all the way to Rubio, Mexico not far from the ranch. Alex indicated there was a plan in place to end the raids, but no details were given. Not knowing what difference one man could make, it was of no consequence. I climbed slowly to my feet. With no real decision to make, I began walking toward the train station. With iron resolve I intended to help in whatever way I could. If Alex needed me I would go. Once more I was being drawn back into Mexico and the unknown beyond the border.

I telegraphed Alex before boarding the train. The ride was long with many stops in the small villages along the way. I was too anxious to sleep until exhaustion took over. The trip took almost four days before I saw the signs of Rubio alongside the tracks. I felt almost naked being back in Mexico without a gun of any kind. The country might be a little more settled, but the fact that bandits or outlaws were still about made me uneasy. *Gringos* were at best only tolerated across the border. This far from the U.S. and Mexican border a *Norte Americano* was a much more rare sight. I did not have to worry about being unarmed for long.

The train had not even stopped rolling before a heavily armed party of men, which had been riding in two cars, had spit out six men onto the boardwalk alongside the tracks. I spotted Alex among them. He was dressed like a prosperous businessman, which I guess he was. He now sported a full beard, which blended well with his curly dark hair. The Winchester rife he carried was new and did not fit with his manner of dress. Ezekiel Holmdahl was beside him. I was most shocked at how much Holmdahl had aged. He was almost completely gray. Dark circles were deeply etched under his eyes. His quick smile and easy manner that I remembered were gone.

A shudder ran through me as I remembered his oldest son had been murdered. God help the man who got between Ezekiel and the men responsible. Both men looked grim and unyielding resolve ran like an electric current between the two men. I made my way to the nearest door as the train slowed to a stop. Alex waved as I stepped down from the train. I returned the wave and stifled a smile at the reunion as I recalled why I was here. "Alex, Ezekiel, I am glad to see you both, but sorry it has to be under these circumstances."

Both men nodded and I shook hands with Holmdahl. Alex and I hugged. His usual bear hug I expected was lacking. "Thank you for coming Oscar. I told Ezekiel you would not let us down. We need all the loyal men we can gather to put an end to this madness." He handed me the .45 caliber Winchester. I checked the new rifle. It was loaded and the finest firearm I had ever held. Alex smiled. "I know you Oscar. You are feeling exposed without a weapon now that you're back in Mexico. Normally we would think of ourselves as past the point of going armed every moment. Times have not changed in Mexico as one would hope. I can't say it has anything to do with the death of Villa's men in 1916, but the attacks are a constant threat."

Alex indicated the cars and I followed him to one. Ezekiel was driving the other. The vehicles were both 1922 Ford Model T touring cars. As we drove out of town citizens waved and smiled at Alex. He was obviously well-respected in the community. Since I had never actually been in the city, I had no way to judge it. Rubio seemed to be a lively spot and growing. "These are nice automobiles. Are there townsfolk who remember you as a child?"

"Thanks, no not many remember me, but the ranch does almost all business in town. I have employed many villagers, part time or full. It is good that you are here. You look good Oscar, a little thinner than I recall. We needed you with us. I hope the trip has not hurt you financially."

"No, I work steady most times. I've been having a good year so far. I told you in every letter that anytime you needed me all you had to do was ask. I'm here and glad of it. I have thought about visiting many times. You look very dapper in suit and beard, although it makes you look older. I don't know what it is you and Ezekiel are cooking up, but when can I hear the details?"

"Soon, we'll discuss business after dinner. Camilla and Abelinda will be happy to see you. They are preparing a great feast for you. Also there is Eva. She is nine now and anxious to see her *Uncle* Oscar again." We both were quiet for awhile as I thought about her pain and loss.

Broaching the subject carefully I said, "Tell me how she is doing Alex? I'll be honest with you, her injury is one of the reasons I came. It weighs heavily on me. It is unthinkable that anyone would harm her."

"She is one tough little girl, cut from the same cloth as her mother. I am pleased to tell you she has recovered sight in her right eye. She worries more about her mother than herself. Camilla took the loss of her son Emil hard. We thought for a few days she had surrendered to insanity. I can't say I blame her. Eventually Ezekiel, who had only left her side to bury Emil reached her with the knowledge that she was needed by the surviving children."

"That is a terrible burden for any family. I'm glad Eva is strong and has regained some sight. Her art is very important to her. Please tell me the details of the attack. Why are you so sure the bandits were still under the command of Villa and not just common outlaws?"

"Don't doubt me Oscar. They were Villa's men. Some of the ranch hands rode with Villa. A few of the bandits were recognized. They killed the guard I had posted first. A moment after the first shot rang out; we were being assaulted from all sides. Another of my men was cut down as he ran for the believed safety of the ranch house. The attack was sudden and deadly. Everywhere we looked there were bandits. I estimated two dozen at least."

Alex drove on as he relived the raid in his mind. I gave him time, knowing there would be more when he was ready. "We killed six of them before the attack ended as quickly as it had begun. After the firing stopped Camilla was screaming as she clutched Eva and Emil to her. She had dragged the children from where they had fallen. We could do nothing for Emil as he was dead. Ezekiel and I forced Camilla to release Eva so we could drive her to town to the doctor."

Alex studied his hands as he drove as if they were covered in blood. "One bandit I shot lived just long enough to confess he had been paid by Villa to raid us. He was ordered to kill everyone on the ranch, and then take everything of value before they burned it down."

I searched my mind but was unable to find any words of true comfort. "I'm sorry Alex. It was a terrible thing. No family should have to witness such a brutality on their own."

He gripped the wheel and spoke with the similar emotions I had felt after reading his letter in El Paso. "Ezekiel and I lead the Army to *San Miguelito*. If that is why Villa attacks us, we share in the blame. I cannot change the past, only prepare for what is to come. If it was only me, I could leave this place and start over. Now the hacienda is once again home to me and my family. Villa will pay for the death and injury to my family. He cut a generous deal with *El Presidente* de la Huerta. He now enjoys womanizing and cockfighting under the protection of his *Dorado's*, or Golden Ones. While he lives on government-granted land and a pension, he continues to send his Villistas out to do his dirty deeds. He is like a plague on the land I love."

When I knew he had finished I said what I had been fretting about since I started the trip back into Mexico. "You know I'll help in any way I can." Fidgeting with the rifle in my hands I voiced my thoughts aloud. "Alex I may have lost whatever ability I had to face men who are determined to kill. I haven't fired a gun since leaving the Army. I remain strong in body due to hard work, but I must admit to a certain amount of mellowing in manner and spirit. The world I travel in is not exactly civilized, but most conflicts are settled with fist, or occasionally with knives. I thought the kind of violence you describe was behind me. What if I can no longer be the man you need me to be? What if I can no longer kill?"

He looked at me seriously. I knew my friend would not judge or pity me. He spoke with no hint of contempt at the possible loss of my nerve. "I don't believe that even for a second. You are one of the bravest men I have ever known. Oscar, for all the years I've known you it was your dogged strength, even when grievously wounded, that carried me through our years of constant fighting. I'll say this, if it's possible that what you say is true, you can stand with us and load our weapons while *we* kill."

As Alex drove up the hill leading to the ranch I got my first look at *San Miguelito* in seven years. The hacienda had been transformed into a shining star in an otherwise colorless country. Horses and cattle crazed in green pastures watered by the river running through the property, only to disappear again under the desert. I saw newly built fortifications of stone close to the house. I assumed the stone works were firing points against further attacks. Smaller stone buildings were higher up I believed were lookouts to observe anyone approaching the house.

"Your ranch looks great Alex. I have not been here since May 1916. If the famous Patton ever came back here he would not recognize the place. Also I'm very impressed with your defenses. I would expect nothing less from an experienced cavalryman such as you."

As we entered the ranch house I was apprehensive. Both times I had been here it was during a period of extreme violence and now the added burden of grief. Camilla, Abelinda, Eva and her younger brother Abe, named for Ezekiel's father, were there to greet me. I then met Little Alex, who was very shy. Eva hugged me fiercely, even though I had not seen her since she was three. As I hugged her back I felt the anger of her injury welling inside me. I fought it down as best I could. She wore a bandage over her left eye but did not seem otherwise hampered by the loss of sight. "Eva I want you to know that your letters and drawings have brought me much pleasure over the years. I've kept every one of them. I am often alone and sometimes read the letters out loud. I often look admiringly at the pictures you've drawn for me."

She smiled radiantly at me and then turned and introduced me to Little Alex, now five, as her mother Camilla and Abelinda hugged me. I had only seen Abelinda a few times in her hometown of Guerrero, where her father had been mayor. I could not recall actually meeting her. She was every bit as pretty as Alex had described.

I held Camilla a while longer and muttered how sorry I was for the loss of her son. I felt her tears on my shirt. "Thank you for coming Oscar. Alex has been frantic waiting for your arrival. I know it will be alright now." She pulled away and inspected me like I had seen her do to Alex after his original return. "You are too thin. You need a good woman to feed you."

Blushing red at the thought I said, "I'll be long in finding a woman who cooks as good as you. All the way over here I was thinking about your cooking." I looked at Little Alex and offered to shake his hand. "Hello Mr. Alejandro, I was in the Army with your pa." He hid warily behind his mother's dress but peeked at me. I reminded myself of what these folks had been through.

Camilla and Abelinda ushered us to a fancy dining table covered with a linen tablecloth and brass candlestick center piece. The Ranch house had moved up in class and become a home as nice as any fine hotel I had stayed seen. Ezekiel spoke first. "We are so thankful you traveled all this way Oscar. Of course we have loyal men here we can count on, but Alex trust no man more than you. I share in that faith."

I worried that I might not be able to live up to their trust. "I am here now. Anything that I can do for your family is yours for the asking."

At my words, Alex and Holmdahl exchanged a glance that set my senses on edge. I was wondering what I had gotten myself into when Alex spoke dismissively, "There will be time for talk of what must be done after supper. We'll sit down to a feast in your honor in a little over an hour." He rubbed his hands together. "Now I have a surprise for you. Let's go out back."

Outside in a small corral behind the house were two beautiful horses. I did not recognize the breed, but I knew fine horses when I saw them. "Those are some kind of pretty Alex."

They are Mexican *Criollo* horses. The type used in the Mexican Revolution on both sides. The breed is directly descended from Spanish horses. I would like to show you more of my home. For old time's sake, let's ride Oscar. "

I was touched by his sentiment and eagerly looking forward to riding again. "I don't want to embarrass myself in front of my old saddle partner, but I haven't ridden a horse since the Army either. I just hope I don't fall off. The hell with it, let's ride."

It was a beautiful ride and the ranch equaled it in magnificent views. From a distance I could see the hill where we had watched the ranch before Patton ordered the attack. Alex showed me the spot place where the river appeared as if by magic from the ground. We rode the length of the river before it disappeared under back under the desert. On a rocky outcropping we dismounted and walked up a dry ravine which I believed had been created by flash floods.

After a walk of no more than ten minutes Alex held up a hand for me to stop. "I wanted you to see my gold claim. Look closely at the broken rock." He pulled a large folding pocket knife from his belt and began digging in the crumbling material. As he worked he said, "I only take from the earth when the need arises. I have not been here more than a half dozen times since I found it as a boy." In another minute of probing the rock he said with satisfaction, "Ah here we go." He held up a marble-sized nugget of shiny metal, and then tossed it to me.

I inspected the nugget. It appeared melted by unknown forces. "I've never seen anything like this. The ranch is prosperous, but you did it on your own, without using much of the gold."

"The gold is only used as needed." I tried to hand the gold back but he shook his head. "No, it's yours. Keep it as a memento of *San Miguelito*, or spend it on a rainy day."

We rode back companionable silence. The sensation of a powerful animal beneath made me feel young and energized, which I had not felt in some time. We stopped at the ranch cemetery and paid respects to Emil and the ranch hands killed in the raid. I looked around and said, "Alex, when eternity comes calling, this is as nice a place as I've ever seen to be laid to rest."

Supper was far and away one of the best meals I had ever eaten. Camilla and Abelinda had prepared a feast just as Alex said they would. When I finally pushed back from the table about as full as a man could get, Camilla served me a generous slice of apple pie. Abelinda brought a steaming pot of coffee to the table. As I immediately tasted the pie I said, "This has been delicious and so kind of y'all. I have not had home cooking in more years than I can recall. I don't know how the men folk on this ranch are all not fat and lazy from the meals."

The women were pleased by my high praise. Alex and Ezekiel exchanged another of those looks before he said, "It's a beautiful night. Take your coffee we'll smoke out on the porch."

Once outside, Alex handed me a *Te-Amo* cigar grown locally by the Turrent family of Veracruz. He had certainly moved up in the world. The mood now became all business as Holmdahl took the lead.

"Oscar, we have come to a crossroads here at the hacienda. It comes down to leaving our home or fighting back. You might remember back when we first met I was living here with Isador Alejandro, Camilla, Eva and Emil. Isador was a bad man and rode with outlaws and Pancho Villa himself. A few of our current ranch hands also rode with Villa." Seeing the look on my face he added, "Yes we can trust them completely. At that time they were young and stupid, chasing riches and glory with a man they thought of as God-like.

Ezekiel looked across at Alex who nodded and took over. "As you know Villa is living in government funded luxury on his ranch outside of *Parral*. Here is the rub. We know from connections we have in *Parral* where Villa is at any given minute, but since he no longer raids personally we can't know when he will send men to attack us again. Our families are in constant peril. I admit to a powerful hate, but we are protecting our families. We cannot risk losing our wives and children. We stop him soon or surrender to hide in the hills like animals."

My ma would have said I was not the sharpest son she had, but I was not born the day before yesterday. I was beginning to have an idea where this was heading. If their minds were set hard I would waste my breath in argument. "I know you two hate Villa. I have no love for the skunk either. I have reasons of my own for wanting him dead. Please consider this, if you two are planning to kill him outright it won't be seen as defending yourselves, but murder. He does not deserve to live, that I understand. I also see that getting yourselves killed or thrown in a Mexican prison for life will leave your family more vulnerable than they are now."

Alex was not to be put aside. "There are certain political circumstances that may play into your decision as it has ours. Powerful forces inside and out of the Mexican government are not keen on having to continue supporting a man as dangerous as Villa. Think of him as a rattler. At any second he might strike out at his supporters to seek greater influence for himself. He has done so before." He paused, "You know the old saying, cut off the head of the snake and the body dies. That is what we intend to do."

Nobody spoke for a while. I carefully considered my next words. The cigar was making me dizzy. I fought to keep a clear head as now was not the time to make a snap decision. Eventually I said, "I understand you might have help, or at least a hands-off acceptance by government authorities. I figure it as a gamble my friends. If you deal the cards and draw aces and eights, you may lose everything. It would not be the first time a government forgot an agreement when it suited their purposes. Think on this; Villa has such an agreement with President de la Huerta his own self. Now you risk trusting like-authorities." I could see they understood the risk, but their minds were set in stone. A fork in the road stood before me clearly defined. I could either throw in with them and take my chances, or run for the border.

They leaned on the corral and waited my decision. I knew there would be no pressure other than that I placed on myself. Finally Alex said, "Of course it is a life-risking decision on all our parts. You are my closest friend, but you have no blood in this feud. Don't believe that we do not realize what we ask of you. Oscar you need to be assured I would accept it without insult if you left on tomorrow's train."

Lunacy was what it was. If there had been a full moon instead of a crescent one at least I would have had something to blame, but my mind was now set as well. "You are not often wrong Alex, but this time you are." He raised his eyebrows but did not argue. "I do have blood in this fight. I've lost two close friends to Villa's path of destruction. Now I have seen others I care about suffer once more at the whim of this same man. Bill and Sean never got to enjoy a long life due to the old bandit's lust for power. I would gladly strangle Villa with my bare hands just for what he did to Eva and Emil. I will ride with you. I only have one request." They both studied me and waited. "I cannot shoot a man from cover. An ambush is probably the best way, but it can never be my way."

Alex spoke up first. "Don't be fretting about that Oscar. Since Villa travels everywhere with his Dorado bodyguards, you'll have plenty of chances to get shot at. One nickname for Villa is *Lion of the North*. We intend to give him his chance, but he'll be *our* big cat ripe for a skinning."

His words about family and having their backs to the wall touched me. Risking your life for others weaker than yourself was honorable if anything was. This would be no vengeance killing, just self-defense of family and home. I felt much reassured by his words. We stood in the quiet night, three men willing to bet their futures on an insane plan that had little hope of succeeding. Eventually I said, "I understand what you are both up against. You have my full support. I would be proud to ride with the both of you."

The tension was suddenly broken by Holmdahl who had not smiled since my arrival. If he intended it as a joke I was unsure. He crushed his cigar under his boot. "Viva Villa my ass!" The three of us howled with relieved laughter, or possibly madness I was not sure which.

# CHAPTER 54

## *A Violent End to a Bad Man*

For more than three months, including the first two weeks of July, I lived at the ranch and fell easily into the routine. Days were spent working hard to mend fences, build cabinets, and even constructing a new out house. Nights were spent playing with the children and enjoying home cooked meals. By the time July 15th rolled around I was saddened to know that my time at *San Miguelito* would be drawing to an end. Since leaving the Army I had been much alone. The sights, sounds and sensations of a full house, filled with loving families had etched a lasting impression on me. My heart seemed heavy in my chest at the thought of returning to my previously lonely life. If I stayed any longer I would find it impossible to leave.

I knew that by joining in the plan to end Villa's attacks on the ranch I risked losing my future. I might never have a home and family of my own. As I had thought many times before when fighting with the Army, I did not want to die in Mexico. A life wasted in a Mexican prison did not set well with me either. I had continued to write my ma but had not mailed the letters. She must be worried by now. However I could not let her know I had returned to this country. If I was killed here she might never know what had become of me. I had grown to love the families at *San Miguelito*, yet I yearned to return home and raise a fresh-faced family of my own in the East Texas pine country. My home, as yet unfounded, was further down the road. In fanciful moments just before sleep, I would think of my life as an unfinished canvas, impatiently awaiting an artist colorful brush strokes.

On the morning of July 17th, we had tearful goodbyes and hugs with those remaining behind at *San Miguelito*. Knowing I might never return was hard on me. I made no promises to those left behind, other than to write when time permitted. At the end, Eva wrapped her arms around my waist and hugged me fiercely. I was too chocked up to say anything. When Eva finally pulled herself free, Little Alex marched up to me and offered his hand. He was standing tall attempting to be brave. I reached for his small hand and shook it. The boy's lower lip quivered with the knowledge of his father and uncle leaving. The children, not knowing the details, must have sensed importance in the trip. The boy's handshake became a hug as well.

Five of us climbed into the two Fords with Holmdahl and Alex driving as before. This time each car was towing ranch-built trailers with supplies and four horses divided between the cars. I was riding in the car with Alex driving. The back seat was loaded with bedrolls and food stores. In the next car with Ezekiel were Manuel Sanchez and Miguel Ortega, former Villistas, who were now loyal hands at the hacienda. Alex drove ahead as we put his ranch behind us. Six loyal men remained stayed behind to protect those at the ranch. "If I never have to be a part of a goodbye like that again I'll die happy. How much did you tell Abelinda and Camilla? "

"Not enough for all the tears back at the hacienda. I suspect they know in their own way. Someday you'll discover that a woman who loves you most times knows what you are thinking. They know or trip is to end this and make us all safer. If Ezekiel and I do not return Ezekiel and I have trusted friends in the town that will see our families safely relocated. If our involvement is ever known, there will be no safety for anyone living at the ranch."

The talk of death was grim and disturbing. It was now always close on the minds of those that lived at *San Miguelito*. I had survived against larger forces before and hoped to do so again. "I expect Pancho Villa is overdue for his final whipping. Back in 1915 when we were near to burning to death in that shack in Glenn Springs, I never thought I would see the dawn anyhow. Yet here we are still alive and ready to fight once more." I paused before saying, "Well we lived then to possibly die just as violently another day."

I had seldom seen Alex lose his sense of humor or good mood. Today he seemed particularly strained. "Eight years ago we had nothing and nobody. Now I have a family and you have yours up ahead. Ezekiel and I are stuck. To do nothing invites more attacks. Yet if our efforts to stop Villa come to nothing, God help us all. I believe there will be no better time than now."

At close to sundown on the 18th, we arrived at our camp about a mile from town. The area was sheltered from wind and casual view by trees and low rolling hills. The spot was known to Alex through previous stays when traveling with his father as a boy. There was room to hide the trucks and trailers off the road in a shallow dry creek bed. The plan was to set up camp then make contact with confederates who lived or were staying in *Hidalgo del Parral*, Chihuahua. *Parral* was not a large village, but an important trade and banking town.

I had much experience of late with setting up camp and I did so now. Alex and Ezekiel began unloading the horses and supplies. Sanchez and Ortega were going to ride into town, blend in with the locals, and get the information on any unexpected circumstances. After their scout they would return to camp. At that time Alex and Ezekiel would return to *Parral* to meet with associates for the final preparations. I was to stay in camp at their request. They did not want me to be seen. The appearance of an unknown gringo might be remembered at a later date and reported.

I was as nervous as a chicken in a coop with a fox prowling about. I broke several matches before I got a small fire started for coffee. The fire was in a one foot deep pit dug at the base of a scrub oak to dissipate the smoke. I gathered deadfall branches to keep myself busy. I never let the rifle get further than an easy grab away. I was wishing I still had the Army-issued Colt 45 when Alex sat down on a half-rotten tree stump. "It's not too late for you to ride away."

I scowled at him and kicked a fist-sized stone. I snapped, "Quit babying me!" You of all people know I get jumpy before a fight. When it counts I'll be as steady as this damn rock."

He looked at me and answered seriously. "I know that. No sane man risked his life, even for a cause he believes in without fear. Now you need to listen to me. Don't be stubborn for once. When this is done I want you to ride north on that *Criollo* you rode before. Don't look for me or the others, just return to El Paso. Keep off the road and away from towns. It is not uncommon for mounted men to still ride in Mexico. However you will not blend in too well. There will be food supplies in the saddle bags along with pesos and American money. You won't need the horse when you return, so take it to our old friends Ronaldo and Lupe Rios."

I did not want to be dismissed in such a way. "I signed on as an equal partner Alex. We all are taking the same risk. I know this is important to you, but I think we should stay together in case someone is wounded and needs help. Another thing, I don't want to take money from you. Considering what is planned, I would think of it as *blood money*."

"That is nonsense. First off the plan is to disappear into the town or escape separately. Any group of riders would be suspect." Now he grinned broadly. "Besides you built cabinets and even an outhouse for my home without pay. Whenever Camilla and Abelinda use those cabinets they'll think of you. Whenever I use the outhouse I'll think of you." Alex never failed to verbally slap me back into a better frame of mind. I knew there was a joke at my expense coming and I was not disappointed. "It's because you can be a grumpy *shit* sometimes Oscar."

The first night came and went without incident. Whatever time Alex and Ezekiel returned I had been out cold. As the morning of the 19th dawned I was up and cooking breakfast while the other men slept in. I did not mind as it gave me time to enjoy the sunrise coming up out of a mist. The ground fog covered everything as far as the eye could see. If we were fortunate to have the same morning blanket on the 20th we could move into position without being seen.

I had noticed times like this before when I was under great stress or facing mortal danger. Every sense in me was alive and I was acutely aware of my surroundings, every color was vibrant. Details were magnified, no matter how small or seemingly insignificant. I believed the sound of a dung beetle passing through the camp could be heard. The sun was reflecting off a red tailed hawk's wings as he circled looking for a meal. The rush of wind across the mighty predator's wings was heard or imagined as I watched. Whispering grass rustled as a jackrabbit darted fifty feet from where I sat. The hare sheltered in front of a rock. When a gust of breeze parted the mist I took up the Winchester and fired. Before the rabbit stopped moving I was on him to finish the job with my knife. I spoke aloud. "Not today Mr. Hawk, you'll have to wait."

Walking back to camp I saw that my shot had awakened the camp. All four men were armed and looking around warily. Alex saw me with my catch gripped by the long ears. I smiled before saying, "Sorry about the shooting, I hope the shot is dismissed as a random hunter. I could not pass up the opportunity of fresh meat roasted over our fire."

"You scared ten years off my life Oscar!" He looked at the direction I had come before abruptly changing his tone. "How far was the shot?"

"It was over by that rock yonder. I saw a hawk circling so I stole his meal." I sat down and started skinning the rabbit. In a few minutes the smell of cooked meat was wafting throughout the camp. My mouth was watering.

Alex sat watching me as he drank coffee and smoked another of his *Te-Amos* cigars. "That was a nice shot Oscar. I expect you can still hit what you are shooting at."

"I'm surprised at my own self. To tell you the truth I did not know I had it in me. It was most likely more reaction than skill. I have been living a rough and tumble existence filled with hard work, using my wits and occasionally my fist, but no guns."

"You know you'll always be welcomed at *San Miguelito*."

"Thanks for that. I know I would be happy there. Had I stayed any longer you would have had to dynamite me off your place. However at one time you felt like America was your home. I still feel the same about my country. How did it go last night? Are we still set for the 20th?"

Tossing the butt of his cigar in the fire he plucked a piece of the meat off the fire and tasted it before he spoke. "Yes, we met with men of some importance. Like you have said they may disown us afterwards, but for now we are useful." Over the next ten minutes he outlined the plan and the men involved. I was taken aback by the news. It was as if we had all fallen or were pushed over the same steep cliff. There would be no stopping until we all ended up in a heap at the bottom. We were too far down the trail. There would be no backtracking now.

That night after supper Alex and Ezekiel went over the plan. Every detail had been seen to like a military campaign. If we did not carry it out with the same type of discipline it had no chance of succeeding. I had a few questions but was satisfied with their preparations. Afterwards all our equipment was loaded into the cars or in saddlebags for our escape, or attempted escape, I reminded myself. I knew sleep would be a long time in coming, if at all, so I walked out away from camp to breathe in of the desert air.

After a few minutes Alex joined me. He put a hand on my shoulder and we stood without speaking. Many nights just like this we had remained awake long after everyone else in camp. The stars were bright and seemed close enough to touch. The North Star aligned me with *Parral* to our south. After this I would return to my old life, seemingly emptier than before.

Alex stirred beside me. "Tomorrow watch yourself mi amigo. I will be sad if you are killed."

I laughed. "What are friends for? Watch yourself. If I'm shot I might take you with me."

On the morning of July 20th before first light we were moving south in the direction of the town. We walked the horses to make less sound. The automobiles were left behind safely hidden. We had four strong horses but five men. Ortega had kinfolk in the town and intended to just walk away to be sheltered locally. He would be on the eyes and ears of talk after we had fled. After daylight began to show itself, I was relieved to see the mist had indeed returned. Crossing the road outside of town we made our way to an abandoned adobe house. The house was in pitiful shape but the location was ideal. It was perfect for our purpose since it stood less than twenty feet from the main town bridge, but away from any other houses.

An attached storage shed on one side became our stable. It was tight quarters for the horses but not as confining as the trailers. We had brought sacks of grain and hay along with jugs of water for the animals. There was not as much as a chair so we sat on the dirt floor. There was no glass in any of the windows only filthy quilts nailed over the opening. Two windows faced out toward the bridge with nothing to the rear in the direction of the town. The house had only one room beside the storage space so we sat cross legged with our backs to the walls.

Time began to drag as each man was left to his own thought for more than two hours. Manuel and Miguel played cards. I stole glances at my pocket watch which just made the time seem to move even slower. At a few minutes before 10:00 o'clock I moved over by Alex. "If you don't think it'll get us discovered, I'd appreciate one of those cigars. I suppose I just want something to do with my hands."

"Sure, here you go." He lit my cigar and sat back lighting one for himself. "Perhaps you should write your ma. As I recall you have bad luck in a fight. I'll see it delivered for you."

"That's not funny. I guess I'll go back and steal all your gold after you don't make it back. In time Abelinda will forget about you and marry a fat lawyer or banker." Before he could respond to my insult we heard a soft hail from outside. As one man we were on our feet and had our rifles aimed at the door leading to the shed. A few seconds later two Mexican men stepped into the door frame with their rifles lifted high to show they were not a threat.

Alex and Ezekiel relaxed and approached the men. The men shook hands and exchanged greetings in Spanish. To me Alex said, "Oscar this is Jesus Herrera, a friend of Ezekiel's." Joaquin had the look of a retired soldier. He was wiry with a thin mustache. His manner was all business. I thought he looked like a Frenchman but his accent was local. The other man was tall and burly. He was dressed in the clothes of poor farmer, but wore them like they were borrowed or recently acquired. He had an air of authority about him. It was not arrogance but rather a sense of confidence in his abilities. Alex turned to the man and said, "This is Commander Felix Lara. He is over the federal troops in *Parral*. He has been chiefly responsible for giving us this chance by ensuring his men are out-of-town on military maneuvers."

Lara's hand swallowed mine in an iron grip. He sized me up before saying, "If Mr. Alejandro vouches for you that is good enough for me. I see a question in your eyes as to why I would risk everything on this quest. I am a former soldier under President Alvaro Obregon when he was Commander-in-Chief of Revolutionary forces. In 1915 at the battle of *Celaya* against Villa forces, Obregon lost his right arm. His presidency has been stable and a time of peace. He replaced President Adolfo de la Huerta. Obregon intends to support Plutarco Elias Calles, now the Minister of the Interior to succeed him as president. Calles was also a former general who fought against Villa. For my beloved Mexico, I cannot stand by so long as there is any small risk that Villa will attempt to seize power. Any such move would cast Mexico back into the dark days of revolution."

His words impressed me. He was unquestionably committed to his cause, whereas I was fighting just to stop the raids on the ranch. It occurred to me that every man here possibly had a different reason for being involved. Whatever the motive, the goal was the same. We had to stop Villa and his men no matter the cost. "It is my great honor to fight beside you Commander Lara. Your sacrifice to your country is something I respect."

"Please, call me Felix. We should not stand on formalities for what could be a brief friendship." He turned to address Ezekiel and Alex and spoke with obvious distaste. "I have a man positioned out-of-sight by the bridge. Meliton Lozoya was the former administrator of the Canutillo hacienda, now in the hands of Villa. Lozoya hates Villa and came to me with the original idea. Since Villa believes Lozoya embezzled from the ranch and owes him a high sum of money, the dislike between them is mutual. Lozoya is too cowardly to take up arms against Villa, but he knows the man. However identification is probably not necessary since his 1919 black Dodge Roadster is the only one in the area. Lozoya will signal with a shout as Villa approaches the bridge."

With everything and everybody now in place, we returned to our waiting. Never filled with patience I paced the floor. No battle or conflict in my life had prepared me for action of this sort or significance. In my past life with the Army there were times that we were vaguely aware that history was being made. The gravity of it all screamed like tomorrow's headline.

Alex walked over to me before saying in a low voice, "Let's sit awhile. I know you have nervous energy to burn but it might be our last time to talk face-to-face in a long while."

I stopped pacing and took a seat in the dirt. I checked the load in the Winchester for the third time and tried to relax. I thought we were as ready it was just the waiting that was getting to me. "I'll leave your rifle in El Paso with the horse. I can't very well carry it around with me. How did you and Ezekiel find out about the plan? It appears it was passed down from the highest levels of Mexican government. How did you two become involved?"

"I am active in business throughout Mexico and even into the United States. Ronaldo Rios sees to my business in El Paso. I breed horses and cattle. On a trip to Durango, I met State Legislator Jesus Salas Barraza. He intended to buy a prized Criollo I had brought to sell. I found him to be a man of high integrity. We shared meals and I invited him to *San Miguelito*. I told him of the attacks and resulting death and wounding of my family. He admitted there was a plan in place to end Villa's days of violence. Of course Ezekiel and I jumped at the chance to protect our families. As you know we are both men who rather act than react. Neither of us favored waiting for the next attack. Instead we joined Barraza to take the fight to Villa."

I thought about his words. The rest of the puzzle pieces now fell into place. "Yes, I see the larger picture now. If the government imprisoned Villa he could be a rallying point to draw new forces to him. Yet publicly President Obregon could not be seen as reneging on the agreement signed by President Huerta before him."

Alex spoke up as I took out my pocket knife and began whittling on a stick. "Now you understand my friend. This desperate move is not about one hacienda and one family. We have much to lose as a country if we fail."

Holmdahl joined us and squatted on his heels. I indicated his friend Jesus who had never stopped watching out the window since he had arrived. We were all jumpy and were startled by every vehicle heard outside. "What is the story on Herrera? He seems rather intense, even considering what we are facing."

"He has lost more than most of us to Villa. He has sworn to kill the man and has tried before. Like many former Villistas he changed sides. In 1919 his father and two brothers were captured and executed on Villa's orders. He has waited his chance ever since."

I looked again at my pocket watch. It was almost 2:00 p.m. The old house had been getting hotter ever since the morning mist had burned off. With no breeze we were all sweating and ready to be shut of the adobe. Felix was now pacing. He saw me looking at him and walked over. "It is not good that there has been no signal yet. The road will be busier soon. I have been here too long and cut off from my contacts. If there is something wrong I would not know and therefore not able to handle the matter."

Alex stood up and spoke reassuringly to the much larger man. "We know Villa usually goes to town on Fridays for banking to pay his Canutillo ranch hands. You know he is also unpredictable and may simply have stopped to meet with one of his many paramours."

"That is true...but still he is as cagy as a wild animal that smells the trap before it is sprung. Villa has not lived this long by being careless. Even now he may suspect something even if he has no reason to do so."

Commander Lara was not to be reassured easily. He was not a man who liked waiting. In my experience most men of action never were. He fixed me with a stern look. "I trust you will be discreet with the knowledge you now possess. In the old days we would not let you ride back to your country with such dangerous information." Seeing the look on my face he smiled and slapped my back. I had been sitting cross legged on the floor and almost fell over with the blow. "Ah the old days are no more. Each of us holds the other's wellbeing in our hands."

Not sure if he was serious or not, I wanted to assure him I was not a threat. I did not know this man and did not want to survive a gun battle, and then get shot in the back as I rode away. "I give you my word commander; I will take today's actions to my grave, be it soon or late.

The others moved off leaving Alex and I alone once more. He stood up and stretched. "Don't forget what I requested of you Oscar. Afterwards we all disappear. I will write you as soon as I return home. That time back in Carrizal if I had not turned up with the traitor Acalan in tow, you would have come looking for me. Please don't think of doing so this time. I will make my way safely home to Abelinda and my family if God wills it. Otherwise there will be nothing you can do. I invited you into this and I want to see you return to your country safely."

I stood up as well. Smiling I said, "I'll do as you request. Know this though, if I make it out of here only to discover you are rotting in a Mexican prison, I'll return with a troop of Texas Rangers to bust down the walls." We hugged unashamedly in front of the others. His usual bear hug was back and made my lungs scream for air. As I pushed him away to catch a breath, we both began laughing at our display of sentiment. Our laughter was cut short as we paused to listen to a car engine heard outside. It was on the far side of the bridge and headed our way.

All seven men took up rifles or drew pistols as we each rushed to the window. I stood between Alex and Holmdahl as we peeked outside. Indeed a black Dodge Roadster was approaching the bridge driving at a slow and steady pace. My heart was jack-hammering in my chest. Was I about to come face to face with Pancho Villa after all the years of chasing him or his men? After a glance at the car we hurriedly crowded into the storage room where a door opened directly onto the street. We were blind now and totally dependent on the signal.

Ezekiel was next to me so I whispered, "Don't be a hero today. Your family needs you. Tell Eva for me I will write her when I get back to El Paso." He nodded at me but said nothing. The strain on his face was unmistakable. Alex freed his right hand from his rifle and gripped my shoulder. He said nothing but his actions said more than any words could. I thought of pa's God and hoped He was listening. I prayed for strength, courage and to do my part.

From outside in the direction of the bridge we heard a shouted unmistakable signal. "Viva Villa!" The time was now. It was a moments that shapes your present and might end any future. In an instant, seven men burst through the door to run the twenty paces to the street.

There was no thought of turning back. No matter the reason for each man's presence, we were to see it through. As one we stopped in the street facing the Dodge as it clamored over the old wooden bridge toward us. Pancho Villa was clearly seen driving. I thought he looked much older than photographs I had seen. Without doubt our positioning and firearms made our purpose clear. Instead of speeding up or turning which we had expected Villa stopped in the rode thirty paces from our position. To my left Jesus swore an oath in Spanish. This was the man who had executed his father and brothers. In reckless anger he snapped a rifle shot. It missed Villa and the Dorado riding in the front seat, but shattered the windshield.

Quicker than I thought possible, an old model pistol appeared in Villa's fist as if by magic. With deadpan calm he shot Herrera next to me. The man's head exploded instantly. Herrera died before he fell, his lust for vengeance unfulfilled by his own hand. The first shot and deadly-quick return fire startled those of us on both sides into action. I fired at the man next to Villa as he lifted a rifle. In the same instant I felt a hot burning sensation in my left leg. I returned fire striking the man in the chest. He fell against the door. To my right began a continuous firing of pistols or rifles. The explosive exchanges echoed off distant buildings, returning to my ears in a staccato-like sound that reminded me of a machine gun.

My next shot hit one of the men in the back seat who had been leaning out the right side of the Dodge Roadster firing a revolver. He was not killed outright, but slumped, then jerked sideways as he was hit at least twice more by Commander Lara. Without being part of the plan we began to advance. I saw Villa take one or more bullet strikes to the body, another and still another. He physically rose up in his seat, but never lost his grip on the gun his right hand. The left literally had a death grip on the steering wheel, his knuckles gone white with the effort. I believed he was dead before a final shot struck him in the head.

It ended quickly after no more than two minutes. Roaring in my ears covered all sound. Three men besides Villa were dead in the car. I was surprised to see the Dodge was still running in the road. Before anyone appeared on the streets, the six of us still alive rushed back to the old adobe. Before entering the storage room I saw the man Felix had said was Meliton Lozoya slink from under the bridge and run away toward town. Commander Lara looked back at Jesus Herrera's body. "I hate to leave any good man behind, but it cannot be helped."

With Herrera's death we each had a horse. I struggled into the saddle favoring my leg. Alex mounted, and then looked down in surprise. "Damn it all to hell Oscar you've been shot!"

Looking at the wound I said simply, "That happens in gunfights. It either passed clean through or just burned me. It'll be my reminder of this day. As you say I am unlucky in battle."

"Leave town quickly but treat your wound when you stop." Now mounted, we clasp hands and waved a salute to the others. Six survivors rode off in a quick hurry in as many directions.

# CHAPTER 55

## *Fleeing Mexico and a Promise Broken*

As Alex had suggested I rode the rest of the afternoon away and deep into the night, but never ran the horse. If I had been seen or pursued I saw no evidence of it. My heart was heavy at leaving Alex and Ezekiel behind. They must make their own way home as would I. The action I had been a part of was abhorrent and not a prideful affair. However I believed with all my being it was what needed to be done. If my friends escaped and their involvement was not discovered it would bring peace to *San Miguelito*. That thought settled my mind a little.

The moon did not rise that night of July 20th 1923. It was so dark I could not see the face of my pocket watch. I supposed the time was after 10:00 p.m. I had been riding with only a few breaks since afternoon. My leg was hurting something awful and was stiff. I struggled mightily to get out of the saddle. It was more of a fall than a smooth dismount. When I ended up in a heap on my back the horse shied away, walking a few feet from where I lay. It might as well have been a mile in my condition. Helplessly I saw lights of a town to the west. The shining illumination beckoned to me but danger waited there even if I could manage to make it.

I was terrified now and fought back panic. I realized if I lost the horse, death by thirst or infection would find me. Or if found I would be arrested and imprisoned. There would be a blistering sun tomorrow as July played out in Mexico. Forcing myself to think, I could not recall if Alex had spoken the name of the horse. I spoke softly. "Hold on a minute mister you and I need each other. We are partners. I'm taking you to a new home. Those folks are nice and will take good care of you until Alex can come fetch you." It worked a little. She shook her head and snorted but did not move further away. I tried whistling to her but my mouth was too dry.

Rolling over I fought my way to my feet. When I put weight on the wounded leg searing pain shot through me. Blood oozed through my pants. I collapsed and was instantly taken back to the afternoon sun in the dusty street of *Parral*; gunfire exploded on either sides of me, Herrera's eyes flew open wide as he was rocked back on his heels, dying in a burst of blood, thick and red as it spattered on my face. I saw to my horror that my hands were covered in blood as well. My mind struggled to understand why blood dripped off my fingers, forming into pools?

There were more like-images, jumbled and disconnected. Eventually I pulled away from the sights and flashes of color. The realization hit me that I must have passed out. When I recovered my wits it was still night and cold in the desert. I was face down and began to crawl to the horse, which was eating dried and sparse grass nearby. One hand over the other I pulled myself up from stirrup to saddle pommel and finally to stand. I ached to let go to sleep or die, slipping silently into darkness. With eyes squeezed shut against the agony in my leg I saw Eva's bandaged face. The child had never given up. Angrily I said, "I won't quit Eva, I promise you."

Leaning heavily on the horse I managed to grasp the reins with one hand and untied the saddle bags with the other, letting them hit the ground. I was sweating despite the cold. Suspecting I was running a fever I set about to make a fire and clean my wound. I took several drinks of water. If the horse ran off now it would be bad luck, but I was too weak to even tie her up. I got a fire started and poured water into an old pot. I took out a hard biscuits and chewed on one as the fire heated. My horse, whatever her name was, drifted closer to the fire.

When the water was boiling I began to wash the wound after first cutting my pants leg from the swollen leg. Below my left knee was a blackened mess. I felt around the backside and found no exit wound. So I reasoned, that lucky bastard Pancho must have got off a second shot. The man next to him had a rifle. The one in the left back seat had not begun shooting at the time. If I had been hit with the larger caliber of the rifle the back of my leg would have been blown out. I was in trouble. With the bullet still in my leg an infection must have set in. If I dared enter a town to find a doctor there would surely be questions. All I could do was cleanse the wound and ride on. Now my head was beginning to throb with the fever. "Damn!"

After eating two more biscuits from my pack I loaded everything back onto *no name* and dragged myself into the saddle. Sensing rather than knowing which direction north was, I started out. I was feeling better and put several miles behind me until I saw the first glimmer of a sunrise. Surprisingly I was actually headed north. Today would be many hours in the saddle. I might still take me days to reach El Paso. The town of *Hidalgo del Parral* was in the southern tip of the State of *Chihuahua*, which bordered El Paso, Texas. I estimated at least a hundred miles of desert lay between me and safety. Grimly I judged the prospect of making it out of Mexico alive was somewhere between slight and no chance at all.

I rode the sun down and believed I either slept or passed out in the saddle a few times. Each instance when I came back to awareness we were still headed north. That puzzled me. During a few stops to rest and feed *No Name* and myself, I was not sure if I could continue further. That night I found a sheltered dry creek bed and built a roaring fire. There was no wood but plenty of dried cow patties from herds of cattle that must pass through the area. The flame was smelly but hot and comforting. Again I boiled water and poured it as hot as I could stand on the wound, which was now inflamed and more swollen from hours hanging off a saddle.

Towns were closer together now. I knew I could be no more than sixty miles away from El Paso. I was weak and believed I was dying. I took strips of rawhide and lashed myself to the saddle before me and No Name started out before dawn. If I passed out again I would probably end up in a buzzard's belly. Now I had to ride further in the desert to avoid people. No Name tugged at the reins as if she knew the way. "Stubborn is what you are." Her ears flickered back at my words but she kept tugging. Eventually feverish, with my head aching so bad I saw blinding flashes of light. I gave in and gave up. "Sorry Eva." No Name was left on her own.

White clean sheets were beneath me. Sun filtered through an open window in a pleasant house. Where was I? Heaven, no, but it certainly was not hell. Something about the room seemed familiar as if I had been here before. I breathed in the fresh scent of flowers and then the memory dropped into place. This was the house overlooking the Rio Grande in El Paso. It belonged to Ronaldo and Lupe Rios, the friends Alex and I had made when they crossed the river into the country. I was back in El Paso and more importantly back in the United States.

How was the question? Suddenly remembering my leg and been shot I abruptly tried to sit up, my hand going quickly to my leg. I feared I had survived only to lose my leg to a doctor's saw blade. A dizzy spell swept over me. I grasp my leg and relief washed over me. It was bandaged but still attached. I wiggled my toes and flexed my foot. The effort caused a burning pain shoot through me, but it was worth it to know everything still worked. Falling back with satisfaction I shouted, "Ronaldo, Lupe, are you out there?"

In a few moments I heard rustling and then footsteps coming toward the door. Ronaldo opened the door and stood there smiling broadly. Ronaldo spoke now with a thick accent. He had known no English when he arrived in 1917, but had worked hard to speak clearly. "Well Senior Draper I think you have returned to us in a bad way. You live still and that is good."

"How did I get here? The last thing I remember was the desert, pain and fever. I was fighting the damn no name horse and then had no more strength."

"It was *Bailaring*, she brought you to us. You were almost dead. I believe in a few more hours it would have been too late."

"Who is Bailaring? I have no idea who that is."

"The Criollo horse senior, she is named Bailaring. It means dancer. Senior Alejandro rode her all the way here from his business in Parral several times. Each time I rode to meet him there he instructed me to ride Bailaring."

I sat up carefully swinging my legs off the bed. I remained on the side of the bed until my head cleared. "Alex, that's why he insisted I ride Bailaring. The horse knew the way better than I did. The man is uncanny with his planning." As a thought struck me I added, "Although he could have provided me the horse's name." My leg was beginning to pound with my heartbeat as blood returned to it hanging from the bed. "What about my leg? Will it be alright?"

He shrugged. "The doctor thinks so. He treated the infection and removed a bullet." Seeing the look of concern on my face he said, "Don't worry Oscar, I told him you were in a hunting accident. A report was made to the local police. I think nothing will come of it." He came to the bed and helped me stand with the assist of a homemade cane. He then encouraged me to take a few trial steps.

My clothes had been washed and neatly left by the bed. I dressed and managed to walk to the next room. It was slow going, but I was too grateful to have both legs attached to complain. "How long Ronaldo?"

He looked confused and said, "How long to get better or how long have you been here?"

"Both, but first when did I arrive?"

"It is July 25$^{th}$ so you have been unconscious for two days." He paused and I wondered what else there was. "Senior you were delirious most of the time. You said many things which would be disturbing to some and I think good news to others. However since they were spoken by a man nearly at death's door, who was mad with fever and infection, it is of no matter. Only Lupe and I heard your babblings."

So I had traveled three days from *Parral* to El Paso. Or rather I had ridden two days and had been taken by Bailarin the last day. I was miffed over not being given the horse's name. I would write an angry letter of protest to Alex. Then I reminded myself that his actions had saved my life. The thought of Alex brought with it troubling worries. Did everyone escape? How would I find out? My thoughts were interrupted when I heard happy voices outside.

Ronaldo was looking out a window smiling at the sight of Lupe and his children approaching. I followed his gaze and saw Lupe carrying a small child with two more walking with her. Rondo was now twelve and Little Eleazar was six. They were fine children and a pleasure to be around. They were one of the reasons I so often stopped here. The children had fast become Americans and were excellent students. The baby was a three month old girl named for Lupe's mother, Maria. She was already the darling princess of the house.

Hugs and kisses were flowing as the boys and Lupe saw me dressed and standing. Lupe talked excitedly about the meal she would prepare for me. As if agreeing with her promise of food my stomach grumbled at the emptiness. After Lupe left to begin preparing the evening meal I looked at myself in a mirror hung in the living room. I saw a pale man, thin, with bloodshot eyes. I looked rough and at least a decade older than my twenty-nine years. MY lack of color was most likely due to my injury, but my rough and tumble life had been extremely hard on my body. Suddenly feeling weary I said to Ronaldo, "Before my strength leaves, let's go outside. I need to feel the sun on my face. Also I have a stubborn dancer to thank for delivering me safely to your home."

Once outside Ronaldo found some oats and I fed Bailaring. Patting her neck affectionately I said, "You saved me girl. I've never ridden a finer horse." A thought hit me. "Ronaldo I asked, "Can you get me copies of the El Paso Times and Herald Post? I also need you to read me those newspapers you get from Mexico. I need to catch up on world events while I recover."

That night I lay full and content from Lupe's meal and the happiness in the house. I was exhausted but satisfied to be alive and on the mend. I went over the shootout in the street with Villa and his men. Questions of what happened afterwards haunted me. Were my friends alive, or imprisoned? Other questions disturbed my rest. Why was there only one car and no other bodyguards? We had expected at least two cars and possibly a third. Thinking about the possibilities I realized if that had been the case none of us would have ridden away. We could have easily faced twelve or more *Dorados*. Eventually I gave in to my fatigue and slept hard.

The next morning I awoke refreshed and filled with new strength. Lupe clucked over me. I began to pretend my recovery was further.

Otherwise she would have treated me like one of her children, fussing over me constantly. I used the cane and walked slowly testing my leg. After a delicious breakfast Ronaldo and I sat on the porch. He handed me the two main El Paso newspapers. I saw little news of Mexico, other than related stories of relations with the nearest neighboring town of Juarez just across the border.

Ronaldo sat nearby on the porch sharpening kitchen knives with a wet stone. When he saw I had finished reading through the two local papers he put down work and said, "News from deep in Mexico is slow to reach us here, but I have a newspaper delivered on the train directly from *Hidalgo del Parral*. Senior Alejandro does much business in Chihuahua. It is good to know the ways of your customers."

He held up the newspaper for me to see. I could only read the date of July 21st, 1917 and one word. The headlines where in large block letters which seemed to scream the capital word *VILLA!* There was a photograph of Villa's bullet riddled Dodge Roadster in the road. I tried to cover my surprise. There was the stark reminder of what I had been involved in covering the front page. I could see by Ronaldo's expression that he knew or suspected I was involved. If I was caught up in Villa's death than he knew that Alex would have been as well.

I had no idea what to say but he spoke first. "It is a good thing I think. Villa was a bad hombre. He is one of the reasons so many Mexicans are now living in America. Lupe and I came to avoid the violence the revolution brought to the land. You cannot ask a mountain lion not to eat you if he is hungry. It is part of his nature and it was so with Villa. Do you want me to read you the story?"

Much relieved at his words I said gratefully, "Yes, all of it please."

He read a ways down the page before beginning to translate. "It says seven gunmen burst from an old abandoned adobe with flames coming from there pistols and rifles. They shot and killed Pancho Villa and three of his *Dorados*. Robbery is not suspected because gold was left undisturbed in Villa's Dodge. An unidentified witness said one hundred and fifty shots were fired into the car in two minutes. Villa was killed with sixteen bullets in his body and four more in the head.

He had a gun in his hand and reportedly killed Jesus Herrera a man known to him."

With shaking hands and voice I asked, "Does it say if any of the other men were captured?"

He read a little further. "Yes, Meliton Lozoya, who was the former manager of Villa's hacienda. The story is that Villa believed he owed him money. It was well known in town that Lozoya hated and feared Villa. Also arrested was an important man, Felix Lara, commander of federal troops in *Parral*. He is suspected of accepting 50,000 pesos to have soldiers and policemen under his command removed from *Parral* on the day of assassination."

The word *assassination* struck my stomach like acid. It fit however. I would have live with it. The arrest of Lozoya pleased me, but not Commander Lara. I did not believe anyone had paid Felix Lara to become involved. He appeared as a gentleman and patriot to me. "Thank you Ronaldo. I believe I'll return to my room now. If you get additional information let me know."

It was still midmorning but I felt tired and slowly began the walk back to my room to nap. I do not know what I believed would be felt after we all went our separate ways. Relief as knowing Alex and his family were safe, but not this guilt. I had hated Villa for so long that I had forgotten he was still a man. In the killing of any man there is a cost to one's self. If there had been any good news it was that Alex and Ezekiel had not been mentioned. However Ronaldo had concluded his reading by saying the investigation was ongoing. The story said there were a large number of as yet unidentified possible conspirators to be uncovered, rounded up and questioned.

Once in my room I lay on the bed thinking. There were seven men shooting at Villa's car. Some carried pistols or rifles. No automatic or semi-automatic weapons were used. Nobody reloaded until after the firing ended. If each man fired six to seven shots that would be no more than forty-two to forty nine shots all together, certainly not one hundred and fifty. Plus Herrera only got off one round. I had no way of being sure but I believed Villa was struck no more than four or five times in the body and only once in the head as far as I saw. The story had said the gunmen had run from the adobe with guns firing. That was not true. We stood before Villa and risked death by his hand or his bodyguards. The story was balderdash. It was pure grandstanding to sell newspapers. The problem was it would be believed.

Throughout the month of August I recovered my strength and stamina. I enjoyed the children's laughter as I would sit on the porch and watch them for hours. On August 14th I received the first letter from Alex, or rather Eva, with a short letter from Alex inside. Eva was drawing again and had included a glowing letter at getting to know me while I was on the ranch. Her picture was very good and I put it up in my room. The letter from Alex was brief and told me nothing of the news I was hungry to hear.

The note said simply…*Your visit was most welcome and came at a fortunate time. We are fine here at San Miguelito. Ronaldo tells me you are mending and will soon leave. As I said before, I think of you every time I use the outhouse. Next year I will move it to our far pasture after indoor plumbing is installed. Best wishes and success always. My God bless and keep you. It remains a rare honor and privilege to be your friend. I am grateful and in your debt, Alex.*

Near the end of August I lined up work elsewhere and was prepared to ride out on the first day of September 1923. I was restless and ready to be on the move. I needed to get back to making a living and still intended to go back home to settle down. Letters from ma always ended with her pleading for me to leave the road and return. On the evening of August 31st I was sitting on the porch with Ronaldo after an excellent send off meal by Lupe. Everything was covered in pure blackness, with no moon or breeze to cool the night.

Ronaldo was sitting quietly smoking a cigarette on a homemade bench. In the darkness, only the glow of his cigarette told me he was there. He cleared his throat and said, "I expect your mind is made up about leaving in the morning. We'll miss you until the next time you come by. I put some money on the table by your bed. You'll need it to get to your next job."

"No Ronaldo, I won't take your money. I owe you and Lupe my life. I'll be alright."

"No Oscar, the money is from Senior Alejandro for work you completed on his hacienda."

Before I could reply there was movement in the dark. I stood up, cursing myself for not having a weapon. Then a voice I recognized sounded from the night. It was Holmdahl. He was speaking Spanish to Ronaldo. He switched to English and said, "Sit easy Oscar, it's me Ezekiel."

He walked out into the open as Ronaldo lit a lantern. I was glad to see him, but disappointed Alex was not with him. We shook hands. "What are you doing away from the ranch Ezekiel?"

"I'm in town on ranch business as a matter of a fact. If Alex had known you'd still be here he would have come and left my sorry butt home with all the womenfolk." His old grin was back and he flashed one now. "Sometimes a man needs to slip away with the boys now and again."

We sat down on the porch as Ronaldo went inside. Not wasting any time he said, "I expect the raids at the ranch are over. Our friend Commander Lara was arrested along with a Durango Congressman, Jesus Salas Barraza, who claimed responsibility for Villa's death. Both men along with Lozoya were convicted and sentenced to life in prison. However, Mexican President Obregon will pardon them after a short time served, or the expected next president, Plutarco Elias Calles. What I'm saying is a dead legend that lived and died by the gun can't hurt us."

"That's great news; your family is safe." Was it worth the risk to see my friends safe from harm? I thought so. I felt good. It was time to go. My way was ripe with promise.

# EPILOGUE

## *One Last Visit*

I finished reading Grandpa Oscar's final letter. Dad and I sat for awhile quietly thinking about what it meant. To me it left behind a heavy burden of guilt. I had not visited Grandpa for the better part of the last two years of his life. His stories had seemed like just one big adventure when I was younger, but now I could see how much he had endured. The one thread that wove through the fabric of his life was loyalty to friends and family. He had asked me to never turn my back on either, living or dead. I had done just that. My best intentions for the future could not erase the last two years of selfish neglect. I regretted letting him down.

Dad sat behind his desk gently rocking as he drummed a pencil lost in thought. The squeak of his chair was loud in the room. I felt like Dad and I we had made a circle and finished much closer. He broke the silence. "I don't expect anyone outside the family will believe the letter. Still we will honor the request made by Alex. I'll mail it to John Ray. He will be anxious to read it. Buddy you should know the stories and letters were a gift. It has been a beautiful and rare insight into what made him think, act and change. I wish I had known him better when I was growing up. It would have explained how he raised his children. Son you should write those stories before they slip your memory. It's important to recall those days and folks who lived it."

"Yes, it started as simple story time but grew into much more. I think I understand the people Grandpa spoke of. They are real to me now. I felt their pain, shared in their hardships and losses. Goodnight Dad." I was filled with the past and the idea of living and experiencing life to the fullest. Most of mine was ahead. I would never stop looking back at those that came before, shaping the world I live in. Thinking about Grandpa's new and refreshed start in 1923 made me smile.

The Air Force was ahead for me and Randy. The future was frightening yet full of new friends, exciting travel, and eventually a family and children of my own. If I could be half the man Dad and Grandpa were I would do alright. I believed Grandpa was not really gone if he lived inside of me and all the others who loved him. I intended to carry what he taught me every day. Before sleep claimed me Grandpa Oscar's last request that I honor family and friends toyed with my mind. I liked Dad's suggestion that I write down Grandpa's stories. I was not sure I knew where to start or was up to the task.

That night I dreamed I was standing outside a large iron gate, black painted and imposing. I realized I was once again outside the Hebrew Rest Cemetery in Fort Worth. It was so real I could feel the heat of a sunny day on my face. Was it a dream? I still cannot say. There were bright colors and the smell of honeysuckle vines growing on the fence. Every sensation indicated the experience was real.

The first thing I saw was sun glinting off the US buckle on Bill's grave. Inside was Grandpa Oscar, Alex and another man I somehow knew was Bill Kubitz. I was confused since I knew Bill was long dead and now Grandpa Oscar too. Yet they stood together, young and in freshly pressed Army uniforms. All three men waved happily. I leaned forward listening as I saw Grandpa speak from across the cemetery. His words seemed to float easily to my ears on the afternoon breeze. I heard every word clearly as if I was standing beside him. "Buddy, I forgive you. Now you must forgive yourself. Hanging on to grief or regret will fester inside you. You are young yet and did not understand. Don't be so hard on yourself, but honor family and friends always. They will be there to give you strength and comfort you when you most need it. Don't forget again." His last words of admonishment were softly spoken but boomed loud inside my head.

I tried to run to him but my legs were frozen, unable to enter the gate. I gripped the cold bars in but they held firm, unyielding to my every effort. The gate was unlocked but too heavy for me to budge or even rattle in my frustration. Sweat poured off my face and stung my eyes. I dared not look away too afraid they would be gone. Giving up my hopeless struggle against the gate I sank to my knees exhausted from the exertion. I reluctantly surrendered my attempts to join them. Finally panting with each breath I said, "I won't Grandpa. This time I'll keep my promise."

He smiled and raised his hand in what I knew was a wave of farewell. I started to lift mine but was abruptly torn from the dream by a far away insistent knocking. Someone was calling my name urgently. Opening my eyes upon waking I was groggy and confused as to where I was. I had just been kneeling at the cemetery. I felt a momentary panic as I relived the images and words spoken in the dream. Attempting to shake off the almost overwhelming sense of loss, I stumbled out of bed recognizing my mom's voice. "Buddy you have a phone call. It's important hurry up."

I tossed on some shorts and stumbled into the kitchen where our only phone was hung on the wall. I sat down on the stool and took the phone Mom was holding. My hands shook and I felt like an anvil was hanging over my head. Mom stood nearby with an expression of sympathy on her face. On the other end of the line I heard soft sobbing. With an inner dread I muttered a hello. "Hello this is Buddy." It was Josephine Leigh calling. She was crying. Her voice sounded weak and was filled with raw emotions. It took a little time to get the story from her. Through her tears she managed to say that Alex, Eleazar Alejandro, my grandfather's dearest friend had died in his sleep the night before. Josephine had said he had been surrounded by his large family and many friends at his beloved ranch when he passed. Alex had left word with Abelinda that Josephine and I should be told of his passing.

With the news I had felt a chill run the length of my spine. The dream, Grandpa, Alex, and Bill all reunited after death. After hanging up the phone I told Mom what Josephine had said. I kept the dream to myself for now as I had much to think about. I wanted to selfishly savor every minute detail before telling anyone. It would take some time before I was ready to share. I needed to sort out what I believed and felt about Grandpa Oscar's last visit. One thing I knew now was that I no longer felt the heavy guilt which had been weighing on me. Grandpa had truly released me from the burden.

Time has a way of slipping by. Before I realized it the year was 1980. I was out of the service, having been stationed in Montana rather than Vietnam, was now married and had a son of my own. I lived only a couple of miles from my parents. I was now a police officer and also attending night classes at a local university. Shift work gave me crazy hours which made it easy to become restless on a day off. Some nights after my son, also named James, and my wife were asleep; I would drive by Dad's house. He often worked late completing a payroll for one of his clients. If the light to his office was on I would knock lightly on his office door. Dad enjoyed the short visits as much as I did. I am sure the break was a good diversion from the tedious accounting work.

Tonight it was a little after eleven o'clock and I was seated comfortably in one of his wooden chairs, my foot propped up on the side of the desk. He was gently rocking back and forth as we spoke of general family news. I could see rolls of calculator tape bunched up and falling behind the old desk. Soft gospel music was playing on his tape player. His squeaking chair reminded me of the cassette tapes he had sent me while I was away in Montana. The squeak could be heard clearly in every tape. The office was small but comfortable. The sweet aroma of cherry pipe smoke lingered in the room from an earlier break.

For some reason Grandpa Oscar had been on my mind today. I believed it was past time to tell Dad about my dream. I had dreamed about my grandfather before and since, but never with the very real feel of that one dream. I told Dad about my guilt and shame at not visiting Grandpa and how I had been released from the guilt after the dream. After I finished Dad sat quietly thinking about what I had said. He did not scoff or doubt me as I feared he might. Instead he took every word as real. We both shed tears unashamedly. Dad believed as I did that the dream was Grandpa's last lesson to me. I agreed. Since the three men had been so close in life, why not meet up in eternity?

Author's note: I'm not a fast writer. It was more than two years in the process of completing the rough draft. I believe all talent flows through God to those who are open to receive His gift. I guess He did not want to overburden my puny human capacity of absorbing His offering by hurrying me along. The hard part is now completed. This has been the single hardest thing I have ever done, but it has also been a journey and true labor of love from the first word to the last. I put so much of myself into Cactus Division I will certainly leave pieces of myself trapped between the pages. Now I will turn off, click off my lamp, dampen the creative side of my brain, and leave it to others to decide if my words deserve to be read and appreciated.

# BIBLIOGRAPHY

## *References*

Harris, L. (1949). *Pancho Villa and the Columbus Raid*. El Paso, Texas: The McMath Company, Inc.

Miles, E. (1993). *Stray tales of the Big Bend*. Texas A&M University, The Centennial Series of the Association of Former Students.

Justice, G. (2001). *Little Known History of the Texas Big Bend*. Odessa, Texas: Rimrock Press.

Dean R. (1994). *The Columbus Story*. Tour Guide & Map. Columbus, N.M.

Unknown author (1916). *VILLA ATTACKS COLUMBUS, N.M. 15 Americans Killed and 9 Wounded When 1000 Mexicans Under Gen. Villa Make early Morning Raid On Border Town; 100 Mexicans Killed*. The Deming Graphic, A Live Paper in a Live Town. (Volume XIV, pp. 1-2, Number XXVIII.

Skeeter, S. (1971). *Pancho Villa: Merchant of Death*. Shooting Times Magazine. Retrieved February 09, 2009, from http://www.darkcanyon.net/pancho_villa.htm

Skeeter, S. (1971). *Pancho Villa & Patton's GUNS*. Shooting Times Magazine. Retrieved: May 16, 2009, from http://www.DocumentsandSettings\Mike\Desktop\PanchoVilla&Patton'sGUNS.mht

Griffith, J. (2008). *In Pursuit of Pancho Villa 1916-1917.* Unknown publication. Retrieved January 01, 2009, from http://www.hsgng.org/pages/pancho.htm

Boardman, M. (2009). *Patton's First Two Notches.* True West Magazine. Retrieved September 13, 2010 from http://www.trueestmagazine.com/stories/patton_s

Boot, M. (2002). *The Dusty Trail.* Chapter 8 of The Savage wars of Peace: Small wars and Rise of American Power. The Wall Street Journal. Retrieved December 17, 2008 from: http://www.opinionjournal.com

Troesser, J. (Unknown date). *Camp Travis & The 90$^{th}$ Division. Cactus Division.* Unknown Publication. Retrieved May 16, 2009 from: http://www.texasescapes.com/WorldWarI/CampTravis.htm

Province, C. (Unknown date). *The M1913 Patton Saber.* The Patton Society, Edited by Charles Province from saber articles by Lt. George S. Patton, Jr. Retrieved January 01, 2009 from: http://www.pattonhq.com/swordhtml

Unknown author and date. *Black Jack Pershing and Pancho Villa.* NW Travel Magazine Online. Retrieved December 17, 2008 from: http://www.u-s-history.com/pagesh1075.html

With grateful acknowledgement to the resources and inspiration of the General George S. Patton Museum, Fort Knox, KY. Also to Pancho Villa State Park, Museum and local Historical Society, and to the City of Columbus, NM for preserving so much of the past to the present.